THE FIRE QUEEN'S APPRENTICE
BOOK ONE

THE
WATERMIGHT
THIEF

JORDAN RIVET

Contact the author at Jordan@JordanRivet.com

For updates and discounts on new releases, join Jordan Rivet's mailing list.

Cover art by Deranged Doctor Design

Editing suggestions provided by Red Adept Editing

Map by Jordan Rivet

The Watermight Thief, The Fire Queen's Apprentice Book 1/ Jordan Rivet – First Edition: February 2019

❀ Created with Vellum

This book is dedicated to Susie Driver.
Thank you for fixing my commas
for ten books and counting.

CONTENTS

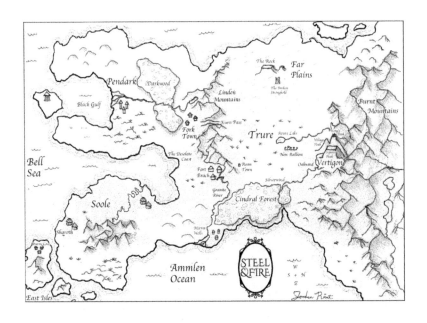

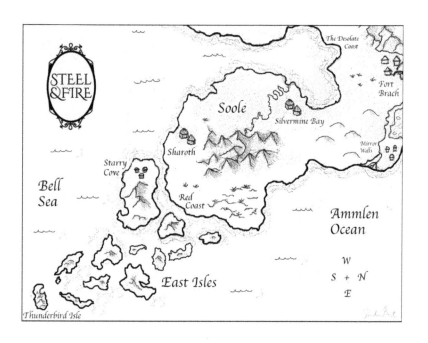

1

Tamri didn't want to steal the dragon. She only needed to borrow it for a little while.

She watched from beneath a canal bridge as the huge creature exited the iron gates, her bare feet sinking slowly into the mud. She'd never been this close to one of the beasts before. It had a reptilian head and a long tail with a barbed knot swinging at the end. The scaled body was dark red, and scarlet feathers covered its wings, making it look like a mix between a lizard and a bird of prey.

The ruins of a grand manor house were visible beyond the dragon's arching back before the iron gates clanged shut. Guards lined the thick stone walls around the manor, protecting its contents, and murky canals circled the island on which it sat.

Tamri got ready to move as the dragon ambled toward her bridge on all fours, its distended belly sagging to the muddy path. It would be vulnerable while crossing the canal, if you could ever call such a beast vulnerable.

The dragon turned its lizard-like head toward her, and the morning sunlight glinted off a mouthful of teeth longer than Tamri's thumbs. She crouched a little lower. It was still well before noon, but a pungent aroma was already rising from the swampy canal. Tamri wiped sweat off her forehead and adjusted a scratchy linen handkerchief over her mouth and nose, waiting for the signal. She felt jumpy, and she wished the dragon would walk faster. Those guards could spot her at any moment.

The dragon's teeth and sheer size were starting to make her think this was a bad idea. But she couldn't back out now. Her friend—and sometimes rival—Pel had recruited her for the job with promises of the biggest score of their lives, swearing it would change her and her grandmother's fortunes for good. He and the others should already be in position.

Tamri and Pel were thieves, but they weren't after gold. They stole Watermight, a valuable magical substance that sprang from underground vents across the city of Pendark and the nearby Black Gulf. Tamri had been born with the ability to Wield the stuff, and she made her living—barely—snatching it up wherever she found it and selling it to more powerful Wielders.

According to Pel, this dragon carried a vast quantity of the substance in its belly. He had assured her it would be worth the extra risk to apprehend the dragon and get it to relinquish its supply.

"The beasts drink Watermight straight from the king's vents," he'd told her. "I reckon we can grab one while it's on the move and take its stash. It'll be easier than trying to get past the guards at the vent itself."

"Won't it breathe fire at us?"

"It can't," Pel said confidently. "You can tell 'cause of the feathers. These ones aren't like the dragons in the stories."

Tamri had been skeptical of Pel's dragon knowledge. The creatures had only appeared in the city a few years ago, accompanied by riders from the north. The foreigners purchased large quantities of Watermight from King Khrillin and carried it off to distant lands in the bellies of the great winged animals. The notoriously fragile substance would drain away or lose potency when carried in barrels or skins for too long, but the dragons had solved that problem. For the first time, the Watermight could be used—and therefore sold—outside of Pendark.

A lot of poor Waterworkers like Tamri figured it wasn't right for the king to sell off their native power, but no one had ever tried to steal it from the dragons before they left the city. Tamri was about to find out for herself if the creatures really were just large flying cargo vessels, as Pel claimed.

The red-feathered dragon lumbered closer to Tamri's bridge. A tall man strode beside it, his blue coat bearing the insignia of the faraway mountain kingdom of Vertigon, but the other guards remained by the stone walls. The dragon and the tall Vertigonian were relatively exposed.

After crossing the canal, the dragon would ascend a wooden platform on the neighboring island and use that to get airborne. All Tamri had to do was intercept the beast and hold it long enough for Pel and the others to extract its Watermight payload.

Oh yes. That's all.

She pulled back into the shadow of the bridge and raised her hands to allow the Watermight she'd been carrying all morning to ooze out of her skin. The silvery-white liquid pooled in her palms for a moment then flowed into the air, twisting into a sinuous line. Lighter than water, finer than silk, the magical substance shone like liquid diamond as Tamri formed it into a long, shimmering cord. She used every drop Pel had allocated her for the job, draining the strength she'd felt while carrying the magic inside her body. Without the Watermight, she was just a scrappy, underfed girl with stringy muscles and no real power to her name. Hopefully today would change that.

Tamri finished her Watermight lasso by spinning a noose at the end then scanned her surroundings. She was supposed to capture the dragon as soon as its clawed feet touched the bridge, but she still hadn't heard the diversion. Pel and the band of gutter kids he'd recruited should be making a ruckus on the opposite side of the island by now.

"Where are those idiots?" she muttered into her handkerchief. She didn't trust Pel far, but this prize should keep him committed. Was he in position or not?

Talons scraped wood. The dragon was on the bridge, shuffling right above her. Boots thudded alongside it. There was still no sign of the others. Tamri was going to lose her chance to act.

She thought fast. There was only one guard—and the dragon was already halfway across the canal. She didn't want her hopes for a new life to amble out of reach. She could barely take care of Gramma Teall as it was.

Praying Pel's team would follow her lead, Tamri pulled her feet out of the mud and scrambled up the embankment, her Watermight lasso already spinning. The silver cord strengthened as it spun, the liquid power coming alive in her hands, making her feel brave.

Her feet hit the first slats of the bridge. The dragon whipped its head around to stare at her as she let the loop of silver magic fly.

"Hey!"

The tall foreign man shouted at her, but the dragon stood between them—and Tamri's Watermight rope was already zipping through the air. The noose landed around the creature's neck and pulled tight.

"Get away from him!"

The foreigner raised a thick metal stick with a knobby golden end glowing with inner fire. Panic shot through Tamri at the sight of that glowing cudgel. That must be Vertigon's deadly Fire magic. She'd never seen it in action.

The Vertigonian started around the dragon. Tamri had put every drop of Watermight she carried into the rope. She couldn't fight him. She looked around wildly for Pel and the others. They should be popping out of the canal, charging from the opposite bank, flinging Watermight razors. They should be helping.

The dragon tugged hard on the cord, yanking her off balance. The Vertigonian ducked as the great scarlet wings swept forward, narrowly missing his face.

"Stay calm, Rook," he called. "I'll get her off if you—"

The dragon spun as if chasing its own tail, forcing the Vertigonian back a step. Tamri's feet skidded on the bridge as the creature hauled her along, circling and squawking and snapping its vicious jaws. She felt dizzy. But she couldn't let go until the others got there.

The Watermight cord sank into her palms, keeping her tethered to the dragon no matter how hard it tried to shake her off. But still no one came to her aid. Those cowards had abandoned her.

The tall Vertigonian made it past the dragon's frantically beating wings and lunged for her, cudgel flashing. Not knowing what else to do, Tamri used the silver rope to haul herself onto the dragon's back and out of his reach. The scarlet feathers on its wings and shoulders were shockingly smooth and difficult to hold. Only the Watermight cord kept her from falling.

She started to slide forward onto the dragon's arching neck and gave the rope a sharp tug to catch herself. At that, the dragon's muscles bunched beneath her, and it gave an indignant roar. Then it launched into the air like a startled pigeon.

For the first few wingbeats, Tamri wasn't sure if she or the dragon was more surprised. *We're flying!* She hadn't thought it could take off with its weighted-down belly. She clung to the Watermight rope for dear life, welding the icy magic directly to her bones, and gripped the dragon's broad scales with her bare feet. Powerful muscles surged beneath her, and the wind whipped her hair into her eyes.

The ground dropped away fast. The muddy island with the walled manor shrank below her, the surrounding canals and swampy landmasses coming into view. A figure in a blue coat waved his glowing cudgel at her as more men rushed toward the bridge. Could that cudgel hurl Fire magic at her?

Panicking at the thought, Tamri kicked her heels into the dragon's sides the way she'd seen Trurens do on their fine horses.

It was the wrong choice. The dragon let out a snarl and shot higher into the sky, its wings nearly knocking her from her precarious seat. Only her ice-hard grip on the Watermight cord kept her from plunging to her death in the canal below. She felt as if her stomach were trailing them by several feet, her heart beating as hard as the dragon's wings. The dragon unleashed a furious roar, loud enough to rattle Tamri's eardrums.

Terror was quickly replacing her surprise of moments ago. She was going to fall. She was going to *die*.

She thought her situation couldn't get any worse—and then the dragon flipped upside down. It barrel-rolled through the sky, over and over, Tamri's whole body flying free like a banner in the wind.

She screamed almost as loud as the dragon. "Put me down!"

The dragon tossed its red-crested head angrily, as if to say, "That's exactly what I'm trying to do."

They came right side up again. Tamri thudded hard onto the dragon's back, jarring her teeth. Her whole body was stiff with terror, but her hands were still welded to the silver rope. The dragon gave her an irate glance over its shoulder, seeming to rein in its fear enough to assess the situation. Then it folded its wings and plunged downward.

"Not so fast!" Tamri shouted.

The dragon dove faster.

The city flashed beneath her. Canals. Mud. Barges. People with dirty feet and shocked faces. Colored flags in the wind. Houses nestled on little islands or perched atop rickety stilts. Squalor and chaos.

The ground got nearer fast. Light shimmered on the canals. Tamri glimpsed her terrified face reflected on the water, surrounded by a red blur. They crossed onto another island crammed with stilt houses. They were too close. *We're going to crash!*

At the last possible instant, the dragon's wings flared wide, and it came to a jolting halt atop a sloped roof.

Tamri flung herself off the dragon's back, and her feet slid on the shingles. Too terrified to think straight, she spun the end of the Watermight cord away from her hands and chained the dragon to the roof. She lurched away from the creature, struggling to regain her balance, and only skidded to a halt when she reached the edge of the sloping roof. She teetered dangerously for a moment. It was a long drop to the canal below.

Behind her, the dragon tried to pull loose, squawking in anger and frustration, but the bond of silvery power held firm. Used to slinging Watermight with desperate speed, Tamri hadn't registered that it would have been smarter to let the dragon go.

Too late now. She was trapped on the roof of a stilt house with the biggest—and angriest—flying lizard she had ever seen.

2

Tamri took refuge behind a grimy brick chimney and tried to get her bearings. Yellow flags decorated the nearby stilt houses, indicating she was in the Boundary District. The houses were bigger and farther apart than down near the Gulf, where she lived. She couldn't even smell the sea from here, just the fetid aroma of the slow-moving canal.

She breathed deeply, trying to calm her racing pulse. She should never have agreed to this job. Pel had grander ambitions than Tamri, figuring a big-enough score could set him up as a Waterlord in his own right. She usually only snatched up enough Watermight to keep her and Gramma Teall eating for another few days. She was all her grandmother had, and she couldn't afford to get killed on some hare-brained job.

She peeked around the chimney at the dragon, whose belly still bulged with Watermight. The portion Pel had promised her would be enough to keep her and Gramma Teall in fish and bread for months if she found the right buyer. But the entire reservoir within the creature's belly? With that much Watermight, Tamri could take her grandmother far away from this stinking swamp of a city and never have to fight for scraps of magic again. And it was perched on the rooftop, within her grasp.

The dragon reared up on its hind legs, tugging at the shimmering cord of Watermight, its feathered wings brushing the slate shingles. The roof shuddered under its weight.

Tamri didn't have a lot of time. Hesitation meant death around here, and she couldn't pass up this opportunity. Tamri might not have Pel's lofty ambitions, but she would do anything to make a better life for Gramma Teall.

Before she could lose her nerve, Tamri emerged from behind the chimney and scrambled toward the dragon. The creature cocked its head, looking decidedly birdlike thanks to a crest of red feathers on its head.

"I didn't mean for this to happen, I swear."

The dragon gave an indignant squawk. Tamri crawled closer, fighting the instinct to run as far and as fast as she could. At least it wouldn't breathe fire at her—if Pel had gotten that part right.

"I didn't know you could take off like that. I thought you needed to jump off something. Please don't eat me."

The dragon ruffled its feathers angrily, not interested in her excuses.

Clutching the shingles with her bare toes to keep her balance, Tamri stretched her hand toward the dragon. "I just want the Watermight. Come on now."

She pulled on the magic in the creature's distended belly, using the innate sense that came with her ability to Wield. A thin stream of silvery-white liquid flowed from the dragon's mouth toward Tamri's outstretched hand. The Watermight glimmered as it curled through the air, lighter than water yet somehow more solid. The liquid stream connected with her palm and began to seep into her skin, making her shiver.

She usually soaked up any power she came across as quickly as possible before another gutter kid like her could snatch it away. She had learned the fierce and dirty art of whipping the substance into her body after too many nights spent starving because someone else got to it first. But she tried to go slowly this time, not sure how the dragon would react.

The Watermight flooded her veins, colder than the waters of the Black Gulf in winter. As it sank deeper into her body, it turned icy, coating her bones, making her feel strong. Her fear of the dragon muted to a dull throb, even though it was close enough for her to smell its cold, meaty breath.

Tamri almost felt bad about keeping all this Watermight for herself, but Pel had only cut her in on the job because she had the fastest whip in the Gutter District. He wouldn't hesitate to take the whole lot if *he* could steal a dragon all by himself.

"Borrow," she reminded herself. "You're only borrowing it."

Tamri managed to draw in a quarter of the Watermight that her small, wiry body could hold before the red dragon realized what was happening. Then it snapped its jaws shut, cutting off the silvery flow, and glared at her with bright bronze eyes. A few silver droplets fell from its mouth and splashed on the shingles. Tamri drew them in too.

The dragon renewed its efforts to escape, scrabbling at the shingles and making the sloped roof shake. A scarlet feather drifted from its frantic wings.

"Calm down," Tamri hissed, crouching lower to stay balanced. "You're going to knock this place right off its stilts."

The dragon gave her a stubborn look then hunkered down like an angry toad, keeping its jaws firmly clamped. Tamri attempted to pry its mouth open with the Watermight, gently at first then gradually applying more pressure. The dragon growled deep in its scaled chest, the power remaining locked inside.

Tamri couldn't force the creature's jaws open no matter how hard she tried. Her magic-wielding skills were rudimentary at best. She was fast, but she had always been too poor to keep any loose Watermight she came across. Eking out a living this way didn't leave much time for practice. She had once dreamed of becoming a Waterworker's apprentice and learning how to use her power properly, but she'd been too busy fighting for her survival—her and Gramma Teall's.

"Please give me that power," she implored the dragon. "The king has plenty more, and I need it."

The dragon snorted derisively and swiped a feathered wing at her, knocking her onto her backside.

"Fine. I'll think of something else."

She scrambled down the sun-warmed shingles and took shelter

behind the brick chimney again, racking her brain for another way to get the Watermight. Force wasn't working. She was beginning to understand why Pel had recruited a whole gang for this job.

She listened to the scraping of the dragon's claws, its agitated growls. Sweat ran down her face, dampening the neck of her threadbare tunic. There had to be a way to make the dragon relinquish the power. *Maybe if I—*

Suddenly a vast shadow swept over Tamri's head, and she nearly pitched off the roof in surprise. The red dragon gave a joyful cry as a second, larger dragon landed beside it. The stilt house shook violently, and only Tamri's grip on the chimney kept her in place. She hugged the grimy brick column, which provided precious little cover from the new arrival.

The second dragon had jewel-blue scales, and its deep chest glinted like a beetle in the summer sun. The wings covering its feathers were whiter than anything else in this city of mud and coal dust. The dragon raised these brilliant wings, the span stretching the full length of the rooftop, and sheltered the smaller red dragon like an elder brother.

Tamri stared the newcomer in its jet-black eye, too shocked to move. It gave a spine-chilling growl.

A figure climbed down from the dragon's back, wearing a blue coat and carrying a glowing golden cudgel. It was the same Vertigonian Tamri had seen before. He was young and tall and powerfully built, with thick, windblown bronze hair and light skin, so unlike the black hair and olive skin Tamri shared with most Pendarkans. He looked furious.

"Release him," he shouted at her. "This blasted roof can't hold both of them."

"Then move your dragon," Tamri shot back. "I'm not done here."

"I don't know who you think you are, but—"

The roof gave a terrible groan, and a few shingles skittered off the slope and dropped into the canal below. Before Tamri could react, the man lunged toward her and seized the back of her tunic. She twisted like a cat caught by the scruff of the neck, sure he was about to toss her into the canal. Instead, he hoisted her onto the back of his beetle-blue dragon and climbed up behind her. And not

a moment too soon. A splintering crack sounded directly beneath them. The dragon raised its white wings and launched off the roof, taking them airborne.

The Vertigonian kept Tamri firmly in place with an iron grip on her tunic, his knees anchoring her thighs. Her bare feet dangled on either side of the dragon's thick, serpentine neck. Below them, the red dragon gave a furious squawk.

"Unleash him, or I'll—"

"Okay, okay." Tamri jerked on the icy cord of Watermight tying the red dragon to the roof, whipping the substance back into her body.

As soon as it was free, the red dragon leapt into the air and soared up to join its compatriot, chattering angrily. A gaping hole had opened in the sloped roof, revealing a cluttered bedroom and part of a fine sitting room. Tamri winced. She wouldn't want to be here when the stilt house's owner returned.

Abruptly she remembered she was sitting on a dragon's back for the second time that day. She clutched frantically at the white feathers lining the dragon's shoulders, wanting to hold on to something.

"Don't grab him so hard," the Vertigonian ordered. "You're pulling his feathers."

The man's fist was still knotted in her tunic. She wasn't going to fall—but there was no escaping, either.

"Why don't you just let me off here?" Tamri said. "No harm done, right?"

"You just stole one of my Cindral dragons." His tone was disbelieving. "You think I'll just drop you off at the nearest water taxi?"

"Uh, maybe?"

Tamri scanned the city below, her stomach lurching at how far away everything was. They were much higher than before. The draft from the dragon's wings buffeted her, sweeping her tangled black hair into the Vertigonian man's face. She'd lost her linen handkerchief somewhere. She felt exposed, with her face to the wind and her captor seated so close behind her.

They left the yellow-flagged Boundary District and crossed over a sea of midnight-blue banners and fine houses. This must be the

Royal District. The bridges between the islands were broader than in the rest of Pendark, and even the canals didn't smell quite as putrid.

The King's Tower rose before them, jutting up like a fist from its own island. A new kind of fear seized Tamri as she realized they were heading straight for it.

"You're taking me to the king?"

"Pendarkan kings dispense justice, don't they?"

"You can't." Tamri twisted, trying to look him in the eye, but their position on the dragon made it difficult. Dread made her feel stiff and ungainly despite the power icing her bones. "Please. I'll give back the rest of the Watermight. You can't take me to Khrillin."

"You're still holding Watermight?" The man sounded startled.

"Of course. Aren't you a Wielder?"

"I am not."

Tamri hadn't tried to use the power against him, assuming he could counter her Watermight with Vertigon's infamous Fire substance, which had nearly torn the continent apart five years ago. Besides, she doubted she could fight him without pitching off the dragon at the first strike. But he didn't know that.

She put on her best threatening voice. "I'll cut off your hands with a Watermight razor if you don't let me down."

"We're fifty feet up," the man said blandly. "Even if you didn't fall, Rook and Boru would never let you escape."

Tamri glanced at the red dragon flying alongside them, and the arching blue neck and white-feathered shoulders beneath her, weighing her chances. Leaping into the void might be preferable to coming face to face with Pendark's ruler.

The King's Tower was drawing closer. Lower battlements bristling with armed men surrounded the tall middle column. Some of those men would be Wielders. King Khrillin was notorious for hiring powerful Waterworkers who might otherwise try to carve out their own territory within the city-state. His followers weren't known for being lenient.

"Please don't give me to the king," Tamri begged, desperate now. The Vertigonian's knee was pressed against her thigh, and she clutched the fabric of his trousers. "I'll do anything."

He was quiet for a beat. She sensed him wavering. She didn't know much about Vertigonians, but maybe he would be merciful. Khrillin surely wouldn't.

"Please."

"I'm afraid it's too late."

They soared over the lower battlement of the King's Tower, and Tamri's heart plunged even faster than the dragon flew. King Khrillin's thugs were waiting for them.

3

Tamri didn't stand a chance. As they landed on the battlements in a clatter of talons, the Waterworkers yanked the remaining power from her body with a violence that left her shaking. She scrambled off the dragon, and the Waterworkers surrounded her, shouting, shoving, and spinning silver power through the air. She lost sight of her Vertigonian captor, and she could barely see the two dragons with so many bigger and taller people closing in around her. She couldn't escape no matter how hard she struggled, and her pleas for mercy fell on unsympathetic ears.

A few chaotic minutes later, she was being dragged into the tower and up a winding staircase to face King Khrillin himself.

The Waterworker serving as Tamri's primary jailer was called Brik, a particularly unpleasant fellow with bad breath, worse teeth, and a cruel grip. The Vertigonian stranger had held her firmly, but Brik squeezed her arms raw as he hauled her into the king's audience chamber.

Tamri had run into Khrillin on occasion back when he was just another Waterlord. She'd sold power to him when he was buying and stolen it when other Waterworkers were paying more. His dominion had encompassed the entire Garment District and a large swath of the Jewel District before he maneuvered his way into the kingship. Famous for throwing extravagant parties for the interesting

14

and influential, he made it his business to know things, and he used the information ruthlessly to achieve his ends. He was widely considered the most powerful Waterworker Pendark had seen in a generation—and its strongest king.

Today, Khrillin was dressed all in black, with fine polished boots, and a silk baldric straining over his broad chest. Black pearls and chips of obsidian were woven into his luxurious black beard, and his skin remained smooth, though he was well into his middle years. He carried himself with grand dignity, his presence radiating power.

"Well, well," he said as Brik dragged Tamri to the center of the audience chamber. "This is our dragon thief? I must say I expected one of the bigger players."

"Some other gutterfeeders tried to cause a distraction, sire," said Brik. "We caught most of them."

Tamri winced, wondering what had become of Pel.

"And what do you have to say for yourself, little gutterfeeder?" Khrillin's deep voice filled the room and rumbled through the soles of Tamri's feet. She resisted the urge to shrink in on herself. "Did you truly think you could get away with the beast?"

"I just wanted to borrow it."

"Borrow."

"That's right. Didn't go as planned."

Tamri scanned the audience chamber as she talked, seeking an escape. It was a windowless room in the dead center of the tower, with sparse but elegant furniture and two exits, both guarded. The king's usual entourage milled in the corners, Waterworkers who were powerful enough to find places at his side but not powerful enough to claim their own districts. A few swirled silvery-white spirals above their hands, showing off their wealth.

The Vertigonian dragon rider who'd caught her stood by a dark-wood table at the side of the room, arms folded across his chest, face impassive. She would find no help there.

A young woman sat at the table, watching the proceedings with interest. Two goblets before her suggested she'd been having a drink with the king when Tamri's arrival interrupted them. Not much older than Tamri, she was tall and freckled, with curly dark hair. Tamri had never seen her before.

"Have you nothing else to say?" The king's booming voice drew

Tamri's attention back to the center of the room. "No explanations or apologies?"

"They're never sorry enough." Brik's hands on her arms went stiff and icy. "Let me teach her a lesson."

Tamri's skin crawled, and she tried not to think about what kind of lesson Brik had in mind.

"I didn't mean any harm."

"Yet harm was done," the king said. "I understand the dragon is distraught, and much of the Watermight it was carrying has been lost."

"What?"

"Oh yes." The king examined the rings on his right hand idly. "A very valuable quantity, I must say."

Tamri glared at him—and at the room full of Waterworkers. She had been careful of the power while the dragon was with her. If someone else took advantage of the chaos to skim some for themselves, it wasn't her fault. Somehow, she doubted Khrillin would believe that.

"What are you going to do to me?"

"No need to fear. We can be reasonable." Khrillin smiled in a way that could almost be mistaken as kind. "You will pay for the missing Watermight and the damages the dragon caused during your little escapade—"

"But—"

He silenced her with a raised eyebrow. "Plus a bit extra for delaying my fine Vertigonian friends, who ought to have departed for the north by now. It—"

"But, sire, I—"

"Do not interrupt me again," the king said, his voice lowering to a dangerous purr.

Tamri clamped her mouth shut, fear worming through her belly. Khrillin gave her a hard stare.

Then he named a sum large enough to make even the other Waterworkers blink.

"I don't have that kind of money," Tamri said faintly. It was as obvious as stating that water was wet or Steel Pentagon fights were bloody. She couldn't hope to repay that much coin if she stole a dragon-full of power every week for a year.

"Then you should not have disrespected our guests."

Tamri tried to stammer out a plea for mercy, panic bubbling up so fast it made her dizzy. This would put Gramma Teall out in the gutter. It would obliterate any hope Tamri had ever had of changing their circumstances, of getting her grandmother the kind of healing and care she needed. It would leave Tamri indebted to Khrillin until her dying day.

Khrillin dismissed her spluttering objections with a wave. "If you cannot pay, perhaps Brik can find a use for you."

"Please, sire, I'll do anything—"

"Brik? Today, if you please."

The thug drew in a wet, pleased breath in Tamri's ear. Then he hoisted her off her feet and pulled her against his sweaty chest. Not pausing to think, Tamri twisted and sank her teeth deep into his hand.

Brik dropped her with a curse. Spitting out the taste of his foul skin, Tamri reached for the Watermight the Waterworkers had been showing off in the corner. The silver power shot toward her from three different hands. She formed it into a whip and lashed it at the nearest door, sending guards diving out of the way.

She yanked the door open with the whip of power and made it four steps before a silver net closed over her and scooped her into the air.

Tamri flailed wildly, knowing it was useless but unable to stop fighting. Fear and desperation convulsed through her as she tried to untangle her limbs from the icy web cutting into her skin. But it was no use. King Khrillin himself had cast the Watermight net—and Tamri's crude ability was no match for his.

No one else had moved as fast as Khrillin and Tamri. The Waterworkers were gaping stupidly at her, and Brik was examining his bleeding hand in irate disbelief. The Vertigonian dragon rider leaned down to whisper to the young woman at the table, watching Tamri with a concerned expression. She bared her teeth at him. It was a little too late for polite concern.

Khrillin drew Tamri back toward him in the net, holding her suspended a few feet off the floor. A silver-white film coated his eyes, not quite hiding the rage burning in his gaze. Tamri's body went cold with dread.

"That was unwise," Khrillin said softly. "Very unwise."

It wasn't just anger in the king's eyes, Tamri realized. Color suffused his cheeks, and he'd turned slightly away from the strangers. He was embarrassed. Her reckless bid for freedom had shamed him in front of his guests. In that moment, Tamri was certain she wouldn't leave this room alive.

Khrillin's voice took on a nasty tone at odds with his earlier grandeur. "You've just earned yourself a punishment worse than even Brik can dream up."

Tamri stiffened, waiting for the first blow.

"Pardon me, Your Majesty," a bright female voice interrupted. "May I have a word?"

Irritation flickered across Khrillin's face for an instant. Then he smoothed his features and turned as the young foreign woman rose from the table and advanced toward him with an energetic stride. She was dressed for travel in trousers and a fine gray coat with discreet yellow flowers embroidered along the lapels.

"I am sorry you had to witness this, my dear Princess Selivia," Khrillin began magnanimously. "I assure you I will dispatch this uncouth—"

"Please don't," the girl said quickly. She blushed and put on a winning smile. "Forgive me for interrupting, King Khrillin, but I believe this girl took our Cindral dragon for a ride after we had already purchased the Watermight it was carrying. That's right, isn't it, Heath?"

"Yes, Princess," said the bronze-haired Vertigonian promptly. "The dragon had already left the vent in the Jewel District."

The girl—the princess?—smiled. "In that case, she was really stealing from me not you, wouldn't you say, King Khrillin?"

The king blinked. "You could certainly make that argument."

"Well, then couldn't you let me determine her punishment?" The princess glanced at Brik, her smile slipping. "I would appreciate it ever so much."

The Watermight net pulsed tighter around Tamri's body, a reflex from its wielder. Khrillin wasn't happy about this development. Even so, Tamri felt a surge of hope. Whether the foreign princess realized she was on shaky ground or not, she wasn't backing down.

Khrillin took a deep calming breath then smoothed his beard and showed his teeth in something like a smile.

"What do you suggest, Princess?"

The young woman tucked a lock of dark, wavy hair behind her ear. "My sister-in-law, Dara, has recently begun a school in Vertigon to train young Wielders in the use of the magical substances, especially our Fire and your Watermight. I think this girl would be a magnificent pupil." The princess smiled at Tamri, who still hung awkwardly from the silver net. "I've never seen someone Wield so fast, and Heath here tells me she made a Watermight cord strong enough to hold a Cindral dragon."

Khrillin's face remained stony. "So the punishment would be . . .?"

"Oh." The princess blushed. "She'd have to live in Vertigon and work for us for a few years, but hopefully that's not overly harsh."

Khrillin didn't answer for several moments. Tamri had been watching the princess in mute incredulity, but she craned her neck in time to catch a calculating glint in Khrillin's eyes.

"I was under the impression Queen Dara only takes younger children," he said at last, a hint of suspicion in his voice. "Those who haven't yet become adapted to the use of a single magical substance."

The princess turned to Tamri. "How old are you?"

"Seventeen." She realized a beat too late that she probably should have lied. She was small for her age thanks to a lifetime of meager eating and could pass for younger. Khrillin would know the truth, though. Besides, she was having trouble believing any of this was really happening.

"I think Dara—the queen—would find it interesting to work with a slightly older student," the Vertigonian princess said. "She herself was nearly nineteen the first time she used Watermight."

"I remember it well," Khrillin said flatly.

An unpleasant current of tension flowed between the princess and the king. He wore an expression that would have made Tamri dive for cover if she weren't still ensnared in the Watermight net. The princess gave him a sunny smile in return, but she was fiddling with the embroidery on her coat, the quick movements of her long fingers betraying her nerves. The air seemed to drain from the windowless space.

Tamri tugged experimentally at the Watermight net, attempting to siphon off enough power to break free while the king was distracted. It was no use. Khrillin was far too strong.

As she shifted against the net, she caught a glimpse of the dragon rider's face. Heath, was it? He was watching the exchange with a stiff-jawed expression, his hand resting on the glowing cudgel at his belt. Tamri was pretty sure he was seconds away from leaping to the princess's defense.

But the young woman seemed determined to batter through the tension with her smile, and apparently Khrillin wasn't willing to risk his lucrative arrangement with her homeland for Tamri's sake. Tamri had heard he arranged the Watermight sales deal with Vertigon's King Siv and his mysterious Fire Queen personally.

At last, he inclined his head. "I don't wish to deny you anything, my dear Selivia. You may take the little urchin back to Vertigon with you, if you think she'll please the Fire Queen."

The princess relaxed a hair. Heath did not.

"It's settled, then," the princess said. "We'll depart tomorrow morning." She glanced at Tamri, her freckled nose wrinkling. "Do let her down. That looks terribly uncomfortable."

"As you wish."

The net unraveled, dropping Tamri roughly onto the ground. Khrillin drew the silvery power in through his ringed fingers, giving Tamri a dark, considering look. She managed to meet his gaze defiantly, even though it made her want to sink right through the stone floor.

Then the king turned to the Vertigonians and plastered on a charming smile. "Shall we see to our dinner now that you'll be staying an extra night, Princess?"

"Oh yes, I would love to visit that place in the Port District my brother told me about."

"It's among my favorites. Their grilled eel and brindleweed are famed throughout the continent. And I know how much you love sugar mushrooms."

"That sounds delightful."

The princess winked at Tamri and returned to the darkwood

table, continuing to chat about food with Khrillin. The tension of moments ago had been shoved down as if it never existed.

None of the Waterworkers or guards knew what to do with Tamri now that the foreign princess had claimed her. She crouched in the center of the room, still not believing what had just happened. Had the princess of Vertigon really just offered her a chance to study Wielding in the legendary mountain kingdom?

A hand landed on her shoulder, and she jumped.

"Easy there." Heath stood over her, wearing an expression of intense disapproval. "Be back here at dawn and pack light. I won't have you slowing the dragons."

"I can go?"

Heath glanced at Brik, who was scowling as though his birthday had been canceled. "Do you want to stay here?"

Tamri had a thousand questions, but with another furtive look at the princess who had saved her from Khrillin's justice, she fled.

4

Tamri left the audience chamber at a run. Her skin smarted from the icy Watermight net, and she couldn't help feeling this was some cruel joke, and Brik would step into her path to begin her real punishment at any moment. She could still smell his foul breath and feel the terror as the Watermight net scooped her up, ending her desperate escape attempt.

As she found her way back to the tower's central stairwell, she glimpsed Pel being hauled down a side corridor. He was babbling to his captors, offering them information, assistance, anything to avoid being punished.

"It wasn't my idea, I swear. I'll lead you to the masterminds if you let me go!"

Tamri picked up her pace, hoping Pel wouldn't spot her. He wouldn't hesitate to pin the whole thing on her. That was just how Pendark was. Friendship didn't get you far, and people never spoke up for each other.

Why had that princess risked Khrillin's ire to defend Tamri, someone she'd never even met? And why had he agreed to the request?

Fearing the king would change his mind, she stomped down the stairwell as fast as she could. Elegant drawing rooms and elaborate archways eventually gave way to crowded barracks with plain wooden doors. At the bottom of the tower, she dashed across the cobblestone courtyard and out the gates, not slowing until she reached the drawbridge leading off King's Island.

She paused to look back at the battlements. A pair of scarlet wings stretched above the stone crenellations. The red dragon screeched, and whether the sendoff was meant for her or not, Tamri took it as her cue to keep moving.

She crossed the wooden bridge and hurried down a busy Royal District street, dodging passersby with her usual agility. Their eyes slid away from her, as if they couldn't bear to look at a grubby little urchin with her bare feet and a muddy tunic. Midnight-blue flags declaring allegiance to Khrillin flew from every shop and balcony, and the boats on the nearest canals displayed similar colors.

Before long, she reached the Market District, where the red flags of the local Waterlady flew proudly. Market District was more canal than island. Tamri slipped onto a flat-bottomed ferry to continue her journey, hiding behind a rotund fruit seller so she wouldn't have to pay the fare. She crouched in the stern, hoping the muscular fellow poling the ferry along the waterway wouldn't notice her. Only when the Royal District disappeared from view completely did she start to believe she'd truly escaped.

The ferry meandered among market barges and smaller shops floating on the swampy water. The fine sandalwood boat where the Red Lady of the Market District oversaw the buying and selling of Watermight looked especially busy today. The canals emitted a rank odor in the late-summer heat, and small creatures floated in the shallows, watching for dropped crumbs.

Gliding along the busy waterway calmed Tamri's anxiety and gave her a chance to think things through. Upon consideration, she was sure Brik's threats and not her Watermight skills had prompted Princess Selivia to speak up for her. Any woman could guess at the kind of "punishments" a man like that would have in mind. But did the princess really want Tamri to study at this magic-wielder school in Vertigon?

The mysterious mountaintop kingdom was hundreds of miles to the north. The most powerful man and woman on the continent, King Sivarrion Amintelle and his Fire Queen, Dara, ruled in Vertigon. Some said she had been the one to sack the land of Trure and burn its cities and fields to ash five years ago. Others said she had defeated an evil Fire sorcerer who would have destroyed Pendark and Soole as well as Trure if he had his way. Pel had even claimed the Fire Queen was responsible for awakening the true dragons and unleashing them on the continent after they'd been asleep for centuries.

The ferry bumped into a dock. Tamri slipped overboard and splashed to shore through the shallows so no one would realize she hadn't paid for her ride. She scrambled out of the water and continued on, the fish and ash smells of the nearby Smokery District enveloping her like a cloud of flies. She took a shortcut along a rocky causeway, holding her breath against the stink.

No matter which rumor was accurate, Queen Dara didn't sound like someone who would take the time to train a bunch of children. All the powerful Waterworkers Tamri had ever encountered were exceedingly cautious about who they taught to Wield. They never knew which apprentice would be the one to rise up and try to seize their power. Even if Tamri had been born to a wealthy family, she might never have been offered a chance to learn. She had figured out most of what she could do with the Watermight on her own.

She left the cloying aromas of the Smokery District behind and turned toward the East Port District. A strong breeze blew in from the Black Gulf, cooling the sweat running down her forehead. The familiar salty air brought her thudding back to reality. No matter how intriguing this Fire Queen and her school were, Tamri couldn't actually go. She would never abandon Gramma Teall.

Her grandmother's hut was only a few blocks from the Gulf, set on rickety stilts that threatened to collapse every time the neighborhood flooded. Technically, this ramshackle neighborhood was part of the Gutter District, the term used for the scattered veins of the city too poor to warrant the attention of a Waterlord.

Despite the stilt hut's location, the sea wasn't visible from here. It had been months since Gramma Teall felt well enough to totter down to the beach without Tamri's assistance. She wished she could be home more, but the Watermight-stealing business got more competitive every day. It was all she could do to keep their heads above water.

Tamri reached the hut and climbed the driftwood steps to her grandmother's porch. Their neighbor, a fisherman who was too old for the work he still did, nodded at her from the next porch, where he was mending brightly colored lures with trembling fingers.

Tamri waved a greeting. "Everything all right, Master Saul?"

"The sun's still rising."

Tamri smiled at the familiar saying. Saul had many. "Have you talked to her today?"

"Aye. She's as feisty as ever," the fisherman called. "And she's having one of her better days. Remembered my name and asked about my son's health."

"Which son?"

"Well, it was Siln, may he rest, but she knew he'd been ill as a youth."

Tamri winced. Saul's eldest son had died in a Watermight struggle years ago. Siln had been the primary provider for his parents and siblings, and his death was the reason the old fisherman still had to go to sea. Gramma Teall must have been remembering an earlier, better time.

"Thanks for looking in on her, anyway," Tamri said.

"Happy to." Saul gave a phlegmy cough. "You look as though you've been fighting in the canals again, girl," he said. "Try not to upset her."

Tamri grimaced at the mud caked to her legs. Angry red lines stood out on her skin from Khrillin's Watermight net. She used a water bucket on the porch to wash up as well as she could and combed her shoulder-length black hair with her fingers before entering the house.

The space was sparsely furnished, with a driftwood table, a few cupboards, and a thin door leading to the only bedroom. Gramma Teall sat in her usual chair by the far window, picking the stitches out of an insignia sewn on a dark-orange coat. Like Tamri, Gramma Teall was small and scrappy, dressed in threadbare clothes. A pewter clasp shaped like a dragonfly held her steel-gray hair back from her wrinkled face.

"There you are," she said, her voice sharp and reedy. "Come in, then. You'll let in the flies."

"How are you feeling?"

Gramma Teall tapped a finger on the shattered hip that kept her housebound. "Spry. You?"

"I had an adventure today."

"Adventures are for rich people, girl. Did you join that fool boy Pel on another scheme?"

"Yes." Tamri sighed. "It was a bad idea."

Gramma Teall chortled. "I'm shocked. Go on, then. Pour us some tea and tell me about it."

Tamri fetched the tea and settled at her grandmother's feet to share what had happened since she left the hut before dawn. While she talked, she pulled another dark-orange garment from the basket at Gramma Teall's side and helped take out stitches with a blunt knife. The Waterlord who favored the shade had recently been murdered—probably by the Red Lady of the Market District or the up-and-comer who controlled half the Boundary District—and the uniforms his people had worn needed to be shorn of his insignia and resold.

Tamri rustled up work like this whenever she could, mostly to give Gramma Teall something to do during her long hours at home. Tamri didn't want her venturing out on her own in case she couldn't find her way back. Even without her troublesome hip, she needed care.

Tamri's greatest and only dream was to make enough money gathering Watermight to take Gramma Teall out of the city one day. She would buy a little cottage overlooking the sea, where she could take care of her grandmother full-time instead of risking death and dismemberment to put food on their driftwood table.

As Tamri described the dragon, the king, and the foreign princess's offer, she wondered if the Fire Queen could teach her skills that would free her family from poverty. Not that she would ever find out. She didn't plan to go near the Vertigonians or the King's Tower ever again.

"That's a tale if I ever heard one," Gramma Teall said when Tamri finished her story.

"It's all true."

"Aye, and would I remember you lying to me if it wasn't, girl?"

Tamri dropped the orange garment into her lap. "I wouldn't do that to you!"

"Mm-hmm. I didn't get to be a hundred and four by being gullible."

Tamri barked a laugh. She was pretty sure Gramma Teall wasn't a day over seventy. "No, you're just too stubborn to die."

"True." Gramma Teall gave a satisfied nod and returned to her work, her hands moving nimbly along the seams. The dwindling light beyond the window caught on her dragonfly clasp. Tamri felt a burst of affection for the old woman, who had cared for her until Tamri was old enough to return the favor.

"I can't go, anyway," Tamri said. "I wouldn't leave you."

"Nonsense." Gramma Teall took another bundle of orange fabric from the basket. "Your momma will look after me. You must go to Vertigon."

Tamri's smile faded. Her mother had died when she was five, before she was even old enough to draw on the Watermight for the first time. As feisty as Gramma Teall seemed, she wasn't well. And as much as Tamri liked the idea of setting off across the continent to learn from a legendary sorceress, it wasn't an option.

She stood, brushing a flake of drying mud off her tunic. "Are you hungry, Gramma?"

"Always."

"Let me see if there's any of that dried—"

The thud of boots on the porch was her only warning. Then the door flew open in a cascade of silver-white power. The hut shook on its stilts as several tall figures stomped inside, already slinging Watermight.

Tamri dove in front of Gramma Teall, reaching for the knife she'd been using to pick out the stiches. But as her fingers closed around the blunt blade, a loop of Watermight lashed around her waist, hoisted her up, and slammed her against the wall. Her head rang from the impact, sparks dancing before her eyes, and the blade dropped from her grasp.

Pinned flat to the wall, she had a good view of the intruders. Brik, a woman with her head shaved bald, and King Khrillin himself were advancing across the hut. Their Watermight-glazed eyes lit the room with an icy glow.

Gramma Teall gave a fierce cry and rose from her chair, her knobby hands reaching like claws. She only managed one step toward Khrillin before the bald female Waterworker flicked her fingers, and a cord of silver power forced Gramma Teall back into her chair. Her skull cracked against the wood.

"Let her go, you slime-eating gutterslug!" Tamri bellowed.

"Silence." Khrillin's whip-crack voice made the whole house shudder. "You exhausted any chance of leniency after that shameful display this afternoon."

"You can't hurt—"

A fist of Watermight punched Tamri in the face before she could finish the sentence, splitting her lip open. A second fist formed directly in front of Gramma Teall, who glared at it as if her gaze alone could destroy the ball of magic.

"You were saying?"

Tamri clamped her jaws shut, shaking with fury and fear. She was plastered against the wall two feet off the ground, rough splinters poking into her skin, completely immobilized.

"That's better." Khrillin went on in an almost conversational tone. "Now, you put me in an uncomfortable position today. Very uncomfortable indeed." He looked around the little hut, with its ramshackle driftwood furniture, and his lips twisted in a sneer. "I couldn't very well deny Princess Selivia's request. The girl is sister to the King of Vertigon and the Queen of Trure, and she is betrothed to a powerful Soolen nobleman. No, I most certainly couldn't tell the little brat no."

Khrillin combed his fingers through his beard. The pearls and gems were still woven into its luxurious depths, glinting in the Watermight glow. He rolled his shoulders as if shaking off an irritant.

"Regardless, you may have inadvertently created an opportunity for me." He stalked toward her, polished boots squeaking. "I would very much like to know what the king and queen of Vertigon intend to do with their little Wielder school. My informants claim it's only a small group of children. But King Siv has deceived me before, and I refuse to fall for it again."

Tamri didn't know what deceit Khrillin was talking about, and she didn't dare ask. She was more worried about Gramma Teall, whose face she couldn't see from where she was splayed against the wall, feet dangling. Gramma Teall's head had dropped sideways. *If they've hurt her . . .*

The truth was Tamri could do nothing. She was utterly powerless.

She glared at Khrillin, imagining setting fire to his fancy beard. "What do you want from me?"

"To pay for your actions today, you will go to Vertigon and attend the Fire Queen's school. You will send regular reports containing everything you learn. And I do not just mean the Wielding skills." Khrillin stepped closer, near enough for Tamri to smell the scented oils he wore on his clothes. "You will find out what the Vertigonian royals are hiding from me."

"You want me to spy?"

Khrillin sniffed. "If you must put it so crassly."

He turned away and began poking through their little kitchen, opening empty cupboards and prodding moldy towels.

"Now, I am not unreasonable," he went on in a lighter voice. "In exchange for your services, I will provide your dear grandmother here with a comfortable home, good food, the best Watermight healers, and a full-time caretaker."

Tamri blinked. "You will?"

"Indeed. Every useful bit of information you send will guarantee another week of easy living for her. You've been her sole support for some time, I hear." He gave a smug smile. "And despite how ferociously she tried to claw my eyes out a moment ago, I understand she is not well."

Tamri dug her fingernails into her palms, wishing she could launch herself at Khrillin. Maybe it was good she was still pinned to the wall. She'd tried enough reckless moves for one day. But even in her agitated state, she knew Khrillin's offer had to be too good to be true.

"What happens if you don't think my information is useful enough?"

"I'm glad you asked." Khrillin opened the tea canister and sniffed its contents. "If you fail to provide regular *substantial* reports or if you tell anyone in Vertigon about this task, your darling granny here will suffer proportionally."

The woman with the shaved head cracked her knuckles, her power still holding Gramma Teall in her chair. Brik was scowling at Tamri so grotesquely it was a wonder he wasn't drooling.

"Can't you leave my grandmother out of this?"

"Oh, I don't think so." Khrillin dropped the tea canister on the table, not bothering to seal it again. "Let her plight motivate you to do your very best sleuthing."

Tamri thought of the bright-eyed princess, who had spoken up for her in a room full of dangerous Wielders. She'd hate to repay her kindness by spying on her family. But she understood refusal wasn't an option, at least not right now. Maybe she and Gramma Teall could steal onto a ship as soon as these three left the hut.

"Okay," she said. "I'll do it."

"I thought you'd say that." Khrillin released Tamri from the Watermight bonds without warning, and she dropped to her knees. She rubbed her arms, which now bore even more angry red lines.

Khrillin strode forward and offered her a hand with a gallant flourish. She hesitated, but she couldn't afford to offend him or give any indication she might not follow through on the agreement. With another look at Gramma Teall's head lolling on her shoulder, Tamri took the king's hand and allowed him to pull her to her feet.

Suddenly, Khrillin's fingernails glowed silver-white, and Watermight laced around Tamri's arm and crept up her elbow. She jerked reflexively, but Khrillin held her tight.

"Do you swear to serve as my eyes and ears in Vertigon, to learn everything you can about King Siv, Queen Dara, and their allies, and to report every word of your findings to me while telling no one of your true purpose?"

Tamri tried to pull away from the silvery snare twining around her arm. A Watermight Oath was binding in a way no other promise could be. Once sworn, there would be no going back on this agreement. But no matter how much she struggled, she couldn't escape Khrillin's grasp.

Gramma Teall raised her head and strained to catch Tamri's eye. She shook her head, mouth tight with concern. She didn't want Tamri to do this. But this might be the only chance Tamri ever had to give her grandmother a better life. No matter how much she scraped and stole, she couldn't pay for a comfortable home, good food, the best Watermight healers, and a full-time caretaker. This could be the chance to change their lives Pel had promised her.

In truth, the decision was easy. Tamri straightened her back and looked up at Khrillin.

"I swear it."

"So may it be."

Abruptly, the Watermight crawled upward from Tamri's arm and looped around her throat like a collar. The power sank into her skin as the Oath took hold, making her neck and jaw go numb, becoming part of her bones. Tamri tamped down a wild jolt of terror. She had made her choice.

At last, Khrillin released her, and she slumped, feeling as if she had just run across half the city. The cold in her neck faded slowly, but she knew she was bound as surely as if she wore an iron shackle. Breaking this promise would freeze Tamri's neck until it shattered like glass.

"That wasn't so bad, was it?" The king wiped his hands with a silk handkerchief. "You will come to the Tower tomorrow, and you will not speak of this to Princess Selivia or her escort. I will send Gyra here to arrange care for your grandmother as soon as you disappear over the horizon."

The bald woman jerked her head in assent, looking at Gramma Teall without expression. Brik massaged the hand Tamri had bitten, looking disappointed he wouldn't be invited to punish her again. She hoped he got an infection.

Tamri looked up at the king, whose eyes still glowed silver. "How long will the Oath last?"

"Until I release you."

"So never?"

"I reward those who serve me well." Khrillin studied her thoughtfully for a moment. "Find me a jewel of information precious enough, and I shall give your freedom and your granny back to you."

"Is that a promise?"

His lips twisted in a cruel smile. "Study hard, Tamri, and do not fail me. The Oath will sense it if you hold anything back." He turned to offer a mocking bow to Gramma Teall. "If you'll excuse me." Then he snapped his fingers at his Waterworkers and strode out into the dusk.

Gyra released Gramma Teall and followed, not sparing another glance for Tamri. Brik stomped across the hut after her, pausing only to spit on the driftwood table.

Tamri waited until the trio descended the porch steps and sloshed away through the muddy street before fetching a drink of water for Gramma Teall and checking her for injuries.

"Don't fuss over me, girl," she said as Tamri removed her dragonfly clasp and parted her steel-gray hair to look for blood.

"I'm so sorry about this," Tamri said miserably. "I don't know how he found us."

"Men like that have their ways."

Tamri gripped the pewter clasp hard, the edges poking her skin. "When I find out who told him where I live—"

"It was probably that scheming boy you think is your friend," Gramma Teall said. "You have bigger things to fret about now. You'd best get packing."

Tamri started to protest, but the mere thought of going back on the Oath made an icy chill tighten around her neck. She was going to obey Khrillin's orders whether she liked it or not.

She brushed Gramma Teall's hair with her fingers—she wasn't bleeding after all—and replaced the dragonfly clasp. "Will you be all right?"

"Of course," Gramma Teall said brusquely. "You go off to study in that . . . what's the burning mountain called again?"

"Vertigon."

"That's right. You go to Vertigon. You do exactly what that salt adder of a Waterlord asks, and don't even think about coming back to Pendark."

"Of course I'll come back." Khrillin had said a valuable-enough piece of information could buy her freedom from the Watermight Oath. She wouldn't be his spy forever.

"My memory is going, girl, not my common sense," Gramma Teall said dryly. "Now that he has leverage, he won't ever let you out of his clutches."

Tamri wanted to argue, to lash out against her own powerlessness. But she would do anything to make sure Gramma Teall wasn't harmed—and Khrillin knew it. But he had also given her just enough hope to keep her going. She would find that "jewel of information" no matter what it took.

She knelt at Gramma Teall's side and took her hand. "I don't care what he does to me," she said fiercely. "I'll come back for you." That was an oath that didn't require Watermight for her to keep.

"Nonsense." Gramma Teall's hands tightened on hers, as tough as old tree roots despite their tiny size. "You won't get another opportunity like this, Tamri. Go see that world out there. Learn how to actually use your power."

"But—"

Gramma Teall silenced her with a sharp look. "Didn't I ever teach you not to interrupt, girl?" She tipped Tamri's chin up, fixing her with an unyielding stare. "Go, and learn enough to make sure no one, not even me, can ever tell you what to do again."

5

Princess Selivia Amintelle stood on a balcony at the top of the King's Tower as daylight faded from the Pendarkan sky. Flashes of silver indicated Watermight being used in the city below, playing beautifully against the rich browns and greens of the delta.

She fanned her shirt briskly, attempting to alleviate the heat. She should have changed into one of her shorter Pendarkan-style dresses before going out to eat, but she'd been distracted by the incident with the young Watermight thief. Despite numerous visits to this muggy southern city, she'd never quite gotten used to the way the heat glued her clothes to her skin and made her hair frizz.

The meal had ended early so Khrillin could disappear on a mysterious errand. Selivia didn't know what to make of his perfunctory treatment of her lately. She had visited Pendark several times a year since Vertigon began purchasing Watermight from Khrillin, and he had always been welcoming, even solicitous.

But this time, something was different. The smiles Khrillin and his supporters gave her were strained, their pleasantries less genuine than on her first visits here. It made her uneasy.

She scanned the purple clouds above the tower, just in case Mav was nearby this evening. He was supposed to return to his usual roost in the Darkwood after their departure was delayed. It was best for him not to spend long in Pendark itself. Too many people still screamed at the sight of his vast black wings and glittering cobalt eyes. They'd be even more scared if they realized Mav was not a benign Cindral dragon, like the ones who could carry Watermight in their bellies. He was the only Fire-breathing true dragon south of the Burnt Mountains.

He was also Selivia's very best friend, and he got lonely and irritable without her.

He'd become agitated more often than usual on this trip, adding to her disquiet. Perhaps he was just jealous because they'd be spending a lot more time apart soon. Hopefully his behavior didn't indicate trouble to come.

Selivia reached into her pocket to touch the last letter she had received from Latch Brach, the young Soolen lord she was to wed in just six months. It was an arranged marriage, one Selivia had negotiated herself in order to persuade Latch's father to end his invasion of her mother's home country of Trure. Selivia had felt positively heroic about it at the time. She'd been only fourteen years old, and her successful negotiations had helped ensure the peace the continent had enjoyed for the past five years. Fortunately, she ended up liking young Latch himself when they met for the first time on the dragon-ravaged slopes of Vertigon. She'd found him gallant and refined and terribly handsome, and he seemed to like her in return.

But that was five years ago. Now that Selivia was actually on her way to the southeastern land of Soole to prepare for their wedding, doubts had begun to assail her.

She and Latch had exchanged letters and gifts over the years, but she still didn't really know him—and she feared they didn't have much in common. Now a grown woman of nineteen, she'd been living a glorious life in the skies, flying Mav back and forth across the continent to ensure the safety of the Watermight-carrying Cindral dragons. She was instrumental in arranging the trade agreement with Khrillin, and the dragon riders hadn't made a single trip to Pendark without her. She had gotten used to seeing the world from the air.

For his part, Latch had spent much of the last few years studying scholarly writing about the magical substances. He was an accomplished Watermight Wielder, and Selivia couldn't understand why he enjoyed combing through musty archives and reading about magic when he could be Wielding it instead. She didn't have the ability to use the magical substances, but if she did, she'd want to be out there actually doing it.

She took the letter from her pocket and traced the neat script on the outside. Latch was an eloquent writer, and she had savored his missives in the beginning. But they had become less frequent over time as he put more of his attention into his research. And she traveled so often that she didn't always receive the letters or respond to them right away.

That was why she was going to Soole so far in advance of her wedding. In the spring, her royal family would travel from their respective domains for the celebration, where they would build relationships and solidify alliances all across the continent. Selivia desperately hoped that by the time they arrived, she and Latch would be properly in love.

The trouble was that she didn't know if Latch would welcome her arrival. She opened the letter and read it for the hundredth time since leaving Vertigon a month ago.

My Dearest Selivia,

Forgive me for being so abrupt in my writing. I am not certain it is wise for you to come to Soole yet. I have learned something in my research, and I may need to investigate. I will send word to Fork Town to confirm if you should join me as planned. Watch out for our pen friends, and bring a copy of Brelling's East Isles journal if you have one.

I remain yours,

Latch

There had been no follow-up message waiting at her usual Fork Town inn. No call for her to join him. No assurances that he'd be pleased to see her. Seeing no reason to wait around in Fork Town, Selivia had gone on to Pendark with the rest of the dragon riders. She hoped a more reassuring letter would be waiting for her on their way back through Fork Town tomorrow.

Selivia reread the line that caused her the most concern. Latch asked her to bring Brelling's "East Isles" journal. The famous travel scribe, who was Latch's favorite writer, had never been to the East Isles, located off the southeastern coast of the Soolen peninsula. In fact, Brelling explicitly warned against going there in his other writings. Latch would know that better than anyone. He had to be trying to tell her something. But why not warn her outright if there was trouble?

She had brought a copy of Brelling's Soole travel journal, carefully packed in her leather satchel. She hoped that was the one Latch had meant and that the reference didn't indicate something was wrong.

But the salutation also wasn't quite right. He didn't normally call her "My Dearest." His greetings had always been more restrained. The hand looked like his, but she had to wonder if the letter had come from Latch at all.

No matter what, the letter bothered her, along with Khrillin's attitude and the increasingly hostile comments she'd been hearing about Soole since arriving in Pendark. She wasn't sure how much longer the peace in the continent would hold. Not getting along with her future husband might be the least of her problems.

A knock sounded on the door to her chamber.

"Princess?" a muffled voice called. "May I have a word?"

Selivia put Latch's letter back into her pocket and reentered the richly decorated sitting room, leaving the balcony door open. She fixed her windblown hair and tucked her shirt back into her snug breeches.

"Come in, Heath."

Her chief dragon rider entered, scanning the sitting room as if checking for hidden enemies. He was the same age as her, but his large size and serious bearing made him seem older. He wore his Amintelle-blue uniform tightly buttoned despite the heat, and his Fire cudgel hung at his belt.

He offered a neat bow, formal despite their long friendship. "I wish to speak with you about your decision earlier today, about that girl."

"She didn't mean to hurt the dragons, Heath. I know you're protective of them."

"She's not the problem," Heath said grimly. "I was watching

Khrillin closely during the incident. He didn't like you challenging him in front of his people."

"It was a small thing." Selivia smiled at his stern tone and skipped over to a small darkwood table to pour him a cup of tea. She still had one box of sugar mushrooms left over. Maybe that would get him to cheer up a bit. Heath took himself and his duties very seriously, and she'd made it something of a personal mission to get him to lighten up.

"Princess—"

"How many times do I have to ask you to call me Sel?"

"Several more, I think, Princess. I'm worried about how King Khrillin has been acting on this visit."

"You're always worried." Selivia pressed a teacup and half a sugar mushroom into Heath's hands. "And you've never liked Khrillin."

"It's different this time." Heath frowned down at her. She was a tall woman, but she still had to tilt her head to meet his eyes. "Can't you tell? He's as accommodating as ever on the surface, but he's not as friendly toward Vertigon as he once was."

"He wouldn't risk his deal with Siv," Selivia said. Her brother had made a peace with Khrillin that was every bit as important as the one she'd secured with Soole.

"Maybe he would," Heath said. "I've been hearing troubling things down in the barracks. Fork Town has apparently been more volatile than usual lately, and Soolen and Pendarkan ships have clashed near the Desolate Coast. No matter what he says, Khrillin still hates Soole."

"Maybe that's all it is, then," Selivia said. "He's starting to see me as a Soolen lady instead of as my father's daughter. They were friends, you know."

"That was over thirty years ago, before Khrillin was the king of the most violent and conniving place on the continent." Heath looked at the balcony door, as if expecting an assassin to leap inside. "It feels different. Please promise me you'll be more careful."

Selivia couldn't contradict him when she'd sensed it herself. A shift in the wind. A change in the air. Khrillin had even ended their dinner early and had her ferried back to the King's Tower without him. Perhaps she could be more cautious.

"Very well. I promise." She took the other half of the sugar mushroom from the box and chewed it thoughtfully. "I wonder if Khrillin thinks I'm planning to end our Watermight contract and buy the substance from Soole instead."

"That could explain some of the hostility," Heath said. "Are you transferring the contract?"

"No." A hint of bitterness snuck into her tone. "Soole is getting a Vertigonian princess. Pendark needs something of equal value to maintain our good relationship."

Heath blinked, and Selivia wished she hadn't said anything. She was used to speaking familiarly with her chief dragon rider, but she hadn't meant to reveal her mixed feelings about her impending marriage. About everything she'd have to give up to become a Lady of Soole.

"You're probably right about that Watermight thief," she said, hoping to change the subject. "I should have spoken to Khrillin privately about the girl instead of insisting he give her to me in front of everyone."

"About that." Heath cleared his throat. "Do we really have to bring her?"

"We couldn't just leave her to Khrillin!" Selivia said.

"Agreed, but that doesn't mean she has to come home with us. She's a criminal."

"I think she'll do really well with Dara."

"We don't know anything about her."

"You'll have plenty of time to get to know her on the way to Vertigon," Selivia said brightly. "You can tell me all about it next time I see you."

Dismay crossed Heath's face, as if he was only now registering that Selivia would be leaving the dragon party at Fork Town and continuing east to Soole instead of returning with him.

The sun had set outside, and shadows were beginning to fill the room. Selivia moved to uncover a Fire Lantern that had been imported all the way from Vertigon to decorate this guest chamber. The golden Firelight filled the elegant room, reminding her of home. She didn't know when she'd next see Vertigon.

"I'll give you a letter to take to Dara about our new friend," she said, fending off the tight pinch of homesickness. "In the meantime, you're in charge of her."

Heath grimaced. "But she's a feral child who—"

"Heath, be nice. I'm counting on you."

He sighed. "Yes, Princess." He took a bite of the sugar mushroom and scrunched up his face at the taste.

She chuckled and patted him on the shoulder. "Poor Heath. You're grumpier than a Soolen sometimes."

"Not sure that's possible." Heath glanced at her hand on his shoulder and then down into her eyes.

Suddenly the world seemed to go still. There was something in Heath's gaze that she'd seen before, something that warmed her cheeks and shortened her breath. Something she was quite certain must never be spoken aloud, for both their sakes.

Heath took a deep breath. "Sel, I need to tell you something." He moved as if to take her hand. "I—"

"Don't!" Selivia stepped back, not quite as smoothly as she meant to, and snatched up her teacup.

Heath looked shocked, but he covered it fast, his face going as blank as stone. It only confirmed what he'd almost said before she pulled away. Neither of them spoke for a few excruciating seconds.

"You'd better go check on the dragons," she said into her tea. "They must be terribly upset after today's excitement."

Silence. Then: "Of course."

Selivia risked a glance at him. A twitch of the mouth and a flicker of the eyelids were enough to tell her Heath was deeply mortified. Her heart gave a painful creak.

He set his teacup gently on the table. "Sleep well, Princess."

She tried to answer and failed. Nothing she could say would help.

After one more unbearable pause, Heath turned and strode for the door, forgetting his usual formal bow entirely. He was gone before Selivia could work up the nerve to call him back.

6

Tamri set out for the Royal District before the sun came up. She'd followed the dragon rider's instructions and packed light, not that she had many possessions. She filled a burlap sack with a few oft-darned tunics and one wide-skirted ankle-length summer dress. She also packed a pair of leather boots that had belonged to her mother, though she couldn't remember the last time she'd worn shoes. It was easier to get mud off bare feet.

"Take my old cloak," Gramma Teall said, limping out the front door after her. "It's cold in the north."

Tamri hugged the thick brown wool, thicker than any blanket she'd ever owned, and tried to think of something suitably meaningful to say. She wasn't sure if they'd ever see each other again—or if Gramma Teall would remember her if they did.

"Saul will check in on you while I'm gone," she said around a lump forming in her throat. "Be nice to him."

Gramma Teall snorted. "I will if he stops proposing marriage."

"Yes, he should really know better."

Gramma Teall looked at her for a moment then reached into her own hair and pulled out the pewter dragonfly clasp. Tamri started to protest, but Gramma Teall waved away her objections and pinned the dragonfly to the brown cloak.

"You're less likely to misplace it than I am," she said, her voice thickening. "Take care of yourself, baby girl."

Tamri kissed her grandmother's cheek and tramped down the driftwood steps, knowing neither of them wanted a tearful goodbye. She paused at the end of their muddy street and looked back at Gramma Teall on the stilt house porch. The sea breeze lifted her steel-gray hair around her face as she raised a thin hand in farewell. Then she gave a resolute nod and hobbled back into the hut.

Tamri left the grubby neighborhood along her usual route, not quite believing she wouldn't return that night. She'd been scrounging up a life for her and Gramma Teall in the Gutter District for years. She'd never imagined some benevolent stranger would spirit her away.

She touched her neck, where the Watermight Oath bound her flesh and bone. This lucky break wasn't without dangers. Still, it might be the only way she'd ever make her grandmother's life more comfortable. If Khrillin kept his part of the bargain, it would be worth the risks.

She reached the Royal District in record time after hitching a ride on the back of an especially speedy water taxi—the kind that used Watermight to speed through the canals. She hopped off just before the Waterworker driving the boat spotted her. Then, wrestling her nerves into submission, she presented herself at the gates to the King's Tower.

A Pendarkan guard escorted her straight up to the battlements, where a narrow walkway overlooked the cobblestone courtyard. It was the same place where she'd landed the day before, though she'd been too busy being trussed up by Brik to take it in. The canals beyond the battlements were turning pink in the light of the rising sun. Despite the early hour, several of the Waterworkers who'd been in Khrillin's audience chamber yesterday were here, along with a dozen more guards carrying spears. The Waterworkers shot angry looks at Tamri, no doubt remembering how she'd snatched away their power in front of the king yesterday.

The Vertigonian princess stood in their midst, wearing breeches and a dusky green coat with white flowers embroidered on the cuffs. Her hair was twisted in a knot on her head, and she carried a leather satchel on her back. When she spotted Tamri, she parted the crowd of guards and Wielders and skipped over to greet her personally.

"It's lovely to see you again—oh, you never told me your name yesterday!"

"It's Tamri," she answered, surprised at the warm greeting.

"I'm so pleased you're traveling with us, Tamri."

"Uh, thank you, uh, Princess."

Princess Selivia smiled brightly. "Lovely weather for flying today," she said. "It'll cool off as we get farther north. I'm not going all the way to Vertigon, but Heath will look after you. You're going to love the school!"

Tamri struggled to find an appropriate response to the princess's chatter. How were you supposed to talk to foreign royalty? A sudden urge to turn and flee seized her.

"I hope it wasn't too much trouble to get ready at short notice," the princess went on, not seeming to notice Tamri's awkwardness. "I'm afraid I'm overdue in—oh look!"

Tamri ducked instinctively at her gasp.

"The dragons are coming!"

Ignoring her startled expression, the princess looped her arm through Tamri's and drew her toward the battlements.

The summer morning was hazy, and the cloudy pink sky sat low on the horizon like a wool blanket. Tamri searched the fuzzy expanse, a nervous thrill buzzing through her. After Khrillin's appearance in her home the night before, she had almost forgotten about the dragons.

A dark shape moved through the clouds, strange and ungainly and silent. Then she saw another. And another. Tamri tried to make out the details through the haze, unsure exactly how many there were.

Abruptly, the clouds seemed to open, revealing the great flying beasts plummeting downward with startling speed.

Tamri stepped back in surprise.

There were five dragons in the flock, each with wings bedecked with feathers and bodies covered in hard, shiny scales. Some had long feathered crests on their heads, which blew back sharply in the wind. All had distended bellies and jaws rimmed in silver, evidence of the Watermight they carried.

The dragons landed in a flurry of wings and scales on the narrow walkway, making the Pendarkan guards jump back and clutch at their spears. Riders in blue uniforms sat comfortably on the backs of the huge flying lizards. They didn't use saddles, though leather harnesses held packs of supplies in place behind each rider.

The dragons looked surprisingly different from one another. In addition to the red dragon Tamri had met before, there was a small sea-green one, a dragon the dark orange of a ripe bitterfruit, and one with slate-gray scales and pale lavender wings. Heath's beetle-blue-and-white dragon was the largest of the five, and it carried itself with a certain dignity suggesting it was their leader.

Heath climbed down from its back, wearing a forbidding expression. He scowled at the spear-carrying guards until he spotted the princess among them. His eyes happened to meet Tamri's, and his frown deepened.

"I'm afraid he was up all night, calming the dragons after your little adventure yesterday," Selivia whispered in her ear. "He's really much nicer than he looks."

Tamri doubted that, but she was more worried about the dragons themselves. Yesterday's "little adventure" hadn't made her eager to mount another one anytime soon.

"Are we riding them the whole way?" she asked, striving for a nonchalant tone.

"Yes, isn't it wonderful?"

The princess released her arm and went over to speak with Heath. He responded to her greeting with polite formality, and the princess's smile became a little strained, as if she was struggling to maintain her cheery disposition. Tamri hung back from the pair, having just made eye contact with the red dragon she'd absconded with the previous day. It glowered at her worse than Gramma Teall in a strop and kept its jaws tightly shut, as if it suspected she might try to seize its Watermight stash again.

Tamri edged away from the creature, though there wasn't much room with five dragons and all the guards and Waterworkers gathered on the narrow walkway. The other dragons and their uniformed riders—two men and two women—paid no attention to her. The creatures shuffled along the battlements, talons scraping, eager to be off at once.

The red dragon was still glaring at Tamri, rustling its feathers like a self-important rooster. She took another step back. Then a large, beringed hand landed on her shoulder.

Tamri jolted in surprise, realizing whom the hand belonged to just in time to keep from swatting it away.

"We meet again." King Khrillin's voice hummed dangerously in her ear. "Remember: you are not to speak of our little arrangement to anyone. The Watermight Oath will sense it if you try."

Tamri's neck went numb, and she felt that invisible icy collar around her throat for an instant.

"I know the rules," she said, unable to keep the defiance from her tone.

"Excellent." The heavy hand disappeared from her shoulder. Then Khrillin raised his voice and spread his arms wide. "Princess, Princess. I am so sorry to see you go. May you have safe travels, and do give my regards to your family."

"It has been a pleasure, King Khrillin." The princess smiled with something short of her earlier brightness. She adjusted the leather satchel on her back, and Tamri got the sense that she was eager to be gone from this place. They had that in common.

"Shall I carry your greetings to my betrothed?"

Khrillin's nostrils flared. "Ah yes. It has been some time since I've seen young Lord Latch." He didn't sound as if he'd enjoyed the experience. "I wish you joy of him."

"Thank you." The princess studied Khrillin, her expression troubled, then she spun away from him. "Let's go, Tamri," she sang. "You're riding with me today. Mav won't bite."

"Mav?"

"That's him now. Please don't be alarmed."

Selivia pointed to the low-hanging clouds. Tamri scanned the expanse, expecting a sixth dragon like the others. But this time when the skies opened, a massive creature thrice the size of Heath's beetle-blue mount swooped toward them.

This dragon had no feathers whatsoever. Its scaly body was deep green, its vast leathery wings as black as a bat's. Cruel black spines crowned its reptilian head, and it moved with a deadly grace that made the feathered dragons seem cuddly by comparison.

The guards and Waterworkers gasped, and even Khrillin took a careful step back. This dragon was so big there was no space for it on the wall. It glided over their heads, casting a vast shadow and making Tamri's spine tingle.

Selivia waved cheerfully at the great creature as it swooped away to fly around the circumference of the King's Tower.

"There's no room for him to land. Come on!" Selivia tugged Tamri forward a few paces then released her to scramble up on the low battlement wall. She teetered above the precipice, wisps of her curly hair floating on the breeze.

"Get ready to jump."

Tamri froze. "What?"

"Now!"

As the dragon swooped suddenly below the battlements, the princess leapt from the wall and landed astride its back. Tamri gaped as the huge dragon soared into the air, the princess's tinkling laughter trailing them. The wind from his huge wings blew Tamri's hair straight back from her face, and she nearly toppled backward. *Does the princess really expect me to—*

"He'll come around for another pass," said someone with a gruff voice nearby. Heath had joined her at the battlements. "Don't make him do a third loop. He's not as accommodating for anyone except the princess."

"But—"

"Here he comes." Heath put his hands around Tamri's waist and hoisted her onto the low wall as if she weighed no more than a sack of fish. "Don't be scared. She'll catch you."

"I'm not scared," Tamri hissed, feeling terrified.

"Then jump." And he gave her a push just as the massive dragon glided beneath the wall a second time.

Tamri plummeted through the air with a strangled yelp and landed hard on the scaled back, pitching over the dragon's other side as her bag of belongings swung wide. Princess Selivia grabbed her arm to keep her from falling off and helped her find her balance. There was no comfortable way to perch on the huge dragon's back. Tamri managed to get one leg on either side and—with nothing else to hold on to—clutched the princess's leather satchel in front of her.

The princess shouted something, and Tamri had to scoot closer to hear her.

"What?"

"I said, 'Isn't he marvelous?'"

"Yes, Princess," Tamri managed.

The princess shouted into the wind, and Tamri had to ask her to repeat herself.

"I said, 'Call me Sel'! No need for that princess business in the air."

Tamri supposed they couldn't stand on ceremony when they were already in such a precarious position. She clung tighter to the other girl, her worries about offending her forgotten.

She was glad she hadn't put on her mother's boots. Her bare feet made it easier to grip the dragon's sides. Its body felt hot through the scales, as if lit with an inner fire. Tamri remembered when Pel had told her dragons with feathers didn't breathe fire. She'd be willing to bet this one did.

Mav took them on another fast lap around the King's Tower. The rising sun flashed off the canals, and shocked faces turned upward from nearby barges and bridges. As Mav completed the circuit and passed the group on the wall again, Tamri caught one final glimpse of Khrillin gazing up at them, a dangerous glint in his eyes.

Then Heath raised his glowing cudgel, and the rest of the dragons launched from the battlements in a tornado of feathers, scales, and wings.

They ascended fast, Mav leading the way, and the canals became small and veiny beneath them. The swamp and squalor aroma of Pendark disappeared, replaced by fresh sea air and the hot-metal scent of the dragon. Tamri felt a wild burst of exhilaration. Pendark was falling away beneath her, with its vicious Waterlords and squalid conditions and blood-soaked streets. Ahead rose a purple-and-green expanse, the vast canopy of the Darkwood and the smudged outline of the Linden Mountains beyond. Tamri had never dreamed she'd be able to see the mountains from the skies above Pendark. They'd seemed as distant as the other side of the Bell Sea.

She glanced down, wondering if she might catch a glimpse of Gramma Teall's hut. But they had already crossed over the Boundary District. Beneath her, a scrub-covered hillside and the scar of the road led away from the city. A wondrous buzz filled her at the sight. She felt giddy and light and terrified all at once. She had left Pendark. She was free.

A cold band throbbed around her neck for a moment, reminding her that wasn't entirely true. But Tamri didn't care. This first exhilarating view of the world beyond Pendark proclaimed that her life would never be the same.

7

They flew all day with only brief stops for food and water. Tamri's body grew stiff from the never-ending buffeting of the wind and the pulse of the dragon's powerful wings. Mav's scales felt hot beneath her, and she gripped him as tightly as she could, her thighs aching from the effort. Her only respite came when he stretched out his wings to glide, smoother than a Watermight-powered canal boat.

Selivia chatted with Tamri as much as the situation allowed, asking about her background and about the landscape north of Pendark. Tamri had never been to the countryside, and she struggled to answer the questions. Luckily, the princess seemed to attribute it to the different perspective from the sky. She must not realize how limited Tamri's world had been until yesterday.

Every once in a while, one of the other dragons pulled forward so its rider could address the princess. The rushing wind and beating wings made it difficult to hear anything, so they waved thin sticks tipped with glowing knobs in patterns to communicate. Heath directed their flight path with his fiery cudgel, visible at a greater distance.

The other dragons weren't as fast as Mav thanks to their smaller size and the Watermight they carried. While they labored onward in a straight line, Selivia allowed Mav to play across the sky, swooping down to explore little clearings in the Darkwood or follow the line of a river or road. These abrupt movements set Tamri's heart spinning, but Selivia only laughed when they plummeted without warning.

The dragons made impressive progress, even weighted down with Watermight. As the sun began to set, the Darkwood gave way to rolling hills quilted with vineyards. The lights of little houses flickered among them. A larger collection of lights indicated a town ahead, with the Linden Mountains standing tall beyond it.

At a signal from Selivia, Mav soared down to the highway stretching between the Darkwood and the town and alighted between two shadowy vineyards. Tamri scrambled off his back with a groan and walked a few paces on wobbly legs. The other dragons had fallen behind since their final stop, leaving them alone on the deserted road.

"Take a minute to stretch," Selivia said, dismounting with more grace than Tamri had demonstrated. "We'll walk the rest of the way into town."

"Did we really cross the entire Darkwood in a day?" Tamri asked, surreptitiously rubbing her backside, which had slowly roasted after hours on Mav's hot scales.

"Didn't you see the lights of Fork Town as we landed?" the princess asked. "I'm so looking forward to a cold drink. Do you have a favorite place to dine there?"

Tamri's cheeks warmed. "I've never been to Fork Town."

"Truly?" Selivia said. "We usually spend two nights there. It can be a bit mad, with so many people traveling through. They don't like us to bring the dragons into town, though."

Mav huffed indignantly, his hot breath stirring up dust on the empty road.

"Where do they go?"

"A converted stable outside of town. Folks can be touchy in Fork Town." Selivia's forehead creased in a frown. "I hear it has gotten worse, though I'm not sure why." She touched her coat pocket absently.

It was growing dark, and their traveling companions still hadn't joined them. Tamri scanned the dusky sky, but it was difficult to discern which shapes were birds and which were dragons. They must have pulled farther ahead than she thought.

The princess remained lost in thought for a moment before shaking her head and hoisting up her leather satchel.

"I'm starving. Let's head into town."

"What about the others?"

"They'll catch up." She patted her dragon's green-scaled chest. "Mav, you can go find your dinner. Remember: no livestock. Wild creatures only."

Mav snorted, and if Tamri didn't know better she'd think he was rolling his eyes.

"Mav," Selivia said warningly.

The huge creature grumbled back at her then shook out his wings and took off, leaving a billow of dust and smoke in his wake.

"Does he understand everything you say?" Tamri asked the princess as they started down the empty road on unsteady legs.

"I believe he understands *more* than we say," Selivia said. "True dragons are frightfully intelligent. Even little cur-dragons are smarter than most other animals. And some people."

"Cur-dragons?"

"They're a bit bigger than dogs. They lived in Vertigon even before the true dragons returned. They make delightful pets."

Tamri shook her head. She still couldn't believe she was really going to Vertigon. It was like a place from one of Gramma Teall's stories, with dragons and Fire Queens and bridges of gold crossing the sky. Were *all* the legends true?

The princess's long strides had carried her ahead. Tamri rushed to catch up, wincing at the soreness in her legs.

"Do you make this flight often?"

"Several times a year since the war," Selivia said. "This will be my last trip for a while. I'm going to Soole from Fork Town."

Tamri wrinkled her nose. "Why would you want to go to that rockeaters' wasteland?"

Selivia raised an eyebrow. "Have you been to Soole?"

"No."

"Then how do you know it's a wasteland?"

"I don't." Tamri wished she'd thought before speaking. "I just . . . Pendarkans don't like Soolens very much."

The princess laughed good-naturedly. "I have noticed. But Soole is to be my home. I'm getting married there in the spring."

Tamri remembered hearing something about that back at the King's Tower. The princess didn't sound especially enthusiastic about the prospect. "Why are you marrying a Soolen?"

"To preserve the relationship between Vertigon and Soole. And Trure, as well. My sister, Sora, is the queen of Trure now."

"Why not marry a Pendarkan?"

Selivia gave her a careful look. "Pendark and Vertigon are already friends, wouldn't you say?"

Tamri kept her face impassive, recalling Khrillin's words in Gramma Teall's hut. He had said King Siv—Selivia's brother—had deceived him. She rubbed at a cold spot on her neck. Khrillin wasn't the type to forgive a slight, even from a supposed friend.

More houses were visible amongst the rows of grapevines now. Tamri wondered what it would be like to live so far from the salty sea air but also from the stench of the canals and the muddy streets. Perhaps Gramma Teall would like a cottage among the grapevines one day, if Tamri managed to collect enough information to buy their freedom.

She glanced at the princess, wondering what kind of information King Khrillin would consider useful. Selivia wasn't anything like Tamri would have expected a young royal to be, especially one on her way to begin a political marriage. Come to think of it, shouldn't she have a group of knights to escort her, or at least a bodyguard? It hadn't seemed important when Mav was with them, but now they were alone with the fading light and the rustling wind. Threats could lurk among the vines or lie in wait around any bend. Yet the princess strode onward through the twilight without fear, chattering to a Pendarkan gutter urchin as if they were old friends.

Suddenly there was a thunderous cry, and a dragon barreled out of the sky in a streak of blue and white and thudded onto the road in front of them.

"Mother of a cullmoran," Selivia muttered. "I was hoping we'd make it to the inn before he caught up."

"Why—?"

"Princess!" Heath leapt off the back of his dragon and marched toward them. "What are you doing? Where's Mav?"

"We're almost to the Fork," Selivia began. "I thought—"

"You thought you'd saunter down a dark road with this stranger? She could have assassinated you!"

Tamri blinked as Heath pointed an accusing finger at her. "I wouldn't—"

"You can't wander around on your own here." Heath sounded almost panicked, as if he had expected to find the princess murdered on the road. "We're not in Vertigon."

"I know that." Selivia drew herself up. "There's no need to overreact."

Heath's face darkened, and his dragon took a careful step back as if sensing his mood.

"Do you remember what we spoke about last night?" he said in a strained voice. "You promised to be careful. I thought you'd have the good sense not to—"

"That is quite enough," Selivia snapped. "You may escort me the rest of the way to town, Lord Samanar, but I will not hear another word of judgment about my *good sense* or what was said last night."

Heath stiffened as if he'd been slapped. Then he executed a deep, painfully formal bow. "Please accept my humblest apologies, Your Highness."

Shame flashed across Selivia's face, as if she hadn't meant to be quite so sharp. But then she jutted out her lip and marched down the road with her head held high. Heath spoke a few quiet words to his dragon then fell in beside her, his back arrow-straight, one hand on his fiery cudgel.

Tamri followed them toward Fork Town, not daring to speak. When powerful people were angry with each other in Pendark, innocent bystanders got killed. She wasn't sure what Heath—*Lord Samanar?*—was so vexed about, and she wasn't going to ask.

Heath's dragon flew off the way Mav had gone as fast as it could. Tamri was sorry to lose the creature's company. It could have served as a buffer against whatever was going on between the princess and the chief dragon rider.

As they walked along, Heath made a point of looking around often, seeking danger among the grapevines. Once, Selivia reached out as if to touch him on the shoulder or say something conciliatory. Then she muttered what sounded like "easier this way" and dropped her hand.

The pregnant silence heightened Tamri's senses as if she were on a Watermight-stealing job. Every footstep was too loud. Every rustle of the nightbirds in the vines made her want to lash out in defense or crouch in the wheel ruts in the road. But her self-preservation instincts were honed toward actual violence not whatever was going on between these two. She might not know much of Vertigonians or royals, but their quarrel clearly wasn't just about the safety of the road.

Tamri breathed a sigh of relief when the vineyards gave way to shops and townhouses and the murmur of voices interrupted the silence. The smell of horse manure, fermenting wine, and chimney smoke replaced the freshness of the countryside as they marched into Fork Town proper.

The bustling trading hub was crammed with inns and taverns and travelers. The highways branching from its center led to Pendark to the south, Soole to the southeast, and Trure and Vertigon to the north by way of Kurn Pass. The three main roads met in a circular intersection, the Fork, which gave the town its name.

At the center of the Fork was a brick platform scrawled with names and symbols, where travelers left their marks when passing through the fabled way station. A bizarre iron statue sat atop the platform. Melted spines and spirals protruded from its torso at odd angles, making it look like a candlewax man who'd tried to dance a jig in a cook fire.

Tamri slowed to look at the statue, and a passing carriage nearly ran her over. She leapt back, clutching her burlap sack to her body. More carriages careened around the intersection at a breakneck pace. Horses and pedestrians wove among them, all eager to get wherever they were going at day's end. Dust clouds hovered like sea fog and settled on sweaty faces and travel-stained clothes.

Tamri's companions didn't see her almost getting flattened, too busy marching politely side by side, which saved her some embarrassment. She was supposed to be a city girl.

Heath held his cudgel in his fist now, as if more determined than ever to ensure Selivia's safety after their argument. Tamri wondered if the Vertigonian princess was truly at risk in Fork Town. She couldn't imagine it was any more dangerous than Pendark. She scanned the crowds for threats, picking out faces and outfits from all over the continent, but no one was paying undue attention to their trio.

Still not speaking, Heath and Selivia skirted the busy intersection and headed straight for a two-story inn called the Waterlord's End. They entered a crowded common room smelling of cured meat and ale. The wooden floors and tables were reasonably clean, and the guests looked prosperous, like wine merchants, silk traders, or maybe even minor Waterworkers. A few looked up at the newcomers then returned their attention to their drinks.

A solicitous man in a spotless apron hurried forward to welcome the princess and inform her the usual rooms were waiting for her entourage.

"That sounds lovely," Selivia said. "Has a letter arrived for me?"

"A letter?" The innkeeper brushed at his apron. "Not here, my lady. Not since your last visit."

"Oh." Selivia frowned and touched her coat pocket. "I was expecting . . . No matter."

She thanked him absently and handed over a few coins. "Would you wait for the others, please, Tamri, and tell Fenn I'm in my usual room? She'll get you set up with somewhere to sleep."

"Oh, uh, sure."

Heath coughed. "Princess, you can't trust this stranger to—"

"I shall retire for the evening," the princess interrupted with a regality that didn't sound at all like her. "I am sure Tamri can convey a message without bringing enemies down on the inn."

Heath looked as if he wanted to object again, but he held his tongue as the princess stalked toward the stairs at the side of the common room. Then he looked down at Tamri with that stern disapproval she'd seen before.

"Fenn is the princess's bodyguard," he said in a tight voice. "She should have been on Mav with her today, but she insisted on bringing you with her instead."

Tamri shrugged. "Okay."

"The princess can be too trusting, but don't assume—"

"You're her sworn man or something, right?" Tamri interrupted. "Aren't you supposed to trust her judgment?"

Heath blinked. "I do trust her—I just—you—" He threw up his hands. "Just tell Fenn where she is. I'll guard her until then."

He marched off after the princess, leaving Tamri alone in the middle of the common room.

The innkeeper in the spotless apron eyed her suspiciously from the polished darkwood bar. Innkeepers could always sense when you didn't have a single coin to your name. She'd been to many similar establishments in Pendark, usually to listen for tips about loose Watermight or to meet buyers. A few of the customers were looking askance at her, too, perhaps wondering what a Pendarkan girl was doing with two foreigners. She wondered if Heath's worries about safety here were well founded.

The inn door opened behind her, a burst of warm, dusty air ruffling Tamri's tunic, and a group of people wearing Vertigonian blue traipsed inside.

"You're with us, right?" A young man a little older than Tamri held out a hand. He had a roguish smile and dark, unruly hair. "We didn't get a chance to meet yet. I'm Taklin."

"Tamri." She didn't take his hand.

The three other dragon riders finished knocking the dried Pendarkan mud off their boots at the door and joined them. They had just come from settling the dragons outside of town for the night, and they were in jovial moods. They nudged elbows and slapped backs in a way that seemed unnatural to Tamri. Pendarkans tended to be careful about whom they touched.

"Which one of you is Fenn?" Tamri asked.

A heavyset woman with thick red hair nodded. She was older and quieter than the others, seemingly the odd person out.

"Princess Selivia asked me to tell you she retired early," Tamri said.

"She went to her room?" Taklin said. "Without supper?"

"Yeah, she and Heath kind of had an argument."

"I'd better go up there," Fenn said.

"Wait! Um . . ." Tamri shifted her feet as they all looked at her at once. "She said you'd find me somewhere to sleep."

"We'll take care of you," said Taklin. "Don't worry about her, Fenn. She's with the dragon crew now."

"Oh, I'm not joining the—"

"I know, I know." Taklin grinned and slapped her on the back before she could duck out of the way. "You're a Wielder. But when you ride with us, you're on our crew."

Fenn marched off toward the stairs, while the others swept Tamri up as if she really were one of them, calling out for food and drink. Before she knew it, she was crammed onto a bench beside a woman called Reya with wild brown hair and thick freckles. Across the table sat Taklin and Errol, a thin man with a smooshed nose and heavy-lidded eyes.

The babble of voices and laughter filled the common room. Tamri's muscles ached from the day's ride, and her stomach was growling, but she felt on edge among these strangers. A lifetime of wariness didn't dissipate easily.

"I don't have any money," Tamri said when the innkeeper set a round of foaming tankards before them.

"Nonsense." Taklin slapped a coin onto the rough table. "The first one's on me. Besides, people love to buy drinks for dragon riders. You won't have to pay for anything once we head out."

"Out?"

Reya nudged her elbow, making Tamri stiffen. "We'll give you the tour of the usual taverns."

"This is the last town before Kurn Pass," explained Taklin after taking a long drink from his tankard. "Anyone going to or from Trure, Pendark, or Soole needs a night of proper Fork Town carousing."

Tamri glanced at the stairs leading to their inn's upper rooms. "Will the princess and . . . Lord Heath . . . approve?"

"Did she call him Lord?" Taklin whistled through his teeth. "That must have been quite the quarrel."

"Yes. Lord Samanar."

The others winced.

"Even worse," Taklin said. "Heath is damn proud of being chief dragon rider."

"As he should be!" Errol pounded his tankard on the table, slopping ale onto his uniform sleeve.

"Aye," Taklin said. "But he's a minor nobleman, too, and he doesn't like people to remember it. His family was on the wrong side of the attempted coup against the Amintelles. Plus, they're not the most dignified of noble houses."

Tamri perked up at the mention of an attempted coup. The Amintelles would be Selivia's family, including her brother, King Sivarrion. Heath's family had acted against them? Interesting. She began making a mental list of facts to send to Khrillin in her first report.

"Just don't let on that you know all the stories," Reya said with a laugh. "Especially the one about his mother and the butler."

Across the table, Errol nodded soberly. "Heath broke my nose for asking if that butler story was true when we first started working with the dragons together."

Reya snorted. "Serves you right."

"I was just curious," Errol said. "Didn't know that was such a sensitive subject."

"His mother?"

Errol shrugged. "I'm not a mind reader."

"Heath's all right," Taklin said. "But the princess doesn't usually poke him where it hurts." He took a contemplative sip of ale. "I wonder what happened between them."

"You're kidding, right?" Reya leaned forward so she could see him past Tamri. "The princess is leaving to get married. A gold fire-stone says one of them tried to make a move."

"You reckon that's it?" Taklin said. "I thought they were only friends."

"Yeah," Errol said, scratching his smooshed nose, "and she's been writing to her Soolen lord for ages."

"Doesn't mean they don't feel something for each other," Reya said. "Heath was the first volunteer when the princess started this whole dragon-riding lark. None of us would have had the guts to join if he hadn't stepped up. They've been through a lot together."

"I always thought he was too tough for feelings," Errol said.

"Do you know any reason he'd be worried about the princess's safety in Fork Town?" Tamri asked. She doubted Khrillin cared whether a minor nobleman had feelings for the princess, unrequited or otherwise. But Heath didn't seem to believe in the friendship between Vertigon and Pendark any more than Khrillin did. "He was carrying that glowing stick of his like they were about to be attacked from all sides."

"Fork Town has its issues," Reya said. "No one usually bothers us, but we're not supposed to bring the dragons into town in case it upsets people. They're too closely associated with the war."

"It's a different crowd here every time too," Errol said. "Pendarkans. Trurens. The occasional Soolen. I met a mercenary from the Far Plains in a tavern here once. She nearly sliced my ears off for smiling at her."

"You don't need to worry, though," Reya said. "We've got your back."

Tamri didn't believe that for a second, but she raised her tankard in thanks anyway.

"All I know," Taklin said, "is that His Chief Dragon Riding Lordship will make us go out to the stables to babysit the dragons if we don't get moving. They're perfectly capable of taking care of themselves." He downed the rest of his ale in a single gulp. "To the Fork!"

8

The dragon riders took the job of giving Tamri a tour of their favorite taverns very seriously. Despite their apparent friendliness, she couldn't fully relax around them. The physicality of their camaraderie was so different from her friendships with the kids she sometimes ran with in Pendark. You just weren't supposed to touch people who weren't family. If she tried to sling an arm around Pel's shoulder the way Taklin did with Reya as they left the Waterlord's End, he'd think she was trying to steal something and shove her into a canal.

The evening progressed in an overwhelming influx of new sights and sounds. Tamri took in everything in flashes. Firelight reflecting on glass steins, long drinks of warm ale, foam on Reya's nose across an olivewood bar, the smells of rabbit stew and vomit. Then fiddlers on the brick platform in the Fork, sending wild music into the night. An inebriated Errol trying to dance with the mangled iron statue. A roughly dressed man with sandy hair muttering curses about Vertigon under his breath as he shoved past. Another with a scar that pulled his mouth into a grotesque smile, watching them with calculating eyes. Tamri tried to point him out to Taklin, but the dragon rider just shoved another drink in her hand and told her to relax.

Tamri stopped drinking at that point, holding on to the bottle to use as a weapon if the fellow with the smiling scar made a move. A sense of looseness and lightness already filled her, as if she didn't need to be wary, and she didn't trust the feeling one bit.

The ale Tamri had already consumed helped to dull the soreness in her muscles, but she deeply regretted it when the ache migrated to her head the following morning.

"Looks like someone had a proper Fork Town revel," Taklin said when she joined the dragon riders for breakfast.

Tamri grimaced and pulled a loaf of bread toward her. Errol was fast asleep with his head on the table, and Reya looked slightly the worse for wear too. Fenn, Heath, and the princess were nowhere in sight.

"Eventful night?" Tamri asked Taklin blearily. He had become shamelessly enamored of no fewer than three different women at various points in the evening. She vaguely remembered one of the women being much more interested in Reya.

"I'll say." Taklin passed her a clay mug full of water. "Good thing we're taking a proper Fork Town day off, though. My dragon won't appreciate it if I hurl on her feathers."

The most difficult stretch of their journey would begin the next morning. They all needed to be well rested when they crossed the mountains through Kurn Pass.

When they'd returned to their shared room at the inn last night, Reya had explained that most people stayed two nights in Fork Town because it was an ideal location for trade, the only major hub connecting Pendark and Soole in the south with Trure and Vertigon on the other side of the Linden Mountains. The tradition of spending the first night carousing made the place infamous, but commerce was the real reason it was a vital stopover.

The dragon riders carried lightweight Fireworks from Vertigon to trade: smaller versions of the glowing sticks they used to communicate, hot stones that stayed warm for a year, and little beads that would erupt into fiery flowers. Reya had assured Tamri she'd see many more wonders made with the Fire in Vertigon. Such things were too expensive for Tamri in Pendark, and she knew precious little about what Vertigon's magical substance could do. That would change soon enough.

"What will the dragons do today?" Tamri asked as she sipped her water and waited for her head to stop throbbing.

"They'll stick to the stables outside town," Taklin said. "They don't like moving more than necessary when they're carrying Watermight." He leaned back, stifling a yawn with his fist. "We'll check on them in shifts throughout the day. Heath's already out there."

Tamri was surprised the Vertigonians weren't more worried someone would try to take the Watermight stash. On the other hand, she supposed you'd have to be really stupid to try to steal from a dragon.

The others dispersed to shop and trade their Fire trinkets with the merchants who frequented Fork Town. Tamri had nothing to trade, of course. She was about to return to her room when Princess Selivia waltzed down the stairs and demanded that Tamri accompany her to the shops.

The princess wore a simple dress of burnished orange, her hair hanging loose around her shoulders. She seemed cheerier than the day before. Perhaps she and Heath had made up during the night. Fenn, the older red-haired woman, shadowed Selivia now, wearing a short sword on her broad hip. The princess's long-time bodyguard stuck close by whenever Mav wasn't around to protect her.

"I'm terribly sorry I abandoned you yesterday," Selivia said as she swept Tamri up from the common room. "Did the dragon riders take care of you?"

"Yes, Princess. Taklin was especially friendly."

"Oh good. I'm afraid I was a dreadful host."

"It's really okay." Tamri certainly didn't expect this sister to kings and queens to fret over her. She glanced at Fenn, but the bodyguard didn't look surprised at the princess's concern for a commoner she barely knew.

Late-morning sunshine greeted the trio as they left the inn. The crowds were out in force, shouting in half a dozen accents and sometimes brandishing weapons at perceived slights. The activity had a chaotic purposefulness, and it was difficult to keep track of any given altercation as they squeezed through the throng.

They crossed the main Fork, dodging the carriages and riders circling the brick platform, and found their way to a smaller side street lined with fine garment shops, wine purveyors, and even a goldsmith.

"I don't mean to make you uncomfortable, Tamri," Selivia said as they strolled along the street. "But I couldn't help noticing you didn't bring many clothes with you."

"Oh, I was told to pack light." Tamri hefted the burlap sack she carried on her back. She didn't mention that it contained all the clothes she owned.

"Did Heath make you—never mind." Selivia smoothed back her hair. "You're from a terribly hot city, but it'll be cold in Vertigon. Let me buy you some warmer things."

"I can't accept that."

"Please! It will be my present to make up for not accompanying you myself."

"But—"

"I insist!"

"I wouldn't fight her on this," Fenn said in a low voice. "She loves dressing people. Letting her get on with it is the kindest thing you can do."

The endeavor did seem to make Selivia happy. They paraded through a succession of shops, where the princess insisted Tamri try on dozens of outfits, sometimes foisting the same item on her in six different colors. Most of the garments were thicker than anything Tamri had worn even in the depths of a Pendarkan winter, and the fabrics were finer too. They made her think of the darning jobs she'd scrounged up for Gramma Teall over the years.

Gyra, the bald Waterworker, must have collected Gramma Teall from the stilt hut by now. Khrillin had said he'd keep her in comfort as long as Tamri's reports proved useful. She hoped he'd give her a room with a view of the sea.

"I really do feel bad about sending you on alone," Selivia said, perhaps noticing Tamri's mood had sobered. She was examining an emerald-green gown with bronze stars embroidered on the bodice. "I'll tell Heath to put an extra safety harness on your dragon."

Tamri blinked. "My dragon?"

"You'll take the little sea-green one Fenn has been riding, and she'll come with me to Soole on Mav. The dragon's name is Laini, and she's lovely. You'll be fine."

Tamri doubted that. It hadn't gone so well the last time she rode a dragon all by herself. But the princess's words reminded her they'd be parting ways soon. She needed to learn something Khrillin could use before she lost her chance.

"What will you do when you get to Soole?"

"I'm not entirely sure." Selivia paused her inspection of the emerald dress to touch something in her pocket. "My betrothed's research keeps him quite busy. I'm not sure how I'll fit in."

Tamri tried to sound only mildly interested. "Research?"

"Latch is a Waterworker, like you," Selivia said. "He also loves to read old books, and he believes a lot of magic-wielding knowledge has been lost. He wants to find it again."

"What kind of knowledge? Like how to make weapons?"

Selivia chuckled. "That's a very Pendarkan thing to say." She held the emerald gown up to her and gasped. "This color looks gorgeous with your skin tone!"

Tamri waited patiently for the princess to say more as she adjusted the velvet skirt and studied the effect from different angles. When you spent most of your life fighting for survival, weapons mattered—especially in the hands of more powerful Wielders. And information about Soolen weapons was exactly the sort of thing Khrillin would value.

As the princess chattered on about her betrothed and his research, Tamri realized Selivia didn't see her as a threat at all. Maybe Heath was right about her being too trusting.

"I've seen Latch Wield, you know," Selivia said. "He's quite talented. Clever too. But I don't want to end up stuffed into a musty archive forever." She wrinkled her nose and examined a loose stitch of embroidery on the gown. "The Brach family works with Cindral dragons, too, but we'll be living in the capital city, not at Fort Brach."

"Fort Brach?"

"It's Latch's family fortress at the base of the Linden Mountains." Selivia waved a vague hand to the east. "It's the one Khrillin captured when he tried to invade Soole."

Tamri coughed. "What?"

"Don't you know about that? I suppose it might have been embarrassing for him. Yes, Khrillin managed to take the fort during the war. My brother convinced him to give it up without a fight by making him think it was about to be attacked by an army of powerful Fireworkers." Selivia made Tamri hold the green velvet dress up while she adjusted her hair, freeing it from where it was tucked behind her ears. "Oh, that's lovely. Such volume!"

"So your brother convinced King Khrillin to give up a fort he'd won and pull out of Soole?" Tamri asked. This had to be the deceit Khrillin had mentioned. She was beginning to understand why he still held a grudge.

"Siv was trying to avoid more bloodshed," Selivia said. "Khrillin left in peace, but it didn't exactly improve relations between Pendark and Soole."

"What did Khrillin do when—"

The door of the shop burst open. Tamri dove behind a table piled with colorful silks, ready to defend herself with her sack full of heavy winter clothes. Fenn stepped in front of the princess and drew her short sword. But it was only Errol, who dashed toward them, long limbs wheeling.

"Princess, come quickly!" He skidded to a halt, grabbing a wooden mannequin for balance. "There's trouble!"

"What kind of trouble?"

"One of the dragons is in the Fork. I don't know how it got there. A crowd is gathering. You have to hurry!"

Selivia tossed a few coins to the shopkeeper and pushed the emerald dress at Tamri.

"I don't—"

"It'll look brilliant on you. Trust me."

Then she darted out into the street with Fenn and Errol. Tamri stuffed the velvet dress into her overflowing sack and followed them toward the Fork.

The shouts reached them first. Then the squawks and squeals of a distressed animal. Tamri forced her way through the gathering crowds to find the sea-green Cindral dragon thrashing about in the middle of the busy intersection, looking confused and agitated. Horses shied away from it, their carriages swerving wide. Two slammed into each other with a deafening crash. Wood splintered. Dust billowed like smoke. Townsfolk gathered to point and stare, delighted by the chaos.

"Oh dear," Selivia said. "This is why they're supposed to stay in the stables. They hate it when people gawk."

Tamri quickly stopped gawking and followed the princess as she tried to force through the onlookers, Fenn at her side. Other people's sweat smeared Tamri's arms as she squeezed through the throng after the princess.

Up ahead, a group of thugs was trying to surround the dragon. There were at least a dozen, dressed in rough clothes and carrying clubs and ropes. One had familiar sandy hair. Another's mouth twisted into a grotesque smile thanks to his scar. They were trying to toss ropes around the dragon's neck and shouting worse than brawling bargemen. Something told Tamri they weren't just going to move the dragon out of the Fork. They wanted it for themselves.

As the thugs closed in, the dragon squealed and retreated onto the brick platform. Her tail whipped back and forth, her feathers fluffing up like a startled chicken.

"Leave her alone!" Selivia cried. "You're upsetting her! Laini!"

Her voice was lost in the cacophony. The thugs circled the platform, still trying to capture the frightened dragon. A thick rope tangled around the creature's wing, making it impossible for her to take off in her frantic state. She squawked in distress, and a flood of Watermight burst from her mouth. This only made the thugs more aggressive in their efforts to subdue her. Another cascade of power spurted from her mouth and sank into the dusty street.

Tamri felt bad for the dragon. She knew what it was like to be surrounded by strangers trying to rip away your freedom. She clenched her fists. Someone had to stop this.

Heath emerged from the inn on the far side of the Fork, brandishing his cudgel, but he was still a long way off. Errol tackled the sandy-haired thug, and he looked as if he might come out of the tussle with another broken nose. The man with the smiling scar shouted orders to the others, who raised their clubs to defend those trying to get more ropes around the dragon. Fenn grabbed the princess, holding her back so she wouldn't try to fight them herself.

More Watermight escaped from the dragon's mouth.

Tamri made a quick decision. "I'll take care of it."

She darted ahead of Fenn and the princess, moving nimbly through the chaos. She figured she could make up for stealing —*borrowing*—the red dragon if she kept this one from being lassoed by the street toughs. She needed the Vertigonians to trust her.

She scampered around Errol and the man he was wrestling,

already pulling on the Watermight the dragon had dropped. The liquid power hadn't sunk too far into the ground, and she drew it back out, taking a liberal portion of dirt with it. She flung the silvery mud into the eyes of the nearest thug and whipped out an icy Watermight razor to sever the ropes of the next two. The men turned, their fists swinging wildly, but they didn't connect the girl scurrying past them with the power lashing at their clubs and ropes. Their eyes rolled with fright as they tried to fend off the magical attack. One tried to hide behind the twisted iron statue.

Angry shouts rose from the crowd, almost drowning out the distressed cries of the dragon. More people were rushing toward the Vertigonians and the would-be dragon thieves.

Tamri tugged up another stream of Watermight from the ground, preparing to deal with anyone who got too close. Panic shot through her at the sight of so many hostile faces. Her fingernails glowed with silver-white power.

"Stop!" a hand closed on her arm, and she lashed out at it, putting a deep score in her attacker's wrist. A second too late, she realized it was Heath.

"I didn't mean—"

Blood welled from the cut in Heath's forearm, shockingly red and bright, but his grip held. "You can't use Watermight here," he said urgently. "We have an agreement."

"But they were trying to—"

"Look out, Chief!" called a new voice. Taklin had followed Heath into the fray, and he was swinging his fists at anything that moved. "They saw her. We need to leave town."

The throng of angry locals was swarming closer. No longer watching the dragon, they were glaring at Tamri and the silver-white glow at her fingertips.

Heath cursed and shoved Tamri toward the frantic dragon.

"Get her in the air. Meet us at Kurn Pass."

"But—"

"Now!"

Tamri obeyed. Once more using the Watermight as a makeshift harness, she scrambled onto the sea-green dragon's back. Then she sliced through the rope tangled in its wing and gave a wordless shout. The dragon launched off the brick platform and into the air.

9

Tamri and the sea-green dragon circled once around the Fork. Below them, Heath advanced toward Selivia, who was trying to placate the growing horde of angry townsfolk. Fenn brandished her short sword at anyone who came too near the princess. Taklin and Reya ran toward the stables where the other dragons were sheltered, and Errol followed, his nose bleeding heavily.

Upturned faces followed the progress of the errant dragon, none of them friendly. Weapons gleamed among the crowds, swords and knives flashing in the sun. A few people even raised half-drawn bows, as if considering whether to try bringing the dragon down. The affable revelers of the night before had been replaced by a hostile mob.

Tamri's actions had apparently exacerbated the chaos. She grimaced. No one had told her anything about not using Watermight in Fork Town. She had just been trying to help.

"Let's get out of here," she called to the dragon, tightening her grip on the Watermight cord anchoring her in place.

The dragon squawked a response and soared higher into the afternoon sky. She was quivering, still distressed by the ordeal. So this was Laini, the dragon she was supposed to ride tomorrow. Tamri gave her a tentative pat on the shoulder, where the sea-green feathers gave way to slightly darker scales.

At her touch, Laini glanced back at her with large golden eyes.

"Uh, could you take me to Kurn Pass, please," Tamri said, remembering what Selivia had said about the dragons' intelligence. "We can wait for the others there."

Laini tossed her head and banked sharply, making Tamri's stomach lurch. When her wings straightened out, they were heading toward the mountains and the sunlit corridor knifing between them.

Tamri twisted in her seat to look back. People still mobbed the Fork, but she couldn't recognize anyone at this distance. None of the other dragons were airborne yet.

A significant amount of Watermight still flowed through Tamri's body, making her feel strong. Laini was smaller and easier to ride than Mav, and Tamri briefly considered running away with her and the power she carried. But the oath bond on her neck pulsed before she could follow the thought far, reminding her of her obligations. Besides, Heath would catch her again if she tried to escape. She remembered the deep cut she'd slashed in his arm and winced. If he hadn't hated her before, he would now.

The sun began to sink as they flew north, and a cool breeze rolled off the mountains, smelling of damp leaves and linden flowers. Fortunately, Tamri had managed to keep her burlap sack on her back when the chaos began. If it got any colder than this, she would definitely need the warm clothes Selivia had bought for her in addition to her grandmother's cloak.

Before long, they reached the narrow channel through the mountains known as Kurn Pass. Laini dove straight for a broad stone ledge overlooking the road and landed in a scurry of talons and feathers.

"Good thinking," Tamri said, sliding off the dragon's back. They could watch for their companions from this ledge without encountering the riders and merchant trains traveling through the pass. "Do you always have this kind of trouble on your travels?"

Laini looked at her with mournful golden eyes and tipped her head sideways. Then she uttered a sound between a whine and a whimper and extended her nose to sniff at Tamri's hand. The dragon still seemed frightened, surprising for such a huge creature.

"You're all right," Tamri said softly. "I know that was scary."

Tentatively, she rested her fingers on Laini's pale-green snout.

The scales felt almost silky. As Tamri stroked her nose, Laini gazed at her trustingly with those liquid gold eyes.

"I won't let anyone hurt you."

Tamri could sense the reservoir of Watermight in the dragon's belly. She thought about keeping the Watermight she'd picked up in the Fork just in case, but it would soon lose its potency inside her body. She let the power pool in her palms and urged the dragon to drink it up again.

"That'll show them they can trust me."

Laini lapped up the liquid magic, gurgling in appreciation, then she lay down, resting her bulging belly on the stone ledge. Tamri sat beside her and reached out to stroke her arched neck. The dragon shuffled closer, nosing at her hair.

Tamri chuckled. "You're kind of sweet, aren't you? I bet my grandma would like you."

Laini huffed contentedly and wrapped one feathered wing around Tamri's body, holding back the mountain breeze. They waited like that, dragon and girl, until the others found them.

The four Cindral dragons and their riders arrived as the setting sun sent long shadows across Kurn Pass, all looking a little battered and frazzled. Errol and Heath had blood on their clothes, and a purple bruise was blooming on Taklin's cheek. Only Reya had escaped unscathed, though her brown hair looked even messier than usual. Mav, Selivia, and Fenn were not with them.

Heath immediately began checking Laini over for injuries, not sparing Tamri more than a stern glance. Taklin, Errol, and Reya seemed to think they'd had a grand adventure. They were already swapping stories of their tussle with the Fork Town thugs.

"They'll never steal from us again," Taklin crowed. "Think they can kidnap our dragons? Ha! I'd like to see them try."

Reya rolled her eyes. "They did try."

"That's not the point," Taklin said. "We fought them off, though I reckon they won't be happy to see us back in Fork Town anytime soon."

"Princess Selivia smoothed things over with the Town Watch

before she left," Errol said, his voice muffled by the handkerchief he was holding to his bloody nose.

"She's gone?" Tamri asked.

Reya nodded. "She and Fenn are on their way to Soole with Mav."

Tamri silently cursed herself for not getting more information before the princess set off. Khrillin would not be impressed. Tamri also hadn't had a chance to thank the princess for her kindness.

"Has anything like that ever happened here before?"

The others exchanged glances.

"No one would have dared anything so blatant a few years ago," Reya said. "Under the circumstances, we didn't think staying at the inn another night would be wise."

"Glad you're here, though, Tamri," Taklin said. "Heath thought he was going to have to chase you down again."

Tamri looked over at the chief dragon rider, who was avoiding her eyes a little too deliberately. He couldn't be happy about the way she'd lashed out at him in the Fork, especially when he already worried about her hurting the princess. She would have to alleviate his suspicions of her somehow, if she wanted to learn anything useful from him. Hopefully the fact that she hadn't tried to escape with Laini was a good start.

Heath went off to settle the dragons while the others built a fire of dried linden branches a few dozen paces from the road. They would have to camp here tonight, as it was too dangerous to fly through Kurn Pass in the dark. They would take turns watching the road in case the Fork Town thugs tried to finish what they started.

They shared a meal of goat jerky and hard cheese as the darkness deepened outside the ring of campfire light. The sky was clear, the flickering light not bright enough to mute the stars. The soothing smells of burning wood and sweet linden flowers surrounded them. Tamri stretched her toes toward the fire. The temperature was dropping. She'd have to get out her boots and new warm clothes before long.

Across the fire, Errol grumbled as he attempted to get comfortable. "Not that it wasn't an exciting day and all," he muttered, "but I thought we'd get another night in a soft bed."

"Why did everyone react so badly when I used Watermight back there?" Tamri asked.

"Fork Town folk get skittish around Wielders," Taklin said. "A lot of refugees moved there after the war in Trure. Saw enough Fire and Watermight violence to last a lifetime. They don't appreciate people flaunting their powers."

He opened a crinkling packet of goat jerky and passed it around the campfire. Errol took a double portion.

"They aren't too happy about the dragons carting magical substances through there every month, either," Taklin went on. "They tolerate us as long as our dragons stay in the stables and their magic stays out of sight."

"Laini's a needy little thing," Reya said. "She probably went looking for Fenn and attracted the wrong kind of attention."

Tamri wasn't sure it was that simple. She had seen those same men—the one with sandy hair and the other with the scarred smile—watching the Vertigonians the night before. And Heath had been worried about threats to the princess. There was something going on here, a deeper undercurrent that could be connected to the souring of relations between Pendark and Vertigon.

"What would those thugs have done with Laini?" Tamri asked.

Taklin uncorked a waterskin and took a swig before passing it to Tamri. "I reckon a lot of people would pay for a captive Cindral dragon."

"Do you ever sell them?"

"We don't own the dragons," came a quiet voice. Heath stepped into the ring of firelight. "They choose to work with us. They're not horses for barter."

He sat down between Tamri and Reya, looking tired. He removed his crisp blue uniform coat and set it carefully on a stone beside him. A grubby scrap of cloth was wrapped around his forearm, but blood still dripped over the back of his hand.

"Looks like a nasty slash you got there, Chief," Errol said.

"I'm fine," Heath said brusquely.

Tamri figured she'd better start convincing him she wasn't one of those threats he was so worried about. She'd spied on Watermight healers at pen-fighting matches, hoping to learn enough to help

Gramma Teall. She'd never gotten further than how to wash and seal a shallow cut, but that ought to win her some goodwill here.

"Uh, Heath?" She swallowed, nervous about addressing the imposing dragon rider. "I know some Watermight healing. I can seal up that wound for you."

He glanced over at her. "Watermight is too valuable."

"It doesn't take much to fix a cut like that." She reached for the cloth on Heath's arm but he pulled it out of her reach.

"We go through a lot of effort to get it to Vertigon. You can't just sling it around."

"Fine," Tamri snapped, irritation at his patronizing tone overcoming her wariness. "Bleed to death, then."

Errol choked on his jerky, and Taklin gave a low whistle.

Tamri ignored them. She knew better than some Vertigonian how dear Watermight was. She had saved it from being wasted today. Thanks to her, it was sitting comfortably in Laini's belly instead of sinking deeper into Fork Town soil.

Heath gave her a flat stare then started poking at the fire with a stick, blood darkening his clumsy bandage. How was she supposed to prove she wasn't a threat if he wouldn't acknowledge her contributions or accept her help?

Everyone ate in uncomfortable silence for a few minutes. The coppery smell of fresh blood joined the aromas of burnt wood and linden flowers. Heath was starting to look pale, even for a Vertigonian.

"Chief, I don't want to cause trouble," Taklin said carefully. "But you're bleeding really bad. Maybe you could let her—"

"No Watermight," Heath repeated.

Taklin lifted his eyebrows, and the others examined their boots and fingernails, seeing no point in arguing with their leader. But Tamri wasn't under Heath's command. She didn't have to put up with his stubbornness, especially when she'd been the one to slice him open.

She grabbed the waterskin and scooted toward him, bracing herself to leap back if he responded poorly.

"At least do a better job of binding this up," she said.

"You don't have to—"

"Yes, I do. Hold this." She shoved the waterskin into Heath's left hand so he couldn't stop her from peeling the rough bandage off his right arm and using it to wipe up the blood. The muscles in Heath's arm tensed as she pressed her fingers into his skin to make sure the wound flowed clean.

"It's a neat cut," Tamri said, trying to hide her nerves. She so rarely touched people she didn't know, and it made her blood race a little too fast. "It'll heal fine, but Watermight would keep it from scarring."

"I don't mind scars." Heath grimaced. "It probably needs stitches, though."

Taklin whispered to Errol that it would be a shame to mar Lord Samanar's noble beauty. Reya rolled her eyes and fetched a needle and thread from one of the packs. She handed them to Tamri with a shrug.

After a moment's hesitation, Tamri gritted her teeth and began to sew up the long cut. She'd learned to sew from Gramma Teall, and she managed to space the stitches evenly from the top of Heath's large hand to just a few inches below his elbow. He didn't utter a sound despite the pierce and pull of the needle.

The task complete, Tamri ripped a clean strip of fabric from the bottom of her own tunic to bind the wound.

"Don't do that," Heath said, sounding startled.

"The princess bought me new clothes today," Tamri said. "I won't miss this one."

He stared at her for a moment then allowed her to wrap the fabric from her tunic around the stitched-up wound without further protests.

"Thank you," he said when she finished tying the bandage, his voice gentler than before.

Tamri met his eyes briefly. "Just don't sneak up on me next time."

"I'll remember that."

Tamri released Heath's arm and scrambled back to her place by the fire.

The next morning, Heath rigged a safety harness on Laini and took the time to advise Tamri on her quirks before their flight through Kurn Pass.

"Laini has a skittish streak, but if you keep calm, she will too." He looked her over critically. "Don't make so many sudden movements."

Tamri glared at him. He made her sound like some kind of feral creature. She supposed he *was* nursing a cut from one of those sudden movements of hers, but it was his own fault for grabbing her in the middle of a scuffle.

"She'll be easier to ride than Mav," Heath said. "She's much less of a showoff."

Laini huffed in what sounded suspiciously like a laugh.

Tamri patted her tentatively on the flank. "She doesn't feel as hot either."

"Mav is a true dragon," Heath said. "That's why he feels hot. True dragons breathe Fire."

"Fire like the magical substance?"

"That's right. Cur-dragons breathe ordinary flame, and true dragons breathe Fire. Cindral dragons like these prefer Watermight."

Heath moved to double-check the harness looping around Laini's chest and under her wings. Whatever he thought of Tamri now, he seemed determined to make sure she survived their journey. That was progress.

"Are there many true dragons in Vertigon?"

"Mav is the only one now." Heath tightened the knots on the harness, speaking more freely with his hands busy. "A swarm of true dragons burned half the mountain to ash several years ago, but the Fire Queen threw them out."

"How?"

Heath shrugged. "Maybe she'll teach you."

Tamri frowned, running her fingers through Laini's soft feathers. She couldn't imagine what it would be like to study with the legendary queen. Could she learn to use the Fire for which Vertigon was famous, alongside her own Watermight? If this power was strong enough to fight off dragons, knowledge of how to use it had to be valuable. Maybe it would even be valuable enough to buy her way out of the oath bond.

"Were you there when the true dragons attacked?" she asked as

Heath showed her where to grab the harness to pull herself onto Laini's back.

"I broke my leg running from them in the first assault and hid in a greathouse during the occupation. I was there when Princess Selivia arrived on Mav. She was the first person to ride a true dragon in centuries." He finished correcting Tamri's hand position on the harness and looked to the southeast, where the princess must even now be soaring toward her betrothed. A stiff breeze blew his thick bronze hair back from his forehead and ruffled his neatly buttoned coat. He had sewn up the slash in the fabric after Tamri sewed up his arm.

When he didn't speak, Tamri cleared her throat, and Heath seemed to remember where he was.

"We're bringing you with us because the princess ordered it," he said, his sternness returning. "Don't give me any trouble. Fork Town isn't the only place where people might not welcome our presence."

"I can keep my head down," she said. "But you have to tell me the rules if you expect me to follow them."

"Fair enough. No Wielding until we get to Vertigon."

"Done."

Heath raised an eyebrow, and Tamri worried her tone had been a little too defiant. She had to work on that.

"We'd better take off," Heath said, giving Laini a final pat. "We have to make it through the pass before nightfall."

"Can't we just go over the mountain?"

"Too tiring for the dragons. Remember this: treat the dragons well, and they'll take care of you."

"Understood."

Heath mounted Boru, his beetle-blue-and-white dragon, then raised his glowing Fire cudgel to signal the others and took off into the bright morning sky. One by one, the other dragons followed. Reya rode the red dragon, Taklin the dark-orange, and Errol the slate-gray with lavender wings. Tamri gripped Laini's harness tight at the base of her sea-green wings and closed her eyes as they leapt into the air after the others.

The five dragons soared through the narrow channel into the Linden Mountains. Kurn Pass wasn't much wider than their wingspans, making clear why they had to do this in the daylight. But Laini flew straight, never coming too close to the sheer stone walls.

With every beat of her vast wings, they got farther from Pendark, farther from the only life Tamri had ever known. They had a long way to go, but excitement began to swirl though her like a stream of Watermight. They were truly on their way now. And the mysterious land of Vertigon awaited.

10

Selivia adjusted her scarf, eyes burning from the wind and the sun, and surveyed the landscape gliding beneath Mav's wings. Soole was a red, rocky land with little vegetation to alleviate the sunlight glancing off the rocks. The journey along the Desolate Coast had been broken up by glimpses of the turquoise sea, but now that they'd left the Coast Road and crossed into the Soolen Peninsula itself, the desert was unrelenting.

She and Fenn made camp each afternoon and departed before the sun rose to avoid the worst of the heat. There was no escape from Mav's hot scales, though. Riding him was like sitting on a Firesmith's forge with bare legs. Sweat and dust caked their faces and clothes, and they had to wash sparingly with the mere trickles of water they found along the way.

Selivia had spent time in the Far Plains, another vast desert, but it had seemed wild and unique, with strange creatures creeping among the rocks and brightly colored banners fluttering from the buildings. This place felt dead.

"Why do people live here?" she muttered. "Why did *I* agree to live here?"

"The coastal cities will be better, Princess," said Fenn, who perched behind her on Mav's back. "It's not all like this."

"I hope not."

Selivia couldn't help feeling apprehensive as she crossed the sunbaked center of her new home. She had originally planned to hug the coast the whole way to Sharoth, but after the incident in Fork Town and the animosity she'd sensed in Pendark, she decided not to delay any longer. Relations among the southern kingdoms had become fragile, and she needed to find out why.

She never imagined Fork Town could become so hostile so quickly. Heath had been right to worry. She wished she'd had time to apologize for not listening before rushing off.

Selivia put Heath out of her mind deliberately, her thoughts turning to what she would find in Sharoth, the capital city located on the peninsula's southern coast. There had been no letter from Latch waiting in Fork Town to confirm whether or not she should complete her journey. She had been debating whether to remain in Fork Town to wait for word when the incident with the dragon decided the matter. She had to find out why the southern lands had become so volatile.

As Mav glided onward over the parched earth, Fenn hung on behind Selivia with her usual placidity. She wasn't the type to fret, but she'd spent extra time sharpening her short sword throughout their journey. She must be nervous about what they'd find in Soole too.

Eventually the desolate land sloped upward to a stubby mountain range. Scattered mines and bleak mountain towns were the only signs of civilization. After a straight flight over the mountains, four days after leaving Fork Town, they approached the capital city of Sharoth.

As Mav flew down from the mountains, Selivia wiped the dust from her eyes and got her first glimpse of her new home.

From afar, the city of Sharoth blended in with the landscape thanks to red clay tiles covering many of the rooftops. As they got nearer, the walls were revealed to be of the purest white stone. Balconies protected by lacy wooden screens adorned many of the houses, and all the screens, doorframes, and window shutters were painted in tasteful colors. The sea spread blue and calm beyond the neat lines of the city. Compared to the muddy chaos of Pendark, the Soolen capital was a work of art.

"Okay, maybe I understand why people live here now," Selivia said as she admired the city nestled between the mountains and the sea. A cool wind blew in off the water, providing blessed relief after their hot journey. She was looking forward to resting at the royal palace and then perhaps going for a dip in the famously temperate waters. *And trying Soolen rawfish!* There were plenty of things to look forward to here. Most importantly, she would get to see Latch after all this time. Her stomach gave an anxious flutter at the thought.

Mav glided over the red clay roofs toward their destination, the Soolen royal palace. It was an elegant structure, crafted with a careful symmetry that was even more apparent from the air. The white stone walls were carved with subtle designs that changed the aesthetic of the building as the afternoon shadows lengthened. It was defensible too. Pretty wooden screens hid armed soldiers guarding the high walls around the palace proper.

This was where Latch stayed whenever he was in Sharoth, where they would live together after their marriage. Selivia's stomach churned, her nerves asserting themselves more insistently as she got closer to her betrothed. She hoped they still liked each other.

Mav flew lower, heading for the palace walls. At the last moment, it occurred to Selivia that the residents of the palace might not be expecting her. Perhaps Latch *had* sent a letter asking her to wait a little longer. It could have gotten lost on its way to Fork Town.

"Wait, Mav. We should go to the gates first and—"

Before she could finish, Mav snorted impatiently and flew right over the palace walls. Shouts rose from the guards as his shadow swept over them. Faces turned upward to follow his flight. Sunlight flashed on swords and spears.

Mav landed in an inner courtyard with a large garden. Tables paired with large blue umbrellas were scattered around the garden, many of them occupied by men and women enjoying iced beverages in the shade. The people stared up at the massive true dragon, shocked into silence at his sudden appearance.

Mav roared a jubilant greeting, and the people began leaping to their feet, knocking over their drinks, and scrambling backward, as if they expected him to begin rampaging among the tables. One woman fainted dead away. Mav gave a throaty chuckle.

"Really, Mav," Selivia muttered. "Didn't anyone teach you manners?"

She slid off Mav's back and strode forward, not allowing her confidence to waver. Fenn scrambled off the dragon with less grace behind her.

Most of the people gasping and clutching at their hearts appeared to be nobles. They had been lounging beneath the blue umbrellas while servants carried trays of cold drinks among them. The Soolens—including many of the women—wore long, flaring vests and trousers tucked into high-topped boots, and both men and women kept their black hair long.

They all gaped at her, unsure what to do about the dragon in their midst.

"I am Princess Selivia Amintelle of Vertigon," she announced. "Would someone please inform Lord Latch Brach I have arrived?"

The nobles exchanged worried glances, a current of tension weaving among them. No one spoke. This wasn't quite the reception Selivia had been hoping for. Her face and clothes were covered in red dust, and she must not look like much of a princess.

"Can anyone direct me to Lord Latch's rooms?"

The Soolens continued to stare at her—well, at her and at Mav looming impressively behind her. He *was* rather distracting.

Selivia was beginning to regret announcing herself when a woman wearing a long vest over flowing white trousers approached her with deliberate steps.

"Welcome, Princess Selivia. I am the steward Piersha. Apologies, but we did not know you were arriving today. We'd have prepared a proper welcome."

"Oh, I don't need any fuss," Selivia said, trying for a breezy tone despite the uneasiness burbling through her. "Is Latch here?"

"Forgive me, Princess." The steward smoothed her vest, which was already perfectly straight. "Lord Latch has not been seen in weeks. We thought perhaps he had gone to meet you."

Selivia froze. "What do you mean, he 'hasn't been seen'?"

Piersha glanced around the courtyard. All the nobles and servants were watching them, and a group of guards had surrounded Mav—albeit from a safe distance. Fenn's hand hovered near her sword hilt.

"Perhaps we should go inside," Piersha said. "Queen Rochelle will want to see you."

"Very well."

Selivia gave Mav a few quiet instructions, then she and Fenn followed the woman to an ornately carved stone archway leading into the palace. She kept her head high, holding on to her confident bearing by a hair. She felt the touch of a hundred eyes on her back.

They entered a wide hall that was dark and blessedly cool after the sunlit desert. The palace interior was tastefully decorated in elegant neutrals with the occasional burst of color: a delicate blue vase, a vermilion carpet, or a stained-glass window. A strain of music drifted through the corridor, creating an air of dignity and sophistication. Selivia felt grubby and out place in her dusty traveling clothes. She really should have freshened up before dropping into the royal palace like a baby bird falling out of a nest.

Piersha summoned a servant to fetch a bowl of cold water and cloths for their faces. A ring of silvery Watermight kept the bowl icy. Selivia wiped the travel grime from her face and hands, hoping being clean would help her feel less like an unwelcome intruder. Her arrival was going differently than she'd imagined. She'd hoped for a grand tour of the palace from her gallant young fiancé—or at least a hello.

"Where did Latch go? Did he leave a message for me?"

The steward's forehead wrinkled slightly. "Apologies, Princess, I shouldn't speak without the queen."

"But—"

"This way, if you please." Piersha dismissed the servant with the water bowl and ushered Selivia and Fenn down a side hallway. The latter kept a hand on her sword, looking ready to draw it every time a servant scurried past or a tapestry fluttered. Selivia felt rather jumpy herself.

They reached a door painted with an understated swirl pattern, and Piersha stopped. "This is the queen's music room. She doesn't like to be interrupted, but I am sure she will speak with you."

Selivia squinted at the door, her eyes still adjusting to the dimness. "Before I go in, could you tell me—"

"I really can't answer your questions." Piersha glanced at Fenn. "And your woman had better wait outside with me."

"But—"

"Princess—"

Piersha cut off their objections and nudged Selivia into the room alone. As the door slammed shut behind her, the faint string music she'd heard from the hall broke off.

Selivia looked around, disoriented by the abrupt treatment. Light slanted through the shutters on the room's only window, sending sharp beams across the floor and casting the rest of the space in shadow.

"Queen Rochelle?"

"So you're here at last," said someone with a rich feminine voice. "I was beginning to wonder if you'd broken your agreement."

Selivia peered into the gloomy corners of the room, trying to make out the speaker. Queen Rochelle was sitting at a large stringed instrument, like a square harp lying flat on a table.

"I wouldn't go back on my word to Latch or to Soole."

"Yet it seems Latch has done exactly that." Queen Rochelle stood and strode forward through the patterned light. She was very tall and muscular, with thick black hair piled on her head and brown skin that remained smooth despite her advanced years.

"I beg your pardon?"

"Latch Brach disappeared five weeks ago."

Selivia's heart stuttered unpleasantly. "Disappeared?"

"Without a trace." The queen loomed nearer. "Do you know where he went?"

"No, Your Excellency." Selivia dipped into a curtsy, though Queen Rochelle had shown no sign of the formal courtesy for which the Soolens were famous. She tried not to shrink away from the imposing woman. "I expected to find him here."

"He writes to you," Queen Rochelle said sharply. "He has done for years."

"Yes, but—"

"And you delayed your arrival after he sent you a letter."

Selivia brushed at the dust on her coat. "I had business in Pendark."

"Of course. Because Vertigon is great friends with Pendark." Queen Rochelle stepped closer—almost close enough to touch— and Selivia realized there actually wasn't a great difference in their heights. But the Soolen Queen had a commanding presence that made her seem eight feet tall. "Did Lord Latch tell you where he was going?"

"No, Your Excellency."

"What do you know of his recent studies?"

"Nothing, Your Excellency."

"Do you have the letter?"

Selivia clenched her fists to keep from reaching for her pocket. "I left it in Vertigon."

Queen Rochelle snorted. "Of course you did."

Selivia already felt five steps behind whatever was happening here. If the queen was trying to intimidate her with these rapid-fire questions, it was working. Selivia straightened her hair, wishing she'd had time to comb it.

"Are you sure Latch didn't go to Fort Brach to visit his family?" she asked.

"Two of his brothers were here last week, asking after him. They haven't had word from him in almost two months." The queen put her hands on her hips, studying Selivia with sharp brown eyes. "You were the last person he wrote to before his disappearance."

"I don't know where he went." Selivia was starting to really worry now. Latch could be in trouble. "Do you think he was abducted?"

"The possibility has been considered," the queen said. "My investigator searched his rooms. There were no signs of struggle, and he seems to have taken some of his belongings with him."

Selivia's stomach churned. She felt lightheaded. She had spent too much time in the hot sun. "Are you suggesting he went back on his word to me? That he left to avoid our engagement?"

"I am not suggesting anything." The queen frowned. "How is King Khrillin?"

Selivia blinked. "Y-Your Excellency?"

"My Pendarkan counterpart. You spent a week in his company, did you not?"

"I—"

"You may have an agreement with House Brach, but I'll warn you that my primary interest is protecting Soole. Becoming Lady Brach will not protect you if you—or your betrothed—see fit to conspire with our enemies."

Selivia struggled to make sense of this turn in the conversation, searching for an appropriate response. She felt as if she were a zur-moth caught in a spider's web. "Enemies, Your Excellency? But I thought—"

"I do not appreciate subterfuge," Queen Rochelle cut in. "What do you know of your betrothed's research?"

"Very little, Your Excellency." That, at least, was the truth.

The queen pursed her lips, and Selivia waited for the next round of questions. But instead of continuing to hammer her with inquiries, Queen Rochelle turned away and adopted a politely formal tone.

"You must be tired after your journey, Princess. My steward will see you safely escorted to your chambers. We will speak again soon."

"But—"

Before Selivia knew what was happening, Piersha appeared at her side, and Queen Rochelle dismissed her with a wave. She returned to her instrument in the shadowy corner, once more filling the room with music as Selivia was ushered from her presence.

Back in the corridor, Selivia shook off Piersha's hold on her arm and paused, attempting to calm her nerves and order her thoughts.

Queen Rochelle had a formidable reputation, but Selivia hadn't expected an interrogation. Her siblings were two of the most powerful monarchs on the continent. She should have straightened her back and demanded answers, as was her right. Instead, the woman had rolled over her like a bullshell, implying first that Latch ran away to avoid their marriage and then that Selivia was conspiring with Latch and Khrillin against the Soolen throne.

She shoved her hands into her pockets to keep from shaking—or maybe yanking the door open to demand an apology. Latch's letter crinkled between her fingers.

The Brach family was wealthy and powerful, and relations had always been strained between them and the Soolen royals. But Latch had made a concerted effort to mend the relationship between his house and the royal family. His betrothal to Selivia was supposed to help, as the queen and Crown Prince Chadrech would value Latch's marriage link to Vertigon. They were supposed to be allies.

But where *was* Latch? He had clearly been worried about something when he wrote the letter suggesting she might need to wait in Fork Town. Why hadn't he written again? He wouldn't leave her, would he?

Piersha cleared her throat. "This way, if you please, Princess."

Selivia jumped. She had been standing still, staring at the pale floor tiles. The queen's music still drifted through the closed door.

Fenn wore a worried frown, but she didn't speak as the Soolen woman escorted them deeper into the palace. Selivia pressed a hand to her forehead, going over everything she and Queen Rochelle had said. She didn't think she had given away any information that could harm Latch. She didn't *have* any blasted information.

They reached a room with a door carved in desert roses. The chamber inside was as elegant as the rest of the palace, with a blond wooden table, turquoise couches, and a window overlooking the sea.

"This is where you will stay," Piersha said. "I shall instruct the servants to bring you refreshments."

She glided away before Selivia could ask any more questions.

"I don't like this," Fenn said as soon as the steward was gone.

"You should have heard the way Queen Rochelle talked to me just now." Selivia filled Fenn in on the conversation. She felt agitated, but she kept her voice down in case anyone was listening at the door. "They should be scrambling to welcome me as the sister of their most powerful ally, but she treated me like an untrustworthy child. I think she expected me to give something away."

"She thinks you know where young Lord Brach is?"

"It certainly seemed that way." Selivia grabbed the other woman's hand. "Do you think he's in danger, Fenn?"

"If he is, you are too." Fenn glanced at the door and lowered her voice. "I think we should take Mav and stay elsewhere."

The suggestion was appealing. Selivia had thought she might have to deal with some awkwardness as she got to know her new husband, but she hadn't expected him to disappear altogether. Added to everything that had happened in Pendark and Fork Town, she had half a mind to fly straight back to Vertigon.

But she had negotiated this betrothal for a reason, and she wasn't going to give up on it so easily. "We won't learn anything if we're not in the palace. We need to find out what's going on."

Fenn grunted. "The young lord shouldn't have brought you into this mess," she said, "especially not without fair warning."

Selivia touched the letter in her pocket. "I think he tried to warn me."

She went to window and pushed open the wooden screen. The lumpy East Isles were visible way out at sea. Storm clouds were building above them, gray and ominous next to the crisp blue ocean. Latch had been trying to tell her something about the East Isles in his letter. She was sure of it. If only he hadn't been so cryptic.

"Let's get cleaned up and start asking questions. I'm not going to let Queen Rochelle scare me."

If she and Latch were going to swear marriage vows to each other, she had to be willing to stand up for him. Besides, his research into ancient magic-wielders could have repercussions well beyond his own safety and the success of their marriage. There could be all kinds of reasons why someone—even the queen—would want him to disappear.

11

I t took a week for Tamri and the others to travel the length of
Trure on dragonsback, following the hard-packed line of the
High Road. Trure was a rolling land of farms and horses and
scattered towns. The people were still recovering after being scoured
by invaders during the war, and the land bore the scars of battle and
destruction.

The dragon riders flew during the day and stayed in little inns or
camped by the roadside at night, careful not to overstay their
welcome. When Taklin asked why they were traveling at a quicker
pace than usual, Heath simply said there might be trouble.

Tamri was becoming comfortable with flying as they got farther
north. She liked the clean wind on her face and the weightlessness
in her stomach as she and Laini soared through the air. She quickly
grew to care for the skittish sea-green creature, who snuggled up to
her whenever they camped under the stars, her wings keeping
Tamri warm.

When they drew near the capital, a sprawling, garden-filled
place known as New Rallion, Heath decided they shouldn't go into
the city. Instead they camped beside the crystal waters of Azure
Lake.

"The old Rallion City was sacked twice during the war," Reya
explained to Tamri as they brushed dust out of their dragons'
feathers by the lake. Her red dragon, whose name was Rook, still

glared at Tamri at every opportunity. "The Trurens are wary of strangers."

"Would they chase us out like the Fork Towners?"

"Could you blame them?" Reya said lightly. "I wouldn't want to have this lot over for dinner, either."

Reya jerked her head toward Taklin and Errol, who were sword fighting with sticks on a rocky bank. The clack of wood and the scuffle of their feet echoed over the mirrored surface of the lake.

"You're just jealous of our skills," Taklin called. "Come on, Reya. Join the fun!"

"Dueling isn't my idea of a good time," Reya said. "Who'd allow themselves to get stabbed on a regular basis?"

"If you're good enough, you don't get stabbed," Errol said.

Reya snorted. "I've seen how bruised up you get after practice. You must be dreadful."

Errol shrugged and turned to Heath. "Sure you don't want to duel, Chief?"

Heath glanced up from where he was mending the leather strap that held his Fire cudgel to his belt. The needle and thread looked comically small in his sturdy hands. "I'm sure."

"How about you, Tamri?" Taklin said. "I reckon you're quick. Wanna duel?"

Tamri shook her head, ducking behind Laini's wing as they all turned to look at her. She found a burr and gently pulled it loose from the sea-green feather. She preferred fighting with Watermight and could use her fists in a pinch, but she'd never handled a real sword.

"Suit yourself," Taklin said. "What do you say, Errol? A bout to ten and the winner has to arm wrestle Heath?"

"I'm not arm wrestling, either," Heath said mildly, keeping his attention on the tiny needle and the strap of leather.

Taklin sighed. "You're no fun at all." He raised his stick-sword to resume the duel.

Despite their playfulness, Tamri sensed uneasiness among the dragon riders. They looked toward the trees lining the lake a little too often, perhaps remembering how they'd been attacked in Fork Town. Plus, there was a stranger in their midst. They couldn't help but be wary.

Tamri took pains to appear nonthreatening. Those she called friends in Pendark wouldn't hesitate to slice her up if they suspected her of betraying them, and she couldn't assume the dragon riders were any different. Yes, they teased each other amiably and invited her in on their jokes, but they weren't family.

Tamri finished combing the burrs from Laini's feathers and was about to fetch her some fruit from the trees overhanging the lake when the dragon nudged her arm deliberately.

"What is it?"

Laini tipped her head sideways then nudged Tamri's arm while moving her wings in a circular pattern.

"I don't know that one," Tamri said. The dragon riders used a basic code to communicate with the Cindral dragons. Apparently, some magic Wielders could understand them in actual words, though Tamri had no idea how that worked.

Laini made the signal again, and when Tamri still didn't understand, she huffed out a cold breath and used her enormous scaled head to nudge Tamri toward Heath, who was still focused on his mending.

"What?"

Laini gave a sharp chirp and pushed her more insistently.

"All right, all right. I'll get him to translate."

Tamri approached cautiously. She had learned Heath was most talkative—and therefore most likely to answer her questions—while his hands were busy, just as Taklin was most talkative when he was eating and Reya when she was in her bedroll for the night. Tamri had been collecting information to send to Khrillin carefully, playing the role of a curious student. Despite Heath's occasional willingness to answer her questions, Tamri still didn't think he trusted her. Unlike the others, he had never tried to engage her in banter or become her friend.

"Heath?"

"Yes?" To Tamri's surprise, he put away the needle and thread and focused all his attention on her, putting her slightly off balance.

"Um, Laini is trying to tell me something. Would you mind . . .?"

The dragon shuffled up beside her and began tilting her head and circling her wings in that deliberate way. Heath watched her for a moment before answering.

"She wants to know if you're coming home to the Roost with us."

"The Roost?"

"It's where the dragons live in Vertigon, on Square Peak. Most of the riders live there too." He turned his stern bronze gaze on her. "She thinks you're one of us."

"That so hard to believe?" Tamri shot back. She patted Laini's neck, striving for nonchalance. "Sorry, sweetie. I have to go off to school."

Laini grumbled deep in her chest and snapped her jaws.

"She's trying to talk you out of it," Heath said.

"I figured that part out on my own." Tamri kissed the dragon's silky scales and whispered nonsense in her ear, relishing her uncomplicated affection.

When she pulled her face away, Heath was watching her.

"What?"

He blinked, as if he hadn't realized what he was doing, and got to his feet. "We have an early start tomorrow. Better let her rest."

Laini chortled something at him. Heath shook his head, not translating whatever the dragon was trying to communicate. He nodded at Tamri and strode off to check on Boru, his beetle-blue-and-white dragon, who was guarding the perimeter of their camp.

Heath seemed to take Laini's affection for her as a vital endorsement, and he acted less hostile toward Tamri as the journey progressed. He even taught her the basic signals he used to communicate with the dragons and riders while in the air.

"This loop means we need to turn." He waved his glowing Fire cudgel through the air, spinning a mesmerizing trail of light. "Two swipes mean we're landing, and—"

"It's not like I can force a dragon to land if she doesn't want to."

Heath frowned disapprovingly at the interruption. "They know the signals. Anyway, you made Rook take off with you."

"And he still hasn't forgiven me."

Heath snorted, lifting the cudgel again. "If I tap my back like this, look behind you. A triple twist means we need to separate and take shelter."

Heath insisted that Tamri demonstrate the movements herself. The Fire cudgel felt warm but not unpleasant in her hands, and she repeated the actions again and again until Heath was satisfied.

She hoped his efforts meant he was becoming less suspicious of her.

The others acted less tense as they got closer to Vertigon, leaving the troubles of the southern kingdoms behind. Only Tamri couldn't relax thanks to the invisible collar around her neck and the mental list of facts she was compiling for her first report. She couldn't forget she had a job to do, and Gramma Teall needed her.

On the final night of their journey, they camped among the trees at the base of Vertigon Mountain, where the Truren High Road met the Fissure Road. It was cool, and Tamri scooted as close to the campfire as she could get without burning Gramma Teall's cloak, which she'd taken to wrapping around her at night, the pewter dragonfly clutched in her fingers.

Laini shuffled over to lie beside her as usual, but Tamri struggled to fall asleep, consumed with thoughts of what tomorrow would bring. She listened to the calls of strange birds and the chatter of unseen creatures among the trees as she tried to imagine what the Fire Queen would be like. Tamri ended up dreaming of a woman like the Red Lady of the Market District, with dark hair threaded with silver and eyes that glowed with cruel power. The Fire Queen waved a larger version of Heath's cudgel and laughed when Tamri tried to escape.

She awoke with a crick in her neck and queasy fear in her belly. It was the eighth day since they left Fork Town, the day of their ascent to Vertigon.

"I'll take Tamri to the castle on Boru," Heath told Taklin as they broke camp by the tree-lined road. "Will you lead the others to the Whirlpool?"

"Yes, sir. We'll get that Watermight delivered without losing a drop." Taklin clapped Tamri on the back—and she almost managed to keep from stiffening at the contact. "Good luck, kid."

"Thanks."

Taklin glanced at the others and lowered his voice. "Hey, there's a girl called Kay at the queen's Wielder school. She's damn cute, and I botched my chance at a first impression. See if you can put in a good word for me, will you?"

"Sure."

"Knew I could count on you, even though you are a dragon thief."

Tamri gave a tight smile, wishing she were as well-meaning as Taklin seemed to think. Today she would begin work on Khrillin's task in earnest.

Reya and Errol wished her luck, too, as they prepared their weary dragons for the final day of travel. They talked about the salt cakes and goat pies they'd eat when they returned home and the friends and family they were eager to see. It had been nearly a month since they left the mountain.

Tamri tried to smother her fear as she said goodbye to Laini. She hugged her scaly neck and smoothed down her crown of sea-green feathers.

"Thanks for looking after me," she whispered, surprised to feel tears welling in her eyes. Somehow this huge flying beast made her feel safe when she couldn't let her guard down around anyone else. "I wish I could keep you."

Laini chortled and nuzzled her neck, meaty breath ruffling her hair. A few tears escaped Tamri's eyes.

When she pulled back, Heath was waiting for her, his expression neither stern nor disapproving for once. It was a mix of surprise and sympathy and something else Tamri couldn't name.

"You can visit her at the Roost if you like," he said. "You don't need to be sad—"

"Are we going or not?" Tamri cut him off, scrubbing her cheek with her sleeve. She had learned a long time ago not to let people see her cry. Weakness meant death in Pendark, and she doubted the Fire Mountain would be any different.

Heath's face closed up like a stone door. "After you."

Tamri hoisted her belongings onto her back and scrambled onto Boru, who was bigger than Laini if not nearly as large as Mav. She rested her hands on his jewel-blue neck, careful not to disturb the fine white feathers at his shoulders. Heath climbed up behind her in a single fluid motion and put a hand on her hip to keep her in place. She welcomed the contact for once, with nothing else to hold on to.

Boru's muscles bunched beneath her, and he leapt into the cold morning air. The ground fell away fast, the wind whipping Tamri's hair around her face. They circled once around the other dragons still on the ground, and then they were off, soaring up the broad green canyon known as the Fissure, which divided one of the three towering peaks of Vertigon Mountain from the other two. A wide river, the Oakwind, ran along the bottom of the Fissure. Mist rose from the water at this early hour, making the whole canyon look hazy and mysterious.

Heath pointed out each of the three peaks as they flew along the Oakwind's silver line. The Fissure separated Square Peak, the widest and flattest of the three, on the right from Village Peak and King's Peak on the left. The shallower Orchard Gorge divided Village Peak from King's Peak, which was the tallest of the three.

Countless bridges crisscrossed the sky over the Fissure and Orchard Gorge, turning the three peaks into a single vertiginous city. The bridges were constructed of wood and stone and rope, not quite the pure-gold highways of the stories. Still, the mountain was larger than Tamri had expected, and her head spun at the thought of crossing those swinging rope bridges.

Boru turned into Orchard Gorge, which was filled with terrace after terrace of fruit trees bearing plums and apples and little green fruits she didn't recognize. The workers tending the trees looked up as the blue-and-white dragon flew overhead.

Boru banked sharply, making Tamri gasp, and continued nearly straight up, skimming the tree-covered slopes of King's Peak to the steep layers of the city proper. People turned to watch as the dragon looped among the bridges connecting the terraces on the lower part of the mountain to those lining Village Peak behind them. Balconies jutted out over the slopes, and the roads looked like staircases as often as pathways. More bridges connected the outcroppings around the midsection of King's Peak.

"You can still see some damage from the true dragon attack," Heath said, bringing his mouth close to Tamri's ear and pointing at a dark scar on the mountainside. "They dug into the Fire access points and destroyed half the buildings in the citadel. We've been rebuilding ever since."

The structures did look new and rather grand. Marble and finely crafted stone had been used more often than wood. Glimpses of blazing gold appeared in swirling patterns on some of the walls and doors.

"What's all that shiny stuff?" Tamri asked.

"Firegold," Heath said. "The nobles love to put it on their greathouses. You'll learn to make it, I expect."

Tamri was awed by the sheer wealth displayed across the mountain. Even when she craned her neck for a glimpse of Village Peak, where she assumed the poorer people lived, she saw fine stone houses and well-kept terrace gardens. Nothing resembled the gutter slums where she'd grown up.

A white haze hung over certain buildings where more glimmers of Firegold appeared in the décor. Those were the Fireshops, where Vertigon's native power flowed from the depths of the mountain.

It was cold despite all the Fireshops. Tamri hadn't put on Gramma Teall's brown wool cloak before she left camp, and she couldn't reach it now. She had gotten used to the wind chill while flying, grateful for the warm clothes Princess Selivia had bought her, but the temperature dropped precipitously as they got farther up the mountain.

"You're shivering," Heath said suddenly.

"Thought the Fire Mountain would be warmer."

"It's still summer."

Most of the people in the streets below weren't wearing cloaks at all. They must be used to it, but Tamri wasn't sure how she'd survive if it got much colder than this.

Heath shifted behind her, adjusting his grip on her waist. "Do you want my coat—"

"What's that?" Tamri interrupted, wanting to divert Heath's attention. She pointed to a large stone building, bigger than any other but unadorned by marble or Firegold. It looked like a flat gray box interrupted only by high windows and an arched entryway.

"King's Arena. It's a dueling venue."

"Oh right. Dueling."

As they continued up the slope of King's Peak, everything got even bigger and nicer. Elegant shops lined the broad avenues, and prosperous-looking people strolled along cobblestone sidewalks or were carried by workers in curtained palanquins. It was like flying over the most expensive part of the Royal District in Pendark without the canal stench. Vertigon smelled of pine, apple trees, and smoke.

They were getting closer to the crown of King's Peak. Closer to the castle. The home of King Siv and his Fire Queen sat on a plateau about a hundred feet above the next nearest building. Built of light-gray stone, the castle had three towers, one obviously newer than the others, and the lower part had a new façade, marble trimmed in Firegold, that shone as if fresh from its maker.

A walled courtyard around the castle contained the blackened stump of what had once been a truly majestic tree. A ring of new trees had been planted around it, but it would be years yet before they peeked over the walls.

Boru landed inside this courtyard, and Heath dismounted smoothly.

"You can just fly right in?"

He shrugged. "They know me."

Still shivering from the cold—and maybe a little fear—Tamri scrambled off Boru's back and landed a bit too hard on the uneven ground.

Heath reached out to steady her. "Don't be nervous. They're—"

"I'm not nervous," Tamri hissed.

He pulled back his hand as if she'd bitten him. "Just trying to help."

Tamri wished her first instinct weren't always to lash out. But Heath didn't know all the reasons she had to be on edge. She hooked her fingers in the rope holding her sack of belongings on her back and willed her pulse to stop racing.

Heath spoke to Boru for a moment. The dragon bowed his head in a dignified farewell then took off into the morning sky to deliver his Watermight cargo.

Heath led the way up the grand castle steps to a pair of double doors made of that same glowing Firegold substance. It seemed an extravagant display of wealth—and a foolish one. Doors like that would be stolen within a week in Pendark.

A pair of men in blue uniforms guarded the doors. One took a crisp step forward, a slim sword swinging at his hip, and held out a hand.

"Welcome back, Lord Samanar."

"Captain Jale." Heath shook the man's hand, and Tamri noticed a Firegold knot on his shoulder indicating his rank. "I bring a letter from Princess Selivia and a . . . delivery for the queen. Is she free?"

Captain Jale looked at Tamri curiously. He was in his late twenties, and he appeared neatly trimmed and thoroughly respectable. "She and the king are in the dueling hall. I'll escort you."

"No need," Heath said. "I know the way."

"Actually, I'd like to ask you about your time in Pendark. I've heard rumors that relations are becoming strained with—"

"Now isn't a good time, Captain," Heath cut in, his tone polite but firm. "I'll visit you later, if you please."

"Of course." Captain Jale looked at Tamri again, this time seeming to take in her thick, dark hair and Pendarkan-olive skin, then gestured to the doors with a shallow bow. "Please proceed."

Heath pulled open one of the large golden doors and ushered Tamri in ahead of him. She found herself in a vast marble entryway hung with tapestries. Another pair of tall double doors stood directly across from the entrance, and corridors led off on either side. Glowing spirals of Fire lit the space, as if a lantern had been deconstructed and stretched across the upper part of the entrance hall. All that foreign magic made Tamri tense. She should have taken a bit of Watermight from Laini that morning.

Heath led the way down the corridor to their left. Sconces containing statues and Fire Lanterns of different designs appeared at regular intervals. The corridor was almost as cold as the outdoors, and Tamri shivered harder than ever as they got deeper into the castle.

At first, their footsteps were the only sound echoing through the broad corridor, which was empty of servants and guards. Then the faint ring of steel against steel reached them. The sound of sword fighting got louder as they approached a simple wooden door halfway down the corridor.

"Tamri," Heath said, pausing at the door and looking down at her. "Before we go in, I need to ask you something."

Strangely, Tamri pictured his large hand on her hip as they soared up the mountainside. Where had *that* thought come from?

She tucked her thick hair behind her ears. "What is it?"

"Are you planning to harm Vertigon?"

She kept her tone neutral. "Harm?"

"Pendark and Vertigon haven't always been on good terms, and King Khrillin . . ." He touched his Fire cudgel, seemingly without realizing it. "I'll allow you to leave right now if your intentions are less than honorable. I refuse to put the king and queen in danger."

Tamri gestured to her small, shivering frame. "How much danger could I possibly be to them?"

"Quite a bit," Heath said. "And I've only seen a hint of what you can do with Watermight."

"I don't want to hurt Vertigon or your precious king and queen." Tamri couldn't say the same for Khrillin, but she spoke the truth. "Coming here wasn't my idea. You know that better than anyone."

Heath studied her for a moment more. His scrutiny made the blood rise in her cheeks. Hopefully he would think she was only nervous about meeting the legendary rulers, not about the job she had to do. She glanced down at Heath's coat sleeve, which hid the wound she'd given him. It must be mostly healed by now.

She jerked her head at the wooden door. "Are we going in or not?"

Heath looked her over once more and then nodded.

"I don't underestimate you," he said as he reached for the doorknob. "And you shouldn't, either. The queen respects people who know their own strength. Pretending to be weaker than you are won't win points with her."

"I'll keep that in mind."

"Good."

He opened the door and led the way into the dueling hall.

12

The king and queen were too busy trying to stab each other to notice Heath and Tamri's entrance.

Three long dueling strips stretched the length of the hall, with wooden dummies covered in stab marks set up at one end. Four tall windows let in thick beams of light, which crossed the width of the strips and fell on a rack full of swords on the opposite wall. The vaulted space smelled of sweat and leather, with just a hint of smoke drifting through the open windows.

The man and woman dueling on the center strip wore white jackets and masks of wire mesh. Both were tall and athletic, and the sweat dampening their dueling jackets suggested they had been at this for a while.

A hit landed with a thwack.

"Point!" shouted a male voice. "That's twenty-seven for me!"

"That was simultaneous."

"Not a chance."

"It was." The woman's voice was serious, focused. "We're still tied."

"Fine. But you have to admit that lunge was a thing of beauty."

"You should have gone for the forearm not the shoulder." She tapped her glove. "You would've had me then."

"Fair enough." The man raised his sword, and the woman mirrored him. "Twenty-seven all. Ready?"

"Duel!"

The man charged forward, and the woman parried his attacks. One. Two. Three. She countered, and only a wide swipe kept her blade from his throat. The tap of boots on stone filled the bright hall. Then the man lunged, aiming his blunt-tipped dueling rapier at the woman's toe. She leapt back nimbly and landed a hit on his mask with a loud clang.

"Sheesh, Dara. You still hit harder than a charging gorlion." He pulled off his mask to run a hand through his dark hair, revealing a handsome face with high cheekbones shadowed by a bit of scruff. The resemblance to Princess Selivia was obvious in his features as well as his bright, good-humored manner. This must be Sivarrion Amintelle, the Fourth Good King of Vertigon.

The woman removed her mask, too, releasing a long golden braid. Her back was to Tamri, hiding her face. "That's what you get for taking half the summer off."

"I've learned my lesson," King Siv said breezily. "Next time I'll make Sora visit me instead of tramping all the way down the mountain to see her in New Rallion."

The queen raised her blade. "Shall we go to thirty, or have I worn you out already?"

He grinned. "Not even close."

Heath cleared his throat, and the pair turned, noticing him and Tamri for the first time. Tamri was surprised to see that King Siv and the Fire Queen were quite young, probably in their mid-twenties.

"Heath! It's about time you got back." The king slung his rapier over his shoulder and strode forward to shake hands with the dragon rider. Thin scars covered his face and hands, and an old burn mark stretched the skin by his ear. "I was beginning to think you had to deliver Sel to Latch's doorstep kicking and screaming like a captive greckleflush."

"No, Your Majesty." Heath straightened his back, and Tamri got the distinct impression that the king's approval mattered a great deal to him. "The princess and I parted ways in Fork Town. She should have arrived in Sharoth by now."

"Good to hear. And how was old Khrillin?"

Heath hesitated. "He didn't seem quite as eager for our business as he has on previous visits, sire. And there was trouble in Fork Town."

"I see." King Siv's grin faded. "That sounds like a conversation best had over a goblet of wine. Would you care to join me in my study? If my lady wife will release me from my training obligations, that is?"

He turned to the tall, golden-haired woman beside him. She was studying all of them, including Tamri, with an intense gaze, an arrow focused on a target. Tamri immediately felt wary. The young king was charismatic, but the Fire Queen had the kind of presence only the most dangerous Waterworkers displayed, the kind that came with power.

"I think that's a good idea," the queen said. "But who is your companion?"

"This is Tamri of Pendark." Heath took a letter out of his pocket and handed it to the queen with a respectful bow. "She is a Waterworker, and Princess Selivia asked that she be allowed to join your Wielder school."

The queen looked Tamri over then read the letter, written in a looping, earnest hand. Tamri couldn't read it from this angle. She tried not to fidget, wondering what Selivia had said about her.

The queen glanced up from the letter. "You stole a dragon?"

"Borrowed it."

King Siv chuckled, looking at Tamri with renewed interest. But Queen Dara was not impressed. She studied her for a moment then returned her attention to the letter. Tamri shivered. Why was it so cold here?

When the queen finished reading the letter, she passed it to her husband and fixed those intense eyes on Tamri again. "You're seventeen?"

"Yes."

"Have you ever tried to touch the Fire?"

Tamri shook her head. Waving a Fire cudgel around a few times didn't count. The Fire was rare in Pendark, more expensive than Watermight. She'd never even seen the substance in its raw form.

The queen's mouth tightened, and Tamri feared she'd be sent home then and there. Dread twisted through her at the thought. Khrillin would never accept such a failure. He would throw Gramma

Teall out in the gutter—if he didn't kill them both. Tamri had to convince the queen to accept her into the school.

She took a step forward. "Princess Selivia told me you were nineteen when you started Wielding both powers, uh, Your Majesty."

"The first time I used Watermight, yes," Dara said, "but the Fire is an incredibly dangerous substance, if you can touch it at all."

"I learn fast," Tamri said, "and I have the quickest whip in Pendark. I'll catch up to the other students."

"It will kill you if you go too fast."

"I can be careful too," Tamri said.

The queen frowned. "I am not sure—"

"I survived Pendark," Tamri said. "I taught myself how to control Watermight. I know how deadly—"

Heath nudged her, just a quick touch at the elbow, and Tamri realized she had interrupted the Fire Queen. She clapped a hand over her mouth.

"You don't have to convince me with words," Dara said calmly. "Wielders' bodies become used to the magical substances over time. Theoretically, we can all use all of them, but if you're already too accustomed to one, the other will hurt you." She brushed a wisp of golden hair back from her face. "Let's just see how you do with a bit of Fire."

Tamri's jaw went slack. "Right now?"

In answer, the queen strode to a small door at the side of the dueling chamber. There was a balcony above it from which people could watch the duelists on the main floor. When the queen opened the door, Tamri glimpsed a table covered in books and papers, and a glowing metal grate set into a fireplace.

The queen raised a hand, and a stream of molten gold flowed from the grate. Tamri gasped as the glittering substance streamed over the table piled with books and out the doorway to the dueling hall. The Fire was spellbinding. It moved like blood: hot, thick, and smooth. It appeared heavier than Watermight, less ethereal, but its magical aura was unmistakable.

The Fire flowed through the air directly to Queen Dara's hands and pooled in her palms, shimmering like satin. Then the liquid magic sank into the cracks in her skin, and for a moment, the Fire Queen's veins glowed gold.

Dara let the door to the study fall shut and rejoined Tamri and the two men. "Hold out your hand."

Tamri clenched her teeth and extended her palm uncertainly. She hadn't expected to be tested so soon.

"Tell me if this starts hurting," Dara said.

The Fire spun out of her fingers and spiraled slowly toward Tamri. The glow lit up the queen's golden hair, the spirals glinting in her eyes. She was beautiful in an intimidating kind of way, and Tamri couldn't tell if her expression was meant to be threatening or not. Heath and the king must still be watching them, but Tamri didn't dare look away from the Fire Queen and the foreign magical substance spiraling closer. Closer. She felt a flutter of anticipation, her heart beating in time with the pulse of the Fire. She wondered if it would warm her up.

Then the molten gold stream connected with the center of Tamri's palm—and the liquid burned her as if it were boiling oil. Tamri gasped in shock.

The Fire Queen pulled the substance back at once.

"Did that hurt?"

Yes. "No."

"Are you sure?"

"Let's try it again."

Tamri held up her hand. If this didn't work, she'd find herself packed off back to Pendark before the sun set. Maybe it would be better the second time.

"Get ready."

The Fire glided closer, as silent as a viper in a canal.

Tamri gritted her teeth as the burning substance connected with her palm. It hurt just as much as the first time, but she clamped down on her reaction. The Fire bored into her, a knife pressing slowly into her skin. She couldn't keep tears from welling up in her eyes.

"Is this okay?" Dara asked.

"It's fine." Tamri blinked away the tears. This had to work. Otherwise, she and Gramma Teall would never get out from under Khrillin's thumb. She couldn't lose this chance. "I can handle more."

Dara looked skeptical, but she made several smaller flows of Fire break off from the main one and snake toward each of Tamri's fingers. The molten magic shimmered, giving off heat and a palpable sense of power.

All five points connected at once, five hot needles pricking her fingers.

Abruptly, Tamri had had enough. She hurled the Fire away from her with the same mental force she used to control Watermight. The Fire scattered into a hundred droplets, spraying like water from a geyser. The droplets flew straight at King Siv.

Time seemed to slow. Tamri's mouth opened in horror. It was too late to take it back.

Then Dara flung up her hand, halting the Fire mere inches from the king's face. The glowing droplets hung in the air, a curtain of deadly rain that could have seared straight through his body.

Tamri stared, shocked at what she had almost done. King Siv looked just as surprised at the near miss. The queen calmly pulled the Fire droplets out of the air, drawing them back into her skin.

Tamri started to release a sigh of relief when hands closed around her arms, nearly lifting her off her feet.

"Your Majesties, I am so sorry." Heath sounded utterly horrified as he restrained Tamri with an iron grip. "I didn't mean to bring an assassin to—I will remove her before—"

"Wait, it was an accident!" Tamri said as Heath dragged her toward the door. She jammed her heel into his toe, trying to wriggle free. "I'm not an assassin."

Heath held her firmly, his face going scarlet. "I believed she meant well."

"It's all right, Heath," Dara said. "She clearly wasn't in control of that attack."

Tamri bristled. "I wasn't trying to attack—"

The Fire Queen looked at her, and Tamri swallowed the rest of her words. The look held calm authority and immense power. Despite her precarious position, Tamri couldn't help wondering what it would be like to see this woman facing off with Khrillin.

Dara turned to her husband. "Are you all right, Siv?"

"As safe as a Soolen bullshell with you around," said the king, rubbing the stubble on his chin. "Almost added to my scar collection, though."

Dara frowned at Tamri. "That was very close."

Tamri shivered at the razor focus in the queen's eyes. She felt as if the woman could see straight through her, all the way to the oath bond on her neck and the mission that had brought her to this mountain. They were going to find out. They were going to kill her. Tamri quaked with fear, with the urge to flee, but she didn't dare look away.

The room became so quiet she could hear Heath's heartbeat behind her. The moment balanced on a knife-edge.

Suddenly there was a squawk, and a winged shape soared down from the spectators' balcony above the door. Tamri jolted in surprise, breaking eye contact with the queen at last.

Everyone turned toward the newcomer, their movements exaggerated as if they'd just been released from a spell. It was a small dragon, featherless like Mav, with scales of dark green and leathery black wings.

The little dragon flew once around the dueling hall then landed beside the king in a clatter of talons. It sniffed at his boots then rose on muscular hind legs to rub its nose on his face, leathery wings rippling.

"Late to the party, as always, Rumy," the king said, scratching the little dragon as if it were a dog. A very scaly dog. "I'm fine. It's hardly the first time Dara has saved my life while you were snoozing."

The dragon gave an affronted snort and dropped onto all fours. It turned its back on the king and trundled over to where Heath still held Tamri prisoner, both elbows pulled back, one of her heels still pressing down on his toe.

Ignoring their awkward position, the dragon began picking at Heath's coat pocket and chattering animatedly.

"Oh, uh, hello, Rumy. It's good to see you too." Heath shifted his hold on Tamri to pull a lumpy treat from his coat pocket. "There you go."

The little dragon gave a delighted chirp and began chomping happily on the treat.

Siv laughed. "Rumy knows who his true friends are."

Heath gave an embarrassed shrug. "Cur-dragons are fickle."

While he was distracted, Tamri considered digging her nails into the cut on his arm to get him to release her, but she doubted that would win her any friends here. Besides, the arrival of the little dragon had cut the tension her accidental outburst had caused.

The queen was studying her thoughtfully, but her eyes no longer held that blade-sharp focus. "At least we know you can Wield the Fire, Tamri."

"I can?"

"The Fire responded to you, though I doubt you realized what you were doing in the moment. You're very fast."

Tamri hardly dared to hope she might salvage the situation. Her palm still smarted from the Fire, but maybe she could get past that little obstacle. She'd accept any discomfort if it meant Gramma Teall would be well cared for, even by Khrillin.

"I didn't mean to hurt anyone," she said, striving for a meek tone. "I have nothing against Vertigon or the king."

"No hard feelings on my part," King Siv said. "Your call, my love."

Dara deliberated for a moment. "I believe you meant no harm. However, you must control impulses like that if you are to study with me. I won't have you hurting yourself or the other students with such wild actions."

Other students? Did that mean she was in?

"I'll be careful," Tamri said. "I want to learn." And it was true. She wanted to learn how to Wield as quickly as the Fire Queen had when she stopped that spray of Fire. She wanted to learn enough to give off an aura of power and authority, too, maybe even enough to face off with Khrillin herself one day.

"Wanting it isn't enough," Dara said. "I expect discipline from my students. The others of your age and strength have had three years to get used to that. You will start at a disadvantage, but you must not rush your training. Discipline. Control. Focus. That is what I require."

Tamri straightened her back as much as she could with Heath still holding her arm and met the queen's eyes. She would focus. She would learn. No matter how much the Fire hurt, she would prove that she was capable of so much more than she had demonstrated today.

This was for Gramma Teall. For their freedom. For herself.

"I'll do it."

13

Queen Dara asked Heath to escort Tamri to the Wielder school a short walk from the castle.

"I'll let Corren, the schoolmaster, know you're coming," she said. "Good luck, Tamri. I'll be seeing you soon."

Tamri bobbed her head, not sure whether she was supposed to curtsy. She could hardly believe that after flinging beads of fiery magic at the king, she would still have a chance to learn from this woman. And spy on her. Tamri couldn't forget that.

She rubbed her palm surreptitiously, hoping the pain the Fire had caused had been some sort of fluke.

The queen strode over to the weapon rack by the wall to remove her dueling jacket and buckle on a fine sword with a jet-black hilt. The little green-and-black dragon scurried over to perch beside her, chittering softly.

King Siv walked Tamri and Heath to the door of the dueling hall.

"We'll have that drink and discuss Pendark later, Heath," he said. "I won't invite Rumy, though. He'll get fat again now that you're back on the mountain."

Heath bowed deeply, still looking embarrassed despite the king's friendly tone. "Sire, I'd like to apologize again for—"

"Nothing to be sorry about." The king clapped Heath on the shoulder. "We'll talk soon."

Heath didn't speak to Tamri as he escorted her out of the castle by the arm. He only released her after they passed Captain Jale at the doors, and then he rested his hand on his Fire cudgel instead. Tamri sighed. He acted as suspicious of her now as he had in Khrillin's audience chamber, as if all the progress they'd made on their journey had evaporated. She wasn't sure why that bothered her.

They crossed the courtyard with the burned stump and the ring of young trees and left the castle grounds on foot, descending a stone staircase, which felt much steeper than it had looked from the air. When they reached the city proper, the road wound down the mountainside in broad switchbacks, sometimes giving way to more staircases. From certain vantage points, they could see Orchard Gorge and the bridges leading to Village Peak in the distance. Many of the fine houses near the castle were under construction, more evidence of the catastrophic attack on Vertigon. Thin wooden scaffolding outlined the walls, and the sounds of hammers and chisels echoed among them.

Plenty of people were about at this late-morning hour, though Vertigon was quiet compared to the busy port city that was Pendark. Few of the passersby were foreigners, but the Vertigonians paid no attention to the scrappy Pendarkan girl being escorted through their fine streets by a tall, stern dragon rider.

Every once in a while, a leather-winged dragon swooped overhead, chattering and squawking. Most of the creatures were even smaller than Rumy. Tamri missed a step when she saw one carrying a brightly wrapped bundle in its talons.

"Cur-dragons," Heath said gruffly. "They carry messages and small packages and melt the snow off the roads in the winter."

"That's what Rumy is?"

"He's half cur-dragon and half true dragon," Heath said. "He and his litter are the only ones I've ever encountered."

Tamri hoped the fact that Heath was talking to her meant he knew she hadn't attacked his precious king on purpose. Heath might not be her friend exactly, but she'd hate to leave things sour between them.

"I really didn't mean to hurt anyone," she muttered as they reached a cracked stone basin that looked as though it had once been a fountain. The main street turned in another switchback, but beyond the fountain, a smaller path descended toward a quieter street lined with greathouses.

Heath led the way past the broken fountain and started down the quiet path. "I should have sent a Fireworker to guard you instead of delivering you to the castle myself. King Siv and Queen Dara are good people, and Vertigon needs them safe."

"I think they can take care of themselves," Tamri said. "And the queen's obviously more powerful than me."

"It's not about whether they can protect themselves," Heath said. "I've worked hard to earn their respect despite—" He broke off, rubbing the back of his neck. "It doesn't matter. I shouldn't have taken the risk."

"So why did you?"

"I believed you meant no harm, and I wanted—never mind."

"What?"

"Nothing. This is it."

They had reached a large greathouse at the end of the path, with a marble façade and a broad porch lined with columns. The roof appeared to be flat, with a stone railing running all the way around it.

They climbed the porch steps and paused at the door. Heath looked down at Tamri, his face unreadable.

"Are you coming in?" She didn't add that she wanted him to. He was her only tether to the life she'd left behind, and even though he'd been suspicious of her from the first moment, his stern presence was strangely comforting.

"I have to get over to the Roost," Heath said. "Master Corren and the students will look after you."

"Will I see you again?" Tamri's cheeks warmed despite the bite in the mountain air. "I mean . . . I don't know anyone here, and I just . . . wondered."

Heath's expression remained guarded. He opened his mouth to speak twice then broke off. The silence felt expectant, and for once Tamri didn't want to interrupt it.

"You should wear your cloak," Heath said at last. "You look cold."

Then he turned on his heel and marched down the steps, leaving her alone at the entrance to the Wielder school.

The door burst open before Tamri could knock. She dove behind a marble column, ready to defend herself with fists and fingernails.

A girl with straw-blond hair and a multitude of freckles bounced out onto the porch. She spotted Tamri straightening up and trying to pretend she hadn't leapt for cover at the sudden noise.

"I was right!" A wide grin split the blond girl's face. "The queen sent a message with the Air telling us you were coming, and I heard it first! I never hear it first."

"That's because you're too busy talking, Kay," came a voice from inside the greathouse.

"Not this time," the blond girl crowed. "Don't just stand there. Come in!"

The girl, who was about Tamri's age, pulled her through the greathouse doors to a wide entrance hall. Tamri shook off her arm automatically, taking in a grand staircase leading to the second level and doorways opening into other wide, well-lit rooms. The place was warm and smelled of baked bread and cinnamon. Small faces peeked around corners, studying Tamri closely and whispering to each other. The children scurried out of sight like gutter mice when Tamri looked at them.

"The little ones are shy now, but you'll wish they'd leave you alone soon," said the blond. She wore black trousers and a fitted red coat, and her pale hair was cut to her chin. "I'm Kay, from Trure. That's Shylla."

Another older girl surveyed them imperiously from the bottom of the staircase. She too wore a red coat and trousers, and her dark hair was piled on her head in an elegant knot. She had olive skin and a glittering, competitive look in her eyes that Tamri knew well.

"You're Pendarkan!"

Shylla only looked at her.

"That makes six of you," said Kay, "but the others are much younger. Shylla's the only one in the older class. You're Tamri, right?"

Tamri nodded, slightly overwhelmed by Kay's quick chatter. "How did you know I was coming?"

"Queen Dara sent a message with the Air. And I heard it first!"

"The Air?"

"It's the third magical substance," Kay said. "We don't have a lot of it here on the mountain, but the queen is trying to get us used to listening for it."

Shylla folded her arms. "We've heard all about you."

Tamri met her aggressive gaze, recognizing the challenge. She hadn't expected to meet another Pendarkan Waterworker here, and it put her on edge. Well, more on edge than usual.

"Have you been in Vertigon long?"

"I was the first Pendarkan student," Shylla said coldly. "My mother controls the Market District back home."

Tamri raised an eyebrow. "I didn't know the Red Lady had a daughter."

"We'll have time for that later," Kay said, flapping her hands excitedly. "You have to meet Master Corren."

She took Tamri's arm again and dragged her toward the front parlor to the right of the entrance hall. The children who'd been watching from the shadows scattered before them. Most appeared to be twelve years old or younger.

"We just have two classes here, the Originals and the Young'ns," Kay said. "The rest of the older students are at the Whirlpool. You'll meet them eventually."

Tamri registered as many details as possible with Kay pulling her along and chattering in her ear. The greathouse was decorated with exquisite care. Tapestries embroidered with Firegold hung from the walls, and Firegold cushions covered the many couches and armchairs. The front parlor was larger than Gramma Teall's whole house, and children filled it almost to overflowing.

Most were Vertigonian, fair-skinned with black, bronze, or dark-red hair. The Trurens, like Kay, had light hair—blond or brown—and light eyes, with tanned skin almost the same shade as their hair. She spotted several young olive-skinned Pendarkans and even a few Soolens with long black hair and dark-brown skin, one a few years younger than her and the others no older than ten. She lost count of the students at twenty-one.

In their midst, a stocky older man with short, graying hair stood up from what appeared to be a loom threaded with Firegold and silk. Several smaller looms surrounded him, each paired with a child-sized stool. He wore a fine coat and had an air of dignity befitting a magistrate.

"You must be our new arrival. I am Master Corren, Firespinner and warden of this fine establishment."

Tamri wasn't sure whether that title warranted a bow, so she just nodded.

"I'm Tamri."

"Welcome, Tamri, to the Wielder School and to our temporary home." He spread his hands wide, the gold embroidery glittering on his sleeves. "As you can see, we've nearly outgrown this place. Construction has already begun on a more permanent campus over on Square Peak."

The children edged closer, as if expecting Tamri to do a trick. She shifted her feet uncomfortably, not sure what to make of this place. It felt more like an orphanage or perhaps an extra-large family than a formal school.

"You're the teacher?" she asked. "I thought this was Queen Dara's school."

"Our queen has many duties," Master Corren said. "I oversee the day-to-day operations and liaise with your other instructors. Most teach their particular skills on a part-time basis, but I make my home here. How much do you know about us already?"

Tamri shrugged. "What you just told me."

Master Corren chuckled. "Sit, and I shall give you a proper introduction. But you must be hungry! Ber, will you fetch a goat pie from the kitchen?"

A boy of around twelve scrambled out from behind one of the couches. Kay ruffled his hair as he darted past.

"My brother," she whispered to Tamri. "He's a first-rate Firespinner already. Sit down. You don't need to be shy."

Tamri sat on a couch by the parlor window. The heavy curtains were drawn back to admit a thick slice of daylight. Master Corren settled into an armchair across from her and rested his boot on his knee, showing off the intricate Firegold details in the leather. The children gathered around him, curious eyes focused on the newcomer. A small boy peeked from beneath the armchair, and two more jostled for position closest to Master Corren's right hand.

The schoolmaster sighed deeply, his barrel chest expanding. "I am a Firespinner by trade," he began, "but Vertigon lost many—nay, *most*—of our Fireworkers during the ill-fated invasion of the Lands Below."

Tamri remembered the scarred land of Trure they'd flown over, the way its citizens were still wary of outsiders. The damage wasn't only due to Vertigon, but Fireworkers had played a large part in the war.

"With so much manpower required to rebuild the city, we no longer had enough Wielders left to train all the apprentices with the potential." Master Corren smiled at the children surrounding him. "The great craftworks that made our city prosper were in danger of being lost. We needed an institution where a small number of Workers could train many apprentices at the same time. I have always taken on multiple apprentices, and Dara—excuse me—Her Majesty the Queen believed I would be a good choice for the position of schoolmaster."

"Are you as powerful as her?" Tamri asked.

Master Corren coughed. "I can't say that I am. The queen and I have not always been on the same side, I must admit, but she entrusted me with this burden and gave me an opportunity to redeem myself." Master Corren shifted and glanced toward the window, as if he hadn't meant to say that much. Tamri filed away the little piece of history in case it could prove useful.

Master Corren regained his composure and smiled benevolently. "Perhaps when the Fireworkers of Vertigon return to their former glory, we will return to the apprenticeship model. Until then, here you find us."

"So you mostly study Fire?" Her hand twitched where the substance had burned her earlier.

"Ah, I'm getting to that. Queen Dara discovered that a Wielder of one magical substance can control them all, providing they do not grow too attuned to the substance originating in their own land. She invited young students of the Work to travel from the lands of our allies to explore these new possibilities."

Tamri looked around at the many non-Vertigonian faces among the students. "Does she keep all the magic Wielders here after their training?"

"Our students are free to depart when they please." Master

Corren glanced at Shylla, who leaned in the doorway with her arms folded. "We offer education and an exchange of magical knowledge. What our students do with it is up to them."

Tamri frowned. Living on the mountain from such young ages would surely make some of the students want to remain after their training ended. Khrillin suspected the Fire Queen's school was more than just a small group of children. What would he say when she told him the Fire Queen was replenishing her depleted forces with the children of her allies?

Ber returned with an earthenware plate piled with steaming goat pie. The smell reminded Tamri she hadn't eaten since they broke camp at the bottom of the mountain. It was hard to believe that was just this morning.

"Please eat your fill," Master Corren said. "Your training regimen will begin in earnest tomorrow. Queen Dara insists her students exercise their bodies as well as their minds. Physical exertion promotes discipline. You will also study art and dragon-care and history and—" Master Corren hesitated and lowered his voice. "Forgive me for asking, but can you read and write? I understand many children from your land—"

"Yes, my grandmother taught me."

Shylla raised an eyebrow, as if she had been skeptical about whether or not Tamri was literate too. She seemed to have pegged Tamri for exactly what she was the moment she walked in the greathouse door. Her imperious air made it clear what the daughter of the Red Lady thought about some gutter kid.

"Excellent," Master Corren said. "Then I hope it won't take you long to catch up with the others in the older class, who we like to call the Originals."

"I'll do my best." Tamri glanced around the large parlor, noticing a few bookcases and desks piled with parchment along one wall. "Master Corren, would it be possible for me to write letters home? My grandmother will worry about me."

"Of course, child. The Cindral dragons carry our correspondence to the Lands Below. A group departs every other week to collect more Watermight."

Tamri remembered Heath's suspicions of her and winced. What were the chances her letters would be opened and the

Vertigonians would learn they didn't just contain reassurances for her relatives?

"What about the Air?" she asked. "Kay was saying you can send messages with it."

"All in good time." Master Corren chuckled. "I am glad to see you are an eager student."

Tamri took a bite of her goat pie to hide a grimace. She'd have to compose her reports for Khrillin carefully until she found a more secure way to send them.

"Kay will be in charge of getting you settled here," Master Corren said. "All students are expected to contribute to the care of the greathouse. You'll receive a chore list along with your uniform and study schedule. Most importantly, you are not permitted to touch any magical substance without the supervision of an instructor or more experienced student."

"But—"

"That part is nonnegotiable," Master Corren said, his tone kind but firm. "I am sure you're used to having all the Watermight you desire at your fingertips, but here we must use it sparingly. It takes a great deal of effort to transport the substance to the mountain and even more to maintain the Whirlpool."

"I've heard the Whirlpool mentioned before," Tamri said, not bothering to correct his assumption about all the Watermight she'd owned. "How does it work?"

"Trine, why don't you take that one?"

A small girl popped out from where she'd been hiding behind Master Corren's broad chairback. She was missing her two front teeth, and she answered in a high-pitched lisp. "The Whirlpool is how we keep the Watermight from drainin' away, Mathter Corren. It keeps the magic thpinning after the dragons bring it."

"Very good, Trine." He looked around at his little congregation, all the children eager to please. "And how do we at the Wielder School help with that task?"

Five hands shot into the air.

"How about you, Malco?"

The little boy hooked his thumbs in the lapels of his red coat and puffed out his chest. "The big kids take turns helping Master Loyil spin the pool so they can practice."

"That's right. All students with enough strength are expected to take a shift assisting the Whirlpool keeper whenever it is full. You'll get your turn, though I daresay you'll need less practice than most."

Tamri wasn't so sure about that. She knew how much power the Cindral dragons had carried on their most recent visit to Pendark. She'd never controlled anything close to that much Watermight.

Shylla was watching her closely, as if she could read her thoughts. She smiled, and the expression was not friendly. Tamri supposed it was too much to hope that her fellow Pendarkan would become an ally.

"Well, we'd better get back to our lesson." Master Corren waved his hands, and the children scattered back to the smaller looms. "The rest of you run along to your chores. Oh, and Tamri?"

"Yes, Master Corren?"

He smiled. "Welcome to Vertigon."

14

Selivia had been in the Soolen royal palace for over a week, but the search for Latch wasn't going well. Every shred of information she collected cost hours of wheedling and eavesdropping and chasing down sources, and she still hadn't figured out what caused Latch's sudden departure from Sharoth.

Part of the problem was her sources. The famously reticent Soolens took time to warm up to people, especially outsiders. Selivia had prepared for this, studying the culture of her future husband's land through books, conversations with Soolen travelers and dignitaries, and of course, through Latch's letters. She had been certain she could charm answers out of someone—if not Queen Rochelle herself—that would explain what had become of her betrothed. But studying a culture and understanding what it was like to exist within it turned out to be entirely different.

She tried to befriend the local lords and ladies, hiding probing questions amidst well wishes and dining invitations, but she underestimated their deeply ingrained sense of privacy and caution. After enduring her concerted efforts to be friends for a few days, people began avoiding her, claiming illness or prior engagements or just ducking out of sight when she approached.

When she managed to corner a lady in the painting gallery: "Would you care to join me for a platter of rawfish, Lady Nille?"

"I'm so sorry, Princess. I'm afraid I'm allergic."

Or a lord in the gardens: "I understand you keep a gorlion in your menagerie, Lord Olar. Might I visit to see—?"

"That won't be possible, Princess. The gorlion escaped last week."

"Oh dear! Is there any chance it can be found or—"

"So sorry, Princess. I believe I hear my wife calling."

"But the gorlion—"

"Farewell, Princess."

The Soolens were unfailingly polite, even when they were avoiding her. In a way, Selivia was glad Queen Rochelle had taken such an aggressive approach the day she arrived. It put her on the offensive, prompting her to push through the culture of social restraint to get information when she might otherwise have tried to be more restrained herself. She couldn't afford to hold back when Latch's life might depend on her.

"I understand your daughter is a steward in the Royal Archives, Piersha." The palace steward tried to stride away, but Selivia caught her arm, ignoring the shocked expression on the elegant woman's face. "I need to speak with her about which manuscripts Lord Latch was studying before he left."

"His papers were collected by the queen's investigator," Piersha said.

"May I see them?"

"I'm afraid I don't know where they are." The steward's face hardened. "And my daughter doesn't, either, so please leave her out of it."

"But—"

"If you'll excuse me, Princess." Piersha all but ran away down the corridor, her long white vest streaming behind her.

Selivia adopted Soolen local dress in an effort to fit in better, wearing long vests and trousers tucked into high-topped boots or sleeveless sheath dresses that made her look even taller than she was. But her efforts to ingratiate herself with the palace inhabitants failed at every turn.

Before the week was out, the nobles and stewards had taken to peeking around corners to see if Selivia was waiting for them. Even the courtyard with the umbrellas, normally a peaceful meeting place for the nobility, had become noticeably emptier since her arrival. It made her grind her teeth every time she crossed it to reach the smaller garden where Mav was staying.

The one thing Selivia managed to puzzle out was that, whether or not anyone knew where Latch had gone, they did *not* want anyone to think they knew. Determined to prove they weren't involved, the residents of the palace simply refused to be seen with her.

"If I hear another Soolen claiming he's allergic to rawfish I might scream," Selivia announced when she and Fenn returned to their rooms after another fruitless effort to get someone to sit down with them. The door carved with desert roses slammed behind her. "It's their national dish!"

Fenn searched the elegant chambers to make sure no one had snuck in while they were out. "How is Mav holding up?" she asked calmly.

"He's moody," Selivia said. "He can tell something isn't right here."

"Perhaps he just doesn't like the food."

"He ought to be grateful it's being delivered to him. He'd have a hard time hunting in that blasted desert."

Fenn's mouth tightened, as if she hadn't quite accepted that Selivia was no longer a child whose language she could correct.

Well, Selivia could blasting curse if she blasting wanted to. Where *was* Latch?

She kept hoping she'd round a corner and there he'd be, looking as dashing as the day they met on the slopes of Vertigon. But frustration and despair were setting in despite her best efforts. She needed a breakthrough.

As soon as Fenn confirmed that no assassins lurked among the potted desert plants decorating their sitting room, Selivia took her letter out of her belt pouch and read through it for the thousandth time.

My Dearest Selivia,

Forgive me for being so abrupt in my writing. I am not certain it is wise for you to come to Soole yet. I have learned something in my research, and I may need to investigate. I will send word to Fork Town to confirm if you should join me as planned. Watch out for our pen friends, and bring a copy of Brelling's East Isles journal if you have one.

I remain yours,
Latch

She was beginning to wish she'd waited in Fork Town after all. But "pen friends" almost certainly referred to the Pendarkans, and there were plenty of them in Fork Town. Latch certainly hadn't warned her of the trouble she'd found there.

She read the final line again. Brelling's East Isles journal. No such book existed. She had confirmed as much with Piersha's daughter at the Royal Archives, a vast, echoing tower full of rolled manuscripts, bound books, and fluted columns. The young woman, whose name was Quell, had refused to disclose what Latch read on his last visit and begged Selivia not to tell her mother they had spoken.

Selivia looked up from the letter. "He has to mean he was going to the East Isles, don't you think?"

"As I said the last twenty times you suggested that," Fenn said patiently, "Brelling wrote many travelogues, including several featuring islands. Lord Latch probably got confused."

"But he *loves* Brelling. He wouldn't make that kind of mistake."

"We cannot go gallivanting off to the East Isles, Princess."

"It's supposed to be lovely this time of year." Selivia pulled open a carved window screen to look toward the distant islands. The storm clouds that often hung over them had spread toward the city, and the scent of rain hung in the air. "Anyway, where else are we going to look? He's obviously not in Sharoth."

"Even if he did travel to the East Isles, there are a dozen of them. We wouldn't know where to search." Fenn sat at the table and took out Brelling's Soolen journal, which had traveled all the way from Vertigon in Selivia's satchel. The water-damaged pages crinkled as she opened it. "And he would have left word if he wanted you to join him."

"Maybe he thought he'd be back by now. If he's in trouble—"

"He is a Waterworker," Fenn said, still perusing the book. "I don't know what trouble he could be in that you could save him from."

Selivia slumped dejectedly onto the low turquoise couch. She wished she could Wield the magical substances. She had communicated using the Air before but only when an Air Sensor drew on the substance and created the link for her. She would never touch magic the way Latch and Dara did. She normally got by on charm and pure enthusiasm, but even those were no match for the Soolens when they wanted to keep something hidden.

A knock sounded on the door.

Fenn was up in a flash with her sword bared. Selivia blinked. Her bodyguard was more worried about their safety than her placidity suggested. The realization made uneasiness worm through her stomach.

Fenn waved for Selivia to remain seated. "Who is it?" she called through the door.

"I wish to speak with Princess Selivia," came a haughty male voice.

"Your name?"

"I don't have to give my name in my own palace."

Fenn grimaced and put her hand on the door. "I will send him away if you wish it."

Selivia sighed, tucking her well-worn letter back in her belt. "Sending him away didn't work so well last time."

Only one person in the palace ever sought her out, and she wished he would leave her alone. He'd accosted her at every opportunity since learning she was in Sharoth.

"I understand you play the harp, Princess. Won't you play for me?"

"You look stunning in those breeches, Princess."

"If Latch doesn't return soon, I may steal you away myself, Princess."

"I hear you love animals, Princess. Would you like to come with me on an expedition to hunt bullshells?"

Her suitor was none other than Chadrech, the Crown Prince of Soole and Queen Rochelle's only son. Selivia had already disliked him after their limited interactions when they were young, but Chadrech's suggestion that they go bullshell hunting was enough to make her hate him.

The knock came again, more insistent this time.

"Let him in, Fenn."

Fenn muttered what sounded suspiciously like a curse of her own and opened the door.

Prince Chadrech sauntered past her into the room. He had a thin face, which he thought far handsomer than it was, and a lean build, like the straw men farmers used to scare away furlingbirds.

"Princess," he crooned, strolling over to where she sat on the low couch. "You are far too pretty to be inside on a day like today."

"I've just returned to my room," she said. "And it looks like it's going to rain."

"Visiting that great beast of yours, were you?" Chadrech said. "He ought to be muzzled, if you ask me."

Selivia stood so he couldn't loom over her. "Did you want something, Prince Chadrech?"

"Only you, dearest."

"I've asked you not to call me that," she said as aggressively as she dared. "I am betrothed to—"

"To a man who doesn't appreciate what an exquisite treasure you are. I would never have left you waiting." Chadrech seized a lock of her hair and twirled it between his fingers. "In fact, I'd have completed our marriage the very day you turned eighteen. Sooner, if the law allowed it."

"Charming." Selivia tugged her hair out of his grasp and retreated to the balcony. It was hot outside despite the storm building in the distance, and sweat broke out on her forehead. The sea rolled below the city, but they were too far up to feel more than a hint of the ocean breeze. "I'm very tired. The heat takes it out of me here. So if you wouldn't mind—"

"Don't be like that, darling," Chadrech said, following her to the balcony. He leaned in the doorway, blocking her access to the room.

"I really must rest, Your Excellency," Selivia said through gritted teeth. Chadrech's position kept her pinned on the balcony and made her feel claustrophobic, despite the broad sea view spreading behind her. "If you'd be so kind as to—"

"Leave us," Chadrech barked.

He was talking to Fenn, who had followed him toward the balcony and was now looming behind him with a glower on her normally placid face.

"Did you hear me?" the prince said.

Fenn ignored the question. Her strong hands twitched nearer to her sword hilt.

"Your Excellency," Selivia said quickly. "It isn't appropriate for—"

"You're in my city, dearest. I decide what's appropriate." Chadrech wiggled his fingers at Fenn. "Out, before I summon my guards to remove you."

Fenn kept her feet planted, her eyes on the prince.

Before her bodyguard could do something drastic, Selivia shoved past Chadrech's elbow and put herself between the two. The prince could have Fenn beaten or worse, but he wouldn't dare strike the Princess of Vertigon.

For a moment, Chadrech's jaw tensed, as if he meant to do exactly that. Then he spread his hands placatingly. "I only wish to talk. You needn't worry about your virtue."

Selivia folded her arms. "Anything you say to me, you can say in front of Fenn."

Chadrech shrugged and strolled over to the table. Selivia sagged in relief. She had spent so much time flying free with the dragons that she had forgotten what it was like to feel cornered.

The prince sat in a finely carved chair and propped his boots on the tabletop. "I have a theory about where your beloved Latch ran off to. Care to hear it?"

"What theory?"

"No need to sound so hostile." Chadrech grinned and stretched his hands behind his head. "Be a doll and pour me some tea, won't you, Fenn?"

Fenn flexed her muscular arms, as if to demonstrate how easily she could crush Prince Chadrech like a doll. But restraint prevailed, and she moved to the sideboard to pour three cups of tea.

Selivia didn't want to indulge this insolent man a moment longer, but she'd made frustratingly little progress since she arrived in the palace. For now, at least, he was the only person willing to talk.

She sat at the table beside Fenn and waited as Chadrech downed half his tea before continuing.

"My mother's stewards had a look through Latch Brach's rooms before you arrived."

"I heard."

Selivia had searched Latch's rooms herself for hints. Queen

Rochelle's investigators hadn't bothered to put his belongings back in place after ransacking it, and they refused to let her look through the items they'd confiscated.

"It was mostly books, taken from a dozen private collections as well as Sharoth's Royal Archives. Some very interesting books they were too."

Chadrech picked up the Brelling journal, flipping through the pages with much less care than Fenn had shown.

Selivia kept her expression neutral. "Latch loves to read."

"I'm sure he does. But some of these books were of a rather dangerous *magical* nature. Your betrothed was following a trail most people would say is better off left cold. If it were up to me, we'd have burned those books the moment they were written."

"Many people are interested in the history of the magical substances." Selivia sipped her tea. "Reading about it is hardly dangerous."

"This one could be."

"This one what?"

"This substance." Chadrech removed his boots from the table and leaned forward, dropping all pretense. "I think Latch was on the trail of a *new* substance that hasn't been used before. Not Air. Not Fire. Not Watermight. Something else."

Selivia shook her head. "That's impossible."

"Is it? Fire comes out of the ground in the mountains. Watermight comes out of the ground near the sea. I don't know about Air, but I'd be willing to bet it comes out of the ground too. If there are pockets of power all over the place, who's to say the ones we know about are the only ones there are?"

Chadrech's tone sounded a little too earnest for Selivia's liking. He was serious. There was a distant rumble, and a gust of wind rattled the window screens.

"What makes you think this is what Latch was studying?" Selivia asked at last.

Chadrech tapped the side of his long nose.

"If you're just going to tease me with vague hints—"

"Tease you? I'd never! I have come to offer you a proposal."

Selivia grimaced. Maybe he was mocking her after all. "I already told you I'm betrothed—"

"Not that kind of proposal." Chadrech adjusted the Brelling book on the table. "A proposal for a little trip. I may know where Latch went, and if he's not back by now, he must have found what he was looking for. I propose we join him."

"We?"

"That's right, my dearest. You, me, and your glowering friend here."

Fenn had started shaking her head before Chadrech even finished speaking, but Selivia was tempted. She was tired of pestering the Soolen nobles for information they probably didn't have and being denied access to the evidence Queen Rochelle had actually collected. Selivia had proved she was capable of dealing with dangerous situations over the years. She hadn't been put in charge of founding the dragon-riding program because she looked pretty on dragonsback.

But she also knew better than to trust a Soolen with secrets, especially *this* Soolen.

"What exactly do you want?" she asked Chadrech. "Don't say you care about Latch's safety."

The prince examined his carefully manicured fingernails. "I want a say in what happens to that magical substance, if it exists. Latch has been sneaking around behind my back for long enough."

"You're going to be the king," Selivia said, feeling queasy at the thought. "If Latch discovers a new substance on Soolen soil, you'd have a say anyway."

"Latch is a Brach," Chadrech said harshly. "We know how far his family's loyalty extends."

A memory of old Commander Brach popped into Selivia's head. Latch's father had been a distinguished man with a polite bearing and a ruthless, bloodthirsty ambition. He had nearly torn the continent apart in his effort to carve out a dominion of his own outside Soole. All because the Brachs were too far from the line of succession. "Latch is not his father."

"Maybe not," Chadrech said. "But would you bet the life of—say —that flying lizard of yours that he will remain utterly loyal to me throughout the entirety of my reign? There are ways, you know. Watermight Oaths you can swear to guarantee Latch has no ambitions beyond serving as the lord of Fort Brach. Do you know your betrothed well enough to make that promise?"

Selivia didn't answer.

Chadrech's lips twisted in an ugly approximation of a smile. "I thought as much. I wouldn't trust him that far, either."

Selivia was out of patience with the prince's sneering ways. "If you know where Latch went, why do you need me?"

"I said I *may* know where he went, but I am not entirely certain." Chadrech stood and walked to the balcony door. The wind blew stronger now, smelling of rain and lightning. "After a careful excavation of Latch's book collection, I've narrowed the search down to two locations. I was hoping you would help me break the tie."

"And if I help, you'll let me go with you?"

Fenn stirred, but Selivia kept her attention on Chadrech. The light from the window cast half his face in shadow.

"That sounds like a fair deal, doesn't it?" Chadrech put a fist over his heart. "I bear you and your future lord no ill will, but I must make sure Latch is not tempted to stray from his loyalties. I suspect you want the same thing." He smirked. "You can even bring your fire-breathing lizard for protection."

Fenn shook her head more insistently and nudged Selivia with her toe. But they didn't have many options. Without access to Latch's books, they couldn't discover his whereabouts themselves. And if Latch really was in danger, he might need the guards the Crown Prince would surely bring for protection. Selivia might as well go too —and that fire-breathing flying lizard of hers could help if Chadrech and his men tried to betray them.

"What are the two locations you've narrowed it down to?"

"A stretch of abandoned silver mines fifty miles inland from the Ammlen Coast or Thunderbird Island, the easternmost of the East Isles."

The rain started then, rapidly drenching the balcony. Chadrech turned at the sound of the water falling across his city. Selivia touched the letter in her belt and thought of the clue it contained. The answer was simple, really. Something had gone wrong with Latch's work. If he was truly meddling with unknown magical substances, he needed help, even if it came from the Crown Prince.

Something about the letter snagged at her senses, like a twig caught in a current, but it was gone before she could grab hold of it.

"Well, Fenn, it looks like we're going to see the East Isles after all."

"Princess—"

"I know you don't like it," Selivia said, squeezing the older woman's shoulder, "but this might be our only chance to investigate those islands."

"Have you an answer?" Chadrech asked, returning to the table.

Selivia downed the last of her tea and stood. "The East Isles. Thunderbird Island, right? I believe that's where he went."

If Chadrech was surprised, he didn't show it. "Lovely. And you'll accompany me?"

Selivia hesitated. She might not like Prince Chadrech, but he was an important ally and the future ruler of her new homeland. She didn't think she could refuse even if she wanted to. Besides, if Latch was messing around with magical substances, he might need Wielders to help him.

"I assume you're planning to bring a few Waterworkers along?"

Chadrech nodded. "My personal guard will prepare for travel the moment I say the word. There are Wielders among them." He looked down his thin nose at Fenn. "They are highly disciplined. I don't accept insubordination from my staff."

The bodyguard gave Chadrech a flat stare.

"I listen to those who speak wisdom, whether highborn or low," Selivia said. "But I don't know enough about the East Isles to search them myself." She faced the Crown Prince, avoiding Fenn's disapproving frown. "Your Excellency, we have a deal."

15

Tamri's first days at the Wielder School were a blur. Instructions, reminders, and introductions spun together like Watermight in a pool. She donned a red coat embroidered with a Firegold spiral on the first morning, and from then on, she was kept busier than she'd ever been in her life. Queen Dara hadn't exaggerated when she said her students worked hard.

In the first week alone, Tamri sweated through daily physical exercises on the greathouse rooftop, with its sweeping views of the mist-filled gorges and smoke-covered peaks. She helped to cook strange Vertigonian foods in the large airy kitchen: pigeon eggs stewed in Fireroot, orchard pies, salt cakes, spiced mountain goat porridge. She spent hours reading about the magical substances in the parlor and watching the other students manipulate the Fire in the basement workshop, though she wasn't allowed to touch it yet. She spent so much time dashing between tasks that she barely had time to write out her reports for King Khrillin.

Tamri wasn't sure what he would consider a "jewel of information," so she wrote down everything she observed about Vertigon. The students who grew up on the mountain took the oddities for granted, and she struggled to make sense of their references and piece together useful bits of knowledge. They were matter-of-fact about the perilous bridges, the flutter and chatter of dragons, and the use of Fireworks in their daily lives.

Tamri had so much to say about the place that she nicked extra ink and parchment from Master Corren's study on the ground floor so no one would notice how much she was writing in the few moments she stole between exercises, lessons, and chores.

She shared a room on the top floor of the greathouse with three other girls: Kay, Shylla, and a Vertigonian girl called Lacy. All were "Originals," part of the older class of a dozen students, aged thirteen and up. This group had come together while Master Corren and the Fire Queen were working out how they wanted their school to function, test subjects for the fledgling academy. Some had started their apprenticeships with other Wielders, but they had been together for over three years now, making them a tight-knit group. The "Young'ns" class, the future core of the school, had more than twice as many students, and they were held to an even more regimented schedule than the Originals. They were the first generation learning to use all the magical substances from the moment their aptitude first manifested.

Tamri was put with the older group despite her late arrival—and her complete lack of Fire knowledge. She was grateful not to have to sit in classes with the ten-year-olds, though it meant she had to work even harder to catch up with her peers.

Kay did her best to help Tamri adjust, but the talkative Truren girl had plenty of her own responsibilities. Tamri struggled along behind her, trying to hide just how overwhelming she was finding the experience.

And then there was the running. It had never occurred to Tamri to go for a run when no one was chasing her. That was where she found herself early in the morning at the end of her first week in Vertigon.

She and the older students were supposed to run across a bridge from King's Peak to Square Peak and back again, while the younger kids ran a shorter route around the district known as Lower King's Peak.

Tamri was more used to quick dashes to safety than long runs, and she had difficulty keeping up with her faster, better-fed classmates. Kay jogged next to her at first, but when they reached the straight expanse of the bridge, her long legs carried her far ahead. Tamri struggled along at the back of the pack, trying not to look at the seemingly endless drop into the Fissure, which was still choked with mist at this hour.

How long would it take to reach the bottom if the bridge gave way? She tried not to think about that, focusing on putting one foot in front of the other and sucking in deep breaths of thin mountain air.

Sweat dripped down her forehead, and her legs ached by the time she passed the bridge's midpoint. She hadn't slept much the night before. She'd been carefully composing a letter that read like an innocuous update for her grandmother but contained all the information she'd gleaned for Khrillin so far. By the time dawn was turning the sky lavender, she'd covered five sheets of parchment in her cramped handwriting.

The letter crinkled in her pocket now, her sweat no doubt smudging the ink. She'd learned there was a letterbox on Square Peak where people could drop off correspondence for the dragon riders to carry on their supply runs to Pendark. Tamri had planned to take a quick detour from their run to deliver the missive, but she underestimated her ability to dart on ahead of the others.

As it was, she could barely keep up with thirteen-year-old Ber. Kay's flaxen-haired little brother ran with a dogged determination, despite being smaller than the other Originals. Unwilling to fall behind him, Tamri forced her legs to keep moving as the bridge swayed beneath her.

An older Vertigonian boy named Dentry dropped back to give her a broad grin. With his ruddy cheeks and bouncing curly hair, he seemed far too energetic for the circumstances.

"How are you holding up, Tam?"

"It's Tamri," she snapped.

"Easy there." Dentry raised his hands. "Someone got up on the wrong side of the bridge this morning."

"Sorry," Tamri wheezed. Her instinct was to keep the other students at arm's length, but they were her best chance to gather information until she saw the Fire Queen again. "Could you tell me why we're doing this? Does running make you a better Fireworker?"

"It's to make us better fighters."

Tamri stumbled, nearly losing her footing on the bridge. "Who are you expecting to fight?"

"Dunno." Dentry pumped his fists, boxing with the thin mountain air. "But Queen Dara won the last war. If she says running helps, then I'm going to run."

Dentry pulled ahead again before Tamri could ask more about the war. Vertigon had been a peaceful land once, according to the history book she'd been assigned, and its secluded mountaintop location allowed the Fireworkers to focus on nonviolent craftsmanship for over a century. But all that had changed five years ago, when King Siv came to power. Apparently the Fireworkers had tried to take over, resurrecting the notion of combat with Fire.

Master Corren talked a lot about rejuvenating the endangered Fire crafts, which were all about making useful objects—Firebulbs, Heatstones, metalworks, Firekettles, textiles—but the students seemed to think learning to fight with the magical substances was their main priority. Yes, Tamri had lots of interesting things to include in her letters home.

The runners reached the end of the bridge and paused by the burned-out shell of an old tavern. Square Peak wasn't being rebuilt as quickly as King's Peak after the true dragon invasion. Used to their scarred land, the students talked and laughed with barely a glance at the ruin. The fittest students had been there long enough to stop breathing heavily by the time Tamri caught up.

"You made it through your first bridge run!" Kay said cheerily. "First half, anyway."

"I wasn't sure she would," Shylla said.

"Go easy," said the boy who had dropped back to run with her earlier. Dentry Roven was the only noble-born member of the Originals, and he seemed to think it made him their leader. "It's her first week."

"I'm fine." Tamri was enough of an outsider without letting on how much she was struggling. She tried to hide her gasps for breath. "Ready to head back now, in fact."

"Not yet." Dentry lunged, stretching out his legs. "We're supposed to pick up some ore from Master Corren's supplier over here. Carrying it back will be good exercise."

Shylla groaned. "Didn't we just do an ore run?"

"We go through it fast," Dentry said.

"What's the ore for?" Tamri asked.

"To use with the Fire, of course," Dentry said. "Most Fireworks include some metal. Fire Blades, Everlights, Fire Lanterns, even Fire-gold threads."

"Get used to finding metal shavings in your shoes and gold dust in your hair," Kay said.

Tamri found it strange that Fireworking as an art was so solid. Fireworks lasted for years when the power was imbued in metal and stone. Master Corren had shown her a Fire Lantern he claimed was over a hundred years old, which still gave off enough light to illuminate his reading chair. Watermight was ethereal and impermanent by comparison. It didn't seem fair—especially when it came to making weapons.

She eyed the others. "Do you all know how to make Fire Blades?"

Dentry chuckled. "Sword smithing is one of the most advanced Works, whether you give your blades a Fire core or not. The school isn't equipped to teach a skill like that, at least not yet."

"I'll bet Queen Dara can do it," said Ber. The earnest younger boy had beaten Tamri across the bridge in the end. "She made her own Fire Blade."

"That isn't quite accurate," said Pevin, another of the Vertigonians, a rail-thin fellow with a few wisps of mustache. "The queen carries a Savven blade. Drade Savven was a legendary sword smith."

"I thought for sure she made it herself," Kay said.

Pevin shook his head. "She gave it the Fire core that makes it so fast and accurate, but it is a Savven. Ask her yourself if you don't believe me."

"When will she come to the school?" Tamri asked. "I haven't seen her since I got here."

Their instructors so far had included Master Corren, a rickety old woman named Madame Mirri, who specialized in Fire Blossoms, and a large stack of books. Other Wielders came in to teach specific skills in short-term workshops, though Master Corren had ambitions for a roster of more permanent teachers. The Fire Queen was the person Khrillin really wanted to know about, though he'd surely make use of her descriptions of the school—and its students' interest in combat—as well.

"She must be busy this week," Kay said, brushing back her

cropped hair. "She usually comes every couple of days to work with us in small groups."

"I'm looking forward to that," Tamri said.

"*You* won't be working with the queen," Shylla said. "Her lessons are too difficult."

"Maybe her Fire lessons." Tamri resisted the urge to rub her palm, which had been tender for days after her brief encounter with the Fire, "but I'm not useless with Watermight. Isn't she supposed to teach us both substances?"

"Eventually," Dentry said. "We have a regular Watermight teacher, Master Loyil, who's also the keeper of the Whirlpool. The queen wants us to have perfect control over each power individually before she'll let us combine them, though. That produces a burst of extraordinary power."

Tamri perked up. "How long does *that* take to learn?"

Dentry pulled back his sleeve, revealing a collection of burn scars. "I'll let you know when it happens."

Shylla's attention was suddenly focused on her well-cut finger-nails, and a blush rose in Pevin's thin cheeks.

Tamri frowned. "Have any of you have actually done it yet?"

"We've all worked with both powers," Kay said. "Just not together."

Tamri wondered if she had time to add that to her letter. If the Fire Queen was trying to build a Wielder army—one capable of extraordinary bursts of power—she was taking her time. Maybe Khrillin didn't have to worry just yet.

Suddenly Tamri's neck went cold, an icy collar pulling tight. The oath bond must sense she was thinking about holding back informa-tion from Khrillin, even just until the next letter. She rubbed at her throat surreptitiously, not wanting her classmates to see her shiver.

I'll still tell him. Ease off.

At least the others were answering her questions. They saw her as a fellow student, plain and simple. Even Shylla's unfriendliness likely indicated nothing more than a desire not to be upstaged by another Pendarkan Waterworker.

"You know what I think?" asked Lacy, the pretty sixteen-year-old Vertigonian girl who shared a room with Kay, Shylla, and now

Tamri. "I bet she'll start teaching the combined powers to whichever of us she selects to go to the wedding."

"What wedding?" Tamri asked. "The one for Princess Selivia?"

"Yes, it's in *Soole* in the spring." Lacy said the name of the southern land as if it were some mythical paradise. "The queen promised she'd take a few of us with her to get some extra experience. Plus, we get to attend the wedding feast." She sighed, twirling a finger through her dark hair. "Can you imagine?"

"It's not about the *wedding*," Kay said. "Think of it: we'd get to go on an adventure with the king and queen!"

"And she'll choose people who need extra training?" Tamri asked.

Shylla snorted. "Of course not. It's a competition to see who's the best Wielder. She said she'll take the strongest students."

"But people have different strengths," Pevin said. "Maybe she'll choose those who are talented in a particular area, not necessarily the ones who are good at everything."

"Aw, you can think that if you like." Kay thumped Pevin on the shoulder hard enough to make him stagger. "But it's definitely a competition to see who's best."

"When will she choose who gets to go?" Tamri asked.

"Why do you care?" Shylla said. "There's no way you'll be in the running."

Tamri wanted to argue or maybe just smack Shylla for her condescension. The other girl hadn't seen her use Watermight. She didn't know what Tamri could do. But she couldn't afford to make enemies. It was safer to let the others assume she wasn't a threat. The students were proving remarkably free with their words. The more she became one of them, the more she would learn.

More importantly, traveling with the royal family could allow her to collect truly significant information. When the Fire Queen selected the best students to bring to Soole, Tamri intended to be among them. She'd make her reports so useful Khrillin would want to build Gramma Teall a cottage with his own hands.

"So where's this ore merchant?" she asked. "Any chance I can deliver a letter along the way?"

16

By the time they made it back to the school, Tamri's arms were shaking from carrying a stack of slim iron bars from Master Corren's supplier. She'd dropped off her letter in a steel box located by the path to the Roost where the Cindral dragons lived. Fortunately, none of her classmates commented on how many sheets of parchment she had rolled into the bundle.

After returning to the greathouse, they ate a quick lunch of tart soldarberries and goat meat on brown bread. The Young'ns had already eaten, and they sprawled all over the front parlor with books, scrolls, and diagrams, their study time overseen by Madame Mirri. The flutter of turning pages and bored sighs whispered through the greathouse along with the occasional burst of giggles.

When Tamri and the others finished their meal, Master Corren summoned them to the basement for a Fire lesson.

The cavernous space beneath the greathouse had been converted into a Fire workshop and classroom. Stone tables illuminated by simple glowing Firebulbs gave the students somewhere to work, and their inelegant creations were displayed on shelves around the walls. Some of the lumps of metal and partially solidified Fire had a recognizable function. Others looked like sandcastles after a tidal wave. The workshop smelled of hot steel and burnt fabric.

In the center, a crack in the stone floor led to a vein of Fire running through the depths of the mountain. At the beginning of each lesson, Master Corren would bring a flood of the substance to the surface and direct it into low stone troughs running among the tables so the students could more easily draw on the Fire for their works.

During her first few Fire classes, Tamri had been told to observe the other students and get comfortable with the space. This time, Master Corren beckoned for her to stand beside him as he called up the Fire. He'd removed his usual Firegold embroidered coat, and he wore a fine silk shirt with just a hint of golden thread at the cuffs.

"The Fire comes from a source called the Spring in the Burnt Mountains," Master Corren explained as the glowing liquid oozed out of the crack in the stone. "It flows through a vast underground river to where it wells up through the mountain. The Well itself is closely protected, and a containment system distributes the Fire through channels in the stone to access points like this one."

Tamri squinted at the stream of molten gold spreading through the troughs and filling the workshop with light. The air warmed quickly, making sweat break out on her forehead.

"So you can only use it if you have an access point?"

"Trace bits of Fire seep through the stones like moisture," Master Corren said. "You can draw on that when you become strong enough, but Works of significance require an access point."

Tamri moved closer to the trough, its radiance so unlike the icy glow of a Watermight pool. The presence of all that power made her spine tingle.

"The rest of you, keep working on your Everlights," Master Corren called to the other students. "Try to keep the glow in the ends only. Tamri, you're with me."

A clatter filled the chamber as everyone collected hunks of unfinished metal and claimed spots at the various stone tables. Then they began pulling Fire from the troughs and into their bodies.

"Why don't they send the Fire straight into the metal?" Tamri asked as she and Master Corren took a spot at one of the tables.

"It becomes more manageable if you draw it into your blood first," Master Corren said. "You can fling it around in a pinch, but when you're creating a Work, you want it to be as smooth and malleable as possible."

At the nearest table, Lacy wrapped her hands around a jagged stick of metal and allowed the Fire to flow into it from her fingers. She stuck her tongue between her teeth, concentrating hard, and the stick melted slowly into a longer, smoother shape. Next to her, a younger boy named Miles transferred the Fire too fast, and his metal bar disintegrated into a puddle.

"Get another, Miles," Master Corren said. "You can try again when that one cools."

"Yes, Master Corren." Miles shuffled toward a bucket full of metal scraps and selected one to bring back to his table.

"Should I get one of those?" Tamri asked.

"We won't start you on metalworking just yet," Master Corren said. "First you need to be comfortable drawing the Fire into your body. Are you ready?"

The memory of the Fire pressing into her hand like a knife back in the castle flashed through Tamri's head. She clenched her fists. "Yes, sir."

Master Corren smiled, pushing back his silk sleeves. "I'll start by handing you about a spoonful of Fire. Allow it to pool in your palms, and when you're ready you can draw it in. Don't worry about speed for now."

Tamri held out her hands, cupped as if to catch raindrops. Master Corren didn't move except for the rising and falling of his barrel chest.

Then a flow of Fire rose from the nearest trough. The sinuous line curled through the air, bloodlike, becoming thicker. Tamri felt the heat as it got closer, but she kept her face carefully blank. She wouldn't make the same mistake as last time.

The Fire poured into her cupped hands, pooling in the cracks in her palms. And it hurt. Blood-drenched mud, did it hurt. Tamri's eyes watered, and her fingers convulsed at the hot pain in her hands.

Master Corren frowned. "Are you all right?"

"Yes, sir," Tamri said promptly.

"Okay. See if you can draw it in." Master Corren's voice was slow, almost hypnotic. "Imagine the Fire sinking into the lines in your palms. Imagine your blood rising up to meet it."

Tamri concentrated on the blistering pool in her hands and frantically tried to draw it into her body. She thought of the Watermight icing along her bones and making her strong. When that didn't work, she thought of the power as a release from the enveloping cold of the mountain, so different from her muggy home.

But it was no use. The Fire still burned.

She thought she was hiding it, but Master Corren's expression became concerned. "If this isn't working—"

"It is," Tamri said quickly. And then, wanting to get it over with as quickly as possible, she bit down on the inside of her cheek and sucked the Fire into her hands in one pull.

The next thing she knew, she was looking up from the hot stone floor. Master Corren knelt over her, sweat glistening in his short gray hair, face pale. The other students crowded around him anxiously. Well, everyone was anxious except for Shylla, who wore a satisfied smirk.

Tamri blinked groggily. "What happened?"

"You passed out," Kay said, sounding half concerned and half impressed. "Are you okay?"

"I think so." Tamri sat up, face flushing, and scooted back from the others. Lying on her back in the middle of the crowd made her feel unspeakably vulnerable. She winced as she put weight on her hands. They ached from her palms to her wrists.

"Well, you got the Fire into you," Master Corren said. "I pulled it out as soon as you fell. If it hurt enough to make you black out—"

"It wasn't that," Tamri said. "I was just tired from running this morning. Maybe I need to drink more water."

Master Corren looked skeptical. "The queen and I expect our students to work hard, but we don't want you to get hurt. We can't continue if your body is already too used to the Watermight."

"Let me try again," Tamri said, trying and failing to hide her desperation. "I'm just dehydrated. And I'm not used to the thin air here."

She kept her hands out of sight in case any burn marks revealed the lie. Even Fireworkers could be burned if they Worked too fast or drew in too much Fire, but that wouldn't help her case now.

Her instructor was still frowning. "I don't think that's wise."

"Aw, give her another chance, Master Corren," Kay said. "It's only her first day."

"Yes," Shylla said, an unkind note in her voice. "Let's see that again."

Master Corren rubbed a thick finger under his eye. "Perhaps we can try once more."

"You won't regret it," Kay said. "Tamri's a tough one."

Tamri gave her a grateful nod. Kay grinned back.

"Very well. Get her some water, please, Ber," Master Corren said, getting to his feet. "The rest of you get back to work."

The other students returned to their tables reluctantly, but Tamri knew they were still watching. The group sensed weakness, whether or not they were aware of it. Tamri refused to show any more.

"Here's the water." Ber appeared at her side with a clay mug, which felt blessedly cool in her hands. She stealthily examined her palm. The skin was a little red from that spoonful of Fire, but she suspected an ordinary person would have a much worse burn. She'd make this work somehow.

"Don't think of it like Watermight," Ber said, too quietly for anyone but Tamri to hear.

"What?"

"The Fire and the Watermight are different. You have to forget what you know about one each time you use the other. It helps."

Tamri studied the boy, whose solemn bearing was so unlike his sister's. She wasn't too proud to take advice from a much-younger student. "Did you start out with one and switch to the other?"

Ber shook his head. "Kay and I came to Vertigon to become Fire-workers, like our father. But I was only ten, and it was easier for me to adjust to both substances. Most of the Originals favor one or the other, but I'm good at both." He said it matter-of-factly, without a hint of bragging or bluster. "It's because I know the powers aren't the same at all."

Tamri handed the mug back to him. "I'll remember that. Thanks."

She stood and faced Master Corren again. The other students watched, only pretending to focus on their own projects. Miles didn't notice when another metal stick melted in his hands.

Tamri held out her hands. "Let's try that again."

"Get ready." Master Corren oozed Fire out of his fingers—the same Fire he'd pulled from her body moments ago—and let it snake toward her in a slow spiral. "Please tell me if it hurts too much."

"I will," Tamri lied.

This time she avoided thinking about the way Watermight froze her bones and instead imagined the Fire was blood. It was a hot, viscous substance that moved and behaved differently than her native power. It still hurt when it touched her skin, but she suppressed the urge to hurl it away from her. She simply let it sit there like an open wound.

The Fire pricked her skin like hot thorns, but she refused to let it get the better of her. She imagined it flowing into her veins, spreading through her palm and down her wrist.

At last, the Fire began to sink into her. She shook with the effort of not pushing it away, not passing out. The prickling sensation traveled down her arm, inch by inch, getting deeper. Sweat bathed her forehead, and black specks clouded her vision. She felt as if she was going to vomit.

But she stayed on her feet. Allowed the power to sit beneath her skin. Held on a little longer. A little longer.

"Okay, Tamri, that's enough," Master Corren said.

At his words, she jerked the Fire out of her hands. Master Corren ducked as it spurted across the chamber like arterial blood.

"We'll have to work on that part," he said. "But that was a good start for today."

A few of the students cheered. Kay banged a piece of metal on her table in celebration, and Ber gave her a solemn nod.

"You did it! Well done!"

Tamri focused on staying upright. The cloud of black specks had become a swarm when the power left her, and she nearly passed out again. As soon as Master Corren strode away to help another student, she sagged against the table and massaged her throbbing hands. She might have done it, but she wasn't sure how many more lessons like that she could take. It was now abundantly clear to Tamri that her body couldn't handle the Fire.

17

The weeks passed quickly at the Wielder School, but the Fire lessons didn't get any easier. It continued to hurt when Tamri drew the power into her veins, sometimes so badly that she felt nauseous or her vision blurred. She didn't dare tell anyone how severe the pain was lest she get kicked out of the school. She managed to avoid blacking out again, and she could usually make it out of the Workshop before throwing up.

To cope with the pain, she kept from touching the power as much as possible. Master Corren chastised her every time he caught her using the substance without drawing it into her body first.

"That's why the melt is uneven," he'd say, pausing to look over her shoulder at the lump of steel she was supposed to be forming into a sphere. "You can't skip any steps."

She would nod and promise to do better, but she dreaded every Fire lesson knowing she'd have to inflict that blistering pain on herself again. Worse were the looks of pity she started receiving from the other students when she couldn't complete her tasks because the Fire was too unwieldy.

"Just don't get sent home," she'd tell herself as she struggled to keep the Fire from splattering all over her worktable. "That's all that matters. And don't pass out again—at least not where the others can see."

She hated being the worst in the class. Gone were her private dreams of becoming a formidable Wielder who could stand up to the likes of Khrillin and the Fire Queen. She felt embarrassed for thinking she might make it to the top of the class, much less become powerful enough to free Gramma Teall from Khrillin's "care."

But she couldn't give up, and she couldn't let anyone see what the lessons were doing to her. So she nursed her tender skin in private and focused on controlling the molten power without first drawing it into her body.

In addition to their Fire lessons, Tamri and the others made regular trips to the Whirlpool to practice with Watermight. Located in a cavern on Square Peak, the Whirlpool could only be reached through a long tunnel lined with Firebulbs. The huge basin glittered like diamonds, producing an icy glow that danced in uneven patterns on the cavern walls. The Watermight had to churn constantly to keep it from draining away. The older students crossed the bridges in pairs to help with this task when the pool was at its fullest.

The keeper of the Whirlpool, and their Watermight instructor, was a soft-spoken healer called Master Loyil. Once employed to patch up the fighters after Steel Pentagon matches, Loyil had left Pendark for a life of peace on the mountain. He lived with a gregarious former pen fighter called Zarr in an alcove just off the Whirlpool decorated with rugs of mountain bear fur and antique Fire Lanterns. Zarr was missing a leg, which had been sliced off at the knee in a long-ago competition. He now walked with an intricately crafted metal leg, which used a Fire core to aid his mobility. He could often be heard moving around the cavern with a metallic clank during lessons. Tamri gathered that Princess Selivia had recruited Loyil and Zarr to maintain the Watermight supply in Vertigon during her first trip to Pendark with the Cindral dragons.

Tamri missed the icy rush of her native power, and the trips to the Whirlpool were like blasts of sea air from home. She would have enjoyed the lessons themselves a lot more if it weren't for Shylla.

The Pendarkan girl was Master Loyil's favorite student—and she made sure Tamri knew it. She often visited Loyil and Zarr to drink tea and eat sugar mushrooms in their alcove, and she was territorial over their attentions. The pair indulged her at every turn, no doubt because of her powerful mother, the Red Lady of the Market District back in Pendark. Loyil was careful not to show too much interest in the newcomer, regardless of her Watermight talents. Tamri almost wished she could tell him about her own powerful Waterlord connection back home—but she didn't like thinking of herself as one of Khrillin's cronies.

Despite Shylla's efforts to monopolize Loyil's attention, Tamri began to build on her skills in a way she'd never been allowed to before. Using the Watermight sparingly, Loyil helped her finesse her ability to seal wounds, project her voice, and make razors of ice to add to the Watermight whips that were her specialty.

When they weren't fine-tuning the more delicate skills, the students practiced controlling large quantities of Watermight by keeping the Whirlpool spinning endlessly. They could add waves to the pool and even practice picking up rocks and tossing them about the cavern as long as they kept the substance moving. If it slowed, the ethereal power would slip away through the cracks in the stone, wasting the effort that had gone into getting it to the mountain in the first place.

Tamri always hoped to catch a glimpse of the dragon riders when she went to the Whirlpool, but they never stayed in the cave after dropping off the power they transported. Tamri wasn't even sure if Heath's crew was still in Vertigon or if they had flown off on another supply run.

Her reports to Khrillin, which she dropped in the letterbox once a week, continued to detail her lessons and any other information she picked up from the other students. She described the weapons that could be created out of Fire, the students' ideas about all the fighting their future held, and this mysterious burst of power that apparently happened when you combined Fire and Watermight properly.

Tamri tried putting a drop of Fire into the Whirlpool to see it for herself one day. She carried the Fire across the Fissure in a piece of hot iron wrapped in a wool scarf, and while Master Loyil was gushing over Shylla's latest healing demonstration, Tamri unwrapped the iron and held it out over the spinning silvery pool. The other students were gathered around Shylla, not paying attention to Tamri's actions.

She concentrated on the bar of iron and the Fire droplet within it. The magic quivered, slippery and difficult to control. It would have been easier if Tamri had drawn the droplet in before forcing it into the metal, but she'd skipped that part, as she often did. The Fire eluded her, a tiny hot beetle scuttling through the metal. She gritted her teeth, tightening her grip on the iron through the wool scarf.

At last, one shimmering gold tear oozed from the metal and dropped to the swirling silver surface. As the two substances met, white light flashed, releasing a puff of pressure barely strong enough to ruffle Tamri's hair. Everyone turned to stare at her.

Tamri stiffened, wishing she could leap into the Whirlpool to avoid their gazes. She decided to pretend ignorance. "What was that?"

A few of the others chuckled, and Tamri's cheeks warmed. They must know what she'd done.

"Fire and Watermight consume each other," Loyil said, a touch of condescension in his tone. "It's all light and air until you learn to combine them correctly. I'm afraid you're not ready for that yet."

"I was just curious," Tamri muttered.

"No matter," Loyil said. "Now, shall we all take a closer look at this lovely seal Shylla made? Perhaps one day you'll be able to do it, too, Tamri."

Tamri bit back a retort. Despite herself, she wanted Loyil to know she wasn't entirely hopeless.

She shoved the iron bar in her coat pocket and joined the group around Shylla, annoyed to feel tears stinging her eyes. She stayed far enough back that she wouldn't have to brush against anyone, twisting the scarf between her hands as if wringing the neck of a poisonous snake. She should have waited until there were fewer people at the Whirlpool. Being the worst Fireworker was bad enough without making a fool of herself in her Watermight lessons too.

Kay came to stand beside her, perhaps noticing her embarrassment. "Don't worry. We've all tried that," she whispered. "I dumped a whole bucket of Fire in there my second week in Vertigon."

"What happened?"

"It let off a flash of light so bright I was seeing purple for a week."

"Did you get in trouble?"

"Oh yeah. The queen yelled at me for wasting so much Fire and

Watermight, and then Master Corren and Madame Mirri made me scrub silverware for a month." Kay glanced down. "Say, is that my scarf?"

Tamri froze. She'd taken the wool scarf, which was white with black stripes, from their shared room. "Uh, I just needed to borrow it. Sorry."

"Keep it," Kay said. "It's getting cold around here, and my mother'll send me another."

Tamri hesitated then wrapped the striped scarf around her neck. "Thanks. I don't have one."

Kay shrugged. "Just tell me next time you want to try something fun. I've been wondering what would happen if you set off a Fire Blossom in the Whirlpool. It would be a wild show."

Tamri grinned. "I'd like to see that, though you'll have to make the Fire Blossom."

"Deal."

As the weeks passed, Tamri feared she wasn't gathering enough information to satisfy Khrillin. She hadn't seen King Siv at all since that first day. Queen Dara came to the school often to work with small groups of students, usually no more than three at a time, but she hadn't summoned Tamri yet.

The queen's instruction would probably be more useful after Tamri sorted out how to manage the Fire-induced pain, anyway. Hiding her difficulties from Master Corren was easier because he was often dealing with a dozen students at once.

The schoolmaster was turning out to be a useful source in his own right, though. He often held forth at the table during meals, a benevolent grandfather regaling his progeny with stories of the important people he knew. Other times, he dined with powerful friends all over the mountain, trying to coax them to serve as guest instructors. The Fireworkers of Vertigon were always busy because so few had survived the war, but Master Corren made it his mission to convince them to give lessons at the greathouse. He had lofty ambitions for the school, and he relished talking about all the wonderful craftsmen who would one day grace its halls. Bit by bit,

Tamri used his words to assemble a record of the various Fireworkers' strengths and weaknesses. And bit by bit, the information made its way to Pendark.

The elderly Fire Blossom conjurer, Madame Mirri, was the only other full-time adult resident of the greathouse. Her primary role was to look after the Young'ns, the large brood of eight-to-twelve-year-olds who represented the future of the school. She sometimes called on the older students to help the younger ones with their lessons, which allowed Tamri to begin making up for the years of instruction she had missed.

But she still felt out of her depth. The pressure of the lessons was suffocating at times, even without the constant battle with searing pain. She missed her grandmother, and she feared her goal of returning to Pendark as a powerful Wielder was getting further out of reach. There didn't seem to be a single subject in which she could truly excel.

Then one morning, when summer was drawing to a close, Kay shook Tamri awake earlier than usual.

"Wake up! It's Dragon Day!"

"What?" Tamri winced at the early-morning light streaming through the narrow window and wrenched away as Kay tried to haul her from bed. In addition to being sore from the Fire, she was still getting used to the casual way people made physical contact in Vertigon—linking arms, nudging elbows, thumping backs. Tamri still couldn't help flinching when the others were too free with their touch.

"Didn't you hear?" Kay crowed. "We're getting a lesson about Cindral dragons today!"

At that, Tamri leapt up and hurried into her clothes, running her fingers through her tangled hair.

"Who's teaching the lesson?"

"Does it matter?" Kay said. "There's a dragon on the roof! Hurry up!"

Tamri looped the black-and-white scarf around her neck and followed Kay to the kitchen to grab bread rolls and hunks of goat jerky.

"It's Dragon Day!" Dentry called when they entered.

"We know!" Kay danced in a circle around the table, ruffling her brother's hair as she passed. Ber sat at the table, finishing his break-fast and calmly ignoring the uproar.

Most of the other students were just as agitated as Kay. This was the first time the dragons had been brought to the school—part of Master Corren's efforts to enlist more teachers. Not all of the students were happy, though. The Vertigonians in particular looked a little green. Their city had been sacked by dragons—albeit not Cindral dragons. Both of Pevin's parents had died in the attack, and sisters Lacy and Liora had lost their older brother. None of them were eating much.

"Where's Shylla?" Dentry asked.

"Probably up there already," Kay said. "She was supposed to help wrangle the Young'ns today. Are you finished yet?"

Dentry stuffed the rest of his roll in his mouth. "Come on, Pevin. Let's get this over with."

The skinnier boy followed, looking pale but determined. Tamri fell in beside him as they made their way to the greathouse rooftop.

"You're not interested in dragons?"

"I wish I could just focus on Fireworking," Pevin said. "I already know I want to be a sword smith not a fighter."

Tamri kept her tone casual. "They use the Cindral dragons to fight?"

Pevin lifted his thin shoulders. "Not yet."

"Who cares what they use them for?" Kay said, skipping up the stairs on Tamri's other side. "We might get to ride them!"

They climbed through the trapdoor at the top of the house, a flood of chattering students surrounding them, and tumbled onto the rooftop, a wide, flat space they often used for their exercises.

Master Corren stood proudly by the stone railing. Beside him perched a familiar Cindral dragon with sea-green feathers and golden eyes.

"Laini!"

Tamri broke away from the others and rushed forward to greet her friend. Laini turned toward her with a joyous squawk. Tamri was halfway to her before she realized Heath was standing next to her, partially obscured by her wing.

"Oh." She skidded to an ungainly halt. "Hello."

Heath looked up from where he'd been adjusting the knots on a training harness and gave her a polite nod.

"Hello, Tamri."

"Heath."

His bronze hair shimmered like gold in the morning sun. She had forgotten how tall he was.

Tamri had thought about Heath and the dragon riders often over the past few weeks, wondering what they were up to and if she'd ever see them again, but she was taken aback by how pleased she was to see Heath's stern, disapproving self in the flesh. It put her off balance.

Laini shuffled her feathers indignantly, jealous of her attention. Tamri lifted a hand toward her. "May I?"

"She missed you," Heath said. "That's why I brought her today."

Tamri hugged Laini around the neck, burying her face in her feathered shoulder. Had Heath really brought Laini just for her? The thought warmed her to her toes and made her feel oddly shy. It was disconcerting to feel so happy to see someone who wasn't family. And she didn't mean Laini.

By the time she pulled back from the dragon, Heath had moved away to talk with Master Corren. The other students watched from a safe distance, hesitant to come any closer to the huge creature.

"She won't bite," Tamri called, patting Laini's neck. "Come and meet my friend."

Kay moved first, her brother following close on her heels.

"We've met a bunch of cur-dragons," she said. "But the Cindral dragons are usually too busy to come around here."

"She's beautiful," Ber said.

Laini fluffed up her feathers like a proud hen and dropped her scaled nose so Ber could stroke it. He whispered quietly to the creature, as if he'd been chatting with dragons for his entire life.

"Gather around, everyone," Master Corren called. "This is Lord Samanar, and he—"

Heath said something in the older man's ear.

"Of course. This is *Master Heath*, and he is going to teach you all about Cindral dragons. We wouldn't have our Watermight without their efforts. Listen closely now, and do exactly as he tells you."

"Thank you, Master Corren." Heath surveyed the students gathered on the roof. He looked rather imposing, and Tamri couldn't blame them for not getting any closer. "The Cindral dragons have been working with us for nearly five years and with the Cindral Forest folk for much longer than that. But they are not pets, and they are not tame."

He walked over to Laini. Kay and Ber scampered back to join the other students. Tamri was about to follow them when Heath stopped her.

"Would you mind helping with a demonstration?"

"Me?"

"If you don't mind." She caught a hint of something in his voice, perhaps a bit of nerves. He must not be used to speaking to large groups, especially groups of little children.

"Okay."

"Thank you." Heath turned back to the students. "Laini here is the nicest dragon on the continent, and she could still decide at any time to stop carrying Watermight for us. We would have to respect her decision. You can't assume dragons think the same way you do." He turned. "Tamri, what's the most important thing I told you about dragons?"

Tamri jumped, not expecting to be tested in front of the others.

"Don't make so many sudden movements?"

Heath coughed, almost a laugh. "That too. What else?"

Tamri thought back to when they'd stood on the rocky ledge on the far side of Kurn Pass.

"Treat them well, and they'll take care of you."

"Exactly." Heath stroked Laini's nose and whispered to her for a moment. Then he said, "Tamri is going to show you all how to mount a dragon using the training harness. Watch where she puts her hands and feet so as not to pull Laini's feathers."

Tamri did as he said, conscious of everyone's eyes on her. But as soon as she was astride the dragon, she remembered the freedom of flight, the way this dragon had carried her far away from her old life. She had almost forgotten that wonderful rush since arriving at the school. She grinned down at Heath, and for a moment, he smiled at her too.

"Pay attention to where Tamri is holding on to the harness,"

Heath said to the children. "Can everyone see how she placed her hands?"

He reached up to touch Tamri's hand, his calloused fingers brushing across hers. For once she didn't feel the urge to pull away.

Then Heath whispered something to Laini, and the dragon launched into the air.

Tamri gasped in delight as she soared into the sky. She clutched the training harness tight, and the wind whipped her hair back from her face, cold and refreshing. Laini carried her higher and higher over the mountain, giving her a perfect view of the slope of King's Peak falling away beneath her and the bridges branching out from the mountainside like extra limbs. Beyond them, the morning mists had cleared away to reveal the deep green-and-purple chasm of Orchard Gorge.

Then Laini flattened her wings to her sides and plunged into a barrel roll. Tamri shrieked as she flipped over and over. The leather harness pulled tight against her hands, making her tender palms ache. She held on, cursing Heath for surprising her with this acrobatic display while at the same time enjoying the furious urgency of flight. She had forgotten how this felt, exhilarating and terrifying all at once.

Laini spread her wings wide and soared for a few glorious, weightless seconds. The world spread beneath Tamri like a painting. The sun warmed her skin, and a fierce, burbling joy made her ribs ache. She had learned to ride a dragon, and she could conquer the Fire too. She wouldn't be weak forever.

Just as she was getting the hang of this again, Laini dove. The children screamed as she streaked toward the greathouse rooftop, a few retreating all the way to the opposite railing. Tamri pressed her face to the scaled neck, her hands clenched into fists around the harness. At the last second, Laini stretched out her wings and came in for a graceful landing.

Heath wore a full-blown smile now. "Did everyone see how Tamri's hand position kept her safe even though she wasn't expecting that?"

He sounds proud! She scowled at him, making his grin widen.

"Good riding form is essential for safety," Heath told the students. "Dragons are stronger than you, and you need to be ready to work with what they give you. You can't force them to do anything. If they want to flip, you'd better hold on."

Dentry raised his hand and waited for Heath to acknowledge him. "Can't magic control them, sir?"

"Only incredibly strong Wielders can restrain dragons with the magical substances." Heath didn't quite look at Tamri. "Don't assume you'll be able to trap them or force them to move."

Tamri blinked. She'd used a Watermight cord to steal the red dragon back in Pendark. She had a fast whip, but the strength of it hadn't really registered. Her failures during her Fire lessons had shaken her confidence. Maybe she wasn't as hopeless a Wielder as she thought.

Heath surveyed the students, one hand resting idly on his Fire cudgel. "Okay, who wants to ride her next?"

No one moved.

"I'll ask Laini nicely not to flip any of you."

The students took a few steps back. Heath grimaced. The dramatic demonstration apparently didn't have quite the effect he had hoped for. Even Kay and Ber didn't volunteer.

Heath shifted his feet awkwardly. His uncertainty in front of the children was kind of endearing, and Tamri took pity on him.

"Maybe we should start with introductions," she said quietly, slipping off Laini's back. "Work up to riding."

"Good idea." Heath turned back to the students, already reaching into his pockets. "How about this: who wants to give her a treat?" He held up a paper-wrapped packet smelling of honey.

Laini preened in the most non-threatening manner possible, and the students ventured closer. Soon, she was surrounded, the children reaching out to gently stroke her wings and offer her bits of their breakfasts. She endured their attention patiently, and before long, the first student—Kay, of course—was begging for a chance to ride her.

Heath spent the rest of the lesson helping the students clamber onto Laini's back using the training harness and leading them in loping steps around the balcony. The bravest went for short flights around the greathouse.

Heath seemed heartened by the results. "Next time I'll bring more dragons and give everyone a chance to fly."

"When will that be, Master Heath?" Malco asked.

Little Trine clung to his coat sleeve. "Will Laini come back too, Mathter Heath?"

"Can you come tomorrow, Master Heath?" several others chorused.

Heath explained the dragons had to rest between their monthly flights to the Lands Below, but he would try to bring them back soon.

"Laini will tell them she enjoyed meeting you all," he assured them. "You can tell she's pleased by the way she's ruffling her feathers."

Master Corren looked pleased with how the lesson had gone too. Tamri overheard him telling Madame Mirri he hoped to make dragon-riding a regular part of the curriculum when they finally moved the school to a larger campus.

"I've been trying to get young Samanar to bring the beasts here for the past year. Not sure what finally changed his mind."

"I've no idea." Madame Mirri said, idly morphing Fire into the shape of a dragon above her wrinkled hands. "He's better with the young ones than you'd think for such a stern lad."

Tamri couldn't help but agree. Heath had overcome his initial shyness around the children, and he was currently lifting little Trine up so she could feed Laini a sticky soldarberry tart she'd been keeping in her pocket. The other Young'ns pestered him with questions, which he answered patiently. Tamri felt a surge of fondness for the dragon rider. He really wasn't as scary and disapproving as he seemed.

Heath caught Tamri's eye over a crowd of eager faces and grinned.

It was well past noon by the time Master Corren clapped his hands and tried to shoo the students back inside for lunch. They all insisted on saying goodbye to Laini, and she crouched for another round of feather strokes and nose pats, clearly enjoying the attention.

In the ensuing chaos, Heath approached Tamri by the balcony railing. She smiled up at him, a fizzy, bewildering warmth beginning to fill her. Then he handed her a rolled-up parchment.

"What's this?"

"From your grandmother," Heath said. "I just got back from

Pendark a few days ago. One of King Khrillin's people asked me to give it to you."

Tamri's smile vanished. "Did you read it?"

"No, I did not." Heath raised an eyebrow. "You're welcome for the hand delivery."

"Sorry. Thanks."

Heath studied her. Was that suspicion in his gaze? Tamri's hands tightened on the parchment, her sweat dampening the paper. All her worries about being found out as a spy came crashing back.

"Well, anyway." Heath leaned on the balcony, trying to be casual and failing. "I guess I'll see you around."

"Will you?"

Her words came out sounding combative, and Heath's shoulders stiffened. The rapport they'd enjoyed during the dragon lesson evaporated like morning mist.

"Not if you don't want to."

He nodded at Tamri and returned to Laini before she could respond. Tamri resisted the urge to follow him. The parchment in her hands reminded her why she wasn't supposed to be making friends here. There was no point in untangling how it had felt to see Heath again, or interpreting the fizzy warmth that had filled her when he smiled.

A few minutes later, Laini took off in a flutter of feathers and scales, carrying Heath away. While her classmates watched the dragon's departure, Tamri ripped open the letter. It was not Gramma Teall's handwriting, though it was signed with her name.

Dear Tamri,

I received your letters. The stories about your school are interesting. I am pleased to hear you are applying yourself to your studies. However, I would like you to write more about your tutor. I am an old woman, and I want to know more about the legendary Fire Queen and her charming husband before I die.

Gramma Teall

Tamri shivered. How dare Khrillin use her grandmother's name to send his demands. She reread the threat in the final line. He wouldn't truly kill Gramma Teall if she failed to provide the information, would he?

She looked up at the sky, rubbing her neck. Laini appeared as small as a bird now as she soared toward Square Peak. King's Peak rose in the opposite direction, the castle invisible from this angle. There had to be a better way to get information about the king and queen. Succeed or fail, studying at the Wielder School wasn't enough.

18

The deck of the ship swayed under Selivia's feet. She held on to a rope to keep from pitching overboard, her knuckles white from the effort. She had good balance after all her time riding dragons, but she'd never been at sea before, especially not in a storm. Beyond the railing, a blurry coastline was just visible through a curtain of rain. Silver-white magic played across the waves, Watermight that Prince Chadrech's men Wielded to keep the ship a safe distance from the rocky shore in the violent weather.

They rarely sailed out of sight of land on their voyage through the East Isles. Starry Cove, the nearest isle to Sharoth and the Soolen Peninsula, was known for its fine beaches and seaside inns. When most people referred to the East Isles, they usually meant Starry Cove. But the archipelago extended well beyond the idyllic island with its well-protected harbor. The more distant islands were rocky and uninviting, surrounded by sharp reefs that made sea travel difficult. Though technically part of Soole, these islands and their scattered residents were largely left to their own devices. Thunderbird Island, the farthest of all from the mainland, was uninhabited and all but inaccessible.

To reach it, Selivia, Fenn, and their Soolen companions were traveling in a schooner called the *Silverliner*. Thirty soldiers and a dozen Watermight Wielders occupied the ship in addition to the sailors. The Waterworkers used spools of their power to guide the vessel and navigate the complex channels among the little islands.

Prince Chadrech's personal guard was larger than Selivia had expected when she agreed to the trip. The soldiers conducted regular exercises on the deck of the *Silverliner,* and she couldn't help being impressed with their disciplined movements and serious faces. She worried about what kind of trouble Prince Chadrech expected to find on Thunderbird Island that would require so many trained fighters, though. She might have agreed to travel with Chadrech, but she didn't trust him.

Mav and Fenn should be enough to protect Selivia herself if things went poorly. The bodyguard stayed close, and the true dragon flew alongside the ship, only peeling away to hunt or to explore the little islands along the way—at least at first.

But on their second day of travel, squalls and rainstorms had begun to batter them, disrupting Mav's flight and putting the *Silverliner* in danger of running aground. The Waterworkers did their best to keep the ship safe, pulling into little coves in uninhabited islands whenever the sea became too rough. The rain was so thick at times that Selivia could barely see the details of the sharp cliffs rising around them.

By the third day, she doubted she'd ever be dry again. She couldn't bear to be cooped up in her cabin all the time, so she lashed herself to the railing and watched the steel-gray waves churning around her. Tongues of Watermight licked along their tops as the Waterworkers held back the worst of the swells. The violent weather made Selivia glad she and Mav hadn't attempted to fly through the East Isles alone.

The weather grew worse on the fourth day. Mav tried to keep up with the ship, but the gale made it difficult for him to track their progress. She shouted at him to rest on the little islands when the effort of fighting the wind became too much. He finally obeyed, crying out to her in a voice lost on the wind before wheeling away through the storm. A flash of lightning glinted on his scales before he disappeared altogether.

"I don't like this," Fenn muttered to Selivia on the fifth day. They were looking out from the shelter of the hatch, hands clenched around ropes, trying to get a glimpse of their scaly friend through the rain. Mav hadn't reappeared, and the wind continued to whip at the sea as if it were trying to get a look at the mud beneath it. "We were supposed to have Mav with us."

"You'll protect me," Selivia said cheerily even though she felt vulnerable without her Fire-breathing companion. Fenn could protect her from brigands and assassins, but she couldn't stand against a dozen Waterworkers and thirty soldiers. "Besides, we're all supposed to be on the same side."

Fenn snorted. "I don't believe that for a second. Chadrech is a snake."

The animosity between the bodyguard and the prince had only increased when they left Sharoth and the royal palace behind. Selivia wished she could disagree with Fenn's assertion.

At the moment, Prince Chadrech was conferring with two Waterworkers by the mast. The first, Captain Boorn, was hefty and had an officer's knot on the shoulder of his slate-gray uniform. The second, Lieutenant Kech, was even skinnier than Chadrech, with long hair that whipped about in the gale. All three men were tied to the mast with Watermight cords for safety. The prince couldn't Wield, so one of the others must have created his tether.

"He wouldn't hurt us," Selivia said. "Not when my brother knows where we are."

She had sent a message to Siv explaining her plans before leaving Sharoth on the *Silverliner*. She wrote down everything Prince Chadrech had said about the new magical substance and promised to keep Siv updated about her whereabouts. Then, after the letter was safely on its way to Vertigon, she told Chadrech what it contained. The prince might be smarmy, but he wasn't an idiot. He would know better than to harm her while Siv—the most powerful monarch on the continent—knew she was in his care.

Just then, Chadrech looked over at the hatch and spotted Selivia and Fenn peeking out at him. He smiled at the princess, ignoring Fenn altogether. It was impossible to hear them over the roaring wind. Selivia hadn't managed to listen in on any of Chadrech's conferences during the voyage, and she was desperate to find out what he planned to do when they found Latch.

"Let's go below," Fenn said. "I don't like the way that prince looks at you."

Selivia scanned the sky once more for signs of Mav then pulled her way back along the rope to get out of the rain.

With the weather delays, the journey, which should have taken three days, lasted seven. Eventually the swells calmed enough that they no longer had to tie themselves to the ship. At noon on the seventh day, they sailed past a spur of rock surrounded by a jagged reef, and Thunderbird Island came into view.

Selivia climbed the forecastle to see it better. The island appeared to be all of stone, taller at one end, and a great expanse of sea separated the hulking shape from the rest of the East Isles. It looked like a vast war ship sitting alone in the Ammlen Ocean.

A mountain rose from the tall eastern end of the island, its top covered in storm clouds. Flashes of lightning lit the clouds from below and cast brief shadows on the stone. As they drew nearer, shapes that could be buildings or rocks became visible around the base of the mountain.

"People used to live here, you know."

Selivia jumped at the voice. Prince Chadrech had come to stand beside her at the railing.

"It was abandoned roughly eighty years ago," he said. "A mine cuts deep into that mountain, and for a while, a mini civilization cropped up here. See there? Those are the ruins of buildings."

Selivia squinted, the gloom making it difficult to distinguish the boxy shapes.

"The town covered nearly every inch of this place," Chadrech went on. "Miners and their families lived stacked on top of each other. There was a market, a blacksmith, even a school."

Hints of grayish vegetation appeared closer to the water, but there were no other signs of life.

"What happened to them?"

Chadrech's mouth tightened. "The mine stopped producing, and they all moved out within the week. You can still see the furniture and clothes they left behind in the buildings. Without the mine providing their living, there was no reason to stay."

Selivia shivered. The details of the ruins were becoming clearer as they got closer. Squat houses. A few broken towers. Empty windows. It was a ghost town now. Was this really where Latch expected to find evidence of a new magical substance?

She glanced back at the less ominous islands they had sailed through. Glimmers of blue sky were visible above them. Mav still hadn't caught up with the ship. He was probably tired from fighting the wind for so long, but she hoped he'd rejoin them soon.

As she turned back, a bolt of lightning forked down from the clouds and struck a ruined tower at the base of the mountain. Thunder boomed, and a cloud of birds burst from the ruins. They rose in a great swarm and looped around and around the tower where the lightning had struck.

"Thunderbirds," Chadrech said. "They lived here even before the mine opened, but they've multiplied over the years. They like stormy places."

Selivia clutched the railing as the birds careened around the smoking tower. They were huge creatures, with wingspans larger than Selivia was tall. Their feathers were the gray of a storm at sea, and jagged white plumes rose from their heads like the spines on a true dragon. One flew a little closer to the ship as lightning flashed again, its cruel beak and fierce golden eyes gleaming.

"Is it safe to be here?"

"Relax, my dearest Selivia." Chadrech sounded a little nervous himself. "They eat fish."

Selivia wasn't sure she believed him. The bird's talons were large enough to close around her arms and carry her off. She wished Mav were here. It shouldn't be taking him this long to regain his strength.

The thunderbird wheeled in a circle about fifty feet from the *Silverliner*, then it sped back to join its fellows in their swooping dance among the lightning bolts. There was a strange energy about this place, crackling like static on a dry day. It felt as if the island itself were alive. Alive, ancient, and not particularly pleased about their arrival.

Prince Chadrech turned away to instruct his men, but Selivia caught his sleeve before he could get far. "What were they mining here, those people who left eighty years ago?"

Chadrech frowned, and for a moment, the sneering prince's arrogance vanished, replaced by utter seriousness. "That, Princess, is a very good question."

The ship headed for a narrow harbor close to the western end of the island. The shoreline was sheer stone except for the inlet, which had a sloping beach of black pebbles, invisible from the sea beyond. The Waterworkers guided them into the harbor slowly, careful of the *Silverliner*'s deep hull. They had used up most of their Watermight fighting the storm, and they stretched it thin to get to a safe mooring.

Scraps of disintegrating wood on the beach suggested there had once been a dock, but it was long gone now, so they went ashore in small boats. The landing party included Selivia, Fenn, Chadrech, eight Waterworkers, and a dozen soldiers. The rest remained aboard the *Silverliner*.

Selivia stumbled as her feet hit the pebble beach, unused to solid ground. She stood for a moment, adjusting to the sensation and breathing in the damp air. The clouds roiled uneasily overhead, and it seemed darker than it should at this afternoon hour. It was colder, too, even though summer was only just turning to autumn. Selivia buttoned up her coat. She had given up on trying to dress like a Soolen, and she wore one of her favorite flying outfits, breeches and a gray coat embroidered with yellow flowers.

The land rising around the harbor was deserted, but deep grooves appeared in the pebble beach near where they had come ashore, as if they were not the first people to alight here recently.

"People used to visit Thunderbird Island to explore the ruins," Prince Chadrech told her as his men examined the marks. "But any treasures have long since been carted off, and many people fear the thunderbirds."

Selivia folded her arms against a sudden chill. Thunder rumbled, shaking the earth. "So those tracks probably belong to Latch and whoever was with him?"

"Likely."

Lieutenant Kech, the skinny Waterworker with the long hair, approached and raised his hand in a salute. "I count enough boot prints for three or four people, Your Excellency."

"Is that all?" Chadrech said. "My mother's investigators couldn't determine how many people were with him when he left, but even he ought to know better than to come here with so few men."

"They were in a longboat," Kech said. "It's hidden up past that rock."

More soldiers and Waterworkers were grouped around a rock at the top of the beach shaped like a giant face in profile. A spur of pale wood stuck out behind it, the prow of Latch's boat.

"Very good," Chadrech said. "Tell Captain Boorn to leave two men on the beach. The rest will come with me."

Kech loped off to join the others, and Selivia leaned down to study the tracks left by her absent betrothed. She felt uneasy. Latch might not be happy to see her in the company of Prince Chadrech and his men. If he was as outnumbered as it appeared, Latch might have no choice but to share his discoveries.

As she straightened from the tracks, Selivia sensed someone watching her. She spun around, her hand closing on her belt knife. A thunderbird perched on an outcropping near where a rocky path led away from the beach. The creature was even bigger up close. Selivia couldn't move for a moment as it looked deep into her eyes.

"Get out of here," Chadrech hissed. He threw a stone at the great bird. "Rock-eating pests."

The thunderbird cried out, the harsh sound reverberating right down to Selivia's toes. Then it took flight and soared into the storm cloud hovering overhead. A single gray feather fluttered down behind it and settled onto the rocky beach.

Selivia went over to pick up the feather, and a bit of static shocked her fingers. Up close, little veins of white were visible in the elegant gray feather. She pocketed it.

"We'd best find shelter before it rains again," Prince Chadrech said. "The footprints head inland, anyway."

His men gathered their supplies and started up the path away from the beach. They wore stony discipline like armor, but they seemed nervous. They kept glancing at the sky, as if expecting rain or thunderbirds to descend on them. Selivia and Fenn followed warily.

The path from the beach wound up a steep incline lined with overhanging rocks. It soon became a staircase of crumbling stone. Selivia picked her way carefully, the slate shifting beneath her soft leather boots. At the top, they came out onto a plateau and found themselves among the ruins of the mining town. Most of the buildings were roughly on the same level, with a few taller towers clustered at the base of the mountain to the east. It was difficult to tell how far up the mountainside the buildings stretched. The storm clouds had crept lower since they left their ship.

"Let's head for that tower with the circular windows," Chadrech said after consulting an old map he carried in his coat. "It seems as good a landmark as any."

He started up the widest road leading away from the beach. It was already getting on into the afternoon. Selivia had a feeling they wouldn't be returning to the ship that night.

No one talked much as they marched deeper into Thunderbird Island. Empty windows watched them from the ruined buildings, and shadows stretched menacingly across the pathways. Selivia wasn't sure if it was the stormy weather or the absence of people that made this place so creepy. She dearly wished Mav had caught up by now.

"I don't like this," Fenn whispered. She carried her bared sword in her hand, and she was scanning the ruins suspiciously.

"But it's kind of beautiful." Selivia strove for a cheery tone. "Imagine what it must have been like when it was full of people."

Fenn looked around darkly. "They sure left in a hurry."

It was true. Broken pieces of furniture were visible through windows and doorways. Stray articles of clothing and even toys lay among the rubble. Chadrech claimed the closure of the mine had led to the island's desertion, but the residents seemed to have packed up awfully quickly.

The storm clouds expanded as they made their way toward the mountain. Rain came in fits and starts, and the wind whipped at their clothes. Lightning crashed again and again. They spotted footprints here and there, where ancient cobblestones gave way to grayish mud. Selivia hoped that meant they were on the right track.

Eventually, they came to a fork in the path, where the main road split into two paths of equal width. One headed uphill, while the other wound away along a flatter plane. A large building that might once have been an inn nestled between the two forks. The roof was gone, and most of the interior walls had collapsed as well, leaving an empty shell.

Chadrech sent his soldiers to scout both routes while the others waited in the cobblestone square in front of the old inn.

"How well do you know this place?" Selivia asked him.

Chadrech didn't answer, his attention on the clouds amassing overhead. He was twisting the old map in his thin hands, his lips tightly compressed.

"Have you been here before?"

Still no answer. Selivia touched the Crown Prince's arm, and he jolted in surprise.

"What?" he said harshly.

Suddenly, Fenn was at her side. "The princess asked you a question."

Chadrech scowled at Fenn then turned to Selivia. His features looked gaunt in the fading light.

"I came here once as a child when my mother was touring the country." He crumpled the map in his fist, not seeming to realize what he was doing. "It feels . . . different."

"In what way?"

"Something in the air." He grimaced. "It's probably just the storm."

Selivia shivered, aware of the crackling energy she'd sensed earlier and the shock of static on the thunderbird feather. "I hope that's all it is."

The scouts returned, and at Captain Boorn's prompting, they approached the prince and snapped off matching salutes.

"Well?" he said impatiently.

"No sign of them up that way," said the soldier who'd taken the uphill fork. "But it's getting mighty dark on the path."

"Not sure they went my way, either," said the other. "I went around two bends and didn't see so much as an overturned cobblestone."

Chadrech muttered a Soolen curse under his breath.

"It's getting dark," Captain Boorn said gruffly. "Could be that we'll see better in the morning."

Chadrech studied the buildings around the square, a frown on his narrow lips. "I suppose this is as good a place to camp as any. Find us a building that won't fall on us."

"Yes, Your Excellency."

The soldiers and Waterworkers searched the nearby ruins and eventually settled on a building constructed from large stone blocks that still had its timber roof. They made camp in the main room, where shelves leaned drunkenly across the space at odd angles. It must have been a shop once. Crumbling fabric was piled in the corners of the room, and scratching sounds hinted at vermin among the rubble.

The soldiers wasted no time breaking apart the shelves and using them to build a fire near the front door. They kept everything neat, making camp in a professional manner. They seemed more comfortable with the rough quarters than Prince Chadrech, who sneered at everything as if this whole trip hadn't been his idea in the first place.

Selivia wondered what had prompted him to make this journey himself. He couldn't Wield magic any more than she could, and he certainly wasn't enjoying himself. She was surprised he hadn't sent Boorn, Kech, and the others to find Latch without him.

Selivia and Fenn spread their blankets on the ground apart from the men.

"Why don't you sleep nearer the fire?" Chadrech said, coming over to the spot they had chosen near the back wall. "No need to hide in the corner."

"I'm quite all right here," Selivia said.

"Are you certain? I brought extra blankets." He gave one of those lecherous smiles he'd deployed back in the royal palace, but his heart didn't seem to be in it.

"The princess will thank you to give her space, Your Excellency," Fenn said. Her words were technically polite enough for the ruler of a foreign nation, but they came out in a snarl.

Chadrech's nostrils flared. "I've had enough of this—"

"She didn't mean anything," Selivia said quickly. "We are all tired, Your Excellency. I hope you'll forgive a little agitation." She put her hand on his arm and gave him her most charming smile even though it made her stomach curdle. Thunderbird Island was making them all much too tense.

Chadrech glowered at Fenn. She stared back at him, unafraid, and that only deepened the hatred in his eyes. He jerked his arm away from Selivia, unmoved by her smile.

"Get some sleep. We'll have a long walk tomorrow."

Selivia waited until Chadrech had rejoined his men before addressing Fenn.

"You need to be more careful. I can't stop him from hurting you."

"Let him try," Fenn muttered.

Selivia squeezed her hand. "You wouldn't want to get yourself killed and leave me all alone, would you?"

Fenn sighed. "I'm sorry, Princess. I feel on edge. I've been waiting for him to turn on us ever since Mav disappeared."

A shiver went down Selivia's spine. "You think Chadrech had something to do with that?"

"I don't know," Fenn said. "But Mav has never left you vulnerable before. I have a hard time believing a thunderstorm would keep him away this long."

Selivia looked at Prince Chadrech, who sat by the fire, sucking unpleasantly at a wineskin. Could he have kept Mav from following them? He had plenty of Waterworkers under his command. Some might be strong enough to capture a true dragon.

"We'll find Latch soon," Selivia said firmly. "Everything will be okay then."

Fenn hesitated long enough to communicate her skepticism. "Get some sleep, Princess. I'll take the first watch."

Selivia jolted awake. The darkness was thick and soupy, and she wasn't sure what had disturbed her slumber. She lay quietly for a moment, listening to the Soolen soldiers breathing, murmuring in their sleep, and shifting in their blankets. Her bedroll felt as hard as stone and just as cold. She wished they'd decided to sleep a little closer to the campfire after all.

The hum of quiet voices drifted through the darkness.

"Saw someone moving on the ridge."

"Are you sure it was Brach?"

"No, Your Excellency, but it was definitely human."

Selivia shifted her head so she could see the speakers. Prince Chadrech was outlined against the lighter darkness of the doorway. Shadows hid the other man, but it sounded like Captain Boorn.

The prince turned suddenly, and Selivia squeezed her eyes shut so he wouldn't see any light reflecting off them.

"Your men know what to do," he said after a long pause. "Make sure he understands the consequences for the princess if he doesn't comply."

"Of course, Your Excellency. And if he decides the power is more important than her life?"

Another pause.

"He won't."

The sound of careful footfalls and rustling fabric replaced the voices. Selivia pretended to be asleep as Boorn woke more of the men, sure someone would hear the hammering of her heart in the stillness. The soldiers packed up their things and crept from the shelter with the same professionalism they'd displayed while making camp. A thin gray light was beginning to seep through the open doorway when the group departed, leaving the prince and a handful of soldiers behind.

So this was Chadrech's plan. He intended to exchange Selivia's life for assurances that Latch wouldn't keep the new magical substance for himself. She had gone along with it, trusting in her status to protect her. Chadrech wouldn't hurt her, not when she had informed Siv she would be traveling with him, but Latch didn't know about her letter. Chadrech was trying to use her as a hostage to secure control over Latch before she even had a chance to speak to him.

We'll see about that, Selivia thought. *I just have to get to him before Chadrech's men do.*

Keeping her eyes shut, Selivia rolled over, sighing sleepily, and settled on her other side. She waited a few seconds to make sure Chadrech wouldn't come over to check on her. She needed to wake Fenn so they could escape. Now, while most of Chadrech's men were out, was their best chance to make a move. She felt a thrill of excitement at the prospect of sneaking away in the night to reunite with Latch. She certainly wasn't going to sit around to serve as a hostage.

But when she opened her eyes, her bodyguard's blanket roll was empty. Fenn was gone.

19

The next morning, Prince Chadrech insisted Fenn had taken ill and returned to the ship.

"And all your men?"

"They are scouting the island. No point in wandering about aimlessly."

They were still at the fork in the path where they'd camped. Only four soldiers and one Waterworker—Lieutenant Kech—remained to guard Prince Chadrech. Selivia couldn't abandon Fenn, so she hadn't snuck away in the night after all. She wouldn't let Chadrech use her as a bargaining chip against Latch, either, though.

Prince Chadrech brought out a deck of cards and played a solitary game while his soldiers patrolled the cobblestone square. He insisted Selivia wasn't a prisoner, but she couldn't go more than a few steps without a grim Soolen warrior stepping into her path.

"I'd like to walk up the hill a little way," she said the third time it happened.

"That would be unwise, Princess." The soldier, whose face bore a myriad of tiny silver scars, was polite but firm.

"But I can't even see the sea through all these ruins." She tried to sidestep the soldier. "I just want to get a better view."

The soldier stepped sideways too. "It is not safe to wander alone."

"Would you like to accompany me?"

"I'm afraid not, Princess."

She tried to step around him the other way, and again he blocked her, his scarred face inscrutable.

Selivia quickly lost patience with this polite little dance. She marched back over to the prince and stood above him with her arms folded, blocking the light from his cards. "I thought we had a deal, Your Excellency. I helped you determine where to search for Latch."

He didn't even glance at her. "And here we are in the East Isles."

"I want to look around."

"All in good time."

Selivia grimaced, wondering how far she could push him. She didn't want to seem petulant rather than assertive. As much as she resented it, she had to be careful with this relationship. This man would be Latch's king—and hers once they were married.

She strove to make her voice sound meek. "Do you know what happened to Mav?"

"Mav, Princess?"

"My true dragon. Did you hurt him?"

"Why would I do that?"

Selivia's cheeks flushed with anger. Did he really think she wouldn't figure out he was trying to use her to control Latch? She *hated* acting meek.

"I'm just worried about him," she said plaintively.

"He'll turn up." Chadrech glanced up at the clouds, which were growing dark again despite the early hour. "You should be more worried about what your betrothed is up to."

"I'm sure whatever he's doing will be for the good of Soole."

Chadrech gave a scornful laugh. "Of course, Princess."

He seemed convinced Latch intended to keep any power he found for himself. Years ago, Latch's father had taken the Soolen Watermight—which had previously been a closely guarded secret—and used it to conquer new territory for himself. But Latch had opposed his father's ambitions then.

Selivia wasn't sure what to do if Latch decided to turn on his country the way his father had. They had been engaged for years, a political alliance designed to tie Soole and Vertigon together. Her family was closer to the Brachs than to Soole as a whole, but the connection between the kingdoms was still important. If the Brachs went rogue, which alliance would be more important to maintain?

A horrible thought occurred to her. If allying with the Kingdom of Soole was more important than allying with the House of Brach, wouldn't the logical step be for Selivia to marry the Crown Prince instead?

Chadrech was still hunched over his cards like a vulture. Selivia shuddered. Latch had better know what he was doing.

She left Chadrech to his cards and approached the shell of the inn, which was as far as the guards allowed her to walk. She could see farther along the two forks in the daylight. The winding one to the left led deeper among the broken buildings, with towers hanging over it on both sides. The uphill path to the right looked relatively straight. It led all the way up the mountainside and into the clouds.

Thunderbirds wheeled through the cloudy sky, occasionally unleashing those bone-chilling cries. The lightning of the night before had subsided, but the air still had that same crackling energy. It felt as if it could erupt again at any moment.

Selivia scanned the ruined town and the craggy mountain, searching for signs of Chadrech's men. They must have brought Fenn with them to meet with Latch as proof they had Selivia. She didn't want to consider any other possibility.

Movement flickered on the mountain, right where the gray stone met the gray cloud. Another thunderbird, perhaps?

She squinted, waiting for another flicker. *There!* It wasn't a bird at all. A man in a white shirt was crouched on a ledge halfway up the mountainside. Chadrech's men all wore slate-gray uniforms. Could it be a member of Latch's party or even Latch himself?

Selivia climbed on top of a fallen wall segment, trying to get a better view.

"Can I help you, Princess?" The guard with the silver scars strode toward her.

"I'm just stretching." She lifted her arms above her head, hoping he wouldn't look toward the mountain.

"Maybe it's best if you go back inside."

"I want a little fresh air."

She twisted her leg behind her in another stretch, risking a glance back at the ledge. The man was gone.

Blast. Was she wrong about the white shirt? Maybe it had been one of Chadrech's men after all, seeking out Latch to deliver his threats.

She turned in a complete circle, finding no sign of the watcher. She had only Chadrech and his guards and the empty ruins for company.

Abruptly she realized it was strangely quiet. The rush of the sea was audible, a gentle roar in the distance. Why hadn't she noticed that sound before?

The birds. Of course. All the thunderbirds had disappeared from the sky. No wonder it was quiet.

The hair rose on the back of her neck. Something was happening—a shift in the air, a pause in the wind. The guards looked up, as if they sensed it too.

Selivia scanned the ledge where the figure in white had been. A low rumble reached her ears, different from the rush of the sea. She climbed down off the fallen wall and walked a few steps up the right-hand path, away from the guards. There was a flicker on the mountainside, like the edge of a white sleeve disappearing behind a rock.

The guard with the silver scars started after her. "Princess, come back—"

Then a bolt of lightning struck the square, turning the whole world white.

Selivia's ears rang, and purple spots danced across her vision. The scent of hot metal tickled her nose. She struggled to make sense of her surroundings through the dust-choked air and her lightning-burned eyes.

The blast had hurled her forward ten feet, scraping the skin off her hands and ripping open the knees of her trousers. Her head felt tender, as if she had stuck a rock in her skull and given it a good shake.

The old inn had collapsed, unable to stand against the blast. The stone wall she'd been standing on a moment ago had been obliterated. Two of the Soolen soldiers were picking themselves up, as rattled as she was. Two more lay dead on the ground, smoke rising from their clothes. One was the man with the silver scars. Lieutenant Kech crouched in the doorway to the ruin where they'd camped, either guarding it or too disoriented to know what he was doing. Prince Chadrech was nowhere in sight.

This might be Selivia's only chance to escape. She struggled to her feet and dashed up the hillside, taking the right-hand path, which would bring her closer to the storm cloud and the ledge where she'd seen the man in white.

Someone might have shouted after her, but her hearing was one sonorous roar. She ran as fast as she could, stumbling over loose rocks and toppled bricks, trying to ignore the pain in her hands and knees.

As she rounded a bend in the road, she chanced a look back. The two surviving soldiers were running after her, their mouths open in unheard shouts.

She took a detour through a row of abandoned houses, dashing through empty doorways and weaving in and out of alleyways, still angling uphill. As she ran, it occurred to her that the lightning had struck exactly where she had been standing a moment ago. Could that be a coincidence?

She had no time to question what had happened. Her hearing was slowly returning, and the footsteps and the rattle of weapons told her Chadrech's men were getting closer.

The ruins were too porous to provide hiding places, and she didn't dare climb to the upper levels of the buildings lest they collapse. It was all she could do to stay ahead of her pursuers.

The men got nearer, shouting her name. Her breath caught in her chest, and her torn knees throbbed as she tried to put some distance between them. But the soldiers were gaining on her.

She refused to let them use her as a weapon against Latch. They might not hurt her directly, but she couldn't be caught. She clenched her fists, her teeth. She had to run faster.

She turned into a sloping alleyway and made it about ten paces before she saw the large stones blocking the other end. The two men entered the alley behind her. There was no time to climb over the stones. She was trapped. The soldiers were going to catch her.

Then a shriek split the air, loud enough to hurt her tender ears. Selivia ducked as two thunderbirds swooped directly over her head, almost close enough for her to grab their tail feathers. Talons flashed, and harsh golden eyes glared as the birds passed much too close.

Selivia came upon a doorway leading off the alley and skidded to a halt. The old door refused to open. She hammered it with her fist, praying the birds wouldn't turn around.

The thunderbirds soared along the alley toward her pursuers, their wingspans wide enough to brush the tops of the walls on both sides. The beat of their wings made the ruins shudder. One unleashed a terrifying song.

Selivia tried to force the door open. She didn't dare climb the rocks at the end of the alley when those creatures might see her. At least their appearance would slow the soldiers down.

Then she heard something even more chilling than the cry of the thunderbirds.

It was the sound of brave men screaming in terror. Footsteps scrambled and scuffled. Steel clashed. There was a ripping sound followed by a splatter. The thunderbirds shrieked. Another man screamed, loud enough to curdle Selivia's blood. Then another rip. A thud. Silence.

Selivia clapped a hand over her mouth to keep from crying out or maybe vomiting. She slid to the ground, back pressed against the door, heart thundering wildly. This couldn't be happening.

There was another horrible shriek. Then the thunderbirds flew past her hiding spot in a rush of feathers and talons and bright-red blood. They soared back the way they had come, back toward the mountain.

Selivia had no idea how long she waited in that narrow doorway. She kept expecting the soldiers to catch up with her. Kept hoping for it. But that eerie silence had returned.

At last, she risked peeking out of the doorway, peering back down the alleyway. She glimpsed a limb clothed in slate-gray, a bloodied shape on the ground. She recoiled in horror. The soldiers were dead. Her pursuers were dead. The thunderbirds had saved her.

Had they done it on purpose? Chadrech claimed they didn't eat human flesh.

Whatever was happening on this island couldn't be natural. The lightning. The birds. Something was very wrong.

She turned from the bodies of Chadrech's men, unable to look at them a moment longer, and hurried to the end of the alley. Holding on to her composure by a fingernail, she climbed over the stones and escaped the nightmarish scene.

She found herself in a narrow road that diverted around a large workshop, perhaps a smithy, before continuing uphill. Keeping to the shadows as much as possible, she continued onward and upward. For good or ill, she would find answers on the mountain.

Rain began to fall, slicking down her hair and turning the world hazy and surreal. Selivia felt as if she were running through a warped mirror world where nothing looked quite as it should. The pattering downpour competed with her pounding footsteps and racing heartbeat. She felt scared half out of her mind, but at least she was free of Chadrech. She might still be able to help Latch.

Suddenly, a thunderbird swooped out of the rain directly over-head. She cringed, but the creature didn't attack. Instead, it careened back and forth, neither striking at her nor moving on. Another joined it. Then another. Feathers and talons glistened with rainwater.

Selivia tried to take shelter in a ruined building. But when she moved toward a gaping doorway, the birds dove at her, shrieking and snapping, preventing her from hiding. She had no choice but to run on, hands flung over her head, certain the foul creatures would rip into her at any moment. Terror filled her, making it impossible to think straight, impossible to breathe.

She ran, and the birds followed, the flock growing with every step. Thunderbirds surrounded her like a dark cloud. Tears filled her lightning-burned eyes. She could barely see the path. She almost didn't notice when she left the last of the buildings behind.

She struggled up the mountainside, rain lashing her face, unable to pause or turn aside lest the birds attack. They didn't touch her with their talons or beaks, but their wings brushed her back, crackling with energy, forcing her onward. They were herding her, guiding her.

Her breath tore at her chest, and she clutched a stitch in her side. She didn't dare slow down, even though the rain made the path slick and perilous. The birds crowed into the storm, harrying her up the rocky mountainside. Stumbling and swearing, she climbed higher.

Just when Selivia thought the birds meant to run her all the way over the mountaintop and down the other side, one of them gave a great shriek and wheeled away from her. The others followed, spinning through the storm, moving as one. Then, as quickly as they had arrived, they were gone.

Selivia sagged to the ground, gasping for breath. Tears filled her eyes, mixing with the rain. The stormy air wrapped close around her like a wet blanket. The world had gone soft and hazy. She was in the clouds, in an alien landscape of water and stone and fear. She could no longer see the ruined city below or any of Chadrech's men. She was utterly alone.

She shivered on her knees for uncountable moments, half fearing the thunderbirds would return to finish her off. In an effort to contain her rampaging fear, she sought the meditative calm she'd learned from the Air Sensors of the Far Plains. She usually imagined colors swirling behind her eyelids, but she couldn't summon them in this world of gray.

Nevertheless, she managed to calm down enough that she no longer sounded like a gasping, dying fish. She was still alive. She would figure something out. She had no choice.

"This could be worse," she rasped. "Not sure how, but it could be."

The rain fell harder, soaking her hair and dripping down the neck of her shirt. She wiped the droplets out of her eyes, shuddering as thunder rumbled through the ground beneath her.

"You'd better be the best husband in history after putting me through all this, Latch."

"I will certainly try," said someone behind her.

Selivia catapulted to her feet, snatching up a heavy rock to hurl in self-defense.

A man emerged from a dark shadow in the mountainside, the entrance to a cave she hadn't noticed before. He was stocky and broad-shouldered, with close-cropped black hair, smooth brown skin, and a short beard. He wore a white shirt, which was soaked through, and a fine sword hung at his belt.

"If you'll still have me, that is."

Selivia gaped at him, sure she was hallucinating. But as he took a step toward her, the stones shifted beneath his boots with a soft clack. He was really there.

Latch had found her.

20

Selivia stared at her betrothed, utterly at a loss for words. She couldn't believe he was actually standing before her, with the rain in his hair and a look of concern on his face. He was as handsome as she remembered, but he looked older, too, more self-assured.

"We should get somewhere less exposed," Latch said. "Are you well enough to walk?"

"Oh, yes." Selivia stopped gaping and hurried to join Latch in the mouth of the cave. She tried to smooth down her hair, which was dripping and tangled and probably looked worse than when she'd spent all day on dragonsback. Despite how many times she had imagined their reunion, she didn't know how to greet him. Should they hug? Kiss?

She settled for a nervous smile. "I'm here!"

"So you are." Latch studied her closely. His manner was reserved, tense. "Your hands are bleeding."

"It's just a few scrapes." Selivia wiped them on her damp trousers.

"We'll get you some bandages down in the camp." Latch took out a Vertigonian Everlight and turned toward the back of the cave. The light glanced off polished stone and discarded tools before illuminating the entrance to a tunnel. "Stay close to me."

Selivia had no intention of doing otherwise. She felt wrung out after her terrifying flight up the mountainside. This was the same Latch she'd exchanged letters with for years. She was safe with him even though she felt as if she were meeting a stranger.

"How did you get here?" Latch asked as he led the way into the tunnel, which sloped downward into darkness.

"Prince Chadrech was kind enough to deliver me."

Once she started talking, the story came out in a garbled rush. She told of her arrival in Sharoth, her efforts to determine his whereabouts, the voyage on the *Silverliner*, and Fenn's disappearance. She was nervous, and she couldn't tell how Latch felt about her arrival. The darkness made it impossible to discern his reactions.

"Then I almost got struck by lightning!" she said when she got to her escape from Chadrech's soldiers. "And that's not even the strangest thing I've seen in the last hour."

"I'm so sorry about that," Latch said. "It's hard to control."

"What is?"

"The Lightning. I was aiming for the building."

Selivia stopped short. "You did that?"

"I was trying to distract them so you could escape, and I'm out of Watermight." Latch turned to face her, holding up the Everlight between them. "The Lightning is the new magical substance I told you about."

"You didn't tell me about a new substance." To Selivia's dismay, her voice cracked. "I had to hear that from Chadrech."

Latch's forehead wrinkled. "But didn't you get my letters?"

"I know you've been studying ancient Wielders, but your last letter was two months ago." Tears sprang up in Selivia's eyes, despite her best efforts to hold them back. "You could have warned me what I was getting myself into."

Latch blinked. "Two months? Sel, I write every week."

"What?" Selivia wondered if her hearing was still messed up from the lightning strike. "The last I heard from you was when you told me to wait in Fork Town and sent a bunch of cryptic messages about pen friends and the East Isles."

"What are you talking about?"

"Your last letter."

"My last letter was about the Lightning. I never said anything about Fork Town." Latch adjusted the sleeve of his damp white shirt.

"To be honest, I didn't expect you for a few months. Didn't you get the one about delaying your arrival until the spring because I wasn't sure how long I'd be at Thunderbird Island?"

"No, I most certainly did not." She really was going to cry. She'd been through so much to get here, and nothing was going how she'd imagined. "You told me to . . . Wait, you call me Sel."

"Should I not?" Latch rolled his shoulders, looking less self-assured than before. "We haven't seen each other for a while, but I thought—"

"Hold on. Let me think." She waved her hands to get him to be quiet. The last letter had been addressed to "My dearest Selivia." Latch had never called her "dearest." But Prince Chadrech had. Selivia groaned.

"Are you all right?" Latch put a hand on her arm and then removed it, as if he wasn't sure whether she'd welcome his touch.

"Chadrech has been intercepting your letters. It must be how he knew where to find you." Selivia recited the letter she'd received and explained how Prince Chadrech used the mention of the East Isles to convince her to accompany him.

Latch scratched his short beard. "Brelling never wrote an East Isles journal."

"I know! That's why I thought it was code. The Crown Prince must have written the letter himself. He was going to trade my life for your new power. He must have been planning this for longer than I realized." Latch must think her foolish and naïve. That was not the impression she wanted to make after all this time. She'd never trusted Chadrech, but she thought she'd have a dragon with her for protection on this journey. "I shouldn't have fallen for it."

"It's okay, Sel. He would have tried to get to me with or without you. I'm just glad you're not hurt."

Selivia appreciated Latch's graciousness, but it didn't make her feel any better. She had brought Fenn into danger too. And who knew where Mav had ended up. She thought of the letter she'd sent to her brother, telling him that she was heading out to sea with Prince Chadrech. She wondered if Siv had even received it.

"What happens now?" she said, dragging her sleeve across her nose. "Chadrech can't use me as leverage anymore, but he has a dozen Waterworkers and a ship full of soldiers out there."

"I'm not afraid of them," Latch said. "With the Lightning, I believe I can fight any Wielder on the continent."

Selivia remembered the smoke rising from the soldiers' bodies back in the cobblestone square and how close the lightning had come to striking her too. "Can you control it?"

Latch hesitated. "Not yet. We observed it for the first few weeks, and we had only just progressed to touching it in small quantities. The substance is volatile. I hadn't planned to draw in anywhere near what it took to make that Lightning bolt for months." His brow furrowed thoughtfully. "It was like shooting an arrow into a windstorm, but it worked."

Selivia suddenly felt queasy. "You're saying you'd never done that before?"

"I'm approaching this as scientifically as possible," Latch said. "Much of the research on the substance has been lost, and we don't know enough about it to use it lightly." He looked at her intently. "But I couldn't let Chadrech hurt you when I had that power at my disposal."

Selivia's cheeks warmed, and she found herself attempting to put her hair in order again. He'd been trying to save her life. She decided not to point out how very close he'd come to frying her in her boots.

"Well, now that I'm here, let's not rush things."

"Agreed." His grave manner loosened, revealing a hint of boyish excitement. "But the Lightning is magnificent. It's nothing like Wielding Watermight, and I think it has the potential to—" Latch shook his head. "Forgive me. You must be tired, Sel. Let's get you bandaged up first."

"I'm okay," Selivia said. "I'd like to see it, if that's possible."

Latch smiled, that boyish pride shining a little brighter. "Of course. Follow me."

They descended through the winding stone passageway, the Everlight providing just enough illumination to keep them from stumbling. Selivia had once spent several days traveling through a tunnel system under the Far Plains Rock, but that had been mostly straight. Here, they got deeper into the earth with every step.

"The miners discovered the Lightning here eighty years ago," Latch explained as they walked. "They dug too deep and struck a vast chasm, bigger than any Watermight vent on the continent. It contained an immense reservoir of power. They called it Lightning, though I believe it's different from the ordinary lightning bolts that result from storms."

"I've never thought of lightning as ordinary," Selivia said.

"Wait until you see this."

The tunnel widened enough for them to walk side by side. Selivia noticed Latch was only a few inches taller than her, but his shoulders had filled out since the last time she saw him. The sword swinging at his hip had well-worn leather wrapped around the hilt, suggesting he hadn't given up on his training regimen despite all the time he spent at his research.

"A Watermight Artist studied the Lightning for a while," Latch went on, "but she ultimately decided it was too dangerous and had the mine closed up. She destroyed most of her notes, but I pieced together enough clues from the Royal Archives to find the chasm."

Selivia didn't like the sound of that. She'd met enough scholars to know they didn't destroy their notes lightly.

"*Is* the Lightning power too dangerous?"

"We are being careful," Latch said. "And after today, I'm pretty sure I can control it with practice."

"What does it do besides blast people off their feet?"

"It's a weapon," Latch said. "But I believe it can be harnessed as a power source as well, one that could lead to all kinds of innovations. That's my primary interest in the substance."

"And what about the thunderbirds?"

Latch frowned. "What about them?"

Selivia described how the giant birds had ripped into her pursuers and guided her up the mountainside. She could still hear those terrible screams. Latch went very quiet as she talked.

"Are you saying you weren't controlling them?" Selivia asked when he didn't speak.

"I don't know," Latch said slowly. "It's possible the power has some link with the thunderbirds. I was certainly focused on your safety while the Lightning was flowing through me. We know Wielders can compel dragons to a limited degree and—I will have to study it further."

They continued downward into the mountain. Latch appeared lost in thought, and Selivia could almost hear his brain humming along as he considered the possibilities if the Lightning and the thunderbirds were indeed linked. But they had more pressing problems.

"What are we going to do about Chadrech and his men?"

"This mine is quite secure," Latch said. "We set up our camp and research station inside. He can sit on his heels outside for as long as he likes."

Selivia doubted Chadrech would sit on his heels for long, especially after going to so much trouble to get here. And he wouldn't be happy about losing her as a bargaining chip after all his efforts to coax her to accompany him here. "How long do you intend to stay?"

"I don't know," Latch said. "The Lightning has so much potential. I could study it for years."

Before Selivia could respond to that, the tunnel opened into a vast cavern, and all thoughts of caution went straight out of her head.

The vaulted ceiling stretched at least thirty feet overhead, with multiple openings in the top like chimneys leading out of the mountain. A strange light played unevenly across them, sometimes purple, sometimes white. A handful of tunnels led away from the cavern, and darker shapes indicated alcoves or smaller caves. The air was dry, and it sizzled with the same strange energy Selivia had felt outside, magnified twentyfold.

A dozen paces from the mouth of their tunnel was a large crack in the stone floor. The flickering purple-white light was coming from within the chasm. A crackling sound reverberated around the cavern, a mix of fire and rain. Selivia's hair stood up on her neck, and goose bumps rose on her skin.

"Careful." Latch took her hand as they approached the chasm. "You don't want to fall in. I don't know how the Lightning affects a non-Wielder."

He seemed to have forgotten Selivia's hand was scraped from her fall, too focused on the crackling power. She bit her lip against the sting, but she didn't pull away. Her hand fit neatly in his.

Together, they moved close enough to peek over the edge into the chasm. Selivia gasped. Purple-and-white light lanced across the vast space, jagged lightning bolts that danced and arched but were never exhausted. She shaded her eyes against the crackling light.

Latch leaned closer, as if drawn by the pulsing energy. "Isn't it beautiful?"

"I've never seen anything like it. You really Wielded that?"

Latch didn't answer. He was staring at the Lightning, mesmerized, almost entranced. The purplish glow played across his face and danced in his eyes.

"Latch?"

She squeezed his hand, and only then did he seem to remember she was there.

"Sorry. Yes, though the scholars call it Casting. Lightning Casting." He turned to face her, the light from the chasm throwing his face into sharp relief. "I'm glad you're here, Sel. It may be sooner than I expected, but I've been wanting to share this with you. I . . . I hope you aren't sorry you came."

Selivia was surprised to hear a note of uncertainty enter his voice. Perhaps Latch had been as nervous about their reunion as she was. But his eyes were steady on hers, flickering with that purple-white power. It made her feel light-headed, being looked at like that.

"I just want to know what you're planning to do with this now that you've discovered it."

"Anything you wish." Latch reached up to touch her hair, his fingers crackling with static. "With this power, we can do anything, Sel. The Lightning will change the world."

21

Tamri didn't sleep well after receiving Khrillin's letter. Even if it were possible to forget his threats toward Gramma Teall, the Watermight bond in her neck gave icy tremors at odd moments, reminding her of his leverage over her. Apparently, all the information she'd sent in her carefully crafted letters still wasn't enough.

She begged Master Corren to let her work with the Fire Queen, but he insisted that she master the basics first. She still avoided drawing the Fire into her skin before beginning her Works, which made even the simplest tasks take thrice as much effort. If she didn't make progress soon, she'd need another way to get information on the king and queen.

Ultimately, it was Tamri's roommates who brought about her next opportunity to spy on the royal couple.

She shared a bedroom on the top floor of the greathouse with Kay, Shylla, and Lacy. Originally designed as a guest room for a single large bed, it was now furnished with two sets of bunk beds. Shylla grumbled that the space was small and cramped, a far cry from her mother's manor house in Pendark. But then Shylla always found things to complain about. The children were stacked on top of each other all over the greathouse, filling every guest room and servants' quarters while they awaited the completion of the new school building on Square Peak.

Kay occupied the top bunk above Tamri's bed. She liked to talk late into the night, sharing stories of her family's farm near Roan Town in Trure and her six siblings, including Ber and her twin sister, Kol. Kay's favorite tale was of when Queen Dara herself had stayed with her family while on a journey with Rumy the cur-dragon and a noble lady called Vine. The event had inspired Kay to become a duelist as well as a Fireworker. Her twin, Kol, had gone to New Rallion to become a lady's maid.

While Kay shared her past freely, Tamri avoided revealing too much about herself. She didn't want to talk about stealing scraps of food and Watermight in the Gutter District while Shylla was listening. And she feared if she started talking about Gramma Teall, she would tell them everything.

Despite her necessary reticence, Tamri and the others were becoming friends. She told herself this was strictly for spying purposes, but she couldn't help enjoying their company.

Lacy, the youngest of the four at sixteen, was from Vertigon. She had a little sister at the Wielder School, Liora, and both girls sometimes invited their friends home to visit their family on Village Peak.

"You should come with us next time," Lacy said to Tamri as they got dressed one morning. "We always have friends over for Eventide."

"Eventide?"

"It's the holiday marking the end of summer. Traditionally, everyone spends two nights visiting friends and giving gifts. Younger folks just go straight to the pub."

"I can't believe it's still summer." Tamri pulled on her red uniform coat and wrapped the black-and-white-striped scarf from Kay around her neck. Vertigon was already colder than it ever got in Pendark. If it weren't for all her hours in the Fireshop, she might never stop shivering.

"Just wait until First Snow!" Kay said with a laugh. "That's another cause for celebration."

Tamri shuddered. She'd heard about snow, of course, but she had never experienced it.

"Eventide is my favorite Vertigonian holiday," Kay said, sitting on Tamri's lower bunk to pull on her boots. "There's a major dueling tournament every year. This'll be my last chance to win the youth division before I age out."

"I'm sure you'll win," Lacy said. "And then Tamri can meet my parents, and we can have salt cakes at Stone Market and—"

"Would you three hurry up already?" Shylla muttered from the doorway. "Dentry and Pevin will finish off the last of the soldarberries if we don't get downstairs."

"Keep your hair on," Kay said, winking at Tamri. "I know it's your pride and joy."

Shylla sniffed and stalked out of the room.

Lacy looped her arm through Tamri's as they trooped down the stairs after her. Tamri managed not to flinch defensively at the contact. Maybe she really was getting used to Vertigonian ways.

"Please say you'll come for Eventide," Lacy said. "Unless you have other friends or family in Vertigon to visit."

"No." For some reason, Tamri pictured a pair of burnished bronze eyes in a stern face. "I don't have anyone else."

"Great!" Lacy gave her arm a quick squeeze before releasing her. "It'll be so much fun!"

———

True to her word, Lacy invited the three girls to Village Peak for the two-day Eventide holiday. They would start by attending the annual dueling tournament to watch Kay compete.

They exchanged their red uniform coats for civilian clothes before leaving the greathouse. Tamri donned a pale-blue coat Princess Selivia had bought her back in Fork Town along with her usual striped scarf. She was looking forward to cheering on her classmate before the evening's festivities. It was also her first chance to cross Orchard Gorge to Village Peak, which she'd only seen from a distance.

Home to Fireshops of various kinds, markets, mines, goat paddocks, and many little wooden houses, Village was the most densely populated of the three peaks. Though humble compared to King's Peak, most of the homes they passed after crossing Fell Bridge were larger and sturdier than the stilt houses of Pendark.

"They used to have the Eventide Open on Square Peak," Lacy

explained as she led Tamri and Shylla through the warren of paths and staircases crisscrossing the Village. "The East Square Dueling Hall was destroyed during the war. They're using the foundations to build our new school."

"I hear dueling is pretty popular," Tamri said.

Lacy rolled her eyes. "It's an obsession. Liora and I took lessons when we were younger, before we learned we were both Fireworkers. I like to watch, but some people are crazy for it."

"Like Kay?" The Truren girl had left their room before the sun rose to get ready that morning.

Lacy chuckled. "Being a Wielder didn't stop her from taking up dueling, but she has way too much energy for one person, anyway."

They reached an area with fewer buildings and joined the crowds heading for the open-air tournament venue. They were jostled closer together as they funneled toward the gates, the atmosphere becoming increasingly festive. Many of the spectators carried banners with the names of their favorite duelists, and music was playing somewhere, trumpets and drums and a tinny sound Tamri couldn't identify.

Lacy insisted on paying everyone's entrance fees. "Consider it my Eventide gift!"

Once through the gates, they found themselves on the bottom level of the dueling venue, which was paved with smooth stones for the competition strips. Wide grassy steps cut into the hillside above it for the spectators, giving them a view of both the dueling competition and the dramatic expanse of the canyon below. The stands were already more than half full, though the events hadn't started yet.

Kay was warming up with the other young competitors near the entrance. She waved cheerily, leaping up and down to loosen her muscles. Her chin-length hair was tucked beneath a strip of black cloth to keep it out of her way.

"I think she's trying to become Queen Dara," Lacy said. "She was a sport duelist, too, you know."

Tamri nodded. "I saw the queen practicing with King Siv up at the castle."

"Well, aren't you special?" Shylla muttered.

Tamri ignored her. She had gotten better at forcing down her desire to put the other girl in her place. Shylla wasn't enough of a threat to warrant that kind of risk.

Besides, this was the first true rest day she'd had since arriving in Vertigon, and she refused to let Shylla ruin it. She'd spent her rare days off working on her reports for Khrillin and delivering them to the letterbox on Square Peak. It was a relief to be outside the narrow world of Wielding lessons and books and spying and bridge runs, at least for a little while. She resolved not to think about Khrillin at all today.

The three girls climbed the steep slope beside the seating area, searching for an empty patch of grass. They passed a couple of younger Wielder students sitting with their parents. Madame Mirri chatted with another elderly woman who could only be her sister, sipping tea from a cup warmed with a band of Fire around the base. Zarr, the former pen fighter, had secured a prime spot in the second row, his metal leg stretched out in front of him on the grass. Master Loyil must be at the Whirlpool. The Watermight had to keep spinning, holiday or not.

"There's Dentry!" Lacy squealed, trying to wave to their classmate and fix her hair at the same time. "I didn't think they'd left the school yet. Oh, he looks so good in green."

Dentry and Pevin had arranged to meet up with them to watch Kay duel. They were saving a large section of a grassy ledge near the top of the hillside venue, marking their territory with blankets liberated from the school. An array of pies and other snacks were piled on top of the blankets between the two boys.

"Happy Eventide!" Dentry called as Tamri, Lacy, and Shylla joined them. "Is Kay ready?"

"Looks like it," Lacy said, shooing Pevin out of the way so she could sit next to Dentry. "Have they announced the first round yet?"

"Nope." He leaned past Lacy to wave at Tamri as she sat cross-legged at the edge of the group. "First time at a dueling competition?"

"Yes. I used to watch Steel Pentagon matches sometimes back home."

"Shylla told us all about those." Dentry tugged at a curl above his ear. Despite his efforts to be the leader of the pack, sometimes he seemed very young. "Do the athletes really fight to the death?"

"Fighting in the Steel Pentagon has gotten a lot of people out of poverty," Tamri said sharply. She had cheered for a death match or two in her time, but she resented the judgment in Dentry's tone. "Besides, Watermight healing means it's not as deadly as you'd think. It can keep a lot of injuries from being fatal, if you can afford it."

"Watermight healing is remarkable, isn't it?" Pevin said. "Shylla fixed me up after a training accident in the school's first year. Master Loyil was too far away to help. I'm healthier now than I was before."

To Tamri's surprise, a blush rose in Shylla's olive cheeks at the compliment. She wondered if all the attention Loyil paid the other Pendarkan was more about her talents than her mother's influence back home.

The picnic-like atmosphere at the dueling tournament bore little resemblance to Steel Pentagon matches, where the weapons were sharpened and the crowds roared for blood. The stands were nearly full now, and everyone seemed eager for the competition to get underway.

"Hey, look!" Dentry said. "It's the king and queen." He pointed to the front row at the bottom of the slope.

Tamri edged forward for a better view. Sure enough, Queen Dara and King Siv were sitting close together on a blanket, with a small picnic lunch beside them. The king wore a midnight-blue coat, festive but not overly ornate, and the queen a simple black dress with blue-and-gold embroidery twining around the sleeves. Two swords lay on the grass behind them, one with a black hilt and one wrapped in gold. Siv was leaning close to whisper in Dara's ear, his hand on the small of her back.

Lacy sighed. "They're so romantic. King Siv is the handsomest man on the mountain. And so charming! If only I were a few years older."

"You still wouldn't have a chance," Dentry said. "He's desperately in love with the queen. Everyone knows that."

"Of course he is." Lacy sighed deeper. "It's a tragedy."

"Why don't they have any children?" Tamri asked. "Aren't kings and queens supposed to produce heirs?"

Dentry shrugged. "They've been a little busy, what with rebuilding after the war and all."

"Queen Dara would have to stop Wielding the Fire while she was pregnant," Pevin said. The others looked at him in surprise, and he blushed scarlet. "It would be too dangerous otherwise."

"I didn't know that," Tamri said.

"Just think what would happen to the baby if it wasn't a Wielder," Pevin said. "She might need to stop using Watermight too."

"I hope she takes a break soon," Lacy said dreamily. "Their babies are going to be beautiful."

Tamri had never heard of childbearing being an issue for Water-workers, though she'd never received a formal education on that front. But Vertigon would need a royal heir one day, meaning the kingdom would be vulnerable for nearly a year while the Fire Queen carried her child.

Now that's the kind of information that'll impress Khrillin.

Even as the thought formed, Tamri felt a twinge of guilt. She frowned. News of this potential weakness could secure Gramma Teall another month in comfort. It could even be valuable enough to buy Tamri's freedom from the oath bond. Why should she feel guilty?

Trumpets blared, interrupting her thoughts. The duels were starting. The crowds cheered wildly as the competitors were introduced, and soon the clash of steel and pounding footsteps echoed across the mountain.

People continued streaming through the gates as the tournament got underway. Additional spectators gathered at the windows and rooftops bordering the venue. It looked as if all of Vertigon had decided to attend the Eventide Open. Tamri watched the people as much as the competition as the stands filled to bursting.

Someone tapped her shoulder, and she jolted away automatically.

"Easy there. I come in peace."

Tamri looked up into a familiar face wearing a roguish smile. "Taklin!"

"One and the same." The dragon rider gave an elaborate bow. "How's magic school?"

"Not bad. How are the dragons?"

"As headstrong as ever. Can we sit with you? Errol is competing today, and he whines when we don't cheer him on." He held up a bundle of sweet-smelling packets wrapped in paper. "We brought refreshments."

"We?" Tamri scanned the hill behind Taklin. Reya was making her way toward them, her arms overflowing with bottles of ale. There was no sign of Heath. Not that it should matter. Tamri smothered her disappointment and scooted aside to make room for Taklin and Reya.

She introduced the two dragon riders to Lacy, Shylla, Dentry, and Pevin. The dragon riders were a little older than her schoolmates, a little more dashing. Impressing her fellow students shouldn't matter when she had bigger things to worry about, but their approval gave Tamri an unexpected burst of pride. Despite herself, she wanted the others to like her.

After a bit of shuffling and rearranging of blankets, the Wielder students and the dragon riders settled in to watch the duels together. Reya took the seat next to Shylla and grinned broadly at her. Shylla smiled back.

"Do you all know a girl called Kay?" Taklin asked the others. "She's a Wielder too."

"That's who we're here to see," Dentry said. "She's down there getting ready for her next bout."

A tournament official was assigning matches to a group of athletes. Kay stood among them, her black bandana fluttering in the mountain breeze.

"She's a great duelist," Dentry said. Then he blushed bright red.

"Is she now?" Taklin said with a sly grin. "I know she's cute, but are you sure she can duel?"

"A gold firestone says she wins the whole thing," Dentry said.

Taklin's grin widened. "You're on."

The duels continued, steel clashing, officials calling the hits, crowds cheering. Vendors hiked up and down the hillside with boxes full of steaming pies, salt cakes, and bottles of ale. The atmosphere in the stands grew increasingly merry as high noon came and went.

The dragon riders and Wielder students exchanged friendly banter, quickly becoming comfortable with each other. Taklin and Dentry competed to see who could cheer louder for Kay, Errol's matches all but forgotten.

Tamri was more interested in the king and queen than the sword fighting. People approached to speak with them during the breaks between duels, and they answered graciously whether the supplicants were nobles in silk coats or miners with patches on their clothes. Tamri wondered if she could get close enough to hear what they were saying. Castle Guards in blue uniforms sat on either side of them, but they appeared to be paying more attention to the tournament than to guarding the king and queen. If only she weren't sitting with such a large group. She needed an excuse to get closer.

The others had finished off the goat pies and cracked open the ale. Dentry and Taklin competed to see who could finish their drinks the fastest and then who could eat the most salt cakes. Next, they challenged each other to collect the most athlete tokens, chips of wood and stone marked with insignias that the athletes gave out to their fans. Soon they each had a large pile of the tokens in front of them.

Reya and Shylla rolled their eyes at the two young men's antics and scooted a little closer together on the grassy slope, talking quietly. Lacy didn't look particularly happy about Dentry's efforts to show that *he* was Kay's biggest fan. She kept twisting the hem of her skirt and letting it unravel dejectedly. She didn't notice Pevin's efforts to engage her in conversation at all.

When Dentry and Taklin moved on to seeing who could balance the most empty bottles on their knees, Tamri knew the competition could only escalate from here.

Taklin was the one to raise the stakes. "Hey Dentry," he called when there was a lull in the dueling. "I dare you to go down there and steal the queen's Savven blade."

"What?"

"Her sword." Taklin gestured down the slope with a mostly empty bottle. "It's just sitting there on the grass."

"She'll melt me like a candle."

"Aren't you Fireworkers supposed to be immune to that? I'm not suggesting you keep it. Just borrow it so we can have a look."

"I'm not stealthy enough for that," Dentry said doubtfully. "Pevin? You're always wanting to examine that sword."

Pevin snorted. "I don't have a death wish."

"Come on." Taklin thumped him on the shoulder. "It's just for a laugh."

"No, thank you," Pevin said primly.

"I'll do it," Tamri said.

The others looked at her in surprise. Even Shylla and Reya stopped whispering to each other and turned to listen.

Tamri tried not to hunch with all those eyes on her. "I bet I can grab the blade, bring it up here for us all to see, and put it back without her noticing."

"Now that would be impressive," Taklin said. "Show us what you learned in your thieving days."

A few of the students frowned at that, making Tamri wince. She hadn't told them about her criminal past. But this might be her only chance to get close to the king and queen.

She stood, casually brushing grass off her trousers. "Like you said, we're just borrowing it."

"I don't know if this is a good idea," Pevin said.

"Of course it's a good idea!" Dentry had consumed too much ale already, and his face was as red as a summer apple. "It won't hurt anybody."

"Yes, go on, Tamri," Shylla said with a twisted smile. "Show us your hidden talents."

"Pay attention," Tamri said, baring her teeth at her. "You might learn a thing or two."

22

Tamri scrambled down the slope beside the stands, feeling the others' eyes on her back. She had no intention of actually taking the queen's sword, of course. She had learned her lesson about reckless thievery. She would get near enough to listen in on the royal couple's conversation and then pretend to lose her nerve. The others would tease her, but she could live with that if it meant overhearing something useful.

She reached the second row, just above the king and queen's position, and edged along the crowded ledge. The spectators barely noticed her. The youth duelists were into the semifinals now, and the adult competitors were in the thick of their elimination matches. Tamri managed to crawl right over Zarr's metal leg without the former pen fighter showing any signs of recognition.

She slowed down as she crept behind the king and queen's bodyguards. One was Captain Jale, whom she'd met that first day at the castle. He was eagerly discussing the duels with the lanky female guard next to him.

"Your brother should have done better against Bilzar Ten last time," Captain Jale said. "Don't you think so, Tora?"

"Errol doesn't have much time to train with his dragon-riding duties. It'll be a miracle if he pulls this off."

"Bilzar has gotten slower lately."

"He's a lot brighter than my brother, though," the woman said dryly. "Let's be honest."

Tamri made it past Errol's sister and the guard captain and stopped directly behind the royal couple.

They were whispering with their heads together again, King Siv resting his hand on Queen Dara's knee. Her long golden braid hung down her back, brushing the wool blanket on which they sat. The fine black rapier—the Savven blade—lay on the grass behind them. The pair was so distracted by each other that Tamri figured she really could steal the sword, if that was all she was after. She hadn't gotten a good look at a Fire Blade yet.

"Your Majesty!"

Tamri pulled back quickly. A man in a blue uniform was hurrying toward the king and queen, a roll of parchment in his hand. Tamri crouched on her heels, trying to look like an innocent spectator while staying near enough to hear the messenger's conversation with the royals.

"A letter just arrived at the castle from Princess Selivia."

"Thank you, Hirram." Siv took the roll of parchment and broke the seal. "I was beginning to wonder whether she made it to Soole."

"Mav is looking out for her," Dara said.

"Maybe, but he's as flighty as she is sometimes." Siv studied the paper for a moment then handed it to Dara to read. Tamri could only see the side of his face, but his expression had grown serious. She shuffled closer, trying to see over Dara's shoulder without being too obvious about it.

"She shouldn't trust Prince Chadrech," Dara said when she finished reading.

"The fellow is slimier than a salt adder in a pigeon's nest, but Sel knows that. She'll be careful." The king grimaced. "It's Latch I'm worried about."

"You think he's trying to get out of the betrothal?"

"He wouldn't break the alliance after everything we've been through. I'm more worried about this discovery of his." Siv scratched one of the many scars on his cheek. "This could upset the balance between the southern kingdoms."

Dara looked down to study the letter again. No matter how Tamri shifted, she couldn't see past her shoulder. What discovery?

Her foot slipped, and a few pebbles slid downhill, pinging against the Savven blade. Dara glanced back at it, but she didn't look up at where Tamri was perched.

A cheer rose from the crowds, loud enough to make the mountain shudder. A duelist ripped off his mask and raised his hands in the air, hamming for the spectators. His opponent was rubbing his arm and scowling.

Tamri willed the crowds to be quiet. She needed to hear more.

"I have half a mind to head to Soole," the king was saying as the noise died down. "I don't like Sel being alone down there."

"Let me try to reach her with the Air before you dash off to the Lands Below." Dara folded the letter and tucked it into her pocket. "I'll get Vine to help me after the tournament."

"Good idea," Siv said. "You know, I think she might win this year."

"She *has* been trying that new technique."

As they resumed chatting about the duels, Tamri focused on the queen's pocket. A corner of the letter was sticking out, creamy white parchment against black fabric. What was this discovery that would affect the southern kingdoms, Pendark included? She couldn't make much sense of the conversation, but if she could grab that letter, it would explain everything.

Tamri hesitated. It was reckless, but she wouldn't have a better chance than this. Before she could talk herself out of it, she slid closer, almost to the edge of the couple's wool blanket. The corner of parchment winked at her from the queen's pocket.

She got closer. Closer. Stretched out a hand. The queen started to turn around.

Panic jolted through Tamri, and she did the only thing she could think of. Her hand closed on the black hilt of the queen's Savven blade. The sword was hot to the touch and heavier than Tamri expected. She'd barely shifted the weapon an inch when the queen's gaze fell on her.

"What are you doing?"

"I'm sorry—I didn't mean to—forgive me, Your Majesty!"

Tamri dropped the sword and threw herself to her knees in front of the king and queen, all but prostrating herself on the grass.

"You were trying to steal my sword?" Dara said incredulously.

"It was a dare. I just wanted to look at it."

She'd known instinctively that grabbing the sword would be easier to explain than why she was stealing their private correspondence.

Dara wore a disbelieving expression. "The Wielder students dared you to do that?"

"They said the sword was hot to the touch, and I didn't believe them." Tamri babbled about her deep contrition, her hands edging closer to the queen's pocket. The pair had shifted around when they realized Tamri was behind them, but she was still quite near. Maybe she could still pull this off.

"I was curious," she said, projecting remorse with all her might. "Please forgive me!"

The king chuckled. "It was a harmless prank, Dara. No harm done. Probably an initiation for the new student."

Dara didn't seem to find it as amusing as her husband did. As she looked up at him, a frown on her handsome face, Tamri reached out with nimble fingers and slipped the letter out of her pocket.

Yes! She crammed the parchment into her coat, heart pounding.

"Even if it was harmless, I expect more of the students," Dara said. "Perhaps I should speak to them."

"Go easy, my love." The king grinned. "It's Eventide."

"I swear it won't happen again," Tamri said. "Please, Your Majesty, don't kick me out of the school."

Dara frowned. "I expected better of you, Tamri, especially after Princess Selivia spoke up for you."

Tamri blushed, feeling the unexpected touch of genuine shame. "It was a foolish idea."

"We've all had our fair share of foolish ideas," King Siv said kindly. "Run along back to your friends and tell them they owe you a drink."

"Yes, Your Majesty."

Tamri bobbed her head and hurried back along the grassy ledge. Many people were looking at her rather than the duelists now, including Zarr. She avoided meeting his eyes, squirming under all that scrutiny. At least she had the letter. Khrillin better feed Gramma Teall from the finest restaurants in Pendark after this.

Her friends were gaping at her with a mixture of shock, horror, and admiration as she rejoined them.

"I thought the queen was going to skewer you with her eyeballs!" Taklin said.

"No one thought you'd actually go through with it," Shylla said.

"That was brilliant, Tam," Dentry said.

"Don't call me that."

"Whatever you say." Dentry raised his hands. "Remind me never to dare you to do anything again."

Tamri tried to fold in on herself as the others gawked at her, the tournament all but forgotten. She seemed to have won their respect and lost the queen's in the same move. She should be feeling triumphant after successfully stealing the letter, but mostly she just wanted everyone to stop staring at her.

"What was the Savven blade like?" Pevin asked.

"Hot." Tamri frowned. "And heavier than it looks."

"What did they say to you?" Lacy asked, her eyes wide. "We thought for sure you were going to be thrown in the castle dungeons."

"The queen disapproved, but King Siv thought it was funny. He talked her out of punishing us. Said you all owe me drinks."

"Hear! Hear!" Reya called. She glanced at Shylla. "I know a place nearby that'll be pretty lively on Eventide. Shall we go after the finals?"

"I'm in," Dentry said. "Anything to get out of visiting my parents' friends and getting my cheeks pinched by old noblewomen."

"Will Kay come along?" Taklin asked. "If so, I'm in too. We're heading back down to Pendark the day after tomorrow. Gotta make the most of the holiday."

"Is Heath going with you?" Tamri asked distractedly. She hadn't seen him since the day he delivered Khrillin's threatening letter.

"Aye." Taklin tipped his head sideways to look at her. "He'll be sorry he missed you."

"Why would he be sorry? He hates me."

"Does he? News to me." Taklin grinned. "Anyway, since you're too stubborn to ask, he's not here today because he had to visit his parents at their respective greathouses for Eventide. Probably getting his cheeks pinched by old noblewomen as we speak."

Tamri shrugged as if it didn't matter, but she'd caught herself looking at the dueling venue gates in case he was just late to join the other dragon riders. She put a hand on her coat pocket. It was probably good Heath hadn't come along. She never would have had the guts to steal from the king and queen in front of him.

In the end, Kay took second place in the tournament, and she heartily approved of the plan to go for a celebratory drink afterward. She found Dentry and Taklin's efforts to impress her highly amusing. Lacy was less pleased with this development, and she spent half the evening moping to Tamri about how Dentry wasn't paying attention to her—all while ignoring Pevin's efforts to share everything he knew about Fire Blades with her. It was almost midnight by the time Tamri managed to sneak out of the pub to read her stolen letter.

A cool breeze carried the aromas of apple cider and cooked meat through the village. People called to each other as they visited one another to fulfill the Eventide tradition, carrying little gifts and steaming plates of food.

Tamri used the light from the pub window to read the stolen message, which was written in eager, looping handwriting. She could almost hear Princess Selivia's breathless voice describing how she arrived in Soole to find her betrothed had disappeared. When she got to the discovery, Tamri knew stealing the letter had been worth every risk she'd taken that day.

Latch may have discovered a new magical substance in the East Isles, something that could be more powerful than Fire and Watermight combined. I am going to find him with Prince Chadrech's help.

Tamri finished the letter and looked up. Lights blazed all across King's Peak on the other side of Orchard Gorge. The castle at the top glowed with the light of a hundred Fire Lanterns.

Had Latch Brach truly found a new magical substance? Such a power, if it existed, would bind Vertigon closer than ever to Soole.

And it would change the balance between the southern kingdoms, as King Siv had said. All of Pendark's Watermight combined might not protect them if the Soolens used this new power against them. She had to warn King Khrillin.

Tamri sat on a barrel outside the pub and began a new letter. She wrote down everything Princess Selivia had said about the magical substance and its possible location in the East Isles. Perhaps Khrillin could send some of his followers on their own research expedition. Her writing took up a full sheet of parchment as she detailed what she'd learned that day.

She hesitated when she recalled what Pevin had said about the queen needing to stop Wielding if she ever became pregnant. She thought of King Siv speaking up for her, just like his sister had done with Khrillin, and she remembered her shame at the Fire Queen's rebuke. Tamri didn't particularly like betraying their secrets.

The pub door burst open, spilling laughter and Firebulb light into the night. Inside, Tamri's friends were crammed around a rough wooden table. Kay raised a mug to toast the holiday, her second-place medal glinting on her chest. Taklin gazed at her admiringly, his own drink forgotten. Pevin and Lacy tapped their mugs together, and Reya leaned in to whisper in Shylla's ear. Dentry had fallen asleep on the table with his curly head on his arms. None of them knew what it was like to fight for scraps or go to bed hungry.

Tamri turned her parchment over resolutely and finished the letter, including every detail she'd learned at the dueling tournament. Perhaps one day she would be powerful enough to make different choices, but right now, she still had a Watermight collar around her neck. Guilty consciences were for people whose grandmothers weren't in danger.

She sealed the letter and addressed it to Gramma Teall as usual. She would send it with Taklin when he left after Eventide. Khrillin would know about the newfound Soolen power and the queen's potential weakness within a fortnight.

23

Selivia was impressed with Latch's operation on Thunderbird Island. He had set up an orderly campsite in a small cave a safe distance from the chasm full of Lightning. The space was cozy, if a little severe, and it provided a welcome retreat from the eerie flickering light in the main cavern.

Both of the men who had accompanied Latch from Sharoth were Waterworkers and fellow scholars. They had been studying the Lightning for weeks, filling notebook after notebook with observations on the substance: how it moved, how it affected different objects that came near it—metal, stone, water, and so on—and of course, how it felt to touch.

The team had a study room of sorts in another cave adjacent to their sleeping quarters. There was an air of industry and purpose about the place. The floor was spread with cushions, and the scholars used boards propped on their knees to write. Vertigonian Everlights provided illumination so they wouldn't get fire anywhere near their papers. Latch and the others spent many hours in this cave, poring over their notes and writing out detailed reports on the day's experiments.

Rosh, a silver-haired old Waterworker who had served Latch's father, was the keeper of the notes. He explained to Selivia that most of the older documents were from the Royal Archives in Sharoth, but they had discovered others in private collections all over Soole.

Despite the wealth of information they'd accumulated, the team had been exceedingly careful about using the Lightning during their first weeks on the island. They didn't touch it at all at first then gradually proceeded to allowing tiny flickers of the substance to dance across their skin. They had only gone so far as to draw it into their bodies a handful of times under carefully controlled conditions. All that changed after Latch used a massive Lightning bolt to help Selivia escape Chadrech.

The other two believed it had been a mistake.

"I mean no disrespect," Rosh said when they discussed it over cups of tea in the study room one evening. "But you could have killed yourself, the princess, and all of us."

"Not to mention the Crown Prince," said the other scholar, a younger man named Melloch, who wore wire-framed spectacles and kept his long hair tied back with a strap of yellow leather. "We're not here to commit treason. I thought the purpose of studying the Lightning in secret was to learn as much as we could before involving the royals." He shot an unkind look at Selivia. "Having them brought to our doorstep changes things."

Latch set down his teacup with a crunch and glared at Melloch. "You don't truly think we should hand the Lightning over to Chadrech, do you?"

Melloch hesitated. "No, my lord."

"We all agreed to proceed with caution in every aspect of our studies," Rosh said, watching the two younger men warily. "I hope that is still your intention, my lord."

Latch's jaw tightened, as if he wanted to argue. But he said, "You are right, of course. I don't want to take unnecessary risks any more than you do." He took Selivia's hand and stared the others down. "Saving the princess was a necessary risk. Do you want to argue otherwise?"

Rosh ducked his head. "No, my lord. I meant no disrespect."

Melloch mumbled a similar sentiment, though he didn't look particularly happy. He took off his spectacles and cleaned them more forcefully than was strictly necessary.

Selivia sensed the precariousness of the situation, perhaps better than Latch did. Her arrival had disrupted their research, and she wouldn't be surprised if the others resented her for it. She hadn't come here to drive a wedge between Latch and his men.

"Can I help with your work?" Selivia asked. "Perhaps I could read through the notes you've compiled, see if I can make any new connections."

"Fresh eyes could help," Rosh said after a brief pause. "Though the Watermight Artist who last studied the Lightning was following a trail left by more ancient scholars. Their language can be difficult to decipher." He touched a stack of crumbling parchment on the ground beside him. "This one is in an archaic version of the Cindral tongue, for example."

"Hmm. It's a shame it's not in Far Plains," Selivia said, examining the swirling symbols on the parchment.

Melloch adjusted his spectacles. "You speak the Far Plains tongue?"

Selivia nodded absently, still focused on the indecipherable script. "I've visited the Far Plains once a year since they achieved independence from Trure. I've even read some older works."

"In that case," Rosh said, "perhaps you'd like to try your hand at a translation."

He moved over to a different stack of papers, these ones in even worse condition. His bones creaked as he bent down to rummage through the parchment until he found a stack bound with a strip of leather.

"Ah. Here it is. I'm not certain the translation of this manuscript we've been using is adequate."

"We've sent for a better one," Melloch said, "but it hadn't reached Sharoth by the time we departed."

"I'll give it a try." Selivia took the stack from the elderly man, wincing at its size. The language was indeed old, and the hand-writing would be a chore to read. But the Soolen scholars were looking at her with interest rather than resentment. She could work with that. "I may need another pot of tea, though."

Rosh insisted on bringing the tea himself, and they got to work on the papers in companionable silence. Selivia settled onto the ground with a cushion under her belly and papers spread out before her. Her sister, Sora, was the scholar of the family, and being absorbed into Latch's endeavors at the cost of her own was exactly what she'd wanted to avoid. But this was about keeping the peace. Besides, she really might be able to learn something useful.

Latch caught her eye and gave her a grateful smile. She grinned back.

Selivia was eager to prove her worth to the group as the days passed, aware that the impression she made on Latch's loyal retainers could have repercussions for the rest of her life in Soole. But an undercurrent of tension remained that even her efforts to be helpful couldn't alleviate.

They were all aware they couldn't continue their research at the same methodical pace they had employed before her arrival. Chadrech's soldiers and Waterworkers were still out there, and no matter how secure the mine was, they would surely attempt to infiltrate or—more likely—storm it. The men slept in shifts and kept watch on the many tunnels leading into the mountain hideout. They all felt the pressure to learn as much as possible about the Lightning before the Crown Prince made his move.

"I don't regret Casting that bolt," Latch told Selivia once when the others couldn't hear. "Now that I know how it feels to use that much power, we can accelerate our research. And we might never have known about the thunderbirds without you."

The possibility that the giant birds might be compelled using the substance became Latch's primary interest after Selivia's arrival. Rosh, Melloch, and the others were skeptical about the link, but Latch was certain the thunderbirds had responded to him that day. He experimented with drawing in bigger and bigger quantities of the power while willing the creatures to land on the ledge outside the main entrance tunnel or to shriek at specific moments. He hadn't yet succeeded in getting them to do anything, but the more Lightning he drew in, the more certain he became that there was a connection.

"The creatures must be drawn to the Lightning, just like with natural thunderstorms," Latch said one afternoon when he and Selivia sat on the outer ledge, sharing dried jerky from a sack. Thunderbirds wheeled and called to each other overhead, paying no attention to the pair on the mountainside. "I think they sense a Wielder's desires when they're immersed in the Lightning. I might be able to compel them to fulfill those desires if I take in as much as I used the day you arrived."

Selivia chewed a piece of jerky thoughtfully. "So when you were trying to get me away from Chadrech by throwing that Lightning bolt at the square, the thunderbirds sensed you wanted me safe?"

"That's my working theory."

"Did you imagine ripping apart those guards?"

Latch grimaced. "No. I'm sorry you had to go through that, Sel. But I can't say I didn't think uncharitable thoughts about what I'd do if you were hurt."

"It was an urgent situation," Selivia said, remembering her terror as she ran through the rain. "Perhaps they responded to that."

"Hmm. That's a possibility."

Latch went quiet, as he often did when he was working out a new theory. He pulled a scrap of parchment from his pocket and began scribbling notes in a faster, sloppier handwriting than he'd used when composing his letters to her. Selivia finished her jerky in silence and left him to it. She knew that by morning, he'd be back at the chasm, thinking urgent thoughts in the direction of the thunderbirds. He could get so wrapped up in a problem that there was no getting through to him, especially when he was in direct contact with the magical substance.

She didn't mind studying with Latch and the others as much as she had feared. They were exploring uncharted territory, and it came with more risks than she had expected when she imagined being stuffed into an archive for the rest of her days. And Latch himself was passionate about the task, which she found surprisingly appealing even though it didn't involve dragons or high-flying adventures.

When they'd first met, Latch had a surly edge to his personality. His father had recently died, and he was suffering from a battle injury. He treated her with courtesy even then, and she'd felt hopeful that she'd grow to love him. But the gruffness had been smoothed away in the intervening years, replaced by thoughtful refinement and intellectual curiosity. She liked these qualities more than she would have anticipated.

And of course, he'd thrown all his careful research aside and risked everything to save her life. She'd be lying if she said that didn't appeal to her too.

But by the end of her first week with Latch and his research team, she was beginning to wonder if Rosh and Melloch were right about the dangers of using too much of the power.

Even without any magical ability of her own, Selivia could sense the Lightning's volatility. It moved erratically, with a frantic, jagged quality. The dancing, rabid light mesmerized her whenever she watched the Wielders experiment with it in the great cavern.

Latch would allow the beams of light to spring from fingertip to fingertip, the tiny lightning bolts shivering back and forth so quickly it looked as though his fingers were webbed, like some strange glowing frog's feet. Sometimes, he shot tiny spears of purple-white light at chunks of stone, cracking them apart with unpredictable force. Other times, the Wielders practiced passing the Lightning between each other's hands, Rosh to Latch to Rosh to Melloch to Latch to Rosh and back to Latch, always in small, controlled quantities. They'd finish each session by directing the Lightning back into the chasm, which contained an almost incomprehensible reservoir of the power.

The others were careful about allowing too much of the substance to enter their bodies. When they did, they would draw in tiny quantities, carry it short distances from the chasm, and then stop to record how it felt. Slowly, they transported the Lightning farther and farther from its source.

But Latch drew in larger amounts than Rosh and Melloch, sometimes much larger, increasing the quantity he held each day. Strange lights flashed and flared in his eyes, getting brighter every time. Selivia hoped he wasn't pushing himself too far. Perhaps he felt more confident since he'd already held so much of the power. Or perhaps he felt the urgency more acutely than he let on. The mountain was still surrounded, after all, and there was no telling when Prince Chadrech would make his move.

Rosh had noticed the methodical increases too. When Latch raised his hand over the chasm and called more and more of the Lightning to him, the old man would purse his lips, straining the wrinkles around his mouth, but he was judicious about speaking his criticism aloud.

Selivia worried Latch was rushing his research, but she sensed the need to understand the power too. That Watermight Artist must have destroyed her notes for a reason eighty years ago, and none of them wanted to unleash something that belonged in the ground.

The more ancient scholars were inscrutable, even with Selivia's understanding of the Far Plains tongue. Sometimes it was difficult to tell whether they were referring to the Lightning or to one of the better-known magical substances. As she found a path through the archaic language, Selivia still struggled to understand what they were talking about.

"Rosh, have you seen this part about a monster?"

"A monster, Princess?"

She was sprawled on the floor with old parchments spread before her, while the Wielders played with little flickers of Lightning at the chasm.

"The language is tricky," she said as Rosh joined her. "The Lightning is said to enchant and entice, leading to the awakening of a monster. The other translation uses the word 'malice' instead of 'monster,' but I'm not sure that's right."

She shuffled the papers and read out a quote.

"The monster is drawn to the power. It revels in the Lightning, as if it were a thunderbird. Once awakened, it cannot be sated."

Rosh frowned, running his finger over the troublesome word. "Some writers have speculated that the Lightning taps into the innate evil in its users. That has largely been influenced by the use of the word 'malice,' I must admit."

"So the monster could be the Wielder or some kind of malicious intent inside the Wielder? We're not talking about a literal creature?"

"I don't believe so." Rosh took the parchment from her to see where she was reading from. "Hmm. If memory serves, this particular Far Plains scholar didn't get much farther in his studies before his colleagues urged him to pull back. Perhaps the malice the power awakened in him was blatant enough that the others recognized it in time."

Selivia thought of the care Latch and the others took with the Lightning. They hadn't done anything monstrous or malicious, at least not intentionally. But the scholars implied it could get worse.

Rosh returned to his own reading, and Selivia reached for the booklet containing the few remaining notes from the Watermight Artist who'd studied here eighty years ago. Despite being written in the common tongue, her notes were even harder to decipher than the ancient manuscripts. Part of the problem was that the notes had been taken from a dozen manuscripts, mostly charred beyond comprehension, and pasted together in a jumble in this booklet.

Some of the notes were merely strange.

It sings to life, and life calls to life, and life ensnares. Only then can it break.

Such lines would be followed by unintelligible scrawls and then single words.

Water. Thunder. Fire. Rain.

Selivia feared they could sit in this cave for years, trying to guess what the unnamed Watermight Artist had been trying to say. But every tenth page or so, she'd find a line that was much less obscure.

The Lightning nurtures aggression. It is a jealous mistress. Anyone who Casts it must be pure of heart and purpose lest it corrupt them.

"No wonder she didn't want others to use it," Selivia muttered. "How many people are truly pure of heart and purpose?"

The more Selivia learned about the Lightning, the more it troubled her. She was already looking forward to the day when they sailed away from here.

She wasn't sure when that would be. The Crown Prince's men had destroyed the longboat Latch had taken to get here. They set up camp in an old granary not far from the black pebble beach and guarded the harbor closely. Selivia and her companions wouldn't be able to leave Thunderbird Island without a confrontation. But so far, Chadrech hadn't forced one.

Sometimes, when the stuffy cave became unbearable and the charred words started running together, Selivia would entice Latch away from his studies long enough to sneak down to the ruined town to spy on Chadrech and his men. She hoped to catch a glimpse of Fenn, but if her bodyguard was still in Chadrech's custody, she must be back on the *Silverliner*.

"He's scared," Latch whispered one morning as he and Selivia knelt behind a pile of rubble, watching Chadrech's granary head-quarters. "He won't risk attacking until he knows everything the Lightning can do."

"Do you think he'd try to kill you? He went to a lot of trouble to try to buy your cooperation without violence." She had foiled that particular outcome by escaping.

"The Brach relationship with the Crown is delicate." Latch traced a line through the dirt, connecting two bricks, like two powerful houses. "Especially since tensions with Pendark are so high right now." He tapped a lump of stone a short distance from the two bricks. "Queen Rochelle won't move against me when I could throw my power behind King Khrillin and give him a path into Soole. Chadrech may not be so cautious."

"And if he's not?"

Latch didn't answer.

Two soldiers emerged from the old granary and scanned the cloudy sky, perhaps watching for rogue thunderbirds. Selivia glanced up, too, checking for signs of Mav. She hadn't seen so much as a talon of her true dragon friend since arriving at Thunderbird Island. Heath always used to say dragons had minds of their own and their autonomy needed to be respected, but Mav was her friend. She couldn't believe he would abandon her.

Right now, she was more worried about what would happen if the delicate relationship between the Brachs and the royals was destroyed.

"Latch?" Selivia lowered her voice. "You only want to study the power, right? You don't want to use it to break away from Queen Rochelle."

"I'm not my father."

"I know. But you also snuck out here behind your rulers' backs. If you were entirely loyal, you'd be sharing your discoveries with the Crown Prince instead of spying on his camp."

Latch was quiet for a long time. Selivia was learning to read his silences. This one suggested he was genuinely conflicted.

"I've been searching for this for years, Sel," he said at last. "I can't just give it up."

"It's dangerous."

"It will be even more dangerous if Chadrech gets his hands on it." Latch met her eyes, speaking with restrained gravity. "I won't use it to harm Soolen lives, but it would be the height of irresponsibility to hand it over."

"But he's going to be your king."

Latch looked over the pile of rubble at the soldiers, who still had their faces turned toward the clouds. Their slate-gray uniforms bore Chadrech's personal insignia.

He sighed. "Let's hope Queen Rochelle has a long and prosperous reign."

Despite Latch's fear that Chadrech would risk the stability of Soole and seize the Lightning directly, the days passed without a confrontation. They continued their accelerated research, and the Crown Prince sat on his hands in the granary. Selivia began to wonder if he was planning to starve them out of the mountain. But then, nearly two weeks after her arrival at Thunderbird Island, he made his move.

24

It happened in the middle of the night. Selivia had fallen asleep with her arms wrapped around a scroll. She was dreaming about riding Mav, with the wind in her hair and the vast world spread out beneath her, when she felt a hand on her arm. She started up in surprise.

"It's me," Latch whispered. "Chadrech's men are on the move."

"Attacking?"

"Rosh saw another ship join the *Silverliner*." Latch kept his voice low, though the others were already awake, strapping on weapons and hurrying out of the cave. "It was delivering more Watermight to Chadrech's Wielders. That must be why he waited this long."

Selivia felt a thrill of fear but also of relief. She had hated waiting, never sure whether they'd be attacked or not. She was ready for some action.

"What's the plan?" she whispered.

"Each of the men will take a tunnel," Latch said. "We're all skilled Watermight combatants. We'll try to take control of the power Chadrech's men are carrying and hold them off with as little bloodshed as possible. I don't want to take Soolen lives if I don't have to."

Selivia remembered the bodies with smoking clothes in the aftermath of Latch's single Lightning bolt and shuddered.

"What about me?"

"I need you to guard our research papers," Latch said.

"That's it?"

"If we fall, don't let them torch anything. This information is too important."

Selivia swallowed the urge to argue for a more exciting role. "I can do that."

"Good." Latch paused, a shadow crossing his face. "I'm so sorry my work has put you in danger, Sel. I wish I could protect—"

"Latch, I'm not a porcelain doll." Selivia reached out in the darkness and squeezed his arm. "I've been through war, same as you. I'll hold the fort here."

"You're remarkable," Latch said gruffly. "I hope you know that."

"Yes, yes." A tight pinch of anxiety tightened in her chest. "But don't you let that insufferable lordling win."

"I won't." Latch took her hand from his arm and gently pressed her palm to his lips. "I'll never let them hurt you."

Selivia's stomach gave a nervous flutter at the ragged edge to Latch's voice. He held her hand for a second longer, scanning her face in the darkness as if memorizing every shadowy detail. Then he released her, tightened his sword belt, and marched out to the main cavern. Selivia scrambled to her feet and followed.

Rosh and Melloch exchanged quick words with Latch and then marched down the tunnels leading away from the cavern. They had fought Watermight battles before, but there was a sense of grim inevitability in their movements. There were more tunnels than men, and they were sure to be outnumbered. They would make a stand on the mountainside, but their chances of keeping their attackers at bay were slim. Neither took any Lightning with them, not knowing how it would react to the Watermight Chadrech's men would use in their attack.

Latch waited for the others to depart instead of going to his assigned tunnel. As their footsteps faded away, he approached the chasm and gazed into its pulsating depths.

Selivia took a few steps closer. Latch wore a considering expression, as if trying to decide on a course of action. She tensed, waiting, as the Lightning source crackled and popped. She wondered if the threat advancing on the mountain was worse than Latch had let on. Perhaps he really was expecting to die out there and that was why he was staring into the chasm with such deadly seriousness.

Suddenly Latch turned to look at her. The erratic light danced around him, making him appear otherworldly and grave.

"Do you trust me, Sel?"

"I do."

She was about to ask what he was doing when he took three quick strides toward her, tipped her chin up, and kissed her.

The warm touch of his lips surprised her. He'd never kissed her before, never done more than hold her hand. His lips were full, his mouth firm and startling against hers. She barely had time to kiss him back before he pulled away.

He looked down at her for a moment, a spark flaring in his eyes. Then he nodded once, marched back to the edge of the chasm, and began to draw on the Lightning.

The light jumped from the crack in the stone to Latch's waiting hands, glowing white, purple, yellow, and blue. Selivia shrank back as a vast quantity of the power lanced into his body, making him shudder. The earth shook under his feet.

He shivered with the Lightning, pulsed with it. Selivia pressed against the cavern wall, getting as far from Latch as she could without abandoning him. He looked as if he could explode into a blaze of light at any moment.

Outside, Chadrech's men must be getting closer, advancing on the tunnel entrances with their bodies full of a different kind of magic. Selivia wished she could see what was going on, wished she could watch it all from dragonsback. But she had promised to guard Latch's research, staying out of the action for his sake. And for her sake, he was about to take another terrible risk.

The air crackled with energy, making Selivia's hair frizz out in all directions. She tasted metal on her tongue. Was this what it had been like when Latch Cast that Lightning bolt before? He was going farther than she'd ever seen—maybe too far.

Just when she was sure he would burst into white light, Latch turned and strode toward the nearest tunnel. She glimpsed his eyes, twin thunderstorms, as he passed. He didn't seem to see her.

Then he was gone, taking the crackling power with him.

Selivia paced back and forth in front of the study cave, listening for hints of what was going on outside, waiting. Occasionally she heard rumbles, felt thunder rolling through the earth. She heard higher-pitched sounds, too, but she couldn't tell whether they were screams or the wind sighing across the mountain. She watched the tunnels, waiting for friend or foe to emerge.

She wouldn't abandon those precious papers, but she wanted to see what was happening. Why had Mav forsaken her? On his back, she could have defended the mountain, could have made sure Latch didn't need to fill himself with that dangerous power to protect her.

But Mav was gone. And she was alone with the little room full of paper and the vast chasm full of power.

She moved a few steps closer to it, shading her eyes against the brilliance. Despite how much power Latch had drawn in, the glow of the chasm hadn't diminished. The beams of light rioted within the earth. What kept the power inside the chasm? Why wasn't it striking up at the mountaintop, blasting its way out of the earth? For all her reading, Selivia still didn't know what terrible force kept this power contained—or what would happen if it ever broke loose.

She turned her back on the chasm, unable to stand the blazing light in her eyes a moment longer.

Thunder rumbled. The stones of Thunderbird Island shook beneath her feet. Somewhere in the distance, that high-pitched sound sighed and whined. She couldn't tell how much time was passing. She felt as if she'd been waiting here her whole life.

Just when she was sure she couldn't take it anymore, Rosh returned. The old man jogged toward her, joints popping, a touch of rain glistening on his silver hair.

"Are you well, my lady?"

"I'm fine." She rushed to clasp his wrinkled hand. "What's happening out there?"

"It was incredible, my lady," Rosh said, his usual scholarly composure missing completely. "The birds, they fought for us. Fought for Lord Latch."

"What do you mean?"

"He walked out of the tunnel blazing with power. I've never felt anything like it in all my days. Then he called on the thunderbirds to aid him. Chadrech's men hadn't even reached us when the foul creatures started diving at them."

"The thunderbirds defended you?"

"They struck with their talons and those knife-sharp beaks whenever the soldiers got too close. The Waterworkers took down a handful, but they were overwhelmed. I would have been, too, if the fiends attacked me."

Selivia shuddered. She could imagine it well enough. The ripping. The screaming. The wet thuds.

"Latch didn't want to kill Soolen soldiers."

Rosh grimaced. "He may have said that, but I don't know how much control he had. It was . . . awe-inspiring."

Selivia felt sick. She had thought Latch would Cast a few Lightning bolts at the enemies to keep them from the tunnels, but this?

She swallowed. "Were there survivors?"

"Yes, but they hightailed it away from the mountain when they realized what was happening, thunderbirds harrying them the whole way."

"And Latch? Is he all right?"

Rosh hesitated. "I am not certain."

Footsteps echoed down one of the tunnels. Selivia turned, hope rising in her throat.

But it was Melloch, not Latch, who emerged from the tunnel. His hair had come loose from the yellow strip of leather, and something dark spattered his spectacles.

"They are retreating," he said as he joined Selivia and Rosh. "Chadrech and his men are returning to the *Silverliner*. They left a small company of soldiers sheltering in the granary, probably to make sure we don't leave."

"Did you see Latch?" Selivia asked.

Melloch wiped off his spectacles and looked around the cavern. "He's not back yet?"

Selivia was proud of the calmness in her voice. "I am going to find him. Guard the study cave, please."

Both men tried to argue.

"Princess, you shouldn't—"

"It isn't safe, yet, Princess—"

She cut them off with a raised hand. "I will be back soon."

"Please," Rosh said. "You don't want to see what those creatures did. And they could still hurt you. He may not have full control."

"I trust Latch," Selivia said. She didn't add that she was fairly certain the thunderbirds wouldn't hurt her when it was Latch's urgent desire to protect her that had prompted him to unleash them. "I'll find him and make sure he's not—"

"I'm here."

Selivia spun around as Latch stumbled back into the cavern. He looked deeply shaken. His skin was ashen, and his hands trembled. Selivia had entertained ideas of greeting him with a proper kiss if he survived Chadrech's attack, but all thoughts of romance disappeared as he crossed the cavern toward them. She was afraid to even touch him.

"What happened?"

"I willed them to protect us, and they did." He looked down at her, his eyes unfocused and his voice wavering. "Their attacks were far more precise than the wild lightning bolts. I didn't expect it to be like that. Those beaks are . . . are so sharp."

Selivia could imagine it well enough. She was glad she hadn't gone out for a look after all.

"But they're gone now," she said. "You saved us."

"I suppose I did." Latch took a deep, steadying breath, as if slowly regaining control of his body.

"What do you think Chadrech will do now?" Selivia asked, including the other two men in the conversation.

"He'll summon reinforcements," Rosh said. "He's not going to give up."

"We don't want another fight." Selivia imagined the talons, the screams, and the thunderbird feathers dipped in blood. "Maybe he'll negotiate."

"I'm not negotiating," Latch said sharply.

Selivia raised an eyebrow at his harsh tone. "And why not?"

"He'll want me to give up the power. But I found it!"

"I don't believe the princess is suggesting you agree to all his demands," Rosh said, watching the young lord with a look of concern that mirrored hers. "Maybe we should talk about it tomorrow."

Latch blinked. "Why?"

"The power may be affecting you. You used so much of it just now."

Latch frowned, allowing flickers of light to crackle along his fingers. Selivia started. She hadn't realized he still had some in his system.

"I have to use it if I'm going to learn to control it," Latch said, his voice distant. "With enough practice, I can get it to obey me."

Melloch took a deliberate step toward Latch and raised a hand as if to take those flickers of light from his fingertips. "Perhaps you should take a break and let us practice Casting for a while, my lord."

"No!"

Melloch adjusted his spectacles, studying Latch's reaction closely. "Interesting."

"What's interesting?" Selivia asked.

"Lord Latch has now directly touched far more Lightning than the rest of us. I wondered if he'd become jealous of it."

"Jealous?" Latch rubbed a shaking hand through his close-cropped hair. "I'm not jealous, just aware of the dangers."

Melloch and Rosh exchanged meaningful glances.

Selivia knew what they were getting at. She recalled the line from the Watermight Artist's notes about the Lightning being a jealous mistress. Latch had read those words dozens of times. He'd written extensively about the potential dangers of the power. But knowing the dangers wouldn't necessarily save him from the Lightning's effects.

"I know what you're thinking," Latch said, giving the two scholars a hard look. "But I'm being careful. Now that Chadrech's gone, let's make the most of this chance to study in peace. I want to know everything there is to know about the Lightning by the time he returns. Now if you'll excuse me, I'd better write down what happened out there before I forget any details."

He turned and shuffled toward the study cave, light still dancing at his fingertips. Selivia watched him go, fear turning her stomach to ice. Latch might have thwarted Chadrech's assault and made a breakthrough with the Lightning in the process, but he had crossed a line today. She didn't know if any of them were ready for the cost.

25

Queen Dara summoned Tamri for a private lesson on the first day of school after Eventide. Tamri went to the basement workshop to wait for her while the other students trooped into the parlor for a history lesson. Tamri had taken extra time to comb her hair and mend a small rip in her uniform, though no amount of tidiness was likely to make up for the terrible impression she'd made on the Fire Queen so far.

When Dara entered the workshop, she wore gray trousers and a plain black coat, and her golden hair was pulled back from her face in a braid. The Savven blade swung at her belt, and she carried a metal bucket full of Watermight.

Tamri didn't wait for the queen to speak. "I'm sorry about what happened at the tournament, Your Highness."

Dara placed the bucket on a stone worktable without speaking. She pulled several lumps of unformed iron out of her pocket and arranged them next to the bucket. Her movements were calm and deliberate, which only made Tamri want to fidget.

"I should have known better." She scuffed her boots on the stone floor. She wasn't sure why she felt ashamed. Getting that valuable letter out of the queen's pocket had been a triumph. "Am I in trouble?"

Dara finished arranging the lumps of iron and turned to meet her eyes. "I told you I had high expectations for my students, but I see more direct supervision was necessary. I should have worked with you individually sooner."

Tamri blushed, pulling at a loose string on her newly mended coat. "It was a stupid thing to do."

"Let's put it behind us," Dara said. "I'd like to see what progress you've made since we met."

She beckoned Tamri closer, her eyes taking on that distinctive focus. Tamri stood up a little straighter.

"Master Corren says you don't like to draw in the Fire."

"It's easier to Wield it outside my body."

"That's not how this usually works," Dara said. "Does it still hurt?"

"No! Not at all."

Dara frowned. "How often do you draw in the Fire?"

"A few times during each lesson." In truth, Tamri hadn't drawn the Fire in at all her last several times in the workshop. She was still trying to force it to obey her without requiring that step. She'd been hoping Master Corren hadn't noticed.

"Do you practice outside of class?"

Tamri shrugged. "We don't have much free time." Master Corren had told her she was now permitted to use a little Fire outside of lessons providing a more experienced student joined her practice sessions, but she hadn't taken him up on it yet.

"You need to make time," Dara said. "This is a vital skill, one that will only improve with training. But enough talking." She waved a hand at the access point and called forth a glowing stream of Fire. It flowed fast and plentifully for her, a servant eager to do her will. "Show me what you can do."

Tamri took a deep breath and approached the trough full of searing power. She pulled up a glimmering stream of Fire, spinning it through the air in a tight spiral to show she could control it without first drawing it into her body. The spiral was a little lopsided but still much better than anything she'd been able to do when she first arrived in Vertigon.

She sent the Fire into a lump of metal on the table, pushing a bit too fast in her eagerness to prove she could. The lump melted into a messy puddle, which spread across the table and dripped iron tears onto the floor.

"I'm sorry I—"

"Try again," Dara said calmly. "This time draw it in first."

Tamri grimaced and drew another thin stream of Fire toward her. The queen watched her closely.

The Fire prickled like hot needles as it touched her palm and sank into her skin. Tamri could only endure it for a few seconds before she pushed it back out again. It flowed a little smoother, but it was frustrating how much it still hurt. She shot it into the second lump of iron, which melted at once, joining the first puddle with a faint hiss.

"Again."

Tamri tried over and over, drawing up streams of power and forcing them into her skin. But the Fire refused to cooperate, and the pain didn't abate. She gritted her teeth to keep from giving herself away, growing increasingly agitated. She wanted to hurl the power faster, to force it to obey her. Why was this so hard?

The Fire Queen watched every failure with that inscrutable calm. She made few suggestions, allowing Tamri to try again and again to get it right.

After her seventh disastrous attempt, Dara held up a hand. "Are you sure it doesn't hurt? Your face—"

"It would work better if I could do it my way," Tamri said, unable to keep the frustration from her voice.

"Perhaps," Dara said. "Or maybe you just need more practice. It's not supposed to be easy. You can't lose focus."

Tamri wiped sweat from her forehead, resisting the urge to argue. *Focus* wasn't her problem.

The queen remained infuriatingly composed. "Let me see you use Watermight."

Sweating and agitated, Tamri turned and whipped the power from the bucket to her hands. She spun it in a loop, relishing the icy speed. Her native power soothed her hands and reminded her she wasn't completely useless.

She broke the Watermight into a dozen silvery strands and used them to snatch up bits of metal from all over the workshop as fast as she'd ever Wielded in her life. She piled them onto the worktable, neatly arranged from largest to smallest.

She looked back at the queen, feeling triumphant. She would have to admit Tamri wasn't entirely incompetent now.

But Dara simply looked back at her, her handsome face giving nothing away.

"Well?" Tamri said impatiently. "What do you think?"

Dara didn't answer, nor did she chastise Tamri for her impertinence. Tamri supposed she *was* being rather bold. She'd already come to expect these Vertigonians not to react with cruelty. If she used the same tone against King Khrillin or the Red Lady of the Market District, she'd find herself sliced into fish food in under a minute.

The Fire Queen didn't punish her or require her to grovel, but she didn't answer Tamri's question, either. She simply studied the line of metal objects on the worktable for a time then said, "I want to show you something, Tamri."

She walked over to the table holding the students' clay water cups. She picked out one of them and dipped it into the Watermight bucket, filling it to the brim. Then she tipped back the cup and swallowed a large mouthful of the silvery power.

Tamri started forward, wondering if the queen had gone insane. Why on earth would she *drink* Watermight?

Dara's eyes took on the white-glazed look of someone holding significant power. Her fingernails glowed silvery-white, glittering as she raised them. Then, as quick as thought, she shot Watermight from her hand, wrapped a cord around Tamri's waist, and lifted her into the air.

Tamri gave an indignant shout and twisted like an angry cat. She hadn't left Pendark to be tossed around. She didn't have to put up with this!

But no matter how fiercely Tamri struggled, Dara's power held her firm.

With a wave of her hand, Dara used the Watermight cord to bring Tamri closer, keeping their eyes level. Tamri was nearly a head shorter than the queen, her boots hanging a few inches above the ground. She forced herself to stop writhing, her body quivering with frustration.

"I learned to Wield late," Dara said. "When I first started using the Fire, holding steel helped me focus." She tapped the hilt of the Savven blade at her belt. "Then a Watermight Artist in Pendark helped me figure out I could use that substance, too, if I swallowed it first. It still hurts to pull it into my skin though not as much as it did five years ago."

She lowered Tamri to the ground and released her. She didn't draw the Watermight back into her body, letting the cord flow around her hands like a silver snake. Tamri wanted to bolt for the door, but she didn't dare move.

"You obviously have potential, Tamri," Dara went on. "If you have a specific block or difficulty like mine, I might be able to help you find a way past it. But that only works if you're honest with me. Now, is there anything you want to tell me about what happens when you touch the Fire?"

Tamri didn't answer. She wanted to be able to Wield Fire as adeptly as she did Watermight. She wanted to be so powerful that neither the Fire Queen nor Khrillin could toss her around whenever they felt like teaching her a lesson. But she couldn't tell the queen the truth. She knew what happened when you let a powerful Wielder learn your weaknesses.

"I just need more practice," Tamri said.

Dara studied her for a moment more, looking disappointed. Then she sighed and gestured to the trough of Fire. "Then go ahead and draw in another measure of Fire, and let's get back to work."

Tamri worked with the queen often after that. Dara seemed to view her training as a challenge. She repeated her warnings not to rush, but she pushed Tamri a little harder each day.

They focused mostly on the Fire, occasionally taking breaks to work with Watermight. Tamri's control was getting better, and the range at which she could seize the Watermight had doubled since her arrival in Vertigon. She was grateful whenever they switched to the silvery power, as Wielding Watermight allowed her to soothe her aching palms and release the tension that built up in her shoulders when using the more painful substance.

After every Fire lesson with Dara, Tamri felt as if she had rolled around in a patch of nettles. She refused to tell the queen how the Fire made her feel, so the queen demanded more and more of her.

Dara was a good teacher, if strict, but Tamri couldn't help pushing at the boundaries she set. The Fire Queen demanded calm, focused actions. But Tamri wanted to Wield faster. She was used to quick, wild motions. They clashed over the best approach, sometimes going so far as to argue. The queen put up with a surprising level of debate from Tamri, but she could still silence her with a look if she overstepped.

Tamri wrote about her progress in regular reports to Khrillin, of course, but in the heat of the lessons she sometimes forgot she was spying on the queen. Khrillin would surely glean plenty of useful information from her letters, anyway, so she put her mind to soaking up all the training she could.

But no matter how often Tamri had lessons with the queen, touching the Fire continued to hurt. The pain plagued her, and her efforts to force the Fire to obey without first inflicting it on her body weren't enough. She began practicing outside of class so she'd do better when the queen summoned her, adding it to her other responsibilities.

Time passed quickly with so much work to do, and a month after their private lessons began, Tamri could hold the Fire in her body for a full ten seconds before the searing started. But it always started. Her attempts to strong-arm the magical substance into submission —and smother her body's response to it—could only go so far.

"That's it, slower, slower."

Dara stood in front of Tamri, holding a glowing sphere of Fire, while Tamri drew small beads of Fire from the sphere, pulling them toward her in a glowing chain. One after another, they dropped into her open palms, scorching her bit by bit.

"I'm going as slow as I can."

"Try to make it smoother, like a heartbeat."

Tamri tugged harder, making the beads pulse out of the sphere and shoot toward her.

"That's too fast!"

The power slipped out of Tamri's control. The glowing sphere wobbled, and the Fire she'd already drawn in expanded, putting pressure on her skin, on her organs. She gasped, feeling like a kettle about to boil over.

Dara didn't try to help, allowing her student to wrestle with the power on her own, to find a path through the problem. Tamri gritted her teeth, imagining the liquid Fire slowing down, running like blood beneath her skin. At last, she managed to bring it back under control.

"That's it." Dara smiled. "Nice and easy."

Tamri smiled back grimly, her teeth clenched so tight her jaws ached. She hadn't hurled the power away. She concentrated on the sphere, which was smaller than a fist now, and drew the last of it toward her.

"I think it's all in."

"Good," Dara said. "Now hold it. Hold it."

Sweat bathed Tamri's forehead as the power simmered inside her. It grew hotter the longer she held it in her body. But this was her tenth attempt at Wielding this much Fire, and she didn't want to fail yet again. She held it, black specks swimming across her vision, her blood about to boil.

"Okay, that's long enough," Dara said. "Now, as gently as you can, release the power into these stones. Do it without touching them this time."

Tamri exhaled, letting globs of Fire drip out of her hands and into the rocks lined up on the worktable. Of all different sizes, the porous stones accepted the flow of the power and began to glow. As the last of the Fire left her, she focused on the rocks themselves, imagining a force pushing in on them, solidifying the shape of the Fire within.

When the power was as stable as she could make it, Tamri released her mental hold on the rocks and slumped against the table. The Fire stayed put. Each rock now gave off a steady warmth.

"Excellent work," Dara said. "Those Heatstones ought to last for weeks or even years. You're making great progress."

"Thank you." Tamri felt a thrill of pride at the queen's words. She rubbed her tender hands surreptitiously. She felt tired after the long Wielding session, but she was much stronger physically than she had been when she first arrived in Vertigon. All those bridge runs and hearty meals were paying off.

"Why don't you keep one of the Heatstones?" Dara wiped her forehead with her sleeve and nodded at the rocks. "You can put it in your blankets to warm your bed."

"Okay, thanks." Tamri already had so many Heatstones in her blankets she could barely move. She'd stolen most of them from the greathouse storage room when the autumn cold became unbearable. But winter was fast approaching, so she picked out another, proud to have a Firework she'd made herself.

"Practice moving the Fire in small beads over the next few days," Dara said as they headed for the door together. "Don't assume because you did something once you'll get it right every time. And use the same Fire quantity we Worked with today."

"If you say so," Tamri said, wincing at the prospect of holding that huge ball of power again.

"Is something wrong?" Dara said.

"No. I'm just tired."

Dara studied her intently for a moment. Tamri wondered whether it would be so bad to admit what was going on. Hiding the pain was getting harder. But she had come to respect the Fire Queen, and she doubted Dara would appreciate hearing Tamri had been lying about the effects of the Fire all along. On the other hand, she might be able to suggest strategies for working through the handicap if she knew the truth. Tamri had tried drinking the Fire, the way the queen did to get Watermight inside her body, but she hadn't been able to keep it down, and it left her unable to taste anything for days afterward.

"You'll get a chance to rest over the next few days," Dara said as they walked up the stairs to the main house. "Siv and I have business to attend to, and I won't be coming to the school for at least a week."

"What kind of business?"

If the queen thought Tamri's question was impertinent, she didn't say so. "We're entertaining visitors from the Lands Below."

"Which lands? If you don't mind me asking."

She laughed. "You'd ask even if I did mind."

Tamri blanched, but there was no sting in the queen's words.

"There's nothing wrong with a little curiosity," Dara said. "They're from the Far Plains and from Trure."

Tamri pictured the vast land of rolling hills and charred fields she'd flown across between Vertigon and Fork Town.

"Is it true a Firewielder sacked Trure years ago?"

Dara's shoulders stiffened, and she paused at the top of the stairs. The sound of chattering and laughing children filtered down the hallway toward them, along with the smell of fresh pies baking in the greathouse kitchen.

Tamri clutched the Heatstone in her pocket, wondering at the grave expression on Dara's face. She'd never seen the Fire Queen look so cold.

"It's true," Dara said at last. "It was a very powerful Firewielder who believed his abilities gave him the right to rule over anyone who couldn't match him."

"What happened to him?"

Dara looked down at Tamri, her intense eyes revealing deep wells of sadness. "Someone matched him."

Tamri felt certain now that Dara had been the one to defeat the Firewielder, like the stories claimed. But why should that make her so sad?

She wanted to ask, but before she could, Master Corren appeared and whisked the queen away for tea and pie. Only when they were gone did Tamri remember she'd been about to tell Dara about the pain the Fire caused. She was glad now that she hadn't. The queen might not kick her out of school at this point, but she might slow down their lessons. And Tamri was hungry to learn. If this woman had vanquished a powerful Firewielder, perhaps she could teach Tamri to defeat a Waterlord king.

———

Kay and Lacy were already in their room when Tamri trudged up the stairs, hoping to get some rest before her shift at the Whirlpool that night. The Watermight supply was getting quite low, but Master Loyil expected the students to help him keep it spinning until it ran out completely.

The two girls looked up when Tamri crossed the room to her bunk.

"Tamri, did you hear?" Lacy said. "We've been invited to a party!"

"Who's we?" Tamri asked, dropping the newly created Heatstone on her pillow.

"All the Originals," Kay said. "One of Master Corren's noble contacts is thinking of sponsoring a wing at the new school, and he wants to show us off to her."

"It's not just a noble contact," Lacy said. "It's Lady Vine Silltine herself!"

"Is that supposed to mean something to me?" Tamri asked.

"Lady Vine is the queen's best friend," Kay said.

"She throws the most glamorous parties," Lacy said. "I never thought I'd actually be invited to one."

Tamri kicked off her boots and flopped back onto her blankets. "It's with a bunch of nobles?"

"You say that like it's a bad thing!" Lacy said.

"Who cares about the nobles?" Kay said. "It's a chance to get out of this place and eat fancy food without being surrounded by little kids. And Lady Vine is nice, though she's a little peculiar."

"What do you mean?"

"You'll just have to meet her." Kay hung her head over the edge of the bunk so she could see Tamri. "Also, she's an Air Sensor. She has given us a few lessons on Air communication. Maybe she'll come to the school more often if she becomes a sponsor."

"Could she teach me to use the Air to communicate with people in Pendark?" Tamri asked. Air, the most nebulous of the magical substances, came from Trure, but some could usually be found floating through the mountain. Using it for messages was one skill she'd been hoping they would learn sooner. She was taking a risk every time she sent a letter with the dragon riders.

"Probably." Kay wrinkled her nose. "If you want to talk over long distances, you can get an Air Sensor to help you transport a message, you know."

"I still want to learn how."

Tamri could never trust an Air Sensor enough to send her reports to Khrillin. At least her letters remained sealed. But having an independent way to communicate would reduce her risk of getting caught. The more time she spent with the Fire Queen and her fellow students, the more she dreaded the prospect of them finding out she was spying on them.

Kay vaulted off her bunk and began digging into her trunk and chattering with Lacy about what to wear to Lady Vine's party. Tamri didn't join them. She would attend the festivities in rags if it meant she could learn this Lady Vine's Air tricks.

26

Tamri didn't understand what an important event Lady Vine's party was until Master Corren canceled their afternoon lessons the day of the festivities.

"You won't be concentrating on your studies, anyway," he said to the class after directing them to put away the Fire Lantern diagrams they were tracing. "We'll finish those drawings later."

"Thank you, Master Corren," Lacy gushed, sending charcoal pens flying as she leapt to her feet.

"Don't thank me," Master Corren said. "I want you all to make a good impression on Lady Vine and Lord Vex." He smoothed out a wrinkle in his silk shirt. "Their support is vital to the future of this school."

"We won't let you down, sir," said Dentry.

"I know you won't. Now run along and get dressed up in your finest."

The students rushed up the greathouse stairs, buzzing about the evening ahead. Even the boys were excited about the prospect of a party at the home of the esteemed lord and lady.

"I've met them, you know," Dentry told everyone as they thundered down the hall to their respective rooms. "My cousin Jully knows Lady Vine well. She goes to the parlors with her and Lord Vex sometimes."

"Who's Lord Vex?" Tamri asked.

"Vex Rollendar. His noble house led the coup against the Amintelles before the war, but he found a way back into King Siv's favor."

"And he's with Lady Vine now?"

"That's right. And the king and queen trust her more than anyone else on the mountain."

"Really?" Tamri said. "Why?"

Dentry threw up his hands. "She's Lady Vine!"

Everyone seemed to think that explained everything. Tamri was eager to meet the fabled lady—and the lord who had recovered from a traitorous past. Master Corren had opposed the king and queen once as well. Tamri couldn't help wondering if they were a little too trusting. No matter what, the party would be the perfect opportunity to learn who wielded power in Vertigon apart from the royals and Fireworkers.

Excitement shook the greathouse to its foundations as the students ran back and forth, commenting on each other's outfits, fighting over hair ribbons and cravats, and searching for missing shoes. The younger children, who weren't allowed to attend the party, generally got underfoot, making the whole process even more chaotic.

Tamri had never attended a fancy event before. She had exactly one dress nice enough for a special occasion, the emerald-green velvet with bronze stars on the bodice that Princess Selivia had bought her in Fork Town. Tonight might be her only chance to wear such a dress. Lacy and Shylla joined forces to wrestle Tamri's thick hair into submission, twisting it into thick ringlets and using a Firestick to set the curls. She was proud of herself for not flinching while Shylla wielded the glowing metal rod so close to her neck. After a moment's consideration, she asked Shylla to help her pin Gramma Teall's pewter dragonfly in her hair.

"It doesn't match," Shylla said.

"I don't care."

Shylla pursed her lips, which she'd painted a striking plum shade. "Fine. But you'd better borrow my bronze dancing slippers." She gathered a few of Tamri's ringlets and secured them with the pewter dragonfly. "No sense in clomping around the dance floor in those old boots."

Tamri blinked. "Thank you." Shylla sniffed and went off to fix her own hair.

By the time everyone was dressed and combed and ready to go, the sun was sinking over the mountain. Master Corren and Madame Mirri, both wearing richly embroidered cloaks, led the way up the cobblestone road and past the broken fountain. The students followed in an eager, giggling mass.

All the Originals had been invited to Lady Vine's party, but Madame Mirri reminded those under sixteen they weren't allowed to drink anything stronger than apple cider. She would be taking the younger ones back to the greathouse after supper. The oldest students, Dentry, Pevin, Kay, Lacy, Shylla, and Tamri, would be permitted to stay until midnight.

"It's not fair," Lacy's sister, Liora, complained as she flounced along in a purple dress that was a bit too loose on her. "I'm fourteen!"

"Be happy you're invited at all," Lacy said. "*I* didn't get to go to House Silltine-Rollendar when I was your age."

"But I don't want to miss the dancing!"

Her best friend, a quiet Soolen girl named Sheen, nodded fervently.

"I'm sure Madame Mirri will let you dance for a song or two," Lacy said.

Liora gasped and clutched Sheen's hand. "Oooh, maybe we'll get to dance with a lord."

"You can dance with me," Dentry said. "I'm a lord."

The two younger girls stared at him for a moment then dissolved into a fit of giggles. Lacy shooed them away, her cheeks stained red, and apologized for her sister's behavior.

"It's okay," Dentry said. Then he gave Lacy a shy smile. "But maybe you'd like to dance with me . . . if you feel like it, that is."

"Oh." Lacy looked like she might faint onto the cobblestone path from happiness. "Yes, maybe I will."

"Good. Yes." Dentry tugged on his curly hair, turning as red as Lacy. "Thank you."

Kay caught Tamri's eye and winked.

The festive mood continued as they descended the wide, winding avenues of Lower King's Peak toward the Silltine-Rollendar greathouse. The autumn air had a cold bite, and Tamri was grateful for Gramma Teall's brown cloak. Beneath it, the green velvet dress felt soft and strange against her skin. She wasn't used to the way her feet kicked the long skirt with every step. But the dancing slippers Shylla had lent her felt almost like going barefoot again, and Tamri relished the firmness of the mountain beneath her toes.

As they passed a large shop with smoke issuing from no fewer than twelve chimneys, Tamri sensed a trail of Fire running through the stone below her. She was becoming more aware of the power's presence throughout the mountain. Contact with the substance might hurt, but the queen's efforts to teach her were paying off. One day soon, she might be able to pull those trace bits of Fire from the stone herself.

They continued on through the busy city streets, fine marble buildings rising on either side. The shop windows displayed expensive textiles, Firejewels, and delicacies from the Lands Below. Muscular servants marched past carrying palanquins, many of them heading in the same direction as the students. Fluttering curtains revealed glimpses of the well-dressed passengers within.

Nerves rippled through Tamri at the sight. Tonight would require different skills from the ones she'd been practicing in the basement workshop. Socializing with wealthy people might be even harder than stealing from them.

"This is it," Lacy said as they rounded a bend and turned down a road leading through a large plum orchard. "The Silltine-Rollendar estate!"

"They built it after the war, you know," Dentry said, chest swelling with importance. "The Rollendar greathouse burned to the ground, and Lady Vine's father still lives in the old Silltine greathouse. He's in poor health, though. She's the true head of the family now."

"I hear she runs House Rollendar too," Lacy said, not to be outdone on the subject of noble gossip. "Lord Vex worships her."

"And for good reason!" Dentry said.

Tamri listened to the pair gossip about the lord and lady as they processed down a sheltered pathway, Firelights guiding their way. Between them, Dentry and Lacy would eventually give her a complete history of Vertigon's nobility. The information might not be as valuable to Khrillin as the things she'd learned about the Fire Queen, but it would beef up her next report.

As they got deeper into the orchard, the trees cut off the sounds of the busy city. The thick foliage was a rich golden red, and leaves drifted down with every breath of wind, littering the orchard floor with autumn colors. The air smelled of overripe plums, damp earth, and the merest hint of smoke.

"Remember to be on your best behavior," Master Corren called over his shoulder to the students, his embroidered cloak swirling around him. "This is an important moment for us."

"We won't let you down," Kay said. "We want Lady Vine to support the school too."

Tamri jogged to catch up with Master Corren. "Sir?"

"Yes, Tamri?"

"Why are you working so hard to get sponsors for the school? Isn't the queen's support enough?"

Master Corren glanced over at Madame Mirri, who was meandering along, occasionally pausing to examine interesting golden-red leaves on the ground. He lowered his voice. "My vision for the Wielder School is that it will become an independent institution. You may have read that Vertigon used to have a Fire Guild that was separate from the king and his Fire Warden."

"I remember something about that. Their powers balanced each other out?"

"Precisely. Right now, the queen is both Fire Warden and monarch, and the Fire Guild is no more. If our school stands alone, I believe Vertigon will be healthier in the long run."

Tamri nodded in understanding. Powerful Wielders constantly warred against each other in Pendark, but Khrillin's consolidation of power over the past five years had changed the dynamic there too.

"Look!" Lacy squealed, pushing between Tamri and Master Corren. "There's the greathouse!"

The stately dwelling was built of pale-gray marble, its flowing lines making it look like a natural extension of the mountainside. Subtle Firegold veins were embedded in the marbling, creating intricate, organic designs that made the whole house shimmer in the dusk. Fire Lanterns swung from the nearest plum trees, drawing out the Firegold details and giving the estate an enchanted air.

The students crossed a broad white-gravel walkway leading up to the greathouse. Music spilled out of the open front doors, and guests were visible on the flat rooftop, enjoying the view of the stars on this crisp fall evening. The clink of glasses mixed with the breeze rustling through the plum trees.

When they were almost to the front steps, a beautiful woman emerged on the columned portico. In her late twenties, she had long, lustrous dark hair, and subtle Firegold streamers glittered in her tresses like stars in the night sky. Her sapphire gown had geometric Firegold shapes embroidered on the bodice and a flowing skirt that swirled dramatically as she descended the steps to greet them.

"Master Corren! And Mirri, dear, it is so lovely to see you both." She pressed their hands in hers. "Your presence is a great gift to me this evening."

"We are humbled by your invitation, Lady Vine," Master Corren said magnanimously.

"The pleasure is entirely mine. Oh! Let me have a look at your students! I'm delighted you brought them." Lady Vine waltzed toward the group, smiling beatifically.

"Lord Dentry Roven, you are getting so tall. Your cousin, Lady Jully, has already arrived. And Kay! I watched you duel at Eventide. Your form has improved marvelously. Is that young Pevin? How is your aunt feeling?"

Everyone responded as articulately as they could manage, dazed by Lady Vine's presence as she greeted them one by one. Lacy looked as if she might burst into tears when Lady Vine complimented her hairstyle.

Tamri revised her assessment of Lady Vine's beauty as she made her way down the line. Though lovely, Lady Vine wasn't actually the prettiest woman Tamri had ever seen. But her lively energy, songbird voice, and knowing smile more than made up for that. She drew the eye, gorgeous in her own unique and enigmatic way. Tamri found herself smoothing her velvet dress, hoping Lady Vine would approve.

"So you are the new student from Pendark." Vine looked Tamri over closely, taking in everything from the pewter dragonfly to the thickness of Tamri's cloak to the nuances of her expression. "I spent several months in your city once. Fascinating place. Tell me, are you in touch with King Khrillin while you're here?"

"I—King Khrillin?" Tamri stammered.

"Yes, is he well?"

Tamri stared at the noblewoman, frantically trying to come up with an answer that wouldn't arouse suspicion. Before she could summon an appropriate response, Lady Vine smiled knowingly and moved on to Sheen, telling the shy Soolen girl how much she was looking forward to her brother's wedding.

Kay elbowed Tamri in the ribs. "You'll catch bees with your mouth open like that."

Tamri snapped her jaws shut, though it was far too late to cover her reaction. What exactly did Lady Vine know about her and Khrillin?

The greetings complete, Vine danced back up the porch steps to address the whole group. "You mustn't stand outside a moment longer. Come into my home! You will add such a lovely energy to the party."

She glided into the greathouse's large front parlor, drawing the students and schoolmasters behind her like ducklings.

The parlor ceilings were quite high, and wide doorways led to other large rooms, giving the house a breezy, open feeling. Discreet Firebulbs lit the space with a gentle glow, and several silver sculptures stretched from the floor to the vaulted ceiling like ice-covered trees. Well-dressed people milled across the pale tile floor, drinks sparkling in their hands.

"You must try the plum tarts," Lady Vine gushed as she led the students across the parlor. "I've already snuck several from the kitchens. Oh, look! It's my dear friend Meza. She taught an Air workshop at your school on her last visit from Trure, didn't she? And Lord Farrow over there might be convinced to support the Wielder School as well, Master Corren. Do say a kind word to him."

Tamri brushed at her velvet skirt nervously as she listened to Lady Vine's chatter. Each word seemed calculated, despite the lady's airy tone. That couldn't have been an idle question about Khrillin. Tamri should return to the school before she got herself in real trouble. She was about to do exactly that—when she caught sight of the food.

A table stretched along the right-hand wall of the parlor, covered with plates piled high with delicacies. In addition to the standard Vertigonian goat and poultry options, there were Far Plains feather cactus, Truren sweet meats and flatbread, Pendarkan eels and brindleweed, and ice-packed rawfish all the way from Soole. A separate dessert table displayed cakes and sweets in a myriad of colors, with a huge platter of Pendarkan sugar mushrooms forming the centerpiece.

"Please help yourselves to as much food as you desire," Lady Vine said to the students. "Our home is open to you, and you are welcome to stroll about or sit and eat wherever you see fit. The stairs are through those stained-glass doors if you'd like to see the view from the roof. Come along, Master Corren, Madame Mirri. There are some people you simply must meet."

Tamri had expected everyone to sit at a long banquet table, but the other guests were piling plates full of food and strolling about with them or sitting at sofas and little round tables spread around the room. The wide-open doorways showed groupings of people in a smaller side parlor, a library, and even the guest bedrooms toward the back of the house. The event had a sort of casual elegance, as if eating and socializing and relaxing and exploring were all part of the same dance.

"Let's get some food already," Kay said. "Then I want to see the rooftop!"

The students collected delicate sea-green porcelain plates and filled them with fine food, mouths watering at the aromas. Tamri took some of everything. She might never attend another dinner like this. She had once snuck into a port lord's manor house during a dinner party, planning to steal Watermight from a garish fountain he used to display his wealth, and glimpsed the elaborate spread on the banquet table. She'd only managed to swipe a small measure of Watermight while the guests were eating, but she had dreamed about the food she'd seen for weeks afterward. This put that meal to shame.

Trying not to drop her overflowing plate, Tamri followed the others to a group of low satin couches arranged in a square beneath one of the tree-like silver sculptures. They balanced the plates on their knees and dug in.

Tamri ate without quarter, forgetting all about Lady Vine's questions about Khrillin, her troubles with the Fire, and even the Watermight bond on her neck. Fortunately, the others found the food as exciting as she did. Only Shylla sniffed disapprovingly when Tamri was the first to clean her plate. She slumped back on the satin couch, wishing she could share a tenth of what she'd just eaten with Gramma Teall.

"Who's up for seconds?" Dentry said.

Tamri gaped at him. "Seconds? We're allowed to have *more* food?"

"She said to help ourselves."

Tamri stared dumbly as Dentry sauntered off to fill his plate again, as if he hadn't just consumed a king's portion of food.

"I'm leaving room for dessert," Kay said, tapping her belly.

"Dessert sounds good," Tamri said faintly.

She followed Kay back across the crowded parlor. None of the other guests were eating quite as desperately as she had. Most were older than the Wielder students, and they drank from tall glass flutes and conversed in dignified tones. A single musician strode among them, playing a lilting tune on a stringed instrument Tamri had never seen before.

All the guests wore silks and satins and fine wool coats. Firejewels flashed at throats and earlobes. Tamri surveyed them doubtfully, unable to tell which were nobles and which were just rich people. They could all know useful information.

"I'm going to look around a bit," she said to Kay.

"Sure thing. Meet you on the rooftop later?" Kay strode off to the dessert table, where a pair of young noblewomen immediately accosted her to talk about dueling.

Tamri left them to it and moved through the room, listening unobtrusively to snippets of conversation. It wasn't all that different from trying to get leads on Watermight buyers back in Pendark, despite the glamorous surroundings. She'd still need to dash for safety if the wrong person noticed her eavesdropping.

Much of what she heard didn't mean anything to her.

"... sure to win the Vertigon Cup this year."

"Not a chance. My money's on Bilzar Ten for another victory."

"He threw another tantrum and offended his sponsor. I doubt he'll be in prime fighting form."

Other observations didn't seem relevant to Khrillin.

"Did you see the blue plums? This has to be the best harvest in years."

"The orchards over on East Slope are still recovering. They had the worst luck . . ."

". . . claimed it came from Purlen, but I know Fork Town wine when I taste it."

Tamri paused behind a pair of older women with Firejewels at their throats, their hair arranged in elaborate knots.

"I swear Lady Tull has gotten prettier since her marriage."

"And have you seen her daughter?"

"Oh yes! She's precious."

"I'm still waiting on that royal baby. Perhaps Lady Vine knows about the queen's plans."

Tamri leaned closer, but the two women began discussing their grandbabies and didn't mention the anticipated royal heir again. She'd seen no sign of the king and queen themselves so far. She wasn't sure if they were supposed to attend this gathering or not.

She recognized a few people as she continued her circuit of the parlor. Master Corren was talking earnestly with a couple of elderly nobles. Zarr and Master Loyil reclined beneath another of those strange silver sculptures, chatting with a young Fireworker who'd once come to the school to teach the students to make Firebulbs. Captain Jale from the Castle Guard stood very straight with his chest puffed out, a pretty young woman with light Truren eyes on his arm.

Lady Vine herself was a vortex of energy in the middle of the room. People surrounded her, knocking glasses and plates as they jostled for her attention. Tamri positioned herself behind a large nobleman who was praising Vine's hospitality in booming tones, hoping to hear something useful. Vine had power, as surely as Khrillin and the Fire Queen, though she wielded hers differently.

"It has been such a joy to host my Truren friends these past days," Vine was saying to the group. "I only wish Queen Sora herself could have visited."

"Is it true the king and queen summoned the Trurens unexpectedly?" asked a robust lady wearing a purple silk gown with purple ribbons woven in her hair. "I heard they traveled in haste."

"Air Sensors do things for their own reasons," Vine said vaguely. Then she gasped in delight. "Oh! You must tell me the name of your jeweler, Lady Atria. Your necklace is simply divine."

The lady in purple blushed with pleasure. "She does excellent work, Lady Vine. And may I say that your gown is ravishing."

"Thank you, Atria, darling. You are too kind."

As the other guests rushed to compliment Lady Vine's dress, too, Tamri gradually got the feeling Vine knew she was listening. The lady's eyes never quite landed on her, but the slightest frown appeared on her lips. She turned to whisper in the ear of a tall, blond man with a long nose, who glanced at Tamri and nodded, his hand resting on the sword buckled over his red coat.

Tamri decided to make herself scarce. She left the main parlor at a jog to explore the greathouse's ground floor. In a smaller side parlor, several elderly men were playing a game of tiles called mijen and chuckling over glasses of brandy. In the library, three young ladies were gathered around a book from Vine's shelves. And in one of the guest bedrooms, where double doors opened onto a balcony overlooking the Fissure, Tamri found Dentry and Lacy having a very earnest conversation. She ducked back out before she could witness anything embarrassing.

It was late by the time Tamri reentered the main parlor. She edged along the wall, keeping an eye out for Lady Vine and her sword-carrying lord. Her friends had vacated the couches beneath the silver sculpture, and a statuesque older woman in a bright-red gown was holding forth in their place, surrounded by admiring younger men. The other students must be up on the rooftop by now. Tamri slipped over to the dessert table, planning to collect some treats before joining them.

She was piling extra salt cakes onto a plate for the others when a familiar voice spoke at her side.

"Are you going to finish all that yourself?"

"Heath!" she sputtered as the tall dragon rider moved up to the table beside her. He wisely hadn't tried to tap her arm to get her attention. "What are you doing here?"

"Hoping for a chance at the salt cakes if there are any left."

"They're for my friends." Tamri blushed, flustered by his unexpected appearance. "I didn't know you were back in Vertigon."

"Just arrived this afternoon. There's a fresh load of Watermight in the Whirlpool for you."

"Thanks. I mean, I guess it's not for me, more for all of us, but—" Tamri's plate shifted, and her salt cakes nearly ended up on the floor. Heath's lips twitched in amusement.

She summoned as much dignity as she could. "How was your trip?"

"I'm training a couple new dragon riders." Heath picked up a plate and began filling it with soldarberry tarts. "Spent most of the time reminding them not to scream every time the dragons make a turn. Not everyone takes to it as naturally as you did."

Tamri laughed. "They must really be dreadful for you to say that."

Heath glanced down at her with a shy grin. He wore his usual blue uniform coat, despite being at a party, the scar she'd put on his arm poking out from beneath the sleeve. His clothes were neat, though, and he'd taken the time to smooth down his thick bronze hair.

He reached past her to grab a salt cake. "How is your Fireworker training going?"

Tamri wasn't sure whether it was his sturdy presence in this glitzy house or the fact that Heath seemed genuinely pleased to see her, but she found herself telling him the truth.

"It's hard. I'm making progress, but the Fire still hurts. I can Wield it outside my body, but that doesn't work as well. I feel like I'm getting stabbed by hot needles whenever I draw it in. I can't tell my instructors, or they might make me stop learning. And I want to impress Queen Dara, but sometimes I can't tell if she approves or if she thinks I'm a lazy student who isn't as committed as . . ."

She trailed off. Heath was staring down at her with a strange look in his eyes. Was he angry? What had she said to warrant that?

"I didn't mean to babble," she began. "I should—"

"The Fire hurts you?" he interrupted.

"Only when I pull it into my skin."

"But isn't that most of the time?"

She shrugged, the plate of salt cakes shifting in her hands. "I guess. And then I'll be sore for a little while afterward, like a sunburn."

"Tamri, you have to tell the queen," Heath said. "She wouldn't want you to keep doing something that causes you so much pain."

"I can't tell her," she hissed, more fiercely than she meant to. "She'll send me back to Pendark!"

"You have to take care of yourself." Heath's face darkened. "Burning Firelord, Tamri. Why do you throw yourself into trouble like your life doesn't matter?" He set down his plate with a thump. "I'm going to tell Master Corren."

"Don't you dare!"

"No Wielding skill is worth torturing yourself."

"I told you that in confidence." Tamri set down her own plate as Heath started to walk away and grabbed his arm. "It doesn't hurt that much."

He continued to march forward deliberately, lifting her right off her feet. She kept forgetting how big and strong he was.

"It's my choice. Stop, you big ox."

Abruptly Tamri realized people were turning to look at them. She went bright red and released Heath's arm. He appeared equally embarrassed.

"Okay." He lowered his voice so the people around them couldn't hear. "I won't tell anyone, but you should."

"I can't get kicked out of school."

"Why is that so important?" Heath brushed a hand through his hair, leaving it messy. "This was supposed to be a punishment for stealing, remember? This could be your way out if you want to go home."

"I can't. You wouldn't understand."

Heath folded his arms and glared down at her. "Try me."

She glared right back, mimicking his stance. He didn't know what it was like to be in a constant battle for your life. Vertigon might have had difficulties in the past, but their streets were safe, their magic was portioned out fairly, and their rulers were benevolent and beloved.

Heath couldn't know what it was like to fight for survival the way she had, and she couldn't reveal how Khrillin had entrapped her.

But his quiet anger over her pain made her want to tell him the truth, or at least part of it.

"It's my grandmother," she said at last. "She's not well. I couldn't compete against the Waterworkers in Pendark, and I thought if I learned to use the Fire, too, it would help me earn enough money to take care of her. I'm all she has."

"I'm sorry," Heath said. "I didn't know." He shifted his boots awkwardly. "What is she like?"

"She's fierce." Tamri grinned, remembering how Gramma Teall had gone for Khrillin's throat with her gnarled fingers. "She can't remember people's names half the time now, but she'll still tell them exactly how to live their lives. And she'll fight like a cornered panviper if anyone threatens the people she loves."

"Sounds familiar."

Tamri looked up. Heath's expression was gentle, and she recognized the same odd mix of emotions as when he'd watched her say goodbye to Laini. As if he genuinely sympathized. Genuinely cared. Without thinking, she reached up to brush a lock of his bronze hair back from his forehead.

She froze as she realized what she was doing, and Heath looked almost as shocked. They stared at each other for a minute.

"You are a puzzle, Tamri of Pendark," he said softly.

She snatched her hand back, her face flushing. What had possessed her to touch him? "I should go meet my friends."

She spun toward the dessert table—and collided with Lady Vine.

"Excuse me, my lady! I didn't see you."

"It's quite all right," Lady Vine said. "But you must tell me where you got your dress. It suits you perfectly. Don't you think it suits her, Heath?"

"I—yes, of course, Lady Vine." His face was brick red, and he appeared every bit as mortified as Tamri felt. "Tamri looks lovely."

"Thank you," Tamri mumbled. "Princess Selivia bought it for me."

Heath blinked. Then, as if the princess's name had cast a spell—or perhaps broken one—he straightened his back, the stern mask closing over his face once more.

"If you'll excuse me, I must greet my mother." He bowed

formally to each of them. "Thank you for your hospitality, Lady Vine. Tamri."

Without returning for his dessert plate, he strode off across the parlor, heading toward the statuesque woman in the red dress.

Lady Vine watched him go with a satisfied smile. "He *has* grown up. I hardly noticed him when he was a young lad, but he has made quite a name for himself in the dragon program." She whirled back to Tamri, grabbing her arm before she could sneak off.

"You must tell me all about your time here, my dear Tamri. Are you getting along with Dara? She can be frightfully serious, but there's no better person to have on your side in a fight, magical or otherwise."

"I—yes, I'm learning a lot from her."

"That's lovely. I do hope you won't take what you've learned and use it to harm her. I'm afraid you would come to regret that very much."

Tamri swallowed, wondering if she'd heard right. "My lady?"

"Khrillin is not the only person with a network of informants spread across the continent." Vine tapped her nose as if they were sharing a private joke. "I understand he has recently become privy to more information on Vertigon than usual. Now, there are a number of ways he could acquire such information, but I will not take it lightly if I find anyone abusing the trust my friends the king and queen have placed in them. Do we understand each other, Tamri of Pendark?"

It took all of Tamri's willpower not to twist free and run for it. She would have bolted already if Vine weren't holding on to her arm.

"I'm sorry, my lady, but I have no idea what you're talking about."

"I do hope that's true." Vine smiled serenely. "In any case, please don't break young Lord Samanar's heart. He guards it ever so closely, and I'd hate to see it damaged."

Tamri choked. "I don't—"

"Enjoy the rest of the party!" Vine sang. "And do grab some of those sugar mushrooms for your friends on the roof. I shall eat them all if there are any left at the end of the night."

Vine sauntered off, leaving Tamri feeling as if she'd fallen off a dragon and was plummeting through thin air.

Numbly, she added the extra sweets to her plate, not daring to disobey Vine now. Did the lady know Tamri was sending messages to Khrillin, or did she only suspect? Tamri moved as slowly as she could, lest any sudden movements reveal the truth. She would have to be more careful than ever with her reports. She didn't want to know what would happen to someone who crossed Lady Vine.

Tamri hurried back across the parlor, planning to join her friends as if nothing had happened. But she stopped at the stained-glass doors and looked around to see if Heath was still there. Additional musicians had appeared around the room, and the Vertigonians were pairing up to dance. But there was no sign of Heath's bronze hair and blue uniform among the lords in their finery. He was already gone.

27

Latch stood at the edge of the chasm, a black shape silhouetted against the purple-and-white glow. Lightning shivered between his hands and the chasm, back and forth, twisting and sparking and splitting. The air crackled with energy, and Selivia felt as if she could be lifted right off her feet at any moment.

She had been trying to get Latch's attention for almost ten minutes. She didn't dare touch him when he was so close to that void of power. No matter how much she shouted at him, he didn't seem aware of her. But there was something he needed to see.

She was reaching for a stone to toss at him when he spoke.

"It's calling me."

"What?"

"It has been trapped for so long, and it needs me." Latch's voice sounded unnatural, as if it, too, were crackling with lightning.

Selivia shivered. It wasn't the first time he'd said such things. When had it started? Not long after the *Silverliner* sailed away, surely. Latch had begun spending more time at the edge of the chasm, ordering his men to stay clear. At first, Selivia thought he was trying to protect them from the eerie, entrancing effects of the Lightning. It had seemed noble then. Now she wished Rosh and Melloch had insisted on sharing the load.

"Latch, there's something you need—"

"I can feel it. Down there. Something more than the power. I have to study it."

Selivia risked moving a few steps closer, her hair rising on the back of her neck. "I think you've studied enough."

Latch ignored her. "I don't know if it created the Lightning or if it's a product of it." He stepped closer to the edge of the chasm, mere inches from the drop now.

"Latch," Selivia said urgently. "Come away from there. Please." This was the worst she'd seen him. In the weeks that had passed since Selivia joined Latch inside the mountain—or was it months?— it had never taken this long to pull him away.

"It'll obey me if I learn to understand it." Latch took another step, the toe of his boot touching the gap now.

Selivia drew in a sharp breath. He wasn't in control. The Lightning called to him, luring him like a siren. What would happen if he stepped over the edge?

Rosh and Melloch were waiting by one of the tunnels leading off the cavern, unwilling to come too close. They understood the pull of the Lightning now.

After chasing Chadrech off Thunderbird Island with the thunderbirds, Latch had become increasingly entranced by the Lightning. Selivia would catch him staring into the chasm, standing a little too near the edge, the purple-and-white glow dancing across his face. She'd have to speak to him several times before he noticed her. Sometimes, she'd catch flashes of irritation on his face, irritation at *her* for calling him away. He often wouldn't realize how much time had passed, and Selivia had to remind him to eat and drink. She wished she'd realized how much danger they were in sooner.

Perhaps they couldn't have stopped it. Latch insisted on drawing the Lightning into his body in larger and larger quantities. When he held it for too long, his thoughtful eyes would grow heated, and his skin would radiate unnatural energy. He began acting suspicious of Selivia and the others, too, as if they were trying to wheedle away the substance for themselves. Rosh and Melloch had given up on trying to use the Lightning at all.

It was perhaps the least of their worries, but Latch hadn't kissed Selivia again, either. The man who'd tipped her chin up and brought his mouth to hers before marching out to defend her was entirely different from the one now swaying at the edge of the Lightning chasm.

Selivia had seen people obsessed with power before, both magical and mundane, but this was different. This wasn't *him*.

A stone broke loose from beneath Latch's feet. Instead of falling, it hovered in the flickering light, strangely still.

Selivia couldn't wait any longer. She darted forward and grabbed Latch's shirt, careful not to touch his skin, and hauled him backward.

A sharp shock went through her as she pulled him away from the chasm. She stiffened at the painful fizzing sensation and stumbled, falling to the ground with Latch beside her. The impact jarred her teeth and made Latch grunt.

"Latch?" She rolled to face him, the fizzing sensation fading quickly from her body. "Are you okay?"

He stared at her, his eyes flickering with unnatural light. "I won't let them take it from me," he muttered.

"No one's taking anything. You need to—"

Suddenly Latch gave a violent shudder. Then he lay still.

"Latch!" Selivia scrambled to her knees. She seized Latch's shirt and pulled him toward her. His head lolled on his shoulders.

"Princess?" Rosh called from a few feet away. "Is he well?"

She didn't answer, knowing her voice would betray her fear. Latch's followers had begun to look to her for leadership as their lord withdrew from them. She had to be strong for them.

"Come on, Latch," Selivia whispered. "You got us into this. It's your duty to get us out again."

At last, Latch's dark eyelashes fluttered on his cheeks, which looked gaunt. He hadn't been eating enough, too absorbed by his studies.

"Sel?" He opened his eyes, blinking up in confusion.

"I'm here."

"What's going on?"

She helped him sit up, positioning herself so she blocked his view of the Lightning chasm. "What do you remember?"

"You were going scouting." Latch rubbed his eyes. "You're back already?"

She didn't bother telling him she had been gone for hours. She'd needed to be out in the fresh air, breathing in the salty aroma of the sea and tramping among the ruins. Living underground on this eerie island was taking a toll on everyone's spirits. And while she was out, she saw their doom approaching.

"There are ships on the horizon," she said. "Prince Chadrech has returned. We need to prepare to defend the mountain or negotiate. The latter is probably our only choice."

Latch started to look toward the chasm, but Selivia took his face in both hands, keeping his eyes on her.

"Latch, the Lightning is doing something to you. You need to stay away from it."

Latch's nostrils flared, as if it was taking effort not to jerk away from her. Selivia held him firmly as he struggled for calm. The gaunt contours of his face were both familiar and strange to her. This was still the man she had sworn to spend her life with, but she missed the brave young soldier who had so enchanted her when they met.

"Okay," he said at last. "You're right. Let's seal off all the tunnels but one. We can send the thunderbirds to patrol the mountainside. I think I can get them to talk with me the way dragons talk to Wielders. I'll go to the chasm and use the Lightning to control them."

Stomach churning, Selivia kept hold of him. He didn't even notice how quickly the chasm drew him back.

"No thunderbirds," she said. "And no Lightning. It's not safe."

Latch took her hands and carefully removed them from his face. "I know what I'm doing," he said. "I'll take the east tunnel. Rosh, Melloch, take the north and south. Sel, I'll meet you at the western exit."

Selivia nodded, ignoring the ache in her chest as he pushed her gently away from him. "I'm on my way."

———

Chadrech's forces took control of Thunderbird Island with the inevitability of a boulder rolling downhill. The ships surrounded the island, guarding it from all possible approaches, while soldiers and Waterworkers occupied the mining town, filling the ruins with the thud of boots and the low rumble of voices.

Before blocking the final tunnel with a barricade constructed from abandoned mining equipment, Selivia crouched on the ledge overlooking the ruined city, trepidation simmering through her. So many of the new arrivals wore silver knots on their slate-gray uniforms, indicating they were Waterworkers. She counted a score of them just within sight of the west tunnel.

The Soolen soldiers wore heavy leather coats over their uniforms, clearly aware of the danger posed by the vicious birds of prey that haunted this island. Even if Latch had complete control of both the Lightning and the thunderbirds, he might not defeat so many. Selivia dreaded what would happen if he tried.

She scanned the overcast sky for Mav. She had considered asking Latch to use the thunderbirds to search for her lost true dragon, but their responses to him were highly unpredictable. They might tear Mav from the sky if they were compelled to search for him. Besides, she didn't want to encourage Latch to use the Lightning any more than he already was. But with that many soldiers occupying the island, they were going to need help.

Latch emerged from the tunnel and knelt on the ledge at her side. His face was grave, but his eyes looked clearer than they had in some time. "We're trapped."

"It sure looks like it," Selivia said.

"They're preparing for a siege. Look there."

Sure enough, the newcomers weren't rushing the mountain. Prince Chadrech must have learned his lesson. Instead, they began repairing the old granary walls and tearing down nearby ruins to build their own barricades. Archers perched on the walls to guard against the thunderbirds. The creatures wheeled through the sky, crying out angrily at the humans who'd invaded their shores.

"We've stored enough water to last for almost two months," Selivia said, "but is there any point in prolonging the inevitable?"

It was clear to her that Chadrech had won. The Lightning power would be his. And now that she'd observed its intoxicating effects, she dreaded what would happen when his army of Waterworkers tried to use it. If Latch had become territorial over the substance, how would a whole battalion of Wielders respond if they tried to share it?

Latch reached out to take her hand for the first time in weeks. "I'm sorry I brought you into this, Sel. This wasn't part of the deal when you agreed to marry me."

"We're supposed to be partners for life, aren't we?" Selivia said. "That includes sieges."

Latch gave a pained smile, his grip tightening on her hand. "You don't have to stay if you don't want to."

Selivia's heart sank at the offer. Latch might have risked drawing in far too much Lightning for her sake, but she still didn't know if he loved her. If he did, would he be so quick to give her up?

"That deal was about more than you and me," she said at last. "Our families are counting on us."

Far below them, a patrol of soldiers was escorting a lean figure toward the old granary. Prince Chadrech himself had returned with his men.

"Queen Rochelle must have given him permission to act against us after all," Latch muttered. "Or at least against *me* after I killed some of his men."

Selivia frowned as the lean figure entered the blocky stone building. The Crown Prince had been careful of how he treated her, even when he was trying to use her as a bargaining chip. No matter what happened with House Brach, he wanted the alliance with Vertigon to hold.

"Maybe the agreement between our families can still help us," she said slowly. "I don't want Chadrech to have the Lightning any more than you do. But we don't have to handle this alone."

Latch gave her an appraising look. "What do you have in mind?"

"You have some Air abilities, right?" Selivia glanced up at the clouds, which were as heavy and dragonless as ever. "Can you feel any of the substance around here? I need to send a message."

28

After her encounter with Lady Vine at the party, Tamri felt certain she was being monitored. She sensed eyes on her back at odd moments—at the Whirlpool, on runs across the bridges, even when she was helping the Young'ns with their lessons—but she couldn't identify her watcher. She wondered if Lady Vine was using the Air somehow.

Tamri condensed her reports as much as possible so her letters wouldn't be suspiciously long and asked her classmates to drop them off in the letterbox when they delivered their own correspondence—never asking the same person twice. When the information wouldn't fit in a single letter, she tucked extra pages inside boxes of sweets, ostensibly for her grandmother. She hoped Khrillin choked on them.

She was beginning to doubt she'd ever discover a "jewel of information" valuable enough to free her from the oath bond. Khrillin hadn't contacted her after she told him about Princess Selivia's letter mentioning a new magical substance, and she couldn't think of anything more important than that. She couldn't find any proof the Fire Queen was training up the Wielder students for combat. Their lessons continued to cover a range of practical Fire crafts, and none of them were taught to Wield Fire and Watermight together to unleash that fabled burst of energy.

At least Lady Vine didn't seem to have informed the queen of her suspicions. Dara continued to work with Tamri, and they made slow, painful progress with the Fire. Whenever her instructors weren't watching, Tamri still avoided letting the substance come near her skin. This forced style of Wielding was becoming more effective, and she was proud of the way her strength had grown.

There was an unfortunate side effect of Tamri's work with the queen, though: feelings of guilt, once vague twinges, now surfaced in force whenever she sat down to write her reports. Tamri admired Dara, and she didn't like spying on her. But she couldn't withhold information without painful stabbing sensations assaulting her neck. And of course, she couldn't endanger Gramma Teall.

As she continued to report the queen's every word, Tamri tried to soothe her conscience by reminding herself that Pendark was still technically Vertigon's ally. But Khrillin had a grudge against King Siv and the Fire Queen, and Tamri was certain he would find a way to exploit every weakness she reported.

Fall was coming to an end now, and the mountain kingdom eagerly awaited its first snowfall. Tamri's classmates had told her the Vertigonians greeted First Snow with toasts and celebrations. She didn't understand why an even colder turn in the weather was cause for celebration. As winter approached, she missed the warm sea air more than ever, and she caught herself thinking fondly of the dank stench of the canals at the height of summer.

Then, on the coldest day of the year so far, Tamri and the others were summoned to the rooftop for a workshop with an Air Sensor.

Master Corren had been bringing in more guest instructors, busy preparing for the move to the new school building. A friend of Loyil and Zarr showed them how to find and purify Firejewels. A soldier with terrible burn scars on his arms gave them a brief, brutal history of the last war. A representative from the Below Lands Trade Alliance lectured them on Firework export tariffs. A Firesmith brought a collection of Fire Blades—much to Pevin's delight—and the students spent the afternoon wielding them against various dummies and slicing through tossed fruits. But this was to be their first Air lesson since Tamri's arrival.

Tamri had read up on the Air, hoping to figure out how to send her messages without Lady Vine catching her. The books Master Corren had on the subject were infuriatingly vague. Philosophy and mysticism mattered more than practicality to Air Sensors. Tamri had spent an hour on the rooftop, trying to Sense the Air, but she just ended up feeling cold and windblown. She hoped this lesson would finally give her the information she needed. But the visiting lecturer turned out to be Lady Vine herself.

"Kindly remove your shoes," Vine said as the students gathered around her on the rooftop. She wore long, flowing trousers, and her hair was pulled up in an elegant knot. "We shall sit in a circle and ready ourselves to welcome the Air."

Tamri thought she was joking about the shoes, but the other students dutifully piled their boots in a corner and joined her on the ground. Tamri followed their lead, wishing she had thought to wear an extra pair of socks.

Vine surveyed them for several moments, breathing deeply, the cold wind ruffling her clothes. Tamri tried not to fidget every time Vine's eyes landed on her.

At last, she spoke. "You must open yourself up to the Air. It may give you the gift of understanding, or it may choose to pass you by. I entreat you not to force it."

Tamri raised her hand. "How does it—?"

"I must ask that you give me the gift of silence, Tamri," Vine said. "All will become clear with time."

"But this is my first Air class, and I don't know what the Air actually is."

Vine smiled dreamily. "It is what it is."

Tamri blinked. "Wait, what is it?"

Kay suppressed a chuckle beside her.

"The Air is a substance of magic," Vine said, her patient tone never wavering. "It does not burn or freeze or flail about like Fire and Watermight. It exists, and its presence may be a comfort and a guide."

"Is it conscious?" Tamri asked.

"Some think so. They listen for prophecy and direction." Vine paused for several more moments. Tamri was about to interrupt the silence with a question when she went on. "I do not question the precise nature of the Air, as questioning can disturb its flow. I simply accept its gifts."

Tamri looked at her classmates to see if they were following this any better than she was.

Kay shrugged and mouthed, "It's always like this."

"You can send messages with the Air, right?" Tamri said.

Vine gave her a knowing smile. "We may ask."

Tamri knew pushing her on this topic was risky, so she gritted her teeth and resolved to observe what Vine was doing in case she could replicate it on her own later. Ideally without so many long pauses.

Vine invited them all to close their eyes and concentrate on the wind.

"Calm your mind. Feel the touch of the wind on your skin, the way it stirs your hair and tugs at your clothes." She drew in a deep, slow breath, and the students imitated her. "The Air originates in the Truren plains, but it is not bound by any nation. Trace amounts can often be found in the mountain regions. It may be enough to grant your requests, or it may slip away on the wind. You must accept whatever course it takes."

Tamri opened one eye to peek at her classmates. Dentry had his eyes shut tight, but he had shifted so his knee touched Lacy's beside him. She was blushing and grinning from ear to ear. Miles was taking deep, gasping breaths, as if trying to suck the passing Air substance into his lungs. Shylla seemed to be doing reasonably well at being calm and accepting, unless she had drifted off to sleep.

Tamri was pretty sure this substance wasn't for her. Calmness and patience weren't exactly her strongest attributes. Queen Dara talked about focus when they were Wielding the Fire, but it still delivered a hot rush of power and made her blood race. Watermight was a razor-sharp weapon, wielded with fierce speed. Sensing the Air was nothing at all like those heart-pounding practices. This skill might be beyond her reach.

The wind got colder, and Tamri hunched against it rather than inviting it in. She really should have worn extra socks. They'd been concentrating on nothing for what felt like hours. She opened her eyes to see if she might sneak away for a few minutes to thaw out her toes.

Suddenly, Vine stiffened as if she'd been struck. "We are

receiving the gift of an example," she said. "A message floats on the wind. Listen closely."

Tamri closed her eyes again, not wanting to miss the message. Her eagerness didn't make concentrating any easier. She thought she heard something, a voice coming from a long way off, but it slipped away before she could make sense of it.

She breathed deeply, attempting to calm her restlessness for once. She wanted to reach into the Air and snatch the message. She wanted to force this disembodied power to obey her the way the Watermight did.

Calm, she told herself fiercely. *Think of Gramma Teall.*

She pictured wrinkly olive skin, strong hands, and gray hair held back with a pewter dragonfly. The image made her want to fight with all the power within reach, but it calmed her, too, reminding her exactly why she was here.

"Vine, is that you?" A voice came to them as clearly as if the speaker were standing in the middle of the circle. Princess Selivia's voice. "Finally! It has been so hard to get a channel these past days. We couldn't reach Dara at all."

"Princess Sel," Vine said. "I am delighted to hear your voice. But right now, I'm instructing a group—"

"It's okay." The princess spoke quickly, sounding anxious. "Forgive me, Vine, but you must get a message to my brother. Tell him we are stranded on Thunderbird Island. I found Latch, and he found the thing he was seeking, but we're surrounded by Crown Prince Chadrech's soldiers, who are trying to take it from us. Fighting our way out will destroy our alliance with Soole, but we can't give the Crown Prince what he wants, either." There was a moment's hesitation, as if she wasn't sure whether to say the next thing. "Latch is different when he uses this—discovery—and we can't risk anyone else having it. Can you tell my brother all of that, Vine?"

"Of course, Princess," Vine said. "Your message is safe with me."

"Thank you. Oh, and tell him Mav has disappeared. Goodbye!"

Tamri opened her eyes as the message ended—only to find Vine looking straight at her. She shivered, feeling an echo of the princess's anxiety as if it, too, were carried on the wind. She didn't dare look away.

"Uh, Lady Vine," Kay said. "Shouldn't you be getting up to the castle?"

"Yes, the princess sounded scared," Lacy said. She was holding Dentry's hand openly. "King Siv needs to know!"

The other students were glancing around nervously, aware of the urgency of the situation.

Vine pulled her attention from Tamri with a sigh. "I'm afraid I must leave you. Thank you for your attention, students. Please keep what you've heard to yourselves."

The students rushed to assure Lady Vine of their trustworthiness and escort her to the door. Dentry hurried off to find a palanquin to carry her to the castle. The others analyzed the princess's message as they pulled on their shoes.

"What do you think 'the thing he was seeking' could be?" Kay asked, stamping her feet into her boots.

Pevin rubbed his nose. "Some kind of treasure?"

"Or maybe a weapon!" Miles said.

"Why would the Crown Prince of Soole try to take it, though?" Lacy said. "That's the future ruler of Lord Latch's own country, but Princess Selivia sounded afraid of him."

"Who knows why Soolens do anything?" Kay said.

As one, they looked around for Sheen, Liora's friend, who was the only Soolen among the Originals. She had disappeared.

"She was here for the lesson, wasn't she?" Lacy said.

"I'm not sure," Pevin said. "She's always rather quiet."

"Do you think she's a spy?" Kay sounded more excited than concerned about the prospect. "She could be rushing off to deliver a secret message to the Crown Prince!"

"Hey!" Liora said. "She's my friend!"

Kay shrugged. "Doesn't mean she's not a spy."

Tamri kept quiet, thinking of the letter she'd stolen at Eventide. The princess and her betrothed must have found the new magical substance on this Thunderbird Island. She had to tell Khrillin. She had already delivered her latest report to the letterbox, this one hidden in a box of salt cakes, and the dragon riders were due to depart for Pendark first thing in the morning. There were still a few hours of daylight left. She might have time to add this new information to the week's report.

She paused with her hands on her bootlaces. She *had* already sent her letter. Did she really want Khrillin to know Selivia and Latch Brach were in peril, possibly putting them in more danger? Couldn't she let this one bit of information wait until the next letter?

Cold pain shot through her neck at the thought, tightening in a ring. She gasped and then tried to cover it with a cough when Shylla looked over at her.

"Go ahead without me," she managed. "I just broke my bootlace."

"Well, hurry up," Shylla said. "It's our turn to make supper."

"Be right with you."

Tamri waited until the others trooped back into the greathouse before she collapsed to her knees, both hands wrapped around her throat.

"Loosen up," she hissed. "I'll send the information next time. My report is already on its way. I can't—"

She shuddered as the cold around her neck deepened. The bond could sense the truth. She still had time to send this news. Withholding the information was a betrayal of her Watermight Oath no matter how she tried to justify it.

But Selivia had saved her life and put clothes on her back. Tamri might have to spy on Selivia's family for Gramma Teall's sake, but she didn't want to put her in danger. It wasn't right. Tamri gritted her teeth and fought back against the bond for the first time, wrestling with the bitter cold in her bones.

The pain worsened, more intense than when she drew in the Fire. She whimpered, forgetting the cold wind when the ice under her skin was so much worse. She couldn't betray Selivia in her hour of need. This was more than a twinge of guilt. She didn't want to keep doing this.

She had to know if there was another way.

Struggling to breathe through her ice-bound windpipe, Tamri hurried back inside the greathouse. She paused on the first landing to loop her striped scarf tighter around her neck in case the bond was visible somehow. Her skin must be blue with the cold.

She raced down to the Fireshop, ducking into shadows to avoid passing students. The younger class was finishing up a Fire Blossom lesson with Madame Mirri. Tamri crouched by the door, fighting tears, and waited for them to file out, chattering animatedly about the pretty shapes they'd made with the Fire.

When the last little Wielder disappeared up the stairs, Tamri stumbled into the workshop and knelt before the stone trough, which still glowed with trickles of Fire. Tamri seized the power with her mind and brought a stream of it as close to her throat as she dared.

The Watermight bond in her neck reacted like a snake tossed onto a cook fire. It writhed beneath her skin, pressing at her veins and cutting off the blood flow to her brain.

Black fuzz clouded her vision, closing in fast. A shadowy dragonfly drifted before her eyes, struggling to stay in flight.

Gramma Teall. Through the haze of her blood-starved brain, Tamri remembered what she risked even if she could break the bond with a burst of Fire.

What was she *doing?*

"Okay, okay!" Tamri released the Fire, hurling it across the room to spatter the far wall. "I'll send the gutter-bleeding message!"

The cold pressure vanished in an instant. Tamri gasped, swaying as blood flooded back to her head. She dropped to the ground and leaned back against the stone trough. Her neck still ached, but the bond was no longer trying to choke the life out of her.

She sat there for a long time, waiting for her head and neck to stop throbbing. She was well and truly trapped. It didn't matter if she no longer wanted to be a spy. It didn't matter if she felt guilty reporting on these Vertigonians who were too trusting to understand how dangerous she could be. Khrillin had her in his grasp, and even the Fire couldn't help.

Her neck gave a faint shiver, reminding her she still had work to do before the night ended.

"I'm going," she muttered. She'd have to skip supper duty. Kay would forgive her even if Shylla didn't. She needed to reach Square Peak before the Roost closed up for the night. Going straight there was the only way to guarantee her message would reach a dragon rider's hands before they left the mountain.

Using all the stealth she could muster, Tamri snuck up to the parlor and grabbed a spare scrap of paper. She hid behind a couch while she scrawled the details of Selivia's message and inserted it between two pages of more mundane chatter for her grandmother. At least she knew Lady Vine would be busy up at the castle.

As soon as the ink was dry, she wrapped her brown cloak tight and slipped out into the cold evening wind. White clouds swirled in the sky with a strange sort of heaviness. Hunching her shoulders against their ominous weight, Tamri tucked the note into her pocket and headed for the nearest bridge.

29

It grew colder as Tamri hurried through the fading light. She jogged across the bridge to stave off the chill, no longer wheezing and struggling as she used to. On Square Peak, she paused to ask for directions to the Roost, eventually ending up on a quiet path that meandered between sloping goat paddocks and rows of houses built into the mountainside.

Children ran among the humble dwellings, bundled up tight against the cold. Tamri passed two girls tossing sticks for a cur-dragon. The smaller of the pair flung her arms around the cur-dragon's neck and pressed her face against its copper-bright scales. The children's mother appeared in a nearby doorway to call them in for supper, revealing a glimpse of a cozy hearth and a rocking chair behind her.

Tamri pulled her cloak tighter around her shoulders and continued on.

The Roost was on the opposite side of the flat-topped mountain from the bridges, and it was dark by the time Tamri drew near. She'd spent plenty of time on Square Peak at the Watermight Whirlpool, but she had never ventured this far beyond it.

She heard the dragons long before the Roost came into view. The rustling of wings and the clatter of talons on stone filled the evening air along with squawks and shrieks and the occasional roar. The houses were few and far between here, leaving the dragons free to make as much of a ruckus as they desired.

Following the thunderous music, Tamri rounded a bend in the path and got her first look at the Roost. A quarry that once supplied stone for the greathouses on King's Peak, the mountainside was stripped away in levels, and wooden shelters like open-air stables now perched atop them. The dragons could curl up inside these nests and shelter from the wind, but they were always free to roam throughout Vertigon as they pleased.

On one level, a row of huts provided living space for the dragon riders and caretakers who preferred to live among their charges. Lights glowing in the windows made the huts look like cozy little lanterns in the darkness. Tamri felt homesick for the ramshackle stilt house she had shared with Gramma Teall, which was about the same size. She had been imagining grander quarters for the dragon riders of Vertigon.

Tamri crept along a narrow cliff-top path toward the row of huts, wishing she'd thought to bring an Everlight to hold back the dark. She touched the note for Khrillin in her pocket, feeling like a trespasser. A thief. She'd hand the letter to the first dragon rider she saw and be gone as soon as possible.

Suddenly, a loud squawk split the night, and a scarlet shape plummeted out of the sky. A familiar dragon landed with a thump directly in front of Tamri, blocking her access to the huts. It was Rook, her old nemesis.

The dragon chattered angrily at her and flapped his wings so hard red feathers showered the path.

"I just need to deliver a message," Tamri said. "I'm not trying to hurt anyone."

The dragon snorted disbelievingly, shifting so his bulk completely obstructed her way.

"Look, I'm sorry I scared you back in Pendark," Tamri hissed. "I never meant to hurt anyone. I'm just trying to take care of—"

The dragon roared at her, forcing her back a step.

"I know, okay!" she shouted, her frayed nerves unraveling. "You don't trust me, and you shouldn't. But I have something I need to do." She picked up a rock and threw it at the dragon, missing deliberately. "Get out of my way!"

She picked up another rock just as the door of the nearest hut opened, and Heath emerged, Fire cudgel raised.

He stopped when he saw Tamri. "Oh, it's you. No wonder Rook is upset." Heath noticed the rock in her hand and raised an eyebrow.

Tamri quickly dropped it back onto the path. "I was only trying to startle him."

Rook snarled at her and scraped his claws on the path, feathers ruffling aggressively.

"Calm down, Rook. She's not as scary as she looks." Heath stuck his cudgel in his belt and advanced toward the dragon, hands outstretched. "That's it. You're okay."

He patted the creature's heaving sides, coming close enough that Rook could have easily taken his head off in a single bite. But Heath's soothing voice and steady hand were enough to calm the red dragon. When it stopped snarling, Heath took something from his pocket and dropped it onto the dragon's tongue. Rook chomped petulantly for a moment. Then, with a final glare at Tamri, he took flight and soared off to the other side of the Roost.

"What did you give him?" Tamri asked as Heath turned back to face her.

"Honey cakes. I always keep a few in my pocket for good behavior."

"I didn't know dragons like sweets."

Heath grinned. "Doesn't everyone?"

He'd rushed outside without his coat, and the top of his white shirt was undone, the laces hanging loose on his broad chest. He seemed at ease here, not at all stern.

Heath is a very handsome man. Tamri wasn't sure she'd ever acknowledged how attractive he was before. The thought staggered her, and for a moment, she forgot why she'd come to the Roost in the first place.

"I didn't expect to see you here," Heath said when she didn't speak. "What do you need?"

"Oh, uh. I just had to add something to my letter." She fumbled in her pocket, shivering from the cold—and maybe a little bit from nerves. "I wanted to catch you before you left."

"More letters? Your grandmother must love hearing from you so often."

Tamri shrugged, abandoning the explanation she'd come up with on her way here. She didn't want to lie to Heath. She'd just as soon say nothing at all.

As she withdrew the letter, a crystal of ice descended from the clouds and drifted to the ground between them. Then another, feather-white and twirling in the cold breeze. Tamri and Heath watched its meandering flight until it too alighted on the path.

Tamri drew in a breath, and all over the Roost, the dragons paused. Silence wrapped around them. Stillness. Waiting. She turned her face to the clouds.

Then the snow began to fall in earnest over Vertigon. The icy flakes dusted the path, clung to Tamri's eyelashes, and glistened on Heath's bronze hair. Wonder filled her. She had never seen snow before. She had never imagined it would dance through the air like that, light and ethereal, its touch on her skin as delicate as it was cold.

Heath cleared his throat, and she realized he was watching her not the snowfall. "Happy First Snow, Tamri."

"Thank you!" She grinned at him, feeling suddenly radiant. "I mean, Happy First Snow. This is my first ever."

"Would you like to come inside?" He gestured to the little glowing hut. "It's traditional to toast the snow's arrival, and it's cold out here."

Tamri remembered Heath wasn't wearing a coat. His lips looked a little blue through the dusting of snow.

"Okay. I'd like that."

She followed him to the hut, and he held the door open for her. Inside the single room was a bed piled with quilts, a thick sheepskin rug, and a large Heatstone. A single Fire Lantern hung from the arched ceiling, casting patterned light over the room.

"I know it's not much," Heath said. "I have a barrel of good cider here. Let me heat some up for a proper First Snow toast. Please make yourself comfortable."

"Thank you." Tamri circled the cozy room, poking through Heath's possessions. He didn't have many, evidence of all the time he spent in the air. A trunk sprawled open in the corner, with a travel pack beside it. A stack of maps rested on a wooden chair pulled close to the Heatstone, as if Heath had been studying them when he heard the commotion outside. "I've never heard of a lord living so simply."

"My father is a lord, but I chose a different path a long time ago."

"Why?"

"I wanted to do something meaningful with my life." Heath kept his attention on the cider, pouring it from a small cask into two tin cups and resting them on the Heatstone to warm them. "Lords spend their time going over accounts, directing servants, and making business decisions. They also have to manage relationships with other nobles and watch out for people maneuvering against them. I'm ... not that great with people."

"You?" Tamri chuckled, and he grinned ruefully at her. She went to the leaded glass window to look outside. The snow was falling faster, obscuring the view of the Roost. The smell of apple cider began to permeate the room, which was beginning to feel like a warm little oven in the middle of the snowstorm.

"What about your family?" she asked. "Do they mind that you live out here with the dragons instead of near them?"

"My parents live separately," Heath said. "They're busy with their own affairs. They would prefer me to use my title, but they can't force me to abandon my occupation. The dragons are my calling."

Tamri frowned at the word, which he used with such simple confidence. His calling. She supposed taking care of Gramma Teall was her calling. She had never thought much beyond that. It had been months since she last poured tea for Gramma Teall or sat on the wood floor beside her rocking chair, but she motivated every action Tamri took, no matter how painful, and every risk.

Heath joined her by the window and handed her a steaming mug of cider, which warmed her fingers instantly.

"Happy First Snow."

"Cheers."

They clinked the tin cups, steam mingling between them, and drank the hot cider together. It was sweet and laced with cinnamon. Tamri had never tasted anything so delicious.

She took another sip, her eyes meeting Heath's over their cups.

"Why did you come here tonight, Tamri?" he said quietly. "Is your note that important?"

He took a step closer, a different question in the way he leaned toward her. The air seemed to go out of the room as Tamri realized how her presence must look to him. She had crossed the Fissure on the coldest night of the year to see him before he left the mountain. He must think she wanted to see *him* specifically, the letter in her pocket just an excuse.

Heath's face was inches from hers, his expression expectant, even hopeful. But she didn't answer his question. Couldn't answer it.

Of course, he would interpret her visit this way. There *was* something between them, still as small and new as a snowflake, a delicate thread spun with genuine care and mutual respect and maybe more. Lady Vine had seen it when she warned Tamri not to break his heart, and Tamri felt it in the quickening of her pulse when he said her name, in the urge to touch him, despite a lifetime of caution, to feel his steady hands on hers, to tell him every last one of her secrets.

She could tell him honestly that she'd wanted to see him before he left.

It would make the perfect cover for sending her note.

But Tamri recoiled at the thought of using this delicate connection between them to get away with Khrillin's dirty business. She wouldn't tell Heath she wanted nothing more than to spend this First Snow evening with him, however true it might be. She refused to use his feelings to enable her betrayal.

She gulped down the rest of her cider, wincing as it scalded her throat.

"I just wanted to send this letter." She pulled it out and stuck it in the travel pack by Heath's trunk, trying to ignore the hurt and surprise on his face. "Thanks for the cider."

"Tamri—"

"Fly safe."

And she dashed out into the snowstorm before he could ask her to stay.

30

Tamri awoke in the middle of the night to the sound of footsteps outside her room. She listened to the stealthy movements, wondering if her classmates were sneaking around for a private tryst.

She had returned to the greathouse late, after her friends were already in their beds. Teeth chattering, she burrowed under blankets with her little Heatstones jabbing her from all sides. It had taken ages to fall asleep. Heath's face loomed before her, wearing that look of hurt surprise, and it was still there when she jolted awake in the darkness.

The footsteps were getting closer. Tamri rolled over to face the door. Whoever was out there paused in the hallway right outside. Kay was snoring loudly in the bunk above her. A quick glance indicated Lacy and Shylla were still in their beds. So if they weren't sneaking back in, who—

The door burst open, and Fire shot across the room and wrapped around Tamri's wrists and ankles faster than any whip she'd ever seen. She cried out in surprise, jerking frantically at the bonds. The Fire held her as firmly as if it were iron.

The Fire Queen herself stood in the doorway, her golden hair loose and glowing around her shoulders. With a brief tug on the fiery cords, she pulled Tamri out of bed, sending Heatstones clattering to the floorboards.

"Let me go!" Tamri struggled harder, trying to twist her hands out of the fiery shackles. Fireworkers were supposed to be able to absorb bonds like these. She sucked one of the shimmering cords into her skin, whimpering at the blistering heat.

"Stop doing that," Dara said, lashing another Fire shackle in its place. "I know it hurts."

"What's going on?" Kay had a dueling sword in hand, no doubt snatched up before she saw who'd entered. The other girls were staring in shock, their blankets pulled up to their chins.

"Queen Dara?"

"I need to speak with Tamri," Dara said. "Stay here, please."

Kay stared at Tamri with wide eyes, but of course she wouldn't raise a hand against the queen. Tamri would find no help from her friends.

"Let's go downstairs," Dara said, using the Fire cords to set Tamri on her feet. "I'll allow you to walk on your own if you release the Fire you're holding."

Tamri had no choice but to obey. She relinquished the Fire she'd pulled from the shackle, shuddering as the heat left her skin. Dara loosened the shackles so they encircled Tamri's limbs without actually touching her and led the way out of the room.

Tamri's thoughts raced as she followed the queen down the stairs. She didn't know exactly what was happening yet. If she was going to get out of this alive, she had to remain calm and think through every action, every word, every glance. It was time to prove she had learned from her mistakes.

In the front parlor on the ground floor, Master Corren, Madame Mirri, and Lady Vine Silltine were sitting around the low table. Heath stood by the front window, his arms folded tightly over his chest, his uniform coat buttoned up to his throat. King Siv was pacing back and forth across the room. He stopped short when Dara and Tamri entered.

"Did she try to fight you?"

"She struggled but nothing I couldn't handle," Dara said. "And she wasn't keeping any magical substances up there except for a bunch of Heatstones."

"Good." The king put his hands on his hips. "You have a lot of explaining to do, my friend."

Tamri gulped as all the Vertigonians turned to look at her. She scanned the room for an escape. This felt too much like when she'd been dragged before Khrillin. But there was no Watermight in the vicinity this time, and her measly skills with the Fire wouldn't save her.

She looked at Heath, daring to hope for sympathy or at least a hint of understanding in his eyes. But he jerked his gaze away to stare out the window at the falling snow, his bearing as stiff as she'd ever seen it. Tamri's heart sank.

"Perhaps it's best if I start," Lady Vine said when Tamri didn't speak. "I suspected King Khrillin was receiving information on us from a new source." She tapped the low table, where papers were spread out before her. Familiar papers, covered in Tamri's handwriting.

Uh-oh. No amount of calm thought would save her from such damning evidence.

"I've had an eye on young Tamri for a while," Vine went on. "Earlier this evening, directly after we received a troubling message involving our Soolen allies—some of Khrillin's least favorite people, I might add—Tamri snuck out of the school. My informant followed her to the Roost, where she delivered a letter to Heath to carry back to Pendark."

"Heath didn't know what was in it," Tamri said quickly. "He wasn't betraying—"

King Siv held up a hand. "No one is suggesting Heath is a turncoat."

"Goodness, no," Lady Vine said. "After you left tonight, I paid Lord Samanar a visit and explained my suspicions. I persuaded him to allow me a glimpse of your recent batch of letters home."

She rose from the couch and glided closer to Tamri. She wore those long, flowing trousers, and her hair was still elegantly arranged despite the late hour. Her expression was curious rather than angry.

"I must say, you are quite clever at hiding useful information in what would look like a genuine update to your grandmother at a glance. You have the knack. Does Gramma Teall even exist?"

"Of course she does," Tamri snarled. "I wouldn't be doing any of this if not for her."

Heath looked at her sharply, and she wished she'd kept her mouth shut.

"I'd like to hear more about your arrangement with Khrillin," King Siv said. "The fellow is about as trustworthy as a povvercat in a pigeon coop, but I didn't think he'd spy on my wife. Has our alliance failed at last?"

Tamri didn't answer.

"You owe us an explanation." King Siv looked at her solemnly. "The game is up, anyway. You may as well tell us what you know."

Tamri wanted nothing more than to tell the truth, to confess her crimes and throw herself on the mercy of the Vertigonians. But the Watermight bond would choke her to death before she got three words out if she tried. Even considering it made the cold awaken in her neck.

She remained silent.

The quick patter of feet sounded in the hall. Madame Mirri left the parlor to return whoever was trying to listen to their beds.

"We have irrefutable proof of your guilt," Lady Vine said, waving at the letters. "In case you think we're bluffing."

"I advise you to explain yourself, young lady," Master Corren said. "You may not have another chance for clemency."

Tamri shrank under their accusing gazes, feeling as hopeless as she had in Khrillin's audience chamber. This time there was no princess to speak up for her. Even the king's good humor faded away as she maintained her silence. He had excused her efforts to swipe the Savven blade as a harmless prank, but he wouldn't vouch for her again.

Queen Dara's quiet disapproval was the worst of all. Tamri had come so close to proving herself to the Fire Queen, so close to winning her respect. Even now, she was giving her ample opportunity to do the right thing. But it was no use.

At last, Dara sighed. "I'm disappointed, Tamri. You could have become a great Wielder."

Tamri was ashamed to feel tears welling up. She kept her head down, refusing to let them see. If she had to be a villain in the eyes of people she had come to like and respect, at least she wouldn't be a weak one. She didn't look up until her eyes were dry.

"What would you like us to do with the little urchin, Your Majesties?" Master Corren asked.

King Siv looked at his wife. "She may still give us information with the right persuasion."

Tamri thought of Khrillin's thug Brik and the kind of "persuasion" methods he would use. She shivered, pulling in on herself as if she could shrink to the size of a mouse and slip away.

"We need to know what Khrillin is up to, but we can't delay our departure," Dara said. "Sel is in danger." She stepped forward, and Tamri could see her strong profile and the golden hair cascading down her back. "We'll have to take her with us to Soole."

Tamri blinked in surprise. Soole? She and Heath exchanged baffled glances, though he quickly looked away when he realized what he was doing.

"Are you sure that's wise?" Master Corren said. "The castle dungeon might be a better place for her."

"Tamri has lived on the mountain and worked closely with us for months," Dara said. "We can't let her out of our sight just yet, and we don't have time to waste on an interrogation."

"Very well," Siv said. "Maybe she'll talk on the way."

"Maybe she will."

Tamri wasn't sure what to feel about this development. She had wanted to be selected for the trip to Soole but not like this. No matter what she learned along the way, there was little chance she could ever send it to Khrillin. She only hoped he wouldn't put Gramma Teall out in the gutter when he stopped receiving her reports.

Despair began to fill her as the implications of what had happened hit her. She'd been caught. She'd failed. She would never buy that cottage by the sea or see Gramma Teall again. She slumped, not caring when the Fire shackles seared her wrists.

King Siv turned to his chief dragon rider, all business now. "Heath, we need to get to Soole as quickly as possible. How many dragons can you muster at short notice?"

"Seventeen," Heath said promptly. "The journey should take two weeks if they each carry no more than two riders. Will that be enough?"

"I hope so." King Siv brushed a hand through his hair. "I'm not entirely sure what kind of trouble we'll find."

"We'll try to reach Sel with another Air channel on our way," Dara said. "Vine, would you like to come with us?"

"You think I'd let you have all that fun without me?" Lady Vine smoothed her hair and smiled airily at them. "Besides, Queen Rochelle is rather fond of me. I may be able to help preserve our alliance if it's truly in peril."

Siv grimaced. "Let's hope Latch hasn't made that impossible."

As the others discussed their preparations, Dara looked down at Tamri. "I suggest you don't try to escape. Heath told me you've been lying about how much the Fire hurts you. Don't think I won't use it against you if you try to sabotage this expedition."

Tamri suppressed a scowl. She had no right to be mad at Heath for giving up her secrets. "I understand."

She didn't bother saying she had no desire to sabotage any of them. The Fire Queen wouldn't believe a word Tamri said now.

"Let's get your things," Dara said. "We fly at dawn."

31

The Fire Queen chose a handful of the older students to bring on the journey to Soole, though they were departing months earlier than planned. Kay, Dentry, and Pevin were deemed advanced enough to make the trip. Tamri wondered if they were really coming along for extra training or if so few Fireworkers remained in Vertigon that the Fire Queen needed the young Wielders to assist with whatever trouble awaited them.

They left Shylla behind, probably because she was Pendarkan and they couldn't risk her siding with Tamri. Shylla directed a truly acrid look at Tamri as she left the greathouse with the others. If they ever saw each other again, it wouldn't be a pleasant encounter.

They departed King's Peak as the sun was rising and soared into the Fissure while it was still mostly in shadow. The snow had continued throughout the night, coating buildings, trees, and bridges in a layer of fine white powder. As the sun rose higher, the snow glistened like diamonds, forcing Tamri to shade her eyes from Vertigon's brilliance.

She was sorry to leave the mountain behind. Despite the pressure she'd been under and the difficulties with her training, she liked Vertigon, with its dramatic heights, crisp air, and glittering magic. She only wished she could leave on better terms.

Tamri rode with the Fire Queen on a dragon she hadn't met before, with dark-gold scales and golden feathers tipped in black.

Laini had given her a slightly wounded look when Dentry and Pevin climbed onto her back instead of Tamri. It wasn't all that different from the wounded looks she received from Dentry and Pevin, who were taking her duplicity personally.

Kay appeared to be reserving judgment. She studied Tamri with a focus that was eerily similar to Dara's. Perhaps she'd picked up on hints about her background in their months sharing a bunk. Kay was assigned to ride with Taklin, who looked too delighted with the arrangement to mind Tamri's status as prisoner and spy.

In addition to the students and Heath's dragon riders, their party included a dozen Castle Guards and four additional Fireworkers, two of whom Tamri had met when they gave workshops at the Wielder School and two who were only a few years older than the students. They had been apprentices during the war that decimated the Fireworker population. Barrels full of raw Fire were strapped to the dragons' backs so all these Fireworkers would have something to Wield if necessary.

Dara charged Kay, Dentry, and Pevin with watching Tamri whenever they made camp. They were not supposed to speak to her, though they came near to bursting with curiosity over what she'd done, especially when they had to shackle her wrists to her ankles with an iron chain each night. But before long, everyone was too tired to be overly inquisitive. Heath set a brisk pace, as if determined to reach Soole in record time. They only slept for six or seven hours per night and spent all day in the bitterly cold air.

Heath resumed his sternest bearing, reminding Tamri of the early days of their acquaintance when she thought he hated her. She finally understood it hadn't been hatred then. Mistrust, maybe. Protectiveness over Princess Selivia. A little awkwardness. But *now* he hated Tamri for real.

The others walked lightly around him, not certain what had made him so terse. Tamri overheard Reya and Errol speculating while they cracked the ice on a frozen pond to collect drinking water.

"I reckon he's worried about Princess Sel," Reya said.

"I thought he was over her," Errol said.

"Doesn't mean he isn't worried." Reya used a tin cup to scoop icy water into a bucket. "They're still friends. And only a girl could make him push the dragons like this. He's normally so careful with them."

"Maybe," Errol said. "I don't think it's the princess that has his knickers in a knot is all."

Tamri wanted to talk to Heath directly, to try to explain, but opportunities proved elusive. He wasn't one of those taking shifts as her guard, and he appeared to be avoiding her deliberately.

Then, on the morning of their third day of travel, Tamri was sitting in the dirt beside Laini, who insisted on sleeping beside her despite her jangling chains, when Heath approached to check the dragon's harness. He didn't look at Tamri as he adjusted the leather strap—the opposite of encouraging—but this might be her only chance to talk to him where no one but Laini could hear.

"Heath?"

He didn't answer. Laini nudged him pointedly, urging him to listen.

"I didn't mean for any of this to happen," Tamri said. "Can we talk?"

"Did you only come to the Roost to deliver that letter?"

Tamri grimaced. "Well, yes, but—"

"Then I don't see what we have to talk about," he said brusquely. "I misinterpreted. That's on me."

Tamri wished she truly had been there to visit him. "If you'd give me a chance to expl—"

"I gave you a chance." He still didn't look at her, but his voice betrayed a hint of emotion. "That day in the castle. I gave you an opportunity to walk away, and you didn't take it."

Tamri winced. "I know."

"My loyalties haven't changed. Unless yours have, there's no point in discussing it further." Heath patted the sea-green dragon, whose shoulders were hunched as if she could sense their mutual misery. "You're all set, Laini. Be careful of the ice when you take off."

He started to walk over to where Boru was waiting for him.

"Heath, wait."

He paused, apparently listening, though his face was turned away. Tamri didn't know what to say. Nothing would make this better. She couldn't reveal the oath bond any more now than she'd been able to that first day, and Heath served a different king from the one holding her leash. But he had offered mercy once. Maybe he would again.

"Will you at least look at me?" She drew in a breath of freezing winter air. "Please?"

Heath stood still for a long time. Tamri didn't interrupt his thoughts or push him any further, sensing his conflict. If she could just get him to undo her shackles, she could handle the rest.

Finally, he turned around and met her eyes directly for the first time in days. "I can't help you, Tamri." He spoke so quietly she almost couldn't hear him over the rustling of Laini's feathers. "Please don't ask me to betray them, if you care for me at all."

Tamri stared back at him, the rawness of the request cutting straight through her. That was when she understood. Heath *would* help her if she asked. But it would require ripping apart everything he'd worked to achieve, everything he was.

She couldn't do that to him. She wouldn't. And that was when she realized how deep her care for him went.

"I'll never ask that of you."

Heath's shoulders slumped. "Thank you."

Laini gave a sorrowful grumble as he walked away.

The weather warmed a little as they flew south, the winter-brown lands passing quickly beneath them. They angled to the southwest over the vast Truren plains, crossing a different part of the country than Tamri had seen on the trip from Pendark. There were few landmarks and fewer people, and they rarely saw anything more populated than a country trading outpost.

Tamri rode with different people each day, and the Vertigonians took pains to separate her from any conversations that might include useful or dangerous information. Queen Dara and Lady Vine both questioned her when they had time, but the oath bond prevented her from explaining why she couldn't answer their questions. Silence was the easiest option.

She hadn't appreciated how much she enjoyed her friendships with her classmates until they weren't allowed to speak to her. With nothing but her own thoughts and her former friends' mournful looks keeping her company, she drew in on herself, traveling in a lonely little bubble. She watched for opportunities to escape, fearing it was only a matter of time before Khrillin learned she had failed and took it out on Gramma Teall. But her guards remained vigilant.

On the eighth day, they reached the Linden Mountains, which were lower here than by Kurn Pass and Fork Town. They flew between the lumpy peaks and descended toward the infamous Fort Brach. The home of Lord Latch and his family was an imposing structure of iron-gray stone with a large town sprawling beneath it, cut through with a wide river. Tamri remembered what Princess Selivia had told her in that Fork Town dress shop. Khrillin had captured this fort once, and King Siv convinced him to give it up. Fort Brach looked like an impressive prize. No wonder Khrillin held such a grudge.

After spending the night in Fort Brach, they followed the Granite River through a sparse wilderness scattered with mines to a village called Mirror Wells. There, the Cindral dragons filled up on Watermight from a closely guarded vent located in a large crater. This Watermight source belonged to the Brachs themselves.

Tamri worked up the nerve to ask Queen Dara about the vent as they flew away from Mirror Wells. The queen insisted she ride with her on the golden dragon now that they'd loaded up on Watermight, knowing Tamri could break her shackles if she got even a spoonful of her native power into her system.

"Why do you buy Watermight from Pendark if the Brachs have a source?"

Dara glanced over her shoulder. "We have a close link with the Brachs because of Latch and Selivia's engagement. We needed something else to foster our friendship with King Khrillin." She paused. "That has been delicate at times, as I'm sure you can appreciate."

"Khrillin can be touchy."

"How long did you work for him before he sent you to Vertigon?"

"I didn't." This simple truth shouldn't violate her oath. "I'd sold Watermight to him, but I wasn't one of his lackeys."

"So why did you take this job?"

Tamri shrugged, lapsing into silence once more.

"We'll have to confront him about you eventually," Dara said. "You might as well answer our questions. We don't want trouble with

Pendark any more than Khrillin does. I am hoping we can still mend our relationship."

Tamri wasn't so sure Khrillin wanted that. But she said nothing.

"We might be able to work out some kind of penance if you cooperate with us." Dara twisted to look at her, golden braid swinging. "I hate losing such a promising student. Wouldn't you like to continue at the school?"

Tamri felt a pulse of longing in her chest. She hadn't yet become the powerful Wielder she wanted to be. She'd progressed enough in Vertigon to give her an edge over the gutter kids—even Pel might be impressed—but there was so much more to learn. Unfortunately, the Fire Queen's offer changed nothing about her circumstances.

Tamri kept silent, and Dara turned her face back into the wind.

They crossed Soole by the most direct path over the desolate red desert, without approaching the capital city of Sharoth. The Vertigonians' relationship with the Soolen queen was tempestuous at times, and they couldn't afford any delays. But they couldn't hide the flight of seventeen Cindral dragons, either. Lady Vine separated from the main group and headed to Sharoth to smooth things over with Queen Rochelle in the meantime.

They reached the sea as the setting sun turned the water to gold and camped on a sandy plateau overlooking the waves. The smell of salty air made Tamri think of Gramma Teall and the cottage she'd hoped to buy her before she got mixed up with kings and queens and dragons. As she went to sleep, shackled to a rock formation with the sea roaring in her ears, she wondered if she had any chance at all of salvaging that dream.

The following morning, she awoke to the sound of agitated dragons. They tossed their heads and clawed at the sand, uttering cries of distress. Heath and the other dragon riders rushed to calm them, while the soldiers searched for what had upset the creatures. Still chained up with no way to defend herself, Tamri grabbed a handful of reddish sand to throw in an attacker's eyes if the worst happened.

A vast shadow passed over their camp. Tamri looked up as a dragon turned in a wide circle overhead, a sharp black crow against

the cloudless winter sky. It was bigger than the Cindral dragons—
and getting nearer. The morning sunlight shone through the
leathery membranes of its huge black wings and reflected off its
dark-green scales. It had no feathers.

"Is that—?"

"Mav!" The Fire Queen climbed onto another rock formation
and waved her arms over her head. "It's Mav."

"Is Sel with him?" King Siv called out.

"I can't tell."

The huge true dragon swooped downward and landed in a puff
of red dust on the plateau. He lashed his tail back and forth, the
thick knot of scales at the end powerful enough to crush a man's
head. He had no rider.

The Cindral dragons, who looked juvenile in comparison, ruffled
their wings and snapped their jaws nervously. Heath walked from
dragon to dragon, soothing them with steady words and honey cakes
from his pockets. Only Boru remained calmly dignified at the arrival
of his larger cousin.

Dara approached Mav and put her hand on his snout, leaning
close to look in his glittering cobalt eye.

"She's speaking to him," Kay said, coming over to sit in the dirt
beside Tamri. Everyone else was too distracted by Mav's arrival to
mind.

"I can see that."

"He speaks back. Some Wielders can communicate with dragons
in words. We're supposed to learn it at school. I guess you'll miss
that." Kay shifted uncomfortably, eyeing Tamri sideways. "Do you
wish you could take it back? Being a spy, I mean?"

Tamri sighed. "All the time."

"So why don't you?" Kay said. "Come over to our side. Tell the
king and queen what they need to know and keep studying with us.
You could be a great Wielder, and I don't think you're evil."

Tamri studied the other girl, who viewed Siv and Dara as *her*
king and queen, even though she'd never been to Vertigon before
the school opened. "Your father is Vertigonian, right? And you're
from Trure, which has a half-Vertigonian queen. Would you turn on
either country to help Pendark just because you liked your classmates and teachers there?"

"I guess not." Kay began scraping patterns in the sand with her finger. "But you don't seem all that loyal to Pendark. Shylla talks about it way more." Kay frowned. "Or were you just hiding it?"

Tamri rubbed a cold spot on her neck, wishing she could tell her former friend the truth of how conflicted she felt about Pendark. Her only true loyalty was to Gramma Teall. "It's not that simple."

Dara was still conversing quietly with the true dragon. She called her husband over to hear what Mav had to report.

"She looks worried," Kay said. "Do you think the princess is all right?"

"I hope so."

The king and queen talked with Mav's great wing sheltering them from view. When they finally emerged to address the others, their faces were grave.

"Mav tells us Princess Selivia is still on Thunderbird Island," King Siv explained, "but there's some kind of presence there that he refuses to go near."

The others stirred.

"What do you mean by a presence?" Heath asked.

"He says it's ancient," Dara said. "Something powerful and territorial. He says it has claimed the island, and he won't challenge it unless he absolutely must."

Heath looked more serious than ever. "He really won't go any closer? Even though the princess is there?"

"He expected her to leave Thunderbird Island on her own," Dara said. "As far as I understand it, he didn't think this 'presence' would pay her any attention, whereas he would be seen as a direct threat."

"He has been staying on a nearby island for the past few months," Siv said, glancing up at the dragon sitting on his haunches, wings folded tight to his sides. "But if she doesn't leave the island soon, he fears a confrontation may be necessary after all."

Tamri exchanged worried glances with Kay. What could be powerful enough to make a true dragon wary of provoking it?

Taklin raised his hand. "Sire, does this mean our Cindral dragons won't go to the island, either?"

"Possibly." Siv looked at Heath. "Any thoughts?"

Heath frowned, studying Mav and then the flock of smaller Cindral dragons. "Let's say you have a dog guarding an enclosure," he said after a moment. "If another dog tries to enter his territory, he'll fight it. A morrinvole, on the other hand, might be able to come and go as it pleases. The guard dog might not even notice a mouse, which would be as harmless to it as the princess is to a true dragon. The question is whether the Cindral dragons are morrinvoles or dogs to this . . . presence."

"If they refuse to take us the whole way, we'll find ourselves a boat," Siv said. "I won't leave my sister to this mystery guard dog."

Mav shuffled his wings, and the Fire Queen placed a hand on his snout to listen again.

"He says he felt the presence in the storm. If it doesn't want the Cindral dragons there, they'll know." She paused. "He also says he'll go to the island if that's what it takes to help Sel, but he doesn't know enough about this presence to be able to promise victory."

"Let's hope we won't need to test him on that," Siv said grimly.

The king and queen conferred quietly with Mav for a moment more, and Kay leaned over to whisper to Tamri. "Mav challenged another true dragon for control of Vertigon during the war. This thing must be ridiculously powerful if he's not sure he can beat it."

"Think it's another dragon?"

Kay frowned, chewing on her lip. "Wouldn't he just say so, then? Hard to imagine Mav not being at the top of the dragon food chain."

"Maybe it's something to do with the magical substances," Tamri said. "Remember Lady Vine saying some people think the Air is conscious?"

"I guess so," Kay said. "Those types can be a bit mad, though."

Tamri could certainly see that. But Lord Latch had gone to the island to study a magical substance. Perhaps it had its own ideas about who could come near its source.

The king and queen finished their discussion and turned back to address the group.

"We have decided to attempt to fly to Thunderbird Island," the king announced. "If anyone wishes to turn back, now is the time. You may not be able to once we reach the island."

Dara's eyes shone with intensity as she looked at their party one by one. "We will not force anyone to join us on this mission."

Heath straightened, a hand on the Fire cudgel at his belt. "Even if the dragons won't go all the way, we will continue on with you."

279

The other dragon riders rushed to agree with their leader.

"Sounds like the princess needs all the help we can give her," Taklin said.

The Castle Guards and Fireworkers also pledged to carry on, with or without the dragons.

Dara turned to the students, including Tamri in her piercing gaze. "We are facing unknown danger, but I respect that you are no longer children. You've worked hard over the past few years, and I may call on you to use your abilities if you feel ready."

"I'm ready, Queen Dara," Dentry said.

"We want to help the princess," Pevin said.

"She faced more danger at a younger age," Kay said. "We can do it."

Tamri added her silent agreement to the chorus. She wanted to find out what Princess Sel and Lord Latch had discovered on Thunderbird Island. If this thing, this presence, was powerful enough to scare Mav, knowledge of it would be priceless. She might have a chance to buy her freedom from the oath bond yet.

"Good," Dara said. "Prepare for departure. I want to see what Thunderbird Island is hiding."

32

Selivia watched Latch from the study alcove. He sat at the edge of the Lightning chasm, staring into its depths. He almost seemed to float on the crackling energy emanating from the chasm. His once-tidy clothes were stained, and she could smell his sweat from twenty feet away.

She hoisted a heavy pack full of old manuscripts onto her shoulder and ventured a few steps closer. "Latch. Can you hear me?"

He didn't respond, as Selivia had known he wouldn't. It had been four days since he'd last spoken to her, a week since he'd moved more than ten feet from the chasm.

They'd had a few good days after the arrival of Prince Chadrech's reinforcements. Selivia and Latch snuck out to spy on the soldiers together, used an Air channel to communicate with Vertigon, and resumed their study of the ancient writings. But the Lightning had lured Latch to the chasm once more. And this time, it wasn't letting go.

"Latch?"

She no longer dared touch him. A beam of light sometimes danced all the way around Latch, as if shielding him from outside influences. Getting too near made her hair frizz out and her mouth taste like metal. She had talked to him, though. Pleading. Raging. Negotiating. But the Lightning had him in its thrall, and she couldn't pull him free.

She also couldn't summon an Air channel without Latch, so she had no idea how far away Siv and Dara were. She couldn't wait for them any longer. Chadrech's men had tried to infiltrate the mountain thrice over the past few weeks. Each time, Latch called on the thunderbirds to defend them. And each time the birds answered his Lightning-immersed call, he was ensnared a little more tightly, until he refused to eat or sleep or leave the chasm's violent glow.

Today, Selivia was taking the only step that might still have a chance of salvaging the situation. She was going to parlay with Prince Chadrech.

Latch would object if he were still coherent enough for that, but he had long since stopped making rational decisions. He'd fought fiercely to defend his discovery, but sometimes it was better to negotiate than to fight.

"Chadrech has agreed to meet with us, Latch," Selivia said, trying one last time to draw his attention away from the chasm. "Don't you want to talk to the Crown Prince? Or maybe punch him in the nose? I know you hate each other."

Even that wasn't enough to shake Latch loose from his trance. She sighed and turned away.

"It's just us, then," she said as she joined Rosh and Melloch by the exit tunnel. Both of them also carried heavy packs full of the scrolls, notebooks, and stray bits of parchment they'd been studying over the past months. Latch's research would be saved, even if he was not.

"Do you have any final suggestions before we meet with Chadrech?" Selivia asked as she started up the tunnel with her forlorn little band. They had held on for as long as they could, but they were days away from running out of food.

"We should surrender," Melloch said, adjusting his spectacles nervously. "We had no business resisting the Crown Prince for so long."

"I'm inclined to agree," Rosh said. "But we should set some terms for what happens next. Lord Latch may react badly if Chadrech's men march in here, even if we invite them."

"I will make sure he understands what we're dealing with," Selivia said.

Chadrech was getting restless. This morning, he had sent a

messenger up the mountainside under a white flag to invite them to treat with him. Even if they hadn't been on the verge of running out of food, she might have accepted the meeting. They had walked too far down a dangerous path already. She only hoped she could convince Chadrech that Latch wasn't himself and hadn't meant to commit treason.

The weather had gotten colder since she'd last been outside. The clouds were especially gray and heavy on this winter's day, and the ominous atmosphere fit Selivia's mood nicely. She wore a thick leather jerkin—one of Latch's—and her hair was tied back to keep it from tangling in the wind. As she descended the steep path to the meeting point with Rosh and Melloch, the thunderbirds swooped overhead, singing their harsh songs.

The Crown Prince met them at the boundary of the ruined town. A dozen soldiers and a dozen Waterworkers accompanied him, all with silvery power showing at their fingernails. Chadrech gestured for all but four to stay among the ruins and strode forward to meet Selivia and her companions on the bare slope.

The prince looked gaunter than the last time she'd seen him, reminding her unpleasantly of Latch. The stay on Thunderbird Island had been rough on his normally immaculate appearance. But he greeted her with his usual leering smile.

"This stalemate has gone on long enough, don't you think, my dearest?"

"You may address me as Princess Selivia."

"Come now, my—"

"I am the sister to two monarchs," she said coldly, "and I will not be spoken to like a pet. I have come to negotiate, but I expect to be treated with the respect I am due as an envoy of a foreign nation."

Chadrech's mouth tightened, his leer vanishing. "Very well, Princess Selivia. Here is my offer: convince Lord Brach to leave this place at once. If you do not, I will attack with all my forces, which are considerable."

Selivia glanced toward the sea, where his ships bobbed in the choppy water. The misty weather made it difficult to see very far, but there had to be at least a dozen vessels out there. Each had carried scores of soldiers and Waterworkers, many of whom now occupied the old mining town.

But they hadn't attacked in force yet, which meant Chadrech was still worried about what Latch would do with the Lightning and the thunderbirds.

Selivia met his eyes without flinching. "If any harm comes to me, you will destroy Soole's alliance with the rulers of Trure and Vertigon."

"Alliance?" Chadrech scoffed. "I've seen little evidence that Vertigon values its relationship with my mother and our Crown."

Selivia adjusted the heavy pack on her back, trying to remain calm. The fates of multiple nations depended on her ability to keep the peace with Soole no matter what Latch did.

"I can assure you we value it highly. What can we do to reaffirm the peace between our nations?"

"Won't your darling Latch be joining us?" Chadrech said, ignoring her question and turning to face the mountain. The wind blew harder, whipping at their clothes and stirring the clouds above the peak. "Tell me: why has he sent you out to negotiate?"

"He trusts me to speak for him." Selivia certainly hoped that was true.

"Is that so? Or is he perhaps unable to answer because he cannot leave the Lightning's influence?"

"I—? Your Excellency?" Selivia tugged at her leather jerkin, exchanging worried glances with Rosh.

Their reactions seemed to confirm something Chadrech already suspected. He gave a knowing little smile. "So he is trapped. Fascinating."

"How did you know?" There was little point pretending he was wrong.

"I have not been idle whilst you've been hiding behind those foul birds," Chadrech said. "I sent for information about the mysterious power of Thunderbird Island. The Royal Archives retained copies of the documents Brach had in his rooms, remember? My scholars have been hard at work on them. I daresay they've uncovered some things Brach missed."

Despite herself, Selivia took an eager step forward. "Did they find out how to control the Lightning safely?"

Chadrech shook his head. "Every Wielder who has tried since the Lightning source's discovery has become ensnared in some way.

The scholars write of how the Lightning awakens the monster within—I am paraphrasing here—a monster that seduces and destroys."

Selivia remembered the fragment she had read about the "monster" or "malice" within. Rosh had favored the "malice" translation and suggested it was a metaphor for the behavior of the Wielder under the Lightning's influence. "I don't suppose your scholars found any suggestions for how to escape the power's influence or control the monstrous impulses it brings up?"

"Most insist the Lightning should be left alone." Chadrech's lips pinched into a tight line. "I'm afraid that's the conclusion I've come to as well."

Selivia blinked. "What are you saying?"

"I am not here to take over the Lightning, my dear Princess Selivia. I'm here to seal it up so its dangers cannot be unleashed on Soole."

She hadn't expected that. *Chadrech* was making a sensible suggestion?

"But what about Latch?"

"If he's trapped, it may be too late."

"I can't accept that," Selivia said. She hadn't heard from Dara and Siv in over a week, but she held out hope that they could still help him. "But you're right about the Lightning. We should leave it where it is. It's too dangerous to use."

"I'm pleased you agree."

Rosh cleared his throat. "Begging your pardon, Your Excellency, but what'll this agreement cost the princess and House Brach?"

Chadrech looked the older man over, sneering at his clothes, which were beyond grimy after months beneath the mountain. "I won't punish House Brach. I daresay you'll suffer enough at the loss of your lord. As for the princess"—Chadrech turned to Selivia —"you could marry me."

Selivia sighed. "This again?"

"I am quite serious." To her surprise, Chadrech dropped to one knee and gave a flourish that was only a shadow of his old arrogance. "Make a new alliance with me, my dear Princess Selivia, and I will promise to seal up the Lightning for the good of Soole, Trure, and Vertigon. Ours will be a romance for the ages if you but say the word."

"I don't even like you."

"Marriage alliances have nothing to do with whether the couple likes each other. You're smart enough to know that."

Selivia could have slapped him, but she forced herself to ignore his smug tone. Chadrech might be one of her least favorite people, but he was still proposing a path that would mean peace for the continent—and giving up a power that other men would grab for themselves.

"You're saying if I marry you, you'll promise not to use the Lightning at all?"

"I think that's reasonable." Chadrech didn't smile, and his expression was unusually earnest. Rain began to fall in patches, misting their faces, and dark clouds roiled overhead. The storm would reach them soon. "What do you say?"

Selivia glanced around the old mining town as she considered the offer. Some of the ruins had been repaired, alleviating the feeling of abandon that had lain thick over Thunderbird Island when she first arrived. The rain fell harder, dripping down the back of her neck.

Her role as a princess of Vertigon was about more than befriending dragons and wearing pretty dresses. She had a solemn duty that had required sacrifices before and likely would again. Her arranged marriage to Latch had helped to end a war, and it had been pure luck that she got along well with him.

She studied Chadrech's gaunt face and his straw-man limbs. Maybe *this* was the true sacrifice required of her. No part of her believed she could come to love Chadrech as she loved Latch.

I do love him. She hadn't realized it before now. She had resented giving up her life in the sky and abandoning everything she'd built over the past five years. And it hadn't been the storybook romance she'd imagined. But she cared for Latch. He was as passionate about his studies as she was about her dragons. He was courteous and thoughtful, and he valued her advice as much as he seemed to enjoy her company. They had faced deadly magic and vicious creatures together, but it was only now, as he was slipping away, that she knew her true feelings.

Chadrech wiped raindrops out of his eyes, remaining on his knees as he waited for her answer. If she refused him and Latch perished, the alliance with Soole would fail. And despite his words, he might still seize the magical substance in that chasm. But if Selivia remained at his side, she could prevent *his* inner malice from being unleashed on the continent. She couldn't forsake her duty. It might be too late for Latch, but it didn't have to be too late for the rest of them.

As Selivia opened her mouth to answer Chadrech's proposal, thunder boomed, shaking the island. She glanced up at the seething clouds, and a colorful flicker caught her eye.

Something was moving in the stormy sky. Several large, living somethings. The creatures were much too big and colorful to be thunderbirds. She saw a flash of white and jewel blue. Scarlet. Sea green. Gold.

Selivia gasped as she realized what those colors meant. A group of Cindral dragons was struggling through the storm, heading toward the island.

"Our betrothal will have to wait, Your Excellency," Selivia said to Chadrech. "We might still have a chance to save Latch!"

33

The weather became increasingly unsettled as Tamri and the others flew over the East Isles archipelago. They camped on the barren islands at night and struggled through the clouds during the day, the wind whipping ominously at feathers and hair. The Cindral dragons grew more tentative with each mile, as if sensing a worse storm ahead. Each morning it took longer to coax them into the air. They were all waiting for the moment when the Cindral dragons, like Mav, refused to go any farther.

On the thirteenth day after their departure from Vertigon, the misty heights of Thunderbird Island appeared in the distance. It looked like a great gray ship rising out of the sea. So that was it. The home of a new magical substance and a territorial presence strong enough to worry a true dragon.

Tamri was riding Laini with Pevin. Queen Dara hadn't wanted the burden of a prisoner when they reached their destination. She had double-checked Tamri's shackles and then entrusted her to the rail-thin boy and the sea-green dragon.

The iron shackles felt cold around Tamri's wrists and ankles, but the wind drowned out the jingle of metal on metal as they got closer to the source of all this trouble. Tamri's heart beat in time with Laini's wings, and she sensed tension in the dragon's powerful shoulders. Pevin was perched behind her with a white-knuckle grip on the safety harness. The air crackled with a strange energy and smelled of salt and steel.

The wind gusted, battering them head-on, as if warning them not to come any closer. But Laini flew onward, surrounded by her dragon brethren, as Thunderbird Island drew nearer. Heath was in the lead on Boru, his Fire cudgel glowing brighter than usual in the grim weather. Mav flew beside him, having decided to risk flying a little closer this time.

For a few minutes, Tamri thought they'd all reach the shore intact. She caught a glimpse of movement, perhaps people or animals on the island. She held tight to Laini, eager to see what Thunderbird Island had in store.

But before she could make out any details about the place, the weather took a sudden violent turn.

The wind picked up speed and took on a howling, screaming quality. The Cindral dragons cried out as they were forced off course, the vicious gale muting their frightened squawks. Rain began to hammer them, flattening Tamri's hair to her face and sliding off Laini's feathers in waves.

The dragons fought to stay airborne, following Heath's glowing cudgel through the maelstrom, still carrying their Watermight burdens. The storm was trying to throw them back. The malevolent presence ruling Thunderbird Island didn't want visitors. The storm had a crackling, unnatural feeling, making Tamri feel as if she were no longer fully anchored in her own body.

She hung on with all her strength as the wind hurled Laini about. Pevin slipped and lurched behind her. She glanced back and found him stiff with fear, his lips peeled back in a rictus. He wasn't used to the dragon and the wild rush of storm and flight. Tamri tried to gesture for him to grab hold of her, but with her hands shackled she couldn't help him without losing her tenuous hold on Laini. She looked around, but no other dragons were near enough to catch Pevin if he fell.

She peered through the clouds, no longer able to see the island. They could be right above it, for all she could tell. She caught glimpses of colorful feathers and churning wings, but she couldn't tell how the other dragons were faring.

Suddenly, a gust caught Laini under the wing and spun her.

Pevin fell sideways, scrambling for the harness with his thin hands, but he couldn't grab hold of it. Tamri threw herself back and managed to catch Pevin's foot, clamping it between her elbow and side, keeping him from tumbling into the raging sea.

With her hands shackled, she couldn't get a better grip. Pevin flopped about like a rag doll in the wind, trying to regain his hold. He hollered a wordless plea for mercy, but the storm showed none. Tamri felt his foot sliding from her awkward hold.

"Laini!" she screamed. "I need Watermight, Laini. Please!"

Laini didn't hesitate. The dragon opened her mouth and released a spurt of silver liquid. Tamri seized control of the Watermight, relishing the sudden rush, and spun it into a tight cord.

In that moment, she knew she could escape. Laini trusted her. If Tamri told her to turn around and abandon this mad flight, she would comply. Tamri could drop Pevin into the sea, and no one would know it hadn't been an accident. She could go home.

But as she pulled the Watermight cord closer, Tamri pictured her friends gathered in a brightly lit pub on Eventide after they'd watched the duels together, their laughter spilling out into the cold mountain air. She'd made a home in Vertigon, too, however temporarily, and her classmates had welcomed her with open arms.

Pevin's foot slipped from her hold. Tamri reacted faster than thought, whipping the Watermight cord around his thin waist to stop his fall. She hauled him back up and bound him securely to Laini so he couldn't fall again.

Pevin gripped the silvery lifeline and shouted something that might have been thanks.

"We'll get through this," Tamri shouted back at him. She had come too far with the Vertigonians to turn back now.

She used more Watermight to shatter the shackles around her wrists and ankles, needing to be agile. She sent another trail of Watermight along the bones of Laini's wings, lending her strength to fight the storm. The silver lines shimmered in the rain and made her feathers glow in the darkness.

Tamri feared it might be too late for such measures. Laini was quivering with fatigue. Tamri sensed her exhaustion as if the Watermight linked them. A swirling mass of cloud surrounded them still, making it impossible to tell which way was up.

"I can't see the island," Pevin wailed.

"Just hold on!"

"We're lost!"

Tamri searched the darkened sky. Lightning cracked between the clouds. The brilliance had a menacing quality, confusing rather than illuminating. Tamri felt the urge to force it away from her, though that didn't make any sense. She had no control over the weather. But this was no ordinary storm.

Thunder boomed, bellowing a warning. They weren't welcome here. But Tamri wouldn't give up. She had work to do, and she wouldn't let Thunderbird Island defeat her.

She glimpsed something gold through the rain, a different kind of radiance.

It was Heath's Fire cudgel. The fiery light shone on Boru's snow-white wings, showing her the way forward.

"We're not lost!" Tamri shouted. "Follow that beacon!"

Laini responded at once, flying toward Heath and Boru with all her might. Other dragons struggled to join them, responding to the fierce golden light. A few people seemed to be following Laini too. The silver glow of Tamri's Watermight lit up her wings in the darkness, helping to pull the others through the storm.

Tamri made out a few faces as the flock of dragons regrouped, every wing beat a struggle. Kay and Taklin. Dentry. The Fire Queen herself. The other Wielders followed Tamri's lead and began drawing out Watermight and reinforcing their dragons' wings to help them make it through the storm.

Tamri felt a burst of pride at the sight and helped to strengthen several more of the creatures using the power Laini provided. She wasn't sure anyone else realized whose idea that had been. She supposed it didn't matter. They were going to stay airborne. But they still needed to find the island.

She looked at Heath, who was rallying the stragglers, waving his fiery cudgel through the rain-drenched night, determined to get them safely to shore. Mav was nowhere in sight, having decided once more not to approach the island. Tamri sensed in Laini a deep aversion to their destination, but the dragon continued on, relying heavily on the Watermight lining her wings and on her trust in Heath and Boru to guide them.

Then, like a colossal dragon's back rising from the sea, the island appeared ahead of them again.

"That's it!" Tamri screamed. "Come on, Laini, you can do it! We're almost there!"

The dragon unleashed a desperate shriek. Tamri bent low over her scales, spreading more Watermight along her wings as she turned her nose into the storm. They could do this. She and Laini might not be the biggest or the strongest, but together they would survive.

34

Selivia dropped her heavy pack beside Rosh and ran down the hillside, heedless of the loose rocks beneath her feet. Hope swelled through her, as strong as a sea wave. They had come for her. Her family would find a way to break Latch loose from his enchantment.

As she ran, the weather worsened, becoming positively vicious. The Lightning was defending its territory—or Latch was defending his discovery. She wasn't sure whether there was a difference between the two at this point. But the dragons struggled onward, their wings glowing silver in the storm.

By the time Selivia reached the black pebble beach, the Cindral dragons were landing in a wet, rumpled, colorful mass. Their passengers scrambled off, staggering on the loose pebbles and looking even more bedraggled than the dragons. Silvery streams of Watermight passed between them as the dragons offloaded the power to the human Wielders. Barrels thudded to the ground, released from their harnesses. One broke open, spilling glowing Fire on the beach until another Wielder drew it in. No sooner did the dragons drop their cargo than they took off again, soaring away from Thunderbird Island as quickly as possible. The storm lifted a little to let them depart.

A large contingent of Prince Chadrech's men marched out to meet the newcomers who had just been dumped on their beach.

The Vertigonians turned to face them, Fire and Watermight showing at their fingertips, steel glinting in their hands.

"Wait!" Selivia darted through the Soolen ranks, trusting that their parlay still held. "It's all right!"

She could see them now. A tall woman with a long golden braid. A man with high cheekbones and scars on his face. A broad-shouldered younger man with bronze hair and a Fire cudgel in his fist. Other faces, both familiar and dear.

Selivia broke through the last of the Soolens and flung her arms around Dara's neck.

"You made it! I thought you got lost. Siv! I'm so glad you're here too."

She released Dara and hurried to hug her brother.

"I hear our alliance with Soole is a little delicate at the moment," Siv said, sheathing his sword and eyeing the soldiers farther up the beach. "Thought you could use some support."

"I'll say," Selivia said. "You'd better talk to Prince Chadrech."

"Talk?" Siv said. "Aren't we supposed to be saving you from him?"

"He's open to a truce." Selivia quickly explained Chadrech's new position on the dangers of the Lightning. "He doesn't want anyone to access it, whether Latch or his own men. You can discuss it with him yourself."

Siv sighed. "I was afraid you'd say that." He lowered his voice so only she could hear. "Is he still as much of a bullshell dropping as I remember?"

Selivia giggled. "He's gotten worse."

"And Latch?"

Selivia's joy at seeing her family faded. "He has been trapped in the Lightning for a week, and he hasn't had anything to eat or drink. I . . . I hope it's not too late."

Dara and Siv exchanged sober glances.

"Any chance we can get out of the rain while we figure out how to help him?" Siv said, his voice taking on a forced brightness Selivia knew well. She was grateful for the effort, however strained.

A long-haired Soolen soldier she recognized as Lieutenant Kech approached the group and offered a formal salute. "His Excellency Crown Prince Chadrech requests your presence at his headquarters."

"We might as well get this over with," Siv muttered. "Lead the way."

Kech guided them up the beach, his soldiers falling in around the newcomers. They weren't exactly hostile, but Selivia sensed the delicacy of their truce. Some of those men had bandages covering what she suspected were thunderbird wounds. They surely blamed Latch and, by extension, Selivia.

The Soolens and Vertigonians climbed the crumbling steps from the beach and entered the old mining town together. Selivia felt unspeakably relieved to have so many friends surrounding her again. The dragon riders had stayed with the group, even though the dragons themselves had departed as fast as their wings would carry them. Heath looked as stern and wary as ever, but Taklin was already chattering animatedly to a pair of grim Soolen soldiers.

Selivia was contemplating what to say to Heath when she caught sight of an unexpected figure near the back of the group.

"Tamri! I'm surprised to see you here. How are you liking the Wielder school so far?"

The young Pendarkan girl stared at her, as if surprised Selivia was talking to her.

"I—the school was great. Princess, I—"

"Tamri here was spying for King Khrillin, Princess," said a curly-haired youth Selivia recognized as her friend Jully's cousin, Dentry. "She's our prisoner now."

"Oh. I didn't expect that." Selivia realized Tamri's hands were bound with a strap of leather from a dragon harness, and she wasn't carrying so much as a belt knife. "But Tamri, Khrillin was so cruel to you. Why would you—"

"I'd rather not talk about it," Tamri said, keeping her gaze lowered.

"She hasn't said much the whole journey, Princess," Dentry said. "It's almost like she can't explain."

"Can't?"

"The others are going to leave us behind," Tamri said. "We'd better catch up."

Selivia frowned. Tamri had been genuinely afraid in the hands of Khrillin's goons. Had that all been an act? She supposed they had bigger worries at the moment.

They trooped up to Chadrech's granary-turned-headquarters, where Selivia introduced everyone, and they began to discuss how to get Latch away from the chasm.

Dara wanted to drag him out by force, assuming minor exposure to the Lightning wouldn't entrap or hurt her. Siv objected to this after hearing how Latch had used the thunderbirds to defend himself. Chadrech maintained his desire to seal up the island and leave Latch for dead, but none of the others would agree to that.

"Mav said there's a strange presence on this island," Dara said at one point. "Any idea what it might be?"

Selivia whirled toward her. "You found Mav?"

"He found us," Dara said. "He sensed a territorial force on the island and believed it would see his arrival as a challenge for dominance. He's been waiting for you on a nearby island. He flew part of the way here with us, but he turned back when the storm hit."

"He could have warned me," Selivia grumbled. "I wonder if this territorial presence has something to do with the 'monster within.'"

"Eh?" Siv said.

"He might be talking about Latch himself. It's like he has merged with the Lightning, and it's acting out his defensive and maybe even malicious urges, with help from the storms and the thunderbirds. I hope you can pull him out of it with your Wielding skills. I couldn't."

"Whatever we do, we'll have to act fast," Dara said. "We brought Fire and Watermight with us, but we had to use up a lot of the Watermight to make it through the storm. The remaining supply won't last long."

"I suppose I might provide more," Chadrech said with a grudging sigh. "But first, we must discuss my terms."

Siv and Chadrech set to negotiating the details of a new agreement, while Dara grilled Rosh and Melloch on everything they knew about the Lightning. The granary buzzed with activity as the various Wielders and soldiers offered their input on the operation ahead. All agreed that they needed to move quickly.

Feeling a little overwhelmed, Selivia took a break from the discussion to step outside for a breath of fresh air.

It was late afternoon now, and storm clouds still churned fitfully above the mountain. Soolens and Vertigonians mingled outside the granary, all of them on edge as their leaders debated their next steps.

Selivia noticed Tamri sitting on a low wall beside the granary, watching the thunderbirds soaring overhead. Her hands were still tied, and a tall, skinny Wielder student stood guard beside her. Despite being a prisoner, the young Pendarkan looked healthier and more self-possessed than she had when they parted ways in Fork Town. She no longer had that starved-cat look.

Selivia went over to sit next to her. "You were really a spy for Khrillin?"

Tamri looked up at her with a resigned expression, so unlike the stark terror that had first drawn Selivia's sympathy when she was hauled before Khrillin.

"Yes, Princess."

"Would you consider coming over to our side? We'd treat you much better than Khrillin and those thugs."

"I can't." Tamri rubbed her neck with her bound hands. "But I never wanted things to turn out this way."

Selivia sighed. She had really thought Tamri would thrive at the Wielder school. She'd believed the best of her, despite Heath's suspicions, and she'd been proven wrong.

Just then, Heath emerged from the granary, where the discussion was still going on. He stopped when he saw her talking to Tamri. He looked as stern as ever, but he didn't avoid meeting her gaze. She hoped that meant their friendship still had a chance to recover.

Selivia left Tamri's side and joined Heath by the granary. The sound of Chadrech and Siv arguing drifted through the door.

"They're still at it?"

"We're making progress," Heath said. "King Siv has only called Chadrech a name under his breath once in the past five minutes."

Selivia smiled. "He has probably thought of six more creative names for him in his head in that time."

Heath's lips twitched, close to a grin.

"Listen," she said. "Can we talk about how we left things?"

"There's no need, Princess," Heath said. "You were under a lot of pressure, and I should have been more understanding. I also shouldn't have let my . . . personal feelings . . . get in the way of my duty."

"Thank you for saying that." Selivia grinned. "You know, that may be the first time you've ever admitted to *having* personal feelings."

"Your friendship is important to me, Prin—Sel. I shouldn't have lost sight of that."

Selivia brushed at a smudge on her leather jerkin to cover her surprise. Heath had always kept a tight leash on himself, determined to be dignified and professional to a fault. She hadn't expected such honesty. "Your friendship is important to me too."

Heath nodded, as if that simple statement was enough, and the remaining tension between them dissolved.

"How is it going with Lord Latch? Did you get along before all that?" Heath gestured at the mountain, where the clouds were growing denser. Lightning flashed fitfully, casting jagged shadows on the rocks.

"It's different from what I expected," Selivia said, "but I have hope for us yet."

"Good," Heath said. "You deserve to be happy."

Chadrech's voice drifted through the door, and Selivia winced. She didn't want to think about what would happen if Latch never escaped the mountain. *Please let him survive this.*

"What about you?" she asked, smothering her fear and adopting a cheery tone. "Any romantic prospects I'll have to interrogate on your behalf?"

Heath's gaze flickered away from her and back again.

"No, Princess. There's no one in particular."

Selivia was pretty sure he'd just looked at someone particular. She turned to survey the Wielders, dragon riders, and soldiers milling outside the granary, but then a Soolen voice called out from beyond where Tamri was sitting.

"Send for the Crown Prince! We caught a spy. A Pendarkan spy!"

Ten minutes later, a large group gathered in a circle around the spy the Soolen soldiers had captured. The prisoner, a lad of perhaps eighteen years, had the olive skin and dark eyes of a native Pendarkan. He moved with the same jumpy, defensive mannerisms Selivia associated with Tamri.

"We caught him trying to sneak past our ships," one of the soldiers explained. "He was with a mean-looking bald woman. She got away after almost taking my head off with a Watermight razor."

"A woman with a shaved head works for King Khrillin," Selivia said. "I've seen her several times."

"So you're another one of Khrillin's spies, are you?" Siv said, crouching on his heels to address the lad directly. "What's your name?"

"Why should I tell you?" he said insolently. "You ain't my king."

"The woman called him Pel," his captor grunted. "I heard her say it along with a string of curses about mud-drenched blood and the like."

"Well, Pel," Siv said. "Are your friends going to cause problems for us?"

"Problems?" Pel grinned at Siv, revealing a gap where one of his teeth had been knocked out. "We were just seeing the sights. This is a historic ruin. We have as much a right to be here as you."

"Sightseers, eh?" Siv said dryly. "How many of you are there?"

Pel's eyes cut to where Tamri sat, not seeming to notice her hands were already tied. He looked around at the menacing circle of soldiers and Wielders then put on a brash smile. "Untie me and get me a drink, and maybe I'll tell you."

Siv asked one of the Soolens to fetch a wineskin, but he didn't untie the boy. He waited until Pel had taken several sips before addressing him again.

"You have your drink. Do you have anything to say that'll convince me to let you go?"

"Tamri works for King Khrillin," Pel said at once. "She has been spying on you."

"Is that all?" Siv waved for Tamri to be brought nearer so Pel could see the leather straps binding her wrists.

Pel cursed, realizing his information was worthless. He clutched the wineskin to his chest as if afraid they'd take it back. Oddly, Tamri appeared neither hurt nor surprised that he had betrayed her so easily.

Siv moved closer to the lad, looming impressively. "You'll have to do better than that."

"There's no others, I swear," Pel babbled. "Apart from Gyra. She's the bald woman who got away. We're scouts, see. We're not planning an ambush or nothing."

"So Tamri told you we'd be here?" Dara turned to her former student. "How did you get a message through? An Air channel?"

"I don't know how to do that," Tamri said. "I haven't sent anything to Pendark since you caught me."

Prince Chadrech snorted. "She's obviously lying."

"They had to find out we were here somehow." Dara's forehead wrinkled in a frown. "I really thought you showed some remorse."

A pained expression flashed across Tamri's face. "I mentioned Lord Latch's research in the East Isles months ago, but I couldn't have told anyone we were heading to Thunderbird Island even if I wanted to."

"We didn't know you'd be here," Pel said. "All the scouting pairs were supposed to search the islands for—" He broke off, realizing what he was saying. "Can I have some more wine?"

Siv ignored him and summoned the leaders to step aside so they could talk without the prisoners overhearing.

Chadrech didn't wait for him to speak first. "Scouting pairs? Pendark has no right to violate our sovereignty like this. When my mother hears—"

"Queen Rochelle will surely put Khrillin in his place," Siv said. "The important thing is that he's not about to descend on us with a hundred Waterworkers. Let's focus on getting Latch out of danger. We can decide what to do about Pendark later."

"I have a plan to retrieve Latch," Dara said. "I may need the help of your Wielders, Prince Chadrech."

"Very well." The prince gave an exaggerated sigh. "That is why I brought them, after all."

Selivia grabbed Dara's hand. "You can really save him?"

"We can try," Dara said. "We'll need to move quickly. The Watermight and Fire we brought ought to protect us long enough to pull Latch out, but we need to be ready to leave the island if it goes badly."

"I convinced Boru to wait a little closer than the other dragons," Heath said. "He'll rally the Cindral dragons, but they barely made it to the island before. I'm not sure they can retrieve us without aid."

"I suppose you may use my ships too," Chadrech said reluctantly. "If you must."

"Thank you, Your Excellency," Selivia said. His willingness to work with them was a testament to just how dangerous he thought the Lightning was. She wished Latch had seen it too.

Chadrech gave her a tight nod, and she recalled how he'd knelt in the mud to offer her a new marriage alliance. After all his help, she would have no choice but to accept if they couldn't save Latch.

Selivia shivered. She wouldn't allow herself to contemplate failure yet. Besides, Dara had a familiar determined look in her eyes. Her plan would work. It had to.

35

Tamri watched the others prepare to advance on the mountain without her. The camp crackled with mistrust as the Vertigonians and Soolens got ready, none too pleased about the joint operation. Many cast suspicious glances at Tamri and Pel—who had been tied up beside her on the low wall—as if they feared more of Khrillin's people would appear and set a match to the powder keg of tension that was this alliance.

The Wielders portioned out the Watermight from the Cindral dragons and the Fire they'd carried all the way from Vertigon in barrels. Dara had taken the Watermight Tamri borrowed from Laini moments after they landed on the black pebble beach and siphoned it into a waterskin for safekeeping. The Fire Queen hadn't commented on Tamri's broken shackles, but she'd ordered Pevin to retie her hands with a strap of leather from a safety harness.

Despite the danger, Tamri wished she were going into the mountain with her friends. Khrillin would surely appreciate the information, and she wanted to see the Lightning in action.

But they're not your friends. It was strange how often she had to remind herself of that.

The Vertigonians paired up with Soolen Waterworkers, who'd brought their own Watermight supply. They were instructed to watch each other for signs that the Lightning was affecting them.

"Don't take unnecessary risks," Dara warned the Wielders as they gathered by the granary, each brimming with their preferred magical substance. "We'll pull Latch out as quickly as possible. Don't try to Wield the Lightning."

Kay raised her hand. "What if we get trapped like Lord Latch?"

"It took weeks for him to become ensnared," said Princess Selivia. She was bouncing nervously on her toes at the Fire Queen's side. "The other Wielders didn't use as much Lightning as he did, and they're fine."

"That's why we're loading up on Fire and Watermight before we go in," Dara said. "Think of how the two substances react to each other." She allowed a bit of Fire to spool out of her fingertips. Then she drew a thin stream of Watermight from the skin she carried on her right hip. The two powers twirled around each other, looping and linking but never touching. "Unless you Wield them in exactly the right manner, they consume each other."

The silvery stream touched the molten gold one, and they vanished in a flash of white light. A weak shockwave rippled outward, ruffling Dara's hair. Tamri remembered dropping the bead of power into the Whirlpool. She'd never learned the trick to Wielding the substances together so they produced real power. Maybe she never would.

"We don't know much about the Lightning," Dara said to the Wielders, "but the other substances should protect you for long enough to finish this. Use them as a shield." She looked up at the sky, where the clouds were billowing unnaturally quickly, as if the island itself were gearing up for battle. Gray-and-white shapes darted among them. "And watch out for the thunderbirds."

Soon the Wielders were raising a strangled cheer and marching away from the granary, leaving the non-Wielders—and prisoners—behind. The wind picked up as they set out for the mountain, howling through the ruins and stirring their coats.

Heath took over the responsibility for guarding Tamri and Pel when the Wielders departed. He was as vigilant as ever, but he didn't stop Tamri from climbing on top of the low wall to get a better view of the mountain. King Siv and Princess Selivia moved to the edge of camp to watch the proceedings along with the dragon riders and

Castle Guards who'd traveled with them. Prince Chadrech stood apart from the Vertigonians, surrounded by his men. He'd insisted on keeping a pair of Waterworkers behind to protect him.

Tamri wasn't sure exactly what had gone on between the Soolen Crown Prince and the Vertigonians, but she could sense the tenuousness of their relationship. She hoped the Fire Queen returned with Lord Latch soon.

She squinted at the base of the mountain, standing on tiptoes and straining for a glimpse of the Wielders. Her heart pounded as if she, too, were marching toward the mysterious power.

Soon, Dara and the others emerged from the town and started up the barren mountainside in the distance. They moved purposefully, in coats of blue and red and slate gray. Tiny glimmers appeared where they allowed the magical substances to play along their fingertips.

As if in response, the thunderbirds began to multiply. The Wielders climbed, and the birds circled closer and closer. Their beaks and talons flashed like lightning, and their eyes glinted fiercely. But they didn't attack. They just watched. Waited.

"Psst!"

Tamri jumped at the sound.

Pel was looking up at her from his seat on the low wall. "You reckon we should escape?"

"We wouldn't get far," Tamri whispered with a nod at Heath. "Unless you brought a dragon."

"I'd never trust those vicious beasts."

"They're not all vicious," Tamri said.

Pel snorted. "Sure."

"Most of them are pretty intelligent." Tamri sensed Heath's eyes on her, but she didn't look at him. She wasn't sure whether he could hear them.

"Whatever." Pel took a swig of the wine the Vertigonians had given him, apparently not interested in the dramatic rescue about to take place on the mountain. "So I heard about your run-in with Khrillin. He really is taking care of your gramma. Gyra says she's living in a care home down in the Jewel District."

"Are you sure?" Tamri suddenly felt light-headed, as if an intense pressure weighing her down had eased.

"Yeah, she's okay," Pel said. "I'd have brought you a letter or something if I knew you'd be here." He gave her a sly look. "Don't think Khrillin knew you'd be here, either."

"I got caught before I could tell him we were coming," Tamri said carefully. "I'd have warned him if I could."

Pel shrugged. "Let's hope he believes that."

Tamri shuddered. She would rather be the Vertigonians' prisoner than Khrillin's after failing him. But at least Gramma Teall was safe for now. Tamri would just have to find a way to convince Khrillin of her loyalty.

Up on the mountain, Dara's Wielders were approaching several shadowy tunnel openings scattered around the slope. Larger flickers of Fire and Watermight began to appear around them, as if they were testing out their shields, readying for the offensive. They were almost in position.

Tamri lowered her voice. "What are you really doing here, Pel?"

"Scouting, like I said. Khrillin was mighty excited to hear the Soolens were looking for a new magical substance. He wanted us to find it in case you never learned more than that."

"I mean why are you working for Khrillin? You were going to be your own man."

Pel shrugged. "Gotta do what it takes to stay alive. You know how it is."

"Yes," Tamri said. "Yes, I know."

The last of the Wielders moved into position by the tunnels. They would all advance at the same moment.

Tamri leaned forward, watching for the signal. The Fire Queen's golden hair stood out against a gray ledge by one of the tunnels. She seemed to be listening for something. Waiting.

The thunderbirds rode the winds overhead, also waiting. Tamri held her breath.

A glimmer of gold appeared. A thin stream of Fire shot upward from Dara's position, speeding toward the peak, and burst into an elaborate Fire Blossom. Spirals of Fire fell all around the mountain, trailing burning stars.

Moving as one, the Wielders deployed their shields and rushed into the tunnels, heading for the mysterious Lightning chasm. Then they were gone, leaving the mountain suddenly dreadfully still.

Tamri imagined Kay, Dentry, and Pevin striding down the tunnels toward the cavern. They would be brimming with Fire, ready to defend themselves from this strange new magic, ready to rescue the Lightning's first victim.

Tamri pulled at the leather strap around her wrists, more from anxiety than an effort to escape. She was too busy watching the mountain to consider making a run for it. Heath and the others were equally entranced.

The Wielders must be getting closer to the center. Soon they would see the white-and-purple glow Princess Selivia had described. Soon they would come within feet of the crackling magic that had drawn them here. Tamri had felt its unnatural energy in the storm that tried to keep them from Thunderbird Island. She couldn't imagine what it would be like to see the chasm itself. She clenched her hands into fists, her bonds tightening at the tension. She barely noticed the leather digging into her skin.

They waited.

Waited.

Then a low rumble started deep within the ground. Small stones clattered and danced on the ancient cobblestones. Tamri's toes vibrated as the whole island shuddered beneath her.

The thunderbirds began to shriek, startling her from her absorption. They careened back and forth, snapping their beaks and fluttering their wings. Tamri's heartbeat quickened with every fearsome cry. The rumbling grew louder, and the ground quaked, shaking her off balance.

Then a blinding flash turned the air white. It lasted for an instant that felt like a lifetime. Tamri's hair rose from her neck, and her eyes burned. She felt as if she were flying, falling.

The sensation passed as quickly as it had come. She realized she was crouched beside the low wall. She really had fallen, still tied up, still alive. Around her, people were staggering, rubbing their eyes, trying to regain their equilibrium.

She squinted at the mountain, trying to make sense of what was happening.

Bolts of lightning were shooting out of every opening in the ground. The clouds convulsed as more lightning forked across the sky. Thunderbirds swarmed through the air, the white in their wings flashing and crackling as if they, too, could hurl magic.

Everyone in the camp was shouting. King Siv called Dara's name, his bellow all but lost in the endless thunder. He drew his sword and ran toward the mountain, which was still expelling lightning bolts in erratic bursts. His guards followed, brandishing weapons of steel that would do no good against that explosion of white-hot power. Selivia shouted at them to wait for her, but Prince Chadrech seized her arm to keep her from running into danger.

Heath took a step forward, as if he, too, wanted to dash up the mountain or perhaps help keep the princess from following her brother, but he restrained himself, keeping to his duty in the midst of the chaos.

Tamri shuddered as shockwave after shockwave rolled over them. She didn't know if the Lightning alone produced those waves of pressure or if it was the Lightning meeting the Fire and Watermight Dara's Wielders had carried into the mountain. Whatever the cause, she could feel the vastness of the power, as if a great creature were thrashing in the mountain's depths. A creature intent on defending itself.

King Siv and his men reached the mountain and were starting up the slope when the lightning finally stopped shooting from the tunnels. When they were halfway up, the first Wielder burst from a tunnel and fled down the mountainside as if chased by nightmares. Tamri drew in a ragged breath. She had feared they were all dead.

One by one, the Wielders emerged, stumbling blindly, trying to keep each other from falling. Some had blood dripping from their noses and ears. Others had burns on their arms and smoke rising from their clothing. All were rubbing their eyes, struggling to find their way.

Then the thunderbirds attacked. As the Wielders fled, the huge birds swooped down on them, clawing and screaming, talons ripping into clothes, into flesh. Beaks flashed, stained with blood. The Wielders flung their hands over their heads, but they had no power left to fend off the vicious creatures. Whatever had happened inside the mountain had consumed their Watermight and Fire, consumed their ability to protect themselves. They could only run blindly down the hill as the birds feasted on their terror.

Tamri saw Pevin go down, two particularly large birds converging on the thin young man who wanted to make swords. Dentry and Kay tried to help him, throwing rocks and sticks at the great birds as they tore into their friend. Beaks flashed as the birds fought back, jealous of their prey.

When they finished with Pevin, the thunderbirds turned their cruel eyes on Dentry and Kay. The pair moved closer together as the vicious creatures swooped toward them.

Tamri couldn't look away, certain she was about to witness the deaths of all three of her friends.

But King Siv and his men reached them first. Taklin charged up the mountain, racing for Kay and Dentry, sword flashing, mouth open in a bellow of rage. He cut one of the creatures down just as it swiped a bloody chunk out of Dentry's cheek. Kay hammered the other with a stone, her dueling skills no use here. Taklin rushed in to help finish off the monstrous bird.

The non-Wielders were fighting thunderbirds all over the mountain, using steel where magic had failed, attempting to cut the vile creatures from the sky. King Siv himself skewered a thunderbird through the breast and hurled it down the slope. The thunderbirds shrieked as their efforts to harry the invaders were thwarted.

Tamri briefly lost sight of her friends amidst the carnage. She scanned the slope until she spotted Kay's pale hair. She and Taklin were hauling Dentry between them, all three bleeding from multiple gashes. Errol and Reya ran beside them, fending off the thunderbirds with their swords, bellowing wordless battle cries.

They didn't go back for Pevin. It was too late. Tamri had saved his life in the storm, only for him to suffer a worse end.

All over the mountainside, King Siv's soldiers were holding off the creatures. They gathered up all the Wielders they could reach and ushered them to the relative safety of the buildings, taking shelter in the half-collapsed ruins. The thunderbirds screeched in anger, and more lightning flashed overhead.

Tamri watched it all in horror, powerless to do anything. She twisted her bound hands, willing her friends to make it down the mountainside. She counted the Wielders as they were brought back to the granary, many with deep scratches on their arms and faces from the thunderbird talons. Only half of them had made it back so far.

Kay, Dentry, and Taklin reached the camp, looking nearly delirious with terror, but too many people were still up there. Too many had suffered the same fate as Pevin.

"Where is Dara?" Princess Selivia joined them by the wall, having succeeded in wrenching away from Prince Chadrech. She grabbed Heath's arm. "Have you seen her?"

"She went into that tunnel by the ledge," Heath said. "She hasn't come out yet."

Selivia gasped. "She's still inside?"

Tamri felt as distressed as the princess sounded. The Fire Queen had to make it out. She *had* to.

"Why is this happening?" Selivia moaned. "I've been staying there for weeks. The Lightning has never acted like this!"

"It's lashing out, defending itself," Tamri said, still concentrating on the slope. The princess hadn't really been speaking to her, but her words made sense. The Fire Queen had brought too much magic into the mountain with her. She was powerful and focused and strong, but this time she'd made a mistake. And she still hadn't come out.

King Siv was almost to the tunnel where Dara had entered, clearly intending to go in after his wife. But lightning was still shivering in the air, striking the mountainside at random. The thunderbirds were regrouping, whirling through the storm, their talons flinging droplets of blood.

"He can't go in when it's like this!" Selivia said. "I have to stop him."

"Wait." Heath caught her arm, preventing her from dashing up the hill after all. "I see something."

Tamri scrambled onto the wall again. He was right. Movement flickered in the tunnel mouth. A glint of gold. Then Dara emerged into the fractured, stormy light. The skin of Watermight was gone from her side, and her face was as white as Vertigonian snow, but she was on her feet. And she was alone.

"Latch is still inside," Selivia said, echoing Tamri's thoughts. "They didn't do it."

King Siv reached Dara in three bounding steps and pulled her arm over his shoulder. He all but carried her away from the tunnel, heading down the mountain.

They only made it a dozen paces when another blast of lightning erupted from the tunnels, as if the Lightning wanted to emphasize they were not welcome. Dara and Siv pitched to the ground and began to tumble down the slope, taking a cascade of rocks and dirt with them. They skidded to an ungainly halt, the king flattening himself on top of his wife to shield her. Selivia covered her eyes.

Tamri froze, watching the spot where the king and queen had fallen, blinking the purple spots from her eyes. They weren't moving.

"Psst, Tamri."

"Be quiet, Pel."

"Tamri, I got a sharp stone. Help me with my ropes, and I'll do yours."

"Not now."

Tamri ignored Pel as he attempted to saw into his bonds. The king and queen were still lying on the ground.

She remembered the day she'd seen them dueling in the castle. She pictured them whispering in each other's ears as they watched the Eventide cup. They were so vibrant, so loving, so much larger than life. She had wanted so desperately to prove herself to the Fire Queen, to show that she could overcome her body's aversion to the Fire and be as strong as her one day. She couldn't be dead.

Movement. Something shifted, blue against the gray slope. Then the king slowly sat up, smoke rising from his coat. A head crowned in gold appeared next as Queen Dara sat up beside him. *They're alive!*

Selivia was shouting, jumping up and down. Heath had his hands in his hair, looking as if he'd run a thousand miles in the moments his beloved king was in danger.

Dara and Siv helped each other to their feet and continued down the mountain. They drew their swords, ready to fight off the thunderbirds, but after that final blast, the foul creatures seemed to lose interest. The remaining survivors were allowed to leave the mountain and struggle toward the camp, where the others hurried to meet them with bandages and water.

In the commotion, Pel nudged Tamri, offering her a sharp rock. Giving her a chance to escape.

Tamri pocketed the stone, still focusing on the mountain. No one else emerged from the tunnels after that final blast. It was over. The Fire Queen and her Wielders had fought the Lightning, and the Lightning had won.

36

Selivia helped tend the wounded while she listened to what had happened in the cavern. She couldn't believe the plan had gone so horribly wrong.

"It was chaos," Dara said. "It's like the island itself decided to fight us."

All the survivors were gathered in the old granary, squeezed together to make enough room. Soolens and Vertigonians, royals and soldiers and Wielders. Too many were nursing burns and gashes. Too many hadn't made it. The thunderbirds still circled threateningly outside. No one would soon forget their nightmarish cries or the way the Lightning flashed on sharp beaks and wicked talons. Selivia doubted she'd ever sleep again.

The power had been lying in wait for them when they reached the cavern, like a cullmoran stalking the Fissure back home. Dara described how the Fire inside her writhed and roiled the closer she got to the chasm. She had been about to order the others to retreat when the Lightning exploded outward, striking every tunnel simultaneously.

"We couldn't get near Latch," Dara said. "I glimpsed him when I reached the cavern, but then the Lightning shot toward me, and I had to concentrate on shielding myself with Fire."

"I did the same with Watermight," said Melloch, who was examining a bloody scratch on his shoulder through cracked spectacles. "It burned up in seconds."

"I just ran," said Kay, her face bloodless. "I can barely remember what I did with the Fire, but it's all gone now."

"Did the power act of its own volition?" Siv asked. His hair was singed, and he would likely have a few more scars after today. He hovered close to his wife, as if afraid she might vanish. "Or did Latch attack you?"

Dara hesitated. Selivia remembered the scholars' warnings about the malice—the monster—that the Lightning awakened in its users.

"I don't know how distinct they are anymore." Dara rubbed her face, where a nasty burn highlighted her cheek. Selivia shivered. Dara's skin wasn't supposed to burn. "Either it's controlling him, or it has unleashed something in him that makes him want to use it against us."

"I warned you of this," Prince Chadrech said. For once, he didn't sound smug. "We should never have come here. Whether Brach is controlling it or not, the Lightning should have stayed buried."

"I think we all agree on that," Selivia said. "But the question is: what do we do now? What's the new plan to retrieve Latch?"

Dara and Siv exchanged glances, neither of them speaking. Prince Chadrech rubbed his gaunt face with a torn sleeve. He'd ripped pieces off his clothes to bandage his men. The nearby Wielders looked down, their expressions defeated.

"Well?" Selivia heard the frantic note in her own voice. "How do we fix this? How do we get Latch?"

"I'll go in," Heath said. "Maybe he—or it—won't react so violently to a non-Wielder."

"In that case, it should be me," Selivia said. "I've been going in and out of that cavern for weeks."

"You already tried to pull him out of the power, didn't you?" Dara said.

Selivia remembered the dancing beams of light and the hair-raising shock lancing through her body. "Well, yes, but—"

"I think it's too late for that." Dara touched the burn on her cheek. "If this happened with Wielders, any non-Wielders might not survive the encounter, much less be able to free him."

"What are you saying?"

Dara met her eyes solemnly. "I'm sorry, Sel, but I don't think we can save him without losing more people."

"Dara is right," Siv said. "We can't let anyone else go in there."

Chadrech nodded, appearing a little surprised to be agreeing with Siv. Heath looked away.

Selivia leapt to her feet. "You're giving up?"

"Not necessarily, but—"

"We have to keep trying."

"We will," Siv said. "I owe my life to Latch several times over. I don't want to abandon him. But we need to take more time to understand what we're facing. And you need to prepare for the possibility that we can't save him."

"No." Selivia had only just figured out she loved Latch. She couldn't give up on him now. "I refuse to believe that."

"We can't do anything with so many injured and those birds out there," Chadrech said. "I say we retreat to a nearby island or even the mainland while we explore other strategies. Perhaps we can search the Royal Archives to see if we missed anything."

"That may be necessary." Dara was tracing the intricate steelwork on her black sword hilt thoughtfully. "We were too rash in the initial assault. And we'll need more Fire and Watermight. The Lightning burned up every drop of the substance we brought with us."

"I can help with the Watermight if not the Fire," Chadrech said.

"Mav will produce more of that," Heath said. "It's the least he can do."

Selivia stared in disbelief as the others discussed the details of their retreat from Thunderbird Island, already talking about transporting the injured to the ships and studying musty documents back in Sharoth.

"We can't just leave," she burst out. "Latch hasn't had any food or water in a week. He'll be *dead* by the time we return!"

Siv's mouth tightened, giving Selivia hope. Latch was his friend. He had helped save Vertigon. Siv wouldn't abandon him.

A thunderbird swooped past the granary window, squawking threateningly.

"I'm sorry, Sel," Siv said at last. "We need to regroup, and we can't do it here."

"But—"

"Get some rest. We leave at first light."

Selivia sat down numbly. She couldn't believe it. They were giving up. They thought Latch was lost.

She wanted to do something, to fix this. She had always been willing to march into danger. She wasn't a Wielder, and she wasn't in line for a crown, but she had done what was required to help the people she loved. But this threat wasn't a warlord with whom she could negotiate or a dragon she could charm into assisting her. No matter how much she wanted to help, her strengths weren't enough.

Only when Chadrech offered her a handkerchief did she realize she was crying.

Tamri watched the tears trail down Princess Selivia's face, sympathy pulsing through her. Selivia had treated her with kindness. She had offered her a chance at a new life. Tamri hated to see the pain in her normally cheery face. If only she could help her the way the princess had helped Tamri that day in Khrillin's audience chamber.

The Vertigonians had all but forgotten about her and Pel in the chaos after the plan failed. When the thunderbirds began circling nearer to their camp, they had all taken shelter inside the granary. Now Tamri and Pel sat against the wall, only a dozen paces from the door. Dentry was their guard, but he didn't watch them nearly as closely as Heath had. Unabashed tears spilled from his eyes, dampening the bandage on his torn cheek. Pevin had been his best friend.

Around them, people were settling in to rest as well as they could in the cramped quarters. Princess Selivia soon dried her tears and rose to help the injured get as comfortable as possible. They would leave the island at first light.

"Well?" Pel hissed at Tamri. "Are we going to do this or not?"

Pel had sawn through his bonds with the sharp rock earlier, but Tamri had convinced him to wait until the others were asleep before they made their move.

"Better if we only have to deal with our guard, not every soldier here."

"Half of 'em can barely walk," Pel said. "I say we run for it."

"We have to choose our moment carefully." Tamri used the rock to sever her bonds then arranged the fragments to make it look as if she were still tied up. "Acting recklessly won't get us far."

Pel raised an eyebrow. "You've changed. The old Tamri would be halfway to the beach by now."

"The old Tamri would have gotten caught."

"Truth." Pel shrugged and followed her lead in positioning his ropes so they looked intact. "All right. We can wait a few hours."

As darkness fell outside the granary and the sounds of fitful slumber rose within, Pel resumed badgering Tamri to escape. But she was no longer sure she wanted to flee.

She'd been close enough to hear the details of what happened inside the mountain, and she had a theory about why the approach had failed. The Fire Queen had decided on her course of action too quickly, perhaps nervous about the Soolens or the thunderbirds or the strange weather. For once, Tamri believed proceeding slowly would have been a better option.

The Lightning had reacted violently to the assault, but it had been a defensive maneuver. The Wielders rushed in, brimming with foreign magical substances, and the Lightning fought back in a way that matched their powerful assault. Tamri had learned that it helped to be small and unintimidating when you had to face the powerful. Having no power could even be an asset at times.

She looked over at Princess Selivia, who was still tending the injured, her leather jerkin smudged with other people's blood. She had spoken up for Tamri when no one else would, using her power to protect a stranger.

Maybe it wasn't too late to repay her. Maybe Tamri could try to save Lord Latch.

An excited buzz filled her at the thought. It was reckless, and she could hardly believe she was even considering it. But she couldn't shake the idea that she might succeed where the Fire Queen had failed.

Moreover, if Tamri entered that mountain, she could learn enough about the Lightning to convince Khrillin to release her. This could be the final "jewel of information" that would impress him so much he wouldn't care she'd gotten caught spying. It might be her only chance to get that jewel now. At the same time, she could return Latch to Selivia.

She rubbed her neck. The oath bond didn't react to the notion. Trying to infiltrate the mountain wouldn't violate her oath. For once, she could choose a dangerous course for herself rather than being forced into it.

She remembered what Gramma Teall had told her. *Learn enough to make sure no one, not even me, can ever tell you what to do again.*

Tamri had many limitations, but she'd learned a lot over the past months. And she was no longer powerless. She was going to do it.

The granary quieted around her. A small group of soldiers and Wielders had gone outside to patrol the area, while the rest drifted into fitful slumber. The thunderbirds were still careening overhead, stirred up by the day's excitement. They'd had enough of strangers on their island. No one would sleep well tonight.

Tamri waited, listening to the crunch of footsteps whenever the patrol passed the outer door. Her heartbeat thundered in her ears, and her palms became slick with sweat. Pel fidgeted beside her, but he was allowing her to take the lead, something he'd never done before.

Dentry still sat nearby, continuing his shift as their jailer as the hour grew late. Tamri was grateful he hadn't been replaced yet. Their chances of success were slim enough, but his grief-stricken condition might make evading him a little easier.

Voices came from the other side of the granary, where the royals were still talking. A steady glow silhouetted them as they used an Everlight to study a map, perhaps planning where they would retreat come morning. Both Selivia and Heath were with them now, fully engaged in the discussion. Still Tamri waited, watching for her moment.

Footsteps crunched outside. The patrol was drawing nearer.

"When I say the word," Tamri whispered to Pel, "run for the beach." She lowered her voice still further. "If you make it back to Pendark without me, promise me you'll check on Gramma Teall."

"Sure. I owe you that much for getting you involved in that dragon business."

"It was my choice," Tamri said.

The footsteps were right outside the door now, heading downhill. Dentry rubbed his eyes, his face puffy.

"Get ready."

Pel shifted, gathering his gangly limbs under him. The patrol started to get farther away.

I'm really sorry about this, Tamri thought. Then she pried up a chunk of stone from the cracked floor, leapt forward, and bashed Dentry over the head. He slumped forward onto the ground.

"Now!"

She and Pel dashed out the doors before anyone realized what was happening. Pel took off running toward the beach. The patrol saw him and raised the alarm. As they pursued Pel down the sloping pathway, Tamri ran the other way. Staying low to the ground, she slipped out of the camp and headed toward the mountain.

37

The wind whipped at Tamri's face as she left the shelter of the ruins and began climbing the bare slope in the darkness. The looming clouds covered up the moon, glowing silver at the edges. She made her way by feel, hoping she wouldn't put a foot wrong and plunge back down the hillside. She removed her shoes not long after leaving camp to make it easier to grip the rocks with her toes. The ground was oddly warm beneath her feet, and she felt the dampness of the rain with every step.

No one had followed her up the mountainside. Hopefully Pel would lead them on a merry chase, and hours would pass before anyone realized she wasn't trying to escape the island. Instead, she was heading closer to its heart.

The tunnels that had been spewing Lightning a few hours ago were quiet, their openings peering like dark eye sockets from the mountainside. The thunderbirds marked her, occasionally swooping overhead to investigate. But they sensed that one small girl picking her way through the darkness wasn't as much of a threat as all the soldiers and Wielders below.

Tamri didn't have a single drop of Watermight or Fire in her blood. She would go in unarmed and hopefully escape the Lightning's notice long enough to pull Lord Latch out.

She headed for the spot where she'd seen the Fire Queen emerge hours ago. The tunnel mouth was still smoking, and glass glimmered around its edges. Tamri pulled back, wondering if she was making a horrible mistake. But Selivia had said the Lightning didn't hurt Latch at first, and he was a lifelong Waterworker—just like Tamri.

She paused at the tunnel mouth and looked back. Thunderbird Island spread below her, a warren of shadows and jagged ruins. The windows of the old granary glowed, and little lights moved farther down the slope, weaving through the streets and alleys, searching. Most of the lights were concentrated close to the beach, where Pel was no doubt realizing it would be more difficult to escape than he thought.

She felt only slightly guilty for using him like that. He'd have tried to escape no matter what she did, and he *had* tried to sell her out.

No one would expect her to go into the mountain. They saw her as a thief, a traitor, a gutter urchin who cared only for her survival. But Selivia had offered her a second chance. Dara had seen her potential and given her an opportunity to become powerful in her own right. Laini had trusted her. And now Tamri wanted to prove she could be something more than a thief fighting over scraps.

She stood up straight, not crouching, not cringing away from danger. And she walked into the smoking tunnel.

She kept her hand on the wall as she made her way into the mountain. It was pitch dark, but the path was smoother than she'd expected. A curious breeze filtered through the tunnel, almost warm enough to make her remove her cloak. Sweat tickled her forehead, and her heart pounded in time with her steps.

She sensed the Lightning long before she saw it. The air hissed and crackled, and her hair tried to crawl up her scalp. Light danced on the tunnel walls, purplish and unnatural, and she felt a familiar thrum. She was pretty sure she'd sensed this same unnatural energy when she and Laini were flying through the storm. Again, she felt the urge to force it away somehow, but she continued onward, putting one bare foot in front of the other.

At last, the tunnel widened, and she paused at the edge of a vast cavern. A handful of other tunnel openings and alcoves scattered around the edges along with broken tools and piles of cracked stone, remnants of the old mining operation.

In the center was the chasm Selivia had described, a deep gash in the stone floor that glittered with purple-white light. The brightness hurt Tamri's night-adjusted eyes, and she didn't dare look too closely. She was pretty sure she'd already made it farther than the other Wielders. Entering without any other magical substances had been the right move.

But where was Lord Latch? She'd expected to find him seated beside the chasm, where Selivia said he'd been for the past week. But however hard she squinted at that glowing crack, there was no sign of the young lord. She edged along the side of the cavern, keeping her back pressed to the wall. Perhaps he had wandered into one of the alcoves. Perhaps he was dead.

Abruptly she sensed a shift in that bizarre energy, as if something was trying to get her attention. She looked up.

A man floated high over the chasm, at least fifteen feet above the cavern floor. Lightning lanced and darted around him, illuminating his dirty clothes, dark skin, and glistening black hair. He was rotating slowly, as stiff as a gargoyle. At first, Tamri thought he was dead. But when he drifted around to face her, a spark of life flickered in his eyes. His pupils were dilated and rolling, flickering with purplish light. He didn't seem aware of her.

Tamri scanned the cavern for something she could use to reach him, an old ladder or a ledge she could climb. He was too far up for her to grab his boot, and she didn't dare touch the Lightning surrounding him. How would she get him down?

Lord Latch rotated toward her again. This time, his gaze fixed on her face, his pupils no longer rolling. A muscle convulsed in his jaw, as if he was trying to speak. She took a step closer, raising a hand in greeting.

Then his lips drew back in a fierce rictus, and a lance of pure white light shot toward her.

Tamri dove aside at the last instant, scraping her hands and knees as she landed. The Lightning bolt exploded against the wall, sending chips of hot stone cascading to the floor.

Tamri staggered to her feet, ears ringing. A hot metallic scent filled her nostrils, and her eyes stung. She could barely tell which way was up.

The Lightning struck again, closer this time, and Tamri suddenly found herself looking up from the ground. She smelled her hair burning and tasted blood on her tongue. Her ears ached, unable to process the resounding boom of thunder that accompanied the strike. The sound seemed to be coming from inside her head and battering it from the outside at the same time.

She struggled to sit up. In the air above the chasm, Latch's mouth was moving, but Tamri couldn't hear him. He looked sorrowful.

More power swelled up from the chasm, the beams of light swirling like a tornado. Tamri scrambled to her feet, unable to find her balance. She staggered a step backward. Then another. And the Lightning struck for a third time.

Tamri had no hope of jumping aside. Without thought, she reached out as if grabbing a whip of Watermight, and her senses caught on the beam of pure energy. As she careened back against the wall, she hurled the Lightning aside with every ounce of strength she possessed.

The bolt diverted and struck the wall beside her. Thunder echoed around the cavern, shaking her body violently. Loose rocks fell, shattering on the floor. Debris choked the air.

Tamri drew in a shocked, dusty breath. It had responded. The Lightning had responded to her.

She marveled at the realization, and the pause nearly cost her life. Two more Lightning bolts shot toward her, splitting and splintering into a dozen smaller points. Once again, she reacted with pure desperation, whipping the Lightning away from her to crack against the cavern wall.

I can do this.

The thought was frantic, barely coherent. She had practiced this. She'd tried over and over again to control the Fire without letting it near her body. Her teachers had told her it was the wrong way to Wield, but here it could save her. All she had to do was keep the Lightning from touching her.

She felt a malevolent presence stirring, as whatever controlled the Lightning realized she wasn't running away. And it was angry. The swirl of energy grew brighter, rising farther and farther out of the chasm.

Tamri darted along the side of the cavern, presenting the Lightning with a moving target. Each time it struck too close, she flung it away from her, whipping the beams of violent energy into the stones around her. More chunks of rock fell, spreading debris across the cavern. The ceiling couldn't possibly hold for much longer.

She was getting the hang of this, though. She didn't try drawing the substance into her body, knowing she couldn't really control it, and she defended herself as fiercely as the Lightning itself.

Dust coated her tongue and throat, and she was pretty sure her feet were bleeding. She couldn't keep this up for much longer. If it didn't kill her, the Lightning would eventually catch her up like Latch. How was she going to get him out of that swirling vortex?

She moved closer to the chasm, searching for a solution, staying ready for the next attack. She had to try something, even something reckless. She was running out of time.

This time when the Lightning struck, she whipped it straight back the way it came. The tornado of crackling energy grew, accepting the power back into itself. Latch spun faster in its center. The Lightning seemed agitated now, annoyed, if such qualities could be assigned to a blazing ball of pure power.

Tamri felt her way blindly, acting on instinct. As the ball of power roiled, she didn't wait for it to strike again. She leapt toward it, reaching out both hands. Then she pulled the Lightning toward her.

The vortex of power responded, shooting crackling beams outward. Tamri deflected these as well as she could, still tugging on that swirl of energy. The vortex heaved toward her, bending out of shape, bubbling outward even as smaller fingers of power shot in every direction. Some of these touched Tamri's skin, shocking and disorienting her. It was too late to stop now.

As the tornado of Lightning teetered and bulged toward her, she dropped to her knees. It was too much. She couldn't balance it. She was going to pull the whole quivering mass onto her head. Latch jerked about in the center, a wooden doll trapped in a whirlpool.

She could no longer deflect the slivers of Lightning. More of them touched her skin, making her nerve endings shiver. It was nothing like the pain of the Fire, nor was it like the Watermight's icy strength. It was too much sensation. Too much energy. Too much power.

Unable to stand it any longer, she flattened herself to the ground and desperately forced the huge bubble of energy upward. The pressure pushed the Lightning off balance, and jagged bolts shot toward the top of the cavern, cracking the ceiling. Tamri's ears throbbed and pulsed, and a wet trickle ran down her neck. She wasn't sure if it was sweat or blood. She was feeling more than hearing now.

The swirling ball of energy spun out of control above the chasm. It pulsed and whirled, lopsided and erratic. Latch floundered in the vortex, spinning, drifting lower. The substance could no longer hold him steady, no longer keep him trapped.

Sensing she didn't have much time, Tamri reached blindly for the space around him, grasping the Lightning substance that held him as if it were the harness on a Cindral dragon. She yanked it toward her, and Latch tumbled downward.

He hit the ground hard, mere inches from the great chasm. Tamri scrambled forward and grabbed his arm. She tried to haul him away from that gaping hole, but he was much too heavy. After controlling all that power, however clumsily, she didn't have the strength in her muscles to move him from the floor.

"Wake up!" she shouted to him, unable to hear her own words. She filled her lungs, and for a moment she felt as if the energy of the Lightning was filling her too, making her body crackle with power. "*Wake up!*"

Latch blinked at her, his eyes flashing white, purple, blue, and gold. Then they cleared to a rich brown.

"Hurry!" Tamri said. "It's out of control!"

Latch lurched to his feet, bewildered, unfocused. She seized his arm, flinging stray Lightning away from them whenever it got too close. Above them, the tornado was regaining its shape, swirling straight upward to the top of the cavern.

As Tamri hauled Latch away from the chasm, something moved deep inside it. Something vast. She paused.

"We need . . . run . . ." Latch muttered.

"Obviously!"

Tamri glanced back into the chasm once more. A jewel-dark glimmer appeared through the flashing beams, as if a great eye had turned toward her, shifting beneath the mass of boiling light. Then it was gone.

Tamri shuddered. It was nothing. Her brain had been shaken up, cooked inside her skull. Turning her back on the chasm, she helped Latch to the nearest tunnel as quickly as she could.

Lightning bolts continued to lance around the cavern, but they no longer struck directly at them. Tamri flung aside any bolts that came too near, not caring where they landed. More rocks fell from the vaulted ceiling. The whole cavern was about to come down on their heads. They had to get out.

Latch leaned heavily on her as they staggered into the tunnel, not fully aware of his surroundings. Tamri hoped his brain wasn't permanently damaged after days caught up in all that power. She hoped *her* brain wasn't damaged after a few minutes. Her head felt like thunder, and her body crackled and popped like a campfire. They'd assess their injuries later. She just wanted to get out of here, to breathe in great gulps of sea air.

They exited the tunnel so suddenly she nearly dragged Latch off the side of the mountain. They skidded to a halt on the ledge.

Storm clouds sat low in the night sky, close enough to mist their faces. Purple light scarred Tamri's vision, and she couldn't see the lights of the camp below. She hadn't been in the cavern for long, but she felt as if days had passed and the others had long since abandoned them.

Latch slumped to the ground, unconscious or shell-shocked. Tamri remained standing, breathing, trying to calm the pounding in her head, her ears, her eyes. As the throbbing slowly abated, she swayed, barely staying on her feet.

She had done it. She had saved Selivia's betrothed, when even the Fire Queen had failed. And she had controlled the Lightning, after a fashion. All that time hurling the Fire away from her had been useful practice after all. She felt a burst of pure pride, of triumph. Then the thunderbirds appeared.

The creatures swooped out of the clouds, their shrieks dull to Tamri's Lightning-blasted ears. The huge creatures wheeled back and forth, getting closer with each pass, as if scouting out exactly which piece of her flesh they wanted to tear into first.

Tamri had no weapons. She reached desperately for a rock, a stick, anything she could use to defend herself and Latch. She pictured Pevin falling to the creatures, the survivors with their gaping wounds and torn flesh.

The thunderbirds dove closer. Tamri had escaped the cavern, but the Lightning's feral servants were going to slay her anyway. She would never see Gramma Teall again.

She clutched her cloak, her hands knotting around the sharp points of the pewter dragonfly.

Then, through her aching, tender ears, she heard a sound that was nothing like the vicious call of the thunderbirds. That fierce cry had once struck fear into her heart, but now it made wild hope leap in her chest. Tamri turned her face to the sky. And out of the clouds came a dragon.

The jewel-blue head appeared first, mouth opened in a roar. White wings spread wide, feathers quivering in the stormy air. Boru soared downward, proud and dignified, unafraid of these pigeons. On his arching back sat a tall man with a glowing cudgel in his hand and grim determination on his face. His stern, beautiful face. *Heath.*

The dragon landed on the mountainside, the wind from his great wings blowing Tamri's hair back from her face. Heath beckoned to her.

"We have to hurry."

Tamri seized Latch's arm. His eyes were open, staring vacantly. "I can't lift him."

Heath dismounted, his movements smooth and powerful, and handed Tamri his cudgel. Then he hoisted Latch onto Boru's back. The Soolen lord's head lolled to the side as Heath used an extra harness to secure him.

Tamri brandished the cudgel at the thunderbirds, but the creatures didn't dare come near with Boru's huge white wings sheltering her. The birds shrieked angrily to each other, giving the dragon a wide berth.

"You next." Heath lifted Tamri by the waist onto the dragon's back then climbed up behind her and tapped Boru's flank. "Let's go."

The dragon gave a great cry and launched into the air. The clouds swirled, and Lightning crackled around them. The energy pulsing throughout the island had changed. It had a wild quality, unlike any mere thunderstorm, and it no longer felt as if a conscious presence was directing it. But it also didn't feel confined to the mountain anymore.

Boru flew as low as possible, skimming along the rocky mountainside and avoiding the storm. His flight was laborious with three riders, but his powerful wings didn't falter. Tamri remembered the first time she'd scrambled onto this dragon, with Heath's knee pressing into her thigh, panic shuddering through her. This time it was exhilarating, euphoric. This time, he had come to save her.

"I thought the dragons refused to get this close," Tamri called over her shoulder.

"Boru trusts me." Heath patted the dragon, and he beat his wings harder as if to prove he wouldn't let Heath down. "When you escaped, we were going to search the water in case you tried to swim for it, but then lightning started erupting from the mountain again. I had a hunch you were to blame."

Tamri grinned. "Thank you for coming for me—or for the princess," she amended. "I guess you wanted to save Latch for Sel—"

"Tamri."

She twisted to look at him. Her shoulder was pressed into his chest, his face close enough to touch.

"Yes?"

He brushed a lock of hair from her forehead with a large, gentle hand, making her nerve endings crackle.

"Your hair is burned," he said softly. "You shouldn't have risked yourself like that."

Tamri shrugged, her shoulders shifting against his chest. She felt unexpectedly emotional at the realization that Heath cared whether she lived or died, even after everything.

"The princess spoke up for me," she replied, her voice a little hoarse. "And I never wanted to be a spy."

Heath studied her, his eyes holding questions Tamri still couldn't answer. She wanted to touch his face, to tell him how often she thought about that night when the First Snow fell around them. But she would only have to hurt him again. The oath bond still circled her neck. Khrillin still had her grandmother. And she finally had information that would buy her freedom, information about the Lightning so intimate she could still feel it sizzling along her skin. In giving Khrillin that information, she would lose Heath anyway. So instead of telling him the truth, she turned away and faced the wind and the storm.

The lights of the old granary were coming into view. It looked just as it had when she left. But Tamri was different now. She had survived the Lightning. She had repaid her debt to Princess Selivia. And one day, she would make Khrillin pay for everything he'd made her do. Tamri could see the edge of freedom, like the first golden slice of dawn, and nothing would stop her from reaching out to take it.

38

S elivia paced back and forth at the edge of their camp, anxiety pulsing through her.

Moments ago, the sky had lit up as if it were noon, Lightning shooting out of the mountaintop, forking wildly into the clouds. The magical substance spiraled out of the peak in an unwieldy column, whirling like a tornado, finally free from containment. Then, as abruptly as it had begun, the blast of Lightning died.

After the eruption, Chadrech urged Dara and Siv to board his ships and leave the island at once. Everyone seemed to think this a good idea, and they began to break camp.

Selivia ignored the bustle of activity, studying the distant mountain. The Lightning wouldn't have acted like that for no reason. Someone must have tried to attack it again. What if they had succeeded?

The clouds drifted fitfully, no longer churning with such violence. Lightning shivered and arched between them, more random than before. Selivia watched. Waited.

The others finished packing the supplies and began carrying the wounded down to the beach. The ships were sailing into the harbor to meet them. Someone called to Selivia that it was time to leave. But she couldn't bring herself to turn away.

And then, just when she was about to give up, she saw the wings. Snow-white feathers. Jewel-blue scales.

"I knew it!"

Selivia jumped up and down as a familiar dragon descended out of the maelstrom.

Heath and Tamri rode on Boru's back, looking windblown and weary. Heath was holding Tamri around the waist, and her feet were bare, clinging to the creature's scales. And in front of them, slung across the dragon's shoulders like a sack of plums was—

"Latch!"

Selivia dashed forward to meet the dragon as it landed. Tamri all but fell off, struggling to balance on her own two feet. Heath dismounted more gracefully and pulled Latch's limp figure off Boru's back.

"You got him! Is he alive? How did you do it? Is he injured? Are you injured?" Selivia babbled.

If Heath and Tamri answered her questions, she didn't hear them. She was too busy wiping dirt from Latch's face and checking him for injuries. He smelled like metal and stone and sweat. His face had a grayish cast, but his skin appeared unbroken.

As Heath lowered him to the ground, Latch's eyes drifted open.

"Sel?" he rasped. "Is that you?"

"I'm here."

She took his hand, and he squeezed, his grip stronger than she expected.

"You were right," he whispered. "I let it trap me ..."

"Shh. Don't worry about that now," Selivia said. "You're safe."

"None of us are safe," Latch muttered. Then his head dropped onto his shoulder.

"What do you mean? Latch? Why are none of us safe?"

But he had lost consciousness. Selivia looked up at the mountain, where Lightning shivered and lanced through the clouds. The thunder was a continuous boom, making her ears ache. Now that she had Latch back, she was ready to leave this place as fast as ship or dragon wings could carry her.

One hour of furious activity later, they boarded the *Silverliner* and left Thunderbird Island behind.

Latch was put to bed in Chadrech's cabin, with Rosh attending him. Selivia hoped all he needed was rest and nourishment after being in the Lightning's thrall for so long. He hadn't yet regained consciousness.

After he was settled, Selivia joined Siv, Dara, and Chadrech on the stern deck. A Fire Lantern hung from the rear cabin, casting a pool of light over them as Thunderbird Island shrank in the distance. A storm still raged above the mountain. The Lightning moved differently now, wildly, as if freed from whatever constraints had kept it concentrated above the peak.

"I think he unleashed something," Dara said. "Upset some sort of balance. Or *we* did."

Siv grimaced. "Any chance the Lightning will stay put on the island if we leave it alone?"

"Somehow I doubt it."

"So what do we do now?" Selivia asked.

"This is still Soolen land," Chadrech said, his old arrogance resurfacing now that he was back on his ship. "All decisions about the Lightning are up to me and my mother."

"We have no wish to impinge on Soolen sovereignty," Siv said, adopting a politely formal tone with visible effort. "We will offer aid, if it pleases Queen Rochelle. My lady wife has had valuable experience Wielding different magical substances. Perhaps Vertigon and Soole can work together to understand this discovery."

Chadrech's narrow jaw worked soundlessly for a moment. Then he inclined his head with equally grudging formality. "We welcome your assistance. Let us hasten to Sharoth. My mother will be surprised to find you larking about in her territory."

"Oh, she'll be less surprised than you think," Siv said. "You remember Lady Vine Silltine, don't you? I expect she's having tea with Queen Rochelle as we speak."

Chadrech's cheeks reddened, and he adjusted his collar. "Who could forget Lady Vine?"

"No one I've ever met," Dara said dryly.

Siv extended a hand. "In any case, I look forward to strengthening our friendship with the Soolen Crown."

Chadrech eyed him for a moment then reached out to take his hand. "Likewise."

JORDAN RIVET

As Siv and Chadrech shook hands, Selivia sensed a turning point in the relationship between Vertigon and Soole. They were no longer just allies of House Brach. For good or ill, the Amintelle family would be bonded more firmly to the Soolen royals than any rulers of Vertigon had been before.

Selivia was relieved she wouldn't have to marry Chadrech in order to forge this partnership. Even so, she couldn't help thinking that King Khrillin of Pendark would not be pleased. Young Pel must have met up with the missing bald woman by now. News of the Lightning would be on its way to Khrillin. Selivia hoped he wouldn't use it as an excuse to break ties with them for good.

Thunderbird Island was receding, but she feared the storm had just begun.

"Now that we're safely underway," Dara said, "I'd like to hear what happened in the cavern." She turned. "Tamri? Will you come here please?"

The Pendarkan girl jumped. She'd been standing farther forward with Heath, out of earshot of their conversation. Selivia supposed Heath was guarding her, but the way they stood side by side didn't look like jailer and prisoner.

Tamri approached cautiously, her quick gaze taking in the king, queen, prince, and princess. Her hair and clothes looked singed, and she was blinking a lot, as if the light from the Fire Lantern hanging in the stern hurt her eyes.

Dara asked her to tell them what happened, and Tamri obliged, describing the vortex of Lightning, the way Latch had been rotating in the air, and her desperate effort to stay alive as Lightning bolts struck at her again and again.

"The Lightning was defending itself," Tamri said. "It lashed out when you went in brandishing Watermight and Fire. I didn't have any power at all. When it came for me, I whipped it away from me without drawing it in or letting it touch me." She tugged a lock of singed hair. "Well, mostly."

"That was good thinking," Dara said.

Tamri shrugged then winced as if her muscles were still tender. "I've had plenty of practice Wielding power outside my body."

"I'd still like to know why you risked yourself," Siv said.

Tamri's eyes flitted toward Selivia. "I wanted to see if I could."

332

Siv shook his head, clearly not believing her. "I suppose you wanted to convince us to trust you again? Or maybe learn about the Lightning for Khrillin?"

Tamri didn't answer. She rubbed her neck with both hands, massaging it as if imagining a hangman's noose. Despite her fear, she looked back at the others with defiance in her gaze.

"Oh, can't we give her another chance?" Selivia burst out. "She saved Latch!"

"I'm willing," Dara said.

Siv began to speak, but Dara put a hand on his arm. They looked at each other for a moment, unspoken communication passing between them. Selivia held her breath, hoping that whatever Dara was saying with her eyeballs was having an effect. At last, Siv nodded.

"Tamri," Dara said, turning to the younger woman. "If you stop reporting to Khrillin, you can stay on at the Wielder school. I'd like your help studying this new Lightning power, since you've had more success with it than the rest of us."

A look of naked longing crossed Tamri's face. But she shook her head. "I can't do that."

"Do you want to return to Pendark?" Dara said.

"No."

"Do you want to study the Lightning?"

Tamri's eyes blazed. "Yes."

"You could leave Khrillin's service. Start anew."

Tamri only shook her head.

"At least tell us why," Selivia pleaded. "You saved Latch for me. I can tell you want to work with us. Is your loyalty to Khrillin that strong?"

Tamri's hands went to her neck again. She was trembling. A tear leaked from the corner of her eye.

"I . . . I can't."

"My queen?" Heath said. "I think King Khrillin is threatening Tamri's grandmother. I overheard her talking with the other prisoner. I believe she has no choice, but if she could, she would accept your offer at once."

Tamri whirled to look up at him. Selivia couldn't see her face, but Heath's expression was clear enough. Admiration. Affection. He'd put Selivia on a pedestal for years, and she recognized that expression. If anything, Heath's eyes were more intense now than they'd ever been when looking at her.

So that's why he went back for her.

"Is it true about your grandmother?" Siv asked. "We can keep it secret from Khrillin. Perhaps you can still send him reports with curated information. Like a double agent."

Tamri shook her head stiffly. Tears flowed freely down her cheeks, and her face scrunched up, as if she was in pain.

Suddenly, Dara gasped. "She has a Watermight bond."

"A what?"

"She literally can't answer." Dara advanced a few steps. "Tamri, stop trying. You don't have to tell us what you were asked to do or why."

Tamri drew in a shuddering breath, wavering, as if about to collapse. Heath steadied her with a hand on her arm.

"What's going on?" Selivia said.

"A Watermight bond can force someone to keep an oath," Dara said. "I had one myself once, though not from Khrillin."

Tamri looked up in surprise. Dara was still studying her carefully. "I'm guessing it's on her neck. Mine was on my sword arm. It would have frozen through and cracked off if I broke the oath."

Selivia pressed a hand to her mouth, looking at Tamri with new eyes. The poor girl was shuddering. No wonder she had been so guarded, so secretive. Selivia could hardly blame her if she was afraid of her neck freezing off all the time.

"Can't you help her?" Selivia said.

"Watermight bonds can be broken," Dara said. "But it usually has to be done by the person who swore the oath, and it's not easy. Unless . . ."

Dara raised a hand, and a thin stream of Fire flowed out of the Fire Lantern and settled on her palm. Dara seemed to be speaking to herself. "If the Lightning weakened the bond in any way, I might be able to . . ."

Tamri took a step forward. "Wait—"

A bead of Fire shot from Dara's hand so fast it looked like a streak of golden light. It hit Tamri in the neck and sank in. Tamri stiffened. Then she cried out and collapsed to the deck.

For one horrible moment, Selivia thought Dara had killed her. But Tamri was still breathing. She crouched on the deck, hands splayed on the planks, and didn't look up.

"What did you do?" Selivia asked, grabbing Dara's arm.

"Just wait," Dara said calmly. "I have a theory based on Tamri's success with the Lightning. It took two magical substances to break my oath bond. After immersing herself in so much Lightning, it's possible hers was weakened. She's always trying to defend herself, and I thought a quick attack with Fire might be enough to help her break the bond herself."

Tamri still hadn't moved from her crouch. Selivia couldn't tell whether or not the oath bond was still intact. Heath knelt beside her, moving as cautiously as if she were a feral animal.

"Tamri?" he said softly.

She whispered something. Selivia moved a little closer. "What was that?"

"It's gone."

Heath rested a hand on Tamri's back, but she jerked violently away from him. Then she was on her feet, baring her teeth at them all.

"It's gone," she hissed. "Khrillin will know. He'll kill her!"

Selivia's heart clenched at the panic in Tamri's eyes. The girl looked around the deck frantically, and for a moment, Selivia was sure she was about to leap overboard to try to swim for it. The rising sun illuminated the white caps on the waves. They were miles from the nearest shore.

"I'm sorry, Tamri," Dara said. "I wasn't sure it would work, but I thought surprise was the only way to—"

Tamri snarled a curse foul enough to make even Siv blink.

"That's enough of that," he said.

"Just let me go." Tamri looked at Selivia then. "Please. I have to get there before he figures it out."

"We'll help you get your grandmother out of Pendark," Selivia said, not knowing what else to say. She turned to her brother. "Won't we?"

Siv hesitated for a beat. "Yes, of course. We owe you after you saved Latch."

Tamri frowned, her eyes hooded. "What's the catch?"

No catch," Dara said. "I didn't mean to put your family in danger. I'll help set things right. And the offer to return to study with me is still open."

Tamri looked up at her, a conflicted expression crossing her face. "My gramma needs me," she said. "But thank you."

"Your Majesties?" Heath said. "I request permission to accompany Tamri to Pendark to retrieve her grandmother. I will try to find out where we stand with King Khrillin in the process."

"That may be necessary," Siv said. He glanced at his wife. "You realize this will create another wedge between us and Khrillin, right?"

"Khrillin carved that wedge himself," Dara said.

Chadrech had been watching the whole exchange with interest. "If you are willing to oppose Khrillin, even in this small matter, I suspect the alliance between Soole and Vertigon will flourish."

Siv sighed. "Let's hope full-on opposition won't be necessary." He turned back to Heath and Tamri, one tall and stern, the other small and scrappy, both equally determined to succeed in their mission. "You'd better get some rest. You have a long journey ahead of you."

"Yes, sire," Heath said.

Tamri didn't move for a moment more, studying them all as if she wasn't sure whether to be angry or grateful. Probably a little of both. She met Selivia's eyes for a beat then bobbed her head to Dara and Siv and turned to follow Heath belowdecks.

As the others dispersed to their respective cabins, Selivia looked back at Thunderbird Island. Lightning was still lancing outward from that vast roiling cloud, spreading out of control. The mysterious substance had knocked the balance in the continent askew after all. This wasn't over.

EPILOGUE

Khrillin folded his arms as he listened to the boy's report. He should never have sent a dimwit like Pel on such an important mission. Though to be fair, he'd had no idea how momentous Thunderbird Island would turn out to be.

"Enough, enough," he said as the boy continued to babble about all the dragons he had seen before he managed to escape and meet up with Gyra. "What of the Vertigonians? Have they taken control of this new power from the Soolens?"

"I reckon so," Pel said. "They're mighty persuasive. They even got Tamri to turn to their side."

"Indeed?"

"Yes, sire."

"Go on."

After a moment's hesitation, Pel spilled the whole story of how young Sivarrion and his extraordinarily powerful bride had managed to win the heart of Khrillin's spy. The girl hadn't said as much to Pel, of course, but Khrillin was adept at reading between the lines. He'd never have achieved his current position without his ability to sense when people were trying to double-cross him. Once, he had fallen for young Sivarrion's charm, choosing to trust the son of his old friend. He wouldn't make that mistake twice.

"She asked me to look after her grandmother too," Pel finished. "But I reckoned I ought to tell you she's trying to put one over on us."

"The girl does have spirit."

The boy waited expectantly, as if he wanted some reward for not holding back the whole of Tamri's story. He would soon learn that absolute loyalty was the minimum required of him now that he served the illustrious Waterlord King of Pendark.

Khrillin wondered if the little gutterfeeder had managed to break her oath bond or if the Fire Queen had done it for her. He couldn't tell from a distance. Dara's experience had inspired him to learn how to create an oath bond in the first place. He would feel quite put out if she had been the one to break it. Or perhaps they'd left the bond intact, and they were planning to use Tamri to feed him information. Either way, the girl herself intended to turn on him.

Little Tamri was about to learn the meaning of loyalty too.

"Pel, go fetch Brik. Hurry now."

"Yes, my king." The lad tugged on his earlobe. "Uh, what about Tamri?"

"You did well in bringing her to my attention." Khrillin smiled. He demanded obedience, but he could give praise where it was warranted. "I believe it is high time I paid Gramma Teall a visit."

ACKNOWLEDGMENTS

This book wouldn't exist without the readers of the *Steel and Fire* series. Thank you for your enthusiasm for the story and for giving me an excuse to return to this world.

I am grateful for the people who put so much time into reading my work and helping me become a better writer: Willow Hewitt, Sarah Merrill Mowat, Rachel Andrews, Jennifer Deayton, Betsy Cheung, MaryAnna Donaldson, Amanda Tong, and Vishal Nanda. Special thanks go to my parents, who read all my books and always have substantial feedback.

On the publishing side, I would like to thank Lynn and Susie at Red Adept Editing for their hard work and professionalism and Deranged Doctor Design for the truly epic cover art.

I'm thankful for the indie writing community online and the authors who have taught me so much and shared in all the triumphs and frustrations of this business. The Author's Corner and the admins of YA Fantasy Addicts deserve all the shout-outs in the world.

Thank you to my advance review team and to all the readers and authors who talk about my books online and help me reach new readers.

Thank you to Wanda for naming Boru and to everyone who suggested so many excellent dragon names.

Thank you, Ryder Lyne, for your kind gift that helped me compile my worldbuilding notes so I could actually write this book.

Thank you to Karen, Cindy, and the gang at my regular Starbucks for never making me feel I've overstayed my welcome.

And last but not least, thank you to my husband, Seb. He's an excellent sounding board, travel companion, cook, and comforter, and a first-rate friend. I'm grateful for him every day.

Jordan Rivet

Hong Kong

January 2019

ABOUT THE AUTHOR

Jordan Rivet is an American author of swashbuckling fantasy and post-apocalyptic adventures. Originally from Arizona, she lives in Hong Kong with her husband. When she's not writing, Jordan likes to read, travel, binge-watch TV shows, and eat other people's cooking.

www.JordanRivet.com
jordan@jordanrivet.com

ALSO BY JORDAN RIVET

Fantasy

STEEL AND FIRE

Duel of Fire

King of Mist

Dance of Steel

City of Wind

Night of Flame

EMPIRE OF TALENTS

The Spy in the Silver Palace

An Imposter with a Crown

A Traitor at the Stone Court

THE FIRE QUEEN'S APPRENTICE

The Watermight Thief

Science Fiction

Wake Me After the Apocalypse

THE SEABOUND CHRONICLES

Seabound

Seaswept

Seafled

Burnt Sea: A Seabound Prequel

Lightning Source UK Ltd.
Milton Keynes UK
UKHW012029170122
397287UK00002B/486